WINONA

broadview editions
series editor: L.W. Conolly

WINONA;
OR,
THE FOSTER-SISTERS

Isabella Valancy Crawford

edited by Len Early and Michael A. Peterman

broadview editions

© 2007 Len Early and Michael A. Peterman

All rights reserved. The use of any part of this publication reproduced, transmitted in any form or by any means, electronic, mechanical, photocopying, recording, or otherwise, or stored in a retrieval system, without prior written consent of the publisher—or in the case of photocopying, a licence from Access Copyright (Canadian Copyright Licensing Agency), One Yonge Street, Suite 1900, Toronto, ON M5E 1E5—is an infringement of the copyright law.

Library and Archives Canada Cataloguing in Publication

Crawford, Isabella Valancy, 1850–1887

    Winona, or, The foster-sisters/Isabella Valancy Crawford; edited by Len Early and Michael A. Peterman.

Prize-winning story originally serialized in a Montreal story paper 1873.

(Broadview editions)
Includes bibliographical references.

ISBN-13: 978-1-55111-709-6
ISBN-10: 1-55111-709-6

    I. Early, Leonard Roy II. Peterman, Michael A., 1942– III. Title. IV. Title: Foster-sisters.

PS8455.R35SW55 2006   C813'.4   C2006-903359-5

Broadview Editions

The Broadview Editions series represents the ever-changing canon of literature by bringing together texts long regarded as classics with valuable lesser-known works.

Advisory editor for this volume: Marie Davis Zimmerman

Broadview Press is an independent, international publishing house, incorporated in 1985. Broadview believes in shared ownership, both with its employees and with the general public; since the year 2000 Broadview shares have traded publicly on the Toronto Venture Exchange under the symbol BDP.

We welcome comments and suggestions regarding any aspect of our publications–please feel free to contact us at the addresses below or at broadview@broadviewpress.com / www.broadviewpress.com

North America
PO Box 1243, Peterborough, Ontario, Canada K9J 7H5
Tel: (705) 743-8990; Fax: (705) 743-8353
email: customerservice@broadviewpress.com
PO Box 1015, 3576 California Road, Orchard Park, NY, USA 14127

UK, Ireland, and continental Europe
NBN International
Estover Road
Plymouth PL6 7PY UK
Tel: 44 (0) 1752 202 300
Fax: 44 (0) 1752 202 330
email: enquiries@nbninternational.com

Australia and New Zealand
UNIREPS, University of New South Wales
Sydney, NSW, 2052
Australia
Tel: 61 2 9664 0999; Fax: 61 2 9664 5420
email: info.press@unsw.edu.au

Broadview Press gratefully acknowledges the financial support of the Government of Canada through the Book Publishing Industry Development Program for our publishing activities.

PRINTED IN CANADA

Contents

Acknowledgements • 7
Introduction • 9
Isabella Valancy Crawford: A Brief Chronology • 62
A Note on the Text • 65
Editorial Emendations • 69
Line-end Hyphenated Compounds in the Original Text • 74

Winona; or, The Foster-Sisters • 77

Appendix A: The Discourse of Womanhood • 287
    1. Eliza Lynn Linton, "The Girl of the Period," *Saturday Review*
       25 (14 March 1868) • 288
    2. "Fast Young Ladies," *Canadian Illustrated News*
       (28 September 1872) • 293
    3. Sara Jeannette Duncan, "Saunterings," *The Week*
       (28 October 1886) • 296
    4. E. Pauline Johnson, "A Strong Race Opinion: On the Indian
       Girl in Modern Fiction," *Toronto Sunday Globe*
       (22 May 1892) • 299

Appendix B: Editorials on Literature and Publishing from
Desbarats's Papers • 309
    1. ["The state of Canadian literature"], *Canadian Illustrated News*
       (13 July 1872) • 309
    2. "Sensation Literature," *The Hearthstone* (3 August 1872) • 311
    3. "Artistic Filth," *The Favorite* (1 February 1873) • 315

Appendix C: Prospectus for *The Favorite* • 316
    1. "Our First Bow," *The Favorite* (28 December 1872) • 316
    2. "Who Will Write for *The Favorite*," *The Favorite*
       (28 December 1872) • 317

Appendix D: Reports of the 1873 Autumn Assizes,
Peterborough, Ontario • 320
1. From "The Assizes," *Peterborough Examiner*
(30 October 1873) • 320
2. From "The Autumn Assizes," *Peterborough Review*
(31 October 1873) • 321

Appendix E: Illustrations • 322
1. "Winona's Return," *The Favorite* (1 February 1873) • 322
2. The Clytie Bust (c. CE 40-50) • 323
3. John Everett Millais, "The Black Brunswicker" (1860) • 324
4. Carlo Dolci, "Madonna of the Veil," c. 1630-86, *Canadian
Illustrated News* (23 December 1871) • 325
5. "A Moonlight Excursion on the St. Lawrence," *Canadian
Illustrated News* (24 June 1871) • 326
6. William Armstrong, "Ice Boats on the Bay, Toronto,"
Canadian Illustrated News (18 February 1871) • 327

Select Bibliography • 328

Acknowledgements

We wish to express our gratitude to the Social Sciences and Humanities Research Council of Canada for a standard grant that enabled us to perform much of the work necessary for this edition of *Winona*, and to the Faculty of Graduate Studies at York University for providing matching funds for research assistance that proved indispensable. We are also grateful for the support of the departments of English at Trent University and York University, the Frost Centre for Graduate Canadian Studies at Trent, and the Graduate Programme in English at York. To those graduate assistants—Kelly Beers, Jennifer Cannataro, Emily Dockrill, Chris Eaton, Brendan Edwards, Janet Friskney, Anna Girling, Jennifer Grant, Darcy Ingram, Brenda Nadjiwan, Lisa Salem-Wiseman, and Jabeen Yusufali—whose labours in library and archival research, transcription, and proofreading made this book possible, we extend particular thanks. We also appreciate the prompt and expert assistance of staff at Trent University's Bata Library, especially Bernadine Dodge, head of Special Collections and Archives, staff members at York University's Archives and Special Collections, Resource Sharing, Map Library, and Printing Services, staff at the Queen's University Archives and the New York Public Library, and John Logan of the Firestone Library, Princeton University.

Special appreciation is due to Jeannine Rivard of the Bibliothèque Nationale du Québec, and to staff at the Thomas Fisher Rare Book Library, University of Toronto, the National Archives of Canada, the British Museum, and National Museums, Liverpool, England for making available copies of primary materials.

Permission by the British Museum and the National Museums, Liverpool, to reproduce illustrations in Appendix E2 (The Clytie Bust) and Appendix E3 ("The Black Brunswicker") is gratefully acknowledged.

Thanks also to our colleagues at Trent and York, especially Ross Arthur, Ian Balfour, Barbara Dodge, Jonathan Edmondson, Ray Ellenwood, Doug Hay, Beth Hopkins, Gordon Johnston, Elwood Jones, David Latham, the late Gordon Roper, the late Michael Treadwell, and Craig Wilson, for advice on the linguistic, literary, and aesthetic aspects, as well as the legal ramifications, of Crawford's novel. We are also grateful to friends and colleagues elsewhere, including D.M.R. Bentley and James Reaney of the University of Western Ontario, Joshua Brown of the Social History Project, City University of New York, Jean Cole, independent scholar, Peterborough, Michael Flavin of Rochester Independent College, U.K., Betty Galvin, writer, Peterborough, Carole Gerson of Simon Fraser University, Burnaby, B.C., Robert Thacker of St. Lawrence University, Canton, N.Y., and the anonymous assessors for Broadview Press, for contributing valuable leads and suggestions.

Introduction

On 27 October 1873, the suit of "Crawford vs. Desbarats" was heard in Judge Adam Wilson's court in Peterborough, Ontario. According to the *Peterborough Examiner,* the defendant had sponsored a literary contest with the promise that the winning stories would be published in his papers "the *Hearthstone* and *Favorite* ... Miss Crawford competed, and after examination was informed by the Editor of the *Hearthstone* that she had been awarded the first prize of $500 for her story entitled 'Winona'" ("Assizes"). While the story had been published, the prize money had not been paid; including what was owed her for other work, plus interest, the plaintiff's claim came to $605.48. After hearing details of the case and a feeble defence, the jury "returned a verdict for plf. of full amount." As things turned out, however, the aggrieved author would see little of this "full amount," for her defaulting publisher had overextended his enterprises during the early 1870s and was sinking towards the low point of an otherwise distinguished career. Having already discontinued *The Hearthstone* at the end of 1872, he would shut down *The Favorite* in 1874 and declare bankruptcy a year later. "Crawford vs. Desbarats" marked the sorry end to a plan that had been announced with fanfare—a plan to foster a literature worthy of the new Dominion of Canada.

Although the plaintiff was Isabella Valancy Crawford (1850–87), one of nineteenth-century Canada's most gifted writers, and the defendant George-Édouard Desbarats (1838–93), a respected Montreal citizen and prominent publisher (his *Canadian Illustrated News* had been flourishing since October 1869), this episode has remained all but lost to literary history.[1] The prizewinning "story" at the centre of the lawsuit was,

---

1   The only previous reference to this lawsuit in published scholarship on Crawford is to be found in Lawrence J. Burpee's 1901 profile. His unidentified source of information may have been verbal, for he mistakes the amount of the prize, which was $500, not $600, and the responsibility for the verdict, which was rendered by jury, not judge; moreover, his assertion that Crawford "pleaded her own case in court so ably that the judge unhesitatingly pronounced in her favor" (577) is questionable, since the *Peterborough Review* identifies the firm of "Boultbee, Fairbairn & Poussette" as her legal representative ("Autumn Assizes"). Burpee further states that Crawford "only received a small portion of the original prize" (577). Maud Miller Wilson's biographical article of 1905 makes no mention of the lawsuit but does refer to the story competition, adding that "after having paid but one hundred dollars of the promised sum, the firm failed, and instead of the five hundred

WINONA; OR, THE FOSTER-SISTERS   9

in fact, a full-length novel and likely one of Crawford's earliest publications. *Winona; or, The Foster-Sisters* appeared serially in twelve installments from 11 January to 29 March 1873 in *The Favorite*, which was, like its predecessor *The Hearthstone*, a weekly "story paper" owned by Desbarats and published in Montreal.

Like most of Crawford's fiction and much of her poetry, *Winona* has never been reprinted—until now. Like the lawsuit that it precipitated, however, it reveals a good deal about the precarious state of literature in post-Confederation Canada. It illustrates the tension between a nascent literary nationalism and the persistent colonial conditions that thwarted such initiatives. It participates in the discourse of womanhood that has been the focus of much recent research on nineteenth-century writing in England and North America. It exemplifies problems that attended representations of "the Indian" in early Canadian literature. It contains fascinating depictions of the Ontario hinterland and the rising metropolis of Toronto in the early 1870s. And it adumbrates the singular, if at this point unfledged, talent that Crawford would later reveal in such acclaimed poems as "The Lily Bed," "The Canoe," and "Malcolm's Katie."

It should be said at once that *Winona* is not a lost masterpiece, although lost it certainly has been for well over a century. Suffused with the clichés of sensational fiction and tailored to the tastes of a popular readership, it clearly represents the weaknesses and compromises endemic in novels written for mass-market periodicals in nineteenth-century North America. Nevertheless, it is a piece of fiction written with intelligence and brio, and it offers rewards as well as embarrassments for admirers of Crawford's later, more accomplished, work. Indeed, it anticipates that work in its representation of women, its ethical vision, its use of Native materials, its exuberant engagement with high as well as popular culture, and its peculiar deployment of irony and romance. It also confirms Crawford's broad knowledge of literature, music, and the visual arts at this early stage of her career through numer-

---

dollars still due, the Crawfords received but a small percentage of that sum" (15 April 1905: 8). No court records of the case have survived, and, unfortunately, Judge Wilson's personal notebooks, now held in the Archives of Ontario, date from the month following the trial. As a result, the primary documents for this affair are brief news reports in the *Peterborough Examiner* and *Peterborough Review* (see Appendix D). For George-Édouard Desbarats's life and career, see Galarneau's *DCB* article (though it is noteworthy that Galarneau does not mention *The Favorite*), and Sutherland 46-58.

ous allusions to writers, singers, painters, sculptors, and their works. A problematical but fascinating mixture of melodrama, scenic delineation, and social satire, *Winona* is of interest both as an example of Canadian popular fiction in the 1870s and as an apprentice work by one of Canada's most important early writers.

Crawford's Life and Writing

Isabella Valancy Crawford was born in Dublin, Ireland, probably on Christmas day 1850, into a well-established family of doctors and barristers[1] Her father, Stephen Dennis Crawford, was, however, one of its less successful scions. After taking medical training and venturing on abortive attempts at emigration to Wisconsin and Australia, he settled in about 1857 with his wife, Sidney Scott Crawford, and five surviving children, in the village of Paisley, near Lake Huron in what was then known as Canada West, setting up practice as a physician. A few years later, in 1861, he left the area under suspicion of having mishandled funds entrusted to him as township treasurer.

By means of a chance encounter with a son of Samuel Strickland, the brother of Susanna Moodie and Catharine Parr Traill, Doctor Crawford moved his family to Lakefield, where for a time he was the community's sole physician. In 1869, having moved several times within Lakefield, he relocated his family again, this time to nearby Peterborough in the newly created province of Ontario where he was one of at least five doctors serving the small city and its environs. While the Crawford children enjoyed lively surroundings in these pioneer towns and the advantage of a stimulating education from cultivated parents, the doctor's financial position appears never to have been secure. Continuing debts, lack of interest in his vocation, rumours about his competence as a physician, and a fondness for drink may all have been factors. It was in these circumstances that Isabella and her younger sister, Emma Naomi, began to write and publish fiction, no doubt moved in part by a desire to supplement the uncertain family income.

The Crawford family's fortunes were singularly ill starred. Before their departure from Ireland to Canada, an epidemic had carried off

---

[1] Biographical work on Crawford is notably uneven in quality and often untrustworthy. The best biography is by Farmiloe; but see also Maud Miller Wilson, Hale, "Antrim," Martin, and Galvin.

seven children. Further losses followed, as it appears that at least two and perhaps three more of the Crawford offspring died in Paisley and Lakefield (Farmiloe 4-5, 12-13, 34). In July 1875, in Peterborough, Dr. Crawford himself succumbed to a heart attack at the age of sixty-seven, and less than six months later, Emma died of consumption at the young age of twenty-one, leaving only Isabella, her mother, and a brother, Stephen, who had gone to the Algoma territory to seek his livelihood. Thrown increasingly upon their own resources, Mrs. Crawford and Isabella moved to Toronto in the spring of 1876, where they lived in a series of boarding houses, eventually settling into rooms above a shop on John Street and surviving in part on what Isabella could earn by writing for local newspapers and the American popular press.

As various critics have observed, Crawford's voluminous production of fiction during these years was, for the most part, a means of earning her bread and butter. In this respect, straitened circumstances affected the pattern of her writing from the beginning until the end of her career. From at least 1872 until her death in 1887, she cultivated two distinct facilities: an ability to produce short and long stories for mass-market fiction "papers," and her literary talent as a poet. The intersection of these elements in her stories and poems remains one of their most fascinating aspects, and can be seen in the melodramatic plot and stylistic verve of *Winona*. A necessary question for admirers of her poetry, then, is how far it is possible to extend that admiration to her fiction.

Crawford's life in Toronto is known only in outline and by way of a few suggestive details. Shortly after her arrival, she joined the Mechanics' Institute, which had just recently extended full membership to women, and thus she had access to books, periodicals, art exhibits, musical performances, and lectures on philosophy, history, and literature.[1] If references in her work are allowable evidence, she must have valued the advantages that the provincial capital had to offer: many of her stories and poems allude to the pleasures of contemporary opera, the glories of European art, and the allure of fashionable life. An able pianist, she likely enjoyed the variety of music—popular, classical, and choral—that could be heard in the provincial capital. At the same time, Toronto sharpened her awareness of social problems: poverty, prostitution, the exploitation

---

[1] For Crawford's membership in the Mechanics' Institute, see Ower; on the Institute itself, see Ramsay, and Murray.

and struggles of labour, and the corruption and hypocrisy of the wealthy and powerful. These harsher features of nineteenth-century urban life are often coupled in her work, in pastoral fashion, with evocations of an unspoiled frontier, and are powerfully treated in a long, unfinished poem written in the 1880s that remained in manuscript for nearly a century after her death when it was published under the title *Hugh and Ion* (1977). Like some of her other later works, this remarkable text shows how far her engagement with social issues had developed in the years following *Winona*.

Crawford's best known work is another long poem, "Malcolm's Katie: A Love Story," first published in the only book by her to appear in her lifetime, a volume printed at her own expense in 1884 by the Toronto bookseller James Bain. *Old Spookses' Pass, Malcolm's Katie, and Other Poems* is a varied collection of blank-verse narratives and monologues, long poems and lyrics, and dialect verse of the kind made popular at the time by American poets such as James Whitcomb Riley and John Hay, and, more locally, by Scots and Irish-Canadian writers such as Alexander McLachlan and James McCarroll. Published in a run of a thousand copies, it sold poorly despite favourable notices by Canadian and British reviewers who saw in it "the mark of genius" ("Library"), "the ring of great promise" (H. Jones), and "a versatility of talent, combined with a descriptive power and a sense of humour, which ought to make their mark" ("Recent Poetry"). In general, these reviews praised Crawford's dialect poetry as the highlight of the book, while expressing mixed opinions about "Malcolm's Katie." Modern critics have concentrated on the latter work, debating the extent to which it celebrates or questions Canadian nationalism, implies a subversion of patriarchal values, anticipates ecological perspectives in our own time, or spins an intricate web of irony, myth, and allusion. While "Malcolm's Katie" fully deserves this scrutiny, other poems in Crawford's book, as well as many fugitive works never reprinted since their appearance in newspapers and magazines, also deserve to be better known. Indeed, the dialect verse that held such appeal to her contemporaries is, though long out of fashion, worth a fresh look.

In 1886 Crawford re-issued *Old Spookses' Pass*, evidently in the hope that it would find more buyers if it could be redistributed under a new cover that quoted the admiring notices garnered on its first appearance. Unfortunately, she did not see the result of her plan: on 12 February 1887, she died suddenly of heart failure at the age of thirty-six. More than one commentator linked her death to the stereotype of the fragile poet that had been famously applied earlier in the century to John Keats, although the fatal blow in Crawford's case was presumed to be disappointment at the commercial failure of her book rather than mortification at a hostile review. In the introduction to his landmark anthology, the expansively titled *Songs of the Great Dominion: Voices from the Forests and Waters, the Settlements and Cities of Canada* (1889), William Douw Lighthall averred, "there is very little doubt that the neglect her book received was the cause of her death" (xxvi). This view of Crawford, like the characterization of her by another late Victorian reader as "this angelic mendicant, craving nothing of life but its finer gifts—this blessed gypsy of Canadian woods and streams" (Wetherald 17) is, of course, nonsense. The matter-of-fact young woman who, at the age of twenty-two, had taken her publisher to court to put her case before a magistrate and jury was, at this point in her career, seasoned by setbacks and misfortune. She continued, almost until the end, to write, plan, and seek out new literary contacts. Little more than a week before her death, she visited the offices of a recently launched journal called *Arcturus*. According to its editor, "[s]he was at that time apparently in the enjoyment of perfect health, and looking forward with hope and confidence to the future. She had several projects of authorship in contemplation, and appeared to be full of literary ambition and enthusiasm" ("Editorial Notes" 84). An earlier letter of inquiry by Crawford was quoted in corroboration of these impressions:

> I feel that I should wish to introduce myself to your notice as a possible contributor to the pages of ARCTURUS. Of course the possibility is remote, as by some chance no contribution of mine has ever been accepted by any first-class Canadian literary journal. I have contributed to the Mail and Globe, and won some very kind words from eminent critics, but have been quietly "sat upon" by the High Priests of Canadian periodical literature. I am not very seriously injured by the process, and indeed there have lately been signs of relenting on the part of the powers that be, as I was offered an extended notice of my book in the columns of the——and the——. This proposal I declined (I suppose injudiciously) as coming in late in the day, and at the heels of warm words from higher literary authorities.

Her exasperation with an unsupportive Canadian literary milieu links Crawford to a number of other early Canadian writers, such as John Richardson, Susanna Moodie, and Charles Mair, who fashioned their careers as literary nationalists only to become disillusioned by what they saw as a persistent lack of encouragement for their work. It also attests both to the continuing vigour of her ambition and the enduring, and spirited, sense of her own worth that she had demonstrated in her lawsuit against Desbarats. It is tantalizing that *Arcturus* refers only in general terms to "several projects" that she had in mind in 1887; whether these involved further popular fiction, or work on the order of "Malcolm's Katie," or both, can only be matter for speculation. Arguably, her death in mid-career was as great a loss to the young literature of Canada as the passing twelve years later of her talented contemporary, Archibald Lampman, at the age of thirty-nine.

Literary Peterborough, James McCarroll, and North American Publishing in the 1870s

Written when Crawford was twenty-one, *Winona* is in all probability one of her earliest publications. Like so much else about her, the question of just when she began to publish has been obscured by scanty evidence and reckless conjecture. Lawrence J. Burpee, for instance, claimed that "[a]t the age of fourteen she wrote stories for *Frank Leslie's Magazine*, and soon became a constant contributor to this and other periodicals" (576). A flamboyant New York publishing magnate, Frank Leslie (1821-80) headed a firm that produced an astonishing array of weekly and monthly magazines and newspapers, often as many as ten at a time, during the second half of the nineteenth century. None of them, however, was titled *Frank Leslie's Magazine*.

Extensive searches have failed to turn up anything by Crawford in Leslie's papers before October 1872, when her novel *Wrecked! or, The Rosclerras of Mistree*, a Gothic romance set in England, France, and Italy, began to run serially in his flagship weekly, *Frank Leslie's Illustrated Newspaper*. After this date, most of her fiction did indeed appear in Leslie's periodicals, notably *Frank Leslie's Chimney Corner*. The family papers of Florence Atwood, a granddaughter of Catharine Parr Traill, Crawford's famous literary neighbour in Lakefield, provide what may be a more accurate indication of when she started to publish:

[The Crawfords] lived in a little house where Mother [Anne Traill Atwood] remembers going with Aunt Kate and Grandmother [Catharine Parr Traill] to take tea with them ... Isabella was the oldest child—at that time about seventeen years old (Mother can't remember the date) very pretty, medium complexion, very pretty hair, which she did in the same style as Empress Eugenie of France—rolled back from the face. Mother doesn't think she [had] written anything up to that time but spoke of writing a book which she was going to call "Lavender & Old Lace." (cited in Martin 392)

This account squares with the fact that, to date, we have almost no concrete evidence of writing by Crawford prior to the 1870s. Dorothy Farmiloe makes an intriguing but improbable case that an anonymous story in the *Peterborough Examiner* in 1865 suggests her style, and there is a manuscript fairy tale in the Crawford archive at Queen's University signed "IVC, N[orth] Douro," thus placing its composition in Lakefield before the family's move to Peterborough. At present, however, her earliest verified publication is a short story, "The Hospital Gondola," which appeared on 13 April 1872 in *The Hearthstone* and was followed by two poems and another story, "Windale's Souvenir," before that paper was terminated at the end of the year. In January 1873, with *Wrecked!* already well underway in *Frank Leslie's Illustrated Newspaper*, *Winona* began to run in *The Favorite*. Other stories and poems soon followed.

The new year of 1873 must have seemed wonderfully propitious to young Isabella. Not only had she won a "national" contest that would see her Canadian novel published by an ambitious new magazine in Montreal, but she was being promoted by *The Favorite* as one of its leading contributors. While that level of recognition presumably reflected her success in *The Hearthstone*'s story competition, it likely owed much to her coincident appearance in *Frank Leslie's Illustrated Newspaper*. With a circulation of about 200,000, that paper had, as a result of its coverage of the Civil War and other major events, become the CNN of its time. Aimed at mobile Americans who travelled by rail and had a taste for fresh pictorial news and serialized fiction, Leslie's weekly newspaper offered sixteen pages of images, notable events, and amusement. To be so prominently featured and to be paid accordingly was to have suddenly risen far beyond the provincial limits of Lakefield and Peterborough and to have the prospect of an income that her family

16 INTRODUCTION

desperately needed. But how did so young and isolated a writer find such favour?

The missing link in the story of Crawford's beginnings as a published writer may well be the influence that James McCarroll (1814-92) was able to exert on her behalf. Irish-born, with strong Peterborough connections and a considerable reputation as a writer in Toronto in the 1850s and 60s, McCarroll had come to Canada in 1831 from County Leitrim. He was seventeen at the time and tried his hand at a variety of occupations, including school and music teaching in the Peterborough-Cobourg area. In the mid-1840s he owned and edited a reform newspaper in Peterborough, establishing close contacts with people there before finding steady work as a civil servant for the Customs Department in 1849. A poet, story writer, humorist, journalist, musician, performer, and drama critic, he placed his writing in many newspapers and magazines in Canada West before gaining a supportive Toronto connection in 1853 through his friend and fellow reformer Charles Lindsay, the editor of a new Toronto newspaper, James Beaty's *The Leader* (later the *The Daily Leader*). That paper would achieve a wide circulation over the next two decades and establish itself as the chief rival of George Brown's powerful Toronto *Globe*. McCarroll contributed some ninety poems to *The Leader* in the 1850s and 1860s, while his comic letters to the eminent federal politician and M.P. Thomas D'Arcy McGee appeared in Toronto satiric papers like *The Grumbler* beginning in 1861. His vivid use of the Irish vernacular under the pen-name of Terry Finnegan (D'Arcy's self-described "lovin cousin") caught the attention of and provided amusement for many Irish-Canadians in the province.[1]

---

[1] Close to ninety poems by McCarroll appeared in the *The Leader* during the pre-Confederation decade. Others appeared in various Canadian magazines and newspapers. Among the poems he identified as from his "Irish Anthology" were several that used the vernacular voice. The Rev. Edward H. Dewart thought highly enough of McCarroll's work to include seven of his poems in his *Selections from Canadian Poets* (1864), ranking him just below Charles Sangster and Alexander McLachlan in terms of number of poems included. McCarroll's Terry Finnegan letters, penned in a ripe and humorous vernacular, appeared not only in *The Grumbler* but also in several other Toronto satiric papers including *Momus* (1861), *The Growler* (1864), and *The Latch-Key* (1863, 1864), the latter two of which were McCarroll's own publications. The "first series" of the Finnegan letters was published as a book in Toronto in 1864. McCarroll also wrote four comic letters for the Editor of the *Peterborough Examiner* in 1863 under pen-name of Lanty Mullins; these were addressed to "Paddy Mahony, Ould Denny's son, Petherboro, Kinnada West." Crawford would have been living in Lakefield at the time of their appearance. See Peterman.

WINONA; OR, THE FOSTER-SISTERS   17

Having become involved in the incendiary enterprise of Fenian politics, McCarroll left Canada under a cloud in 1866, and by 1872 was working in New York for Frank Leslie. During the years in which Isabella Valancy Crawford's novels and stories began to appear in *Frank Leslie's Illustrated Newspaper* and *Frank Leslie's Chimney Corner*, his editorial hand is apparent in both papers. As an expatriate "Canadian" now engaged in New York journalism, he was interested in using his editorial role to promote Canadian writing and other achievements. Indeed, in what might be seen as a kind of phantom signature, he included on at least three occasions in 1873 one of his own unsigned poems alongside serialized portions of Crawford's novel *Wrecked!* (22 February, 8 March, 29 March).[1] He also seems to have left a similar clue in *The Hearthstone*, where his poem "A Royal Race" is printed on the same page as Crawford's story "The Hospital Gondola" (13 April 1872), her apparent debut as a published writer.

The Crawford-McCarroll connection may have developed as much from female influence and friendship as from mutual Irish-Canadian interests. In the early 1870s three of McCarroll's four daughters were still living in Peterborough. While one daughter was married, the other two were single women who, having inherited their father's musical passion, made their livings as local music teachers. Though hard evidence of their connection with Crawford is lacking, it is possible to envision a supportive social circle among these young, mostly unmarried, and cultivated women—the McCarroll sisters, Isabella and Emma Crawford, and another aspiring author, Mary Muchall, Catharine Parr Traill's third daughter, whom Crawford would doubtless have known earlier through her connections with the Traill family in Lakefield. Both Mary Muchall and the two Crawford girls were listed as prospective "Peterboro', Ont." authors, along with "Susanna Moody" of Lakefield,

---

[1] There is a dearth of family archival material for both Crawford and McCarroll. However, a letter from McCarroll to Charles Lindsay dated 12 May 1873 and written under the letterhead of "Frank Leslie's Publishing House" reports that "I have been in this office for some time now, and filling, you may be assured, no very secondary position. You may have some idea of our establishment when I assure you that we have the *largest engraving one in the world*, and that, as I am informed, we keep forty power presses running day and night throughout the year" (Lindsay Papers [MU 1923, file 5]). McCarroll had included a profile of Lindsay in a *Chimney Corner* series entitled "Self-made Men of Our Time." "[S]o enormous is the circulation of this journal that," he promised Lindsay, "you will find your way into every civilized land on the face of the habitable globe."

in the first issue of Desbarats's *Favorite* (28 December 1872). Indeed, both Susanna Moodie and Catharine Parr Traill were old friends of McCarroll, through earlier publishing ventures in Moodie's case and through Peterborough connections in the 1840s in Traill's case. Like Isabella, Mary Muchall was an aspiring writer in the 1860s and '70s whose work appeared in both *The Hearthstone* and *The Favorite*, and who sent sketches to Leslie's papers. In fact, two of Muchall's stories were published, although anonymously, by Leslie in the early 1870s.

Once her own career was launched, Crawford, like many of her contemporaries, wrote prodigiously, encouraged by the opportunities made available by a voracious and competitive periodical market. To date, three of her serialized novels, over thirty stories of various lengths, and more than one hundred and thirty poems have been found in a dozen American and Canadian newspapers and magazines published between 1872 and 1887. Titles mentioned in contemporary sources indicate that at least three more novels appeared in periodicals that have either vanished or remain unidentified.[1] Moreover, the Queen's University archive contains a mass of fiction in manuscript for which no publication in Crawford's lifetime has been traced: some 30 shorter pieces, including prose sketches, stories and fairy tales, and no fewer than nine draft novels in various states of composition.

From at least the period of *Winona* until her death, then, Crawford wrote busily and published steadily, except perhaps for an interval of some 20 months in 1877 and 1878 during which only two or three short poems are known to have appeared in print. This output indicates both dogged industry and imaginative fertility, but it was by no

---

[1]   The three serialized novels by Crawford that have been located are all works of the early to mid-1870s: *Wrecked! or, The Rosclerras of Mistree* (1872-73), *Winona; or, The Foster-Sisters* (1873), and *Hate* (1875), which appeared in *Frank Leslie's Chimney Corner*. A later novel, *A Little Bacchante; or, Some Black Sheep*, was serialized in the Toronto *Evening Globe* in January 1886, but few numbers of this evening edition of the paper have been preserved and only the ninth chapter of the novel, "In the Presence of the Tempter" (21 January 1886), has actually been found (see *Varsity*, "A Talented Lady Dead," and Petrone 11). Other works whose published texts remain untraced are "Monsieur Phoebus; or, Some of the Adventures of an Irish Gentleman," "A Kingly Restitution," and "A Wicked Old Woman," which are mentioned in prefatory notes to poems by Crawford published in the Toronto *Evening Telegram* in the early 1880s ("Verses," "At the Opera—A Fragment," "'He Arose and Went into Another Land'"). Both "Monsieur Phoebus" and "A Kingly Restitution" are extant in manuscript among the Crawford papers at Queen's University.

means unusual. To take the examples of three well-known American writers, Harriet Beecher Stowe (1811-96) published more than 40 books and 300 sketches and stories during her lifetime, Mrs. E.D.E.N. Southworth (1819-99) over 60 novels that appeared initially as serials, and Louisa May Alcott (1832-88) 39 books in various genres and 138 pieces of shorter fiction, including several thrillers serialized in mass-market periodicals, among them *Frank Leslie's Illustrated Newspaper*.[1]

Three patterns emerge from the record of Crawford's publications, so far as it can be pieced together. First, it appears that she preferred to publish fiction in the United States—though this may be merely the consequence of James McCarroll's encouragement and his association with Leslie's periodical mill—while favouring Canadian venues for her poems. Second, she tended to limit "Canadian content" to work published in Canada. Put another way, she catered to the American market by setting stories either in the United States or in glamorous, often aristocratic, European locations. And third, she seems to have stuck with individual publishers until circumstances or a change in personnel led her to seek an alternative, as there is little overlap in the periods at which her poems, on the one hand, and stories, on the other, appear in specific newspapers and journals.

This fidelity to her publishers—serial monogamy is perhaps a better description—was fairly typical of the age. Susan Coultrap-McQuin has described the relationship between nineteenth-century American women writers and their publishers in terms of the ethos of "the Gentleman Publisher," as a relationship based on trust, mutual respect and loyalty—essentially a species of benevolent paternalism on the part of members of the publishing firm. It was only toward the end of the century that publishing became more impersonal, aggressive, and strictly businesslike —more "modern," as it were—in its treatment of authors. While it is difficult to judge how far this custom of loyalty applied to Crawford, it seems clear that she established a reliable and congenial relationship with her Leslie editors, likely through McCarroll's close attention to her interests. For his part, McCarroll seems to have maintained a connection to the Leslie operations until about 1880.

The limited evidence available suggests that the conditions of

---

[1] For Stowe, see Hildreth; for Southworth, see Coultrap-McQuin 51; for Alcott, see Payne and Stern.

20 INTRODUCTION

Crawford's arrangement with the Leslie corporation led her to forego book-publishing opportunities. She sold her individual copyrights to Leslie, exchanging the welcome immediacy of payment for the corporation's right to republish her stories at its discretion. She seems to have shared with McCarroll the view, encouraged by Leslie and his ilk, that if one wished to make ready money from writing, the best way was to write to the narrative formula of the successful story papers rather than to seek the less certain and likely less-profitable road of book publication. Leslie certainly took advantage of his copyright control, republishing several Crawford stories in his new magazines, *Frank Leslie's Pleasant Hours* and *Frank Leslie's Popular Monthly*. By contrast, as noted above, Crawford's only book, her collection of poems, was published at her own expense in 1884 in Toronto. Without the evidence of surviving correspondence, we can only speculate about her relationship with Leslie's editors and James McCarroll in particular. That it was, on the whole, more satisfactory than the treatment she received from editors in Canada seems a legitimate inference from the debacle involving Desbarats and the astringent remarks she voiced in her letter to *Arcturus*.

The Story Papers, George-Édouard Desbarats, and Canadian Literary Nationalism

The "story papers" that published Southworth, Alcott, Crawford, and a host of now mostly forgotten writers emerged in North America in the 1830s and 1840s to meet the needs of an expanding reading public created by increased population, literacy, and leisure time, advances in printing technology, and the mass market made possible by railway distribution.[1] These weekly papers satisfied their readers' craving for cheap fiction in every sense of that adjective, and by the 1870s had occupied the open terrain between the Sunday supplements of daily newspapers and the "literary" monthlies such as *Harper's* and the *Atlantic*. While they might include other material such as editorials, practical advice on housekeeping and agriculture, poetry, and "tidbits," their columns of closely packed print were mostly filled with serialized novels and short fiction. Typically, a serial would be featured under the

---

[1] The following account of the North American story papers is indebted to Mary Noel's witty and informative *Villains Galore ... The Heyday of the Popular Story Weekly*.

paper's gaudy masthead, accompanied by a dramatic if not lurid illustration that sprawled across the middle three of five long columns on the large folio page. With three or four—and in an extreme case, as many as nine—serials running simultaneously, these story papers mixed famous authors with newcomers, oriental romances with westerns and detective fiction, and reams of hastily-produced pulp with occasional (mostly pirated) works of substance and quality.

Through the middle decades of the century the most successful of the American story papers such as *The Flag of Our Union*, the *Saturday Evening Post*, and the *New York Ledger* conducted a feverish and often vainglorious rivalry, freely reprinting material from both domestic and foreign publications, vying for serialized versions of the work of their most celebrated contributors, and conducting story competitions to attract new writers. By the 1870s, writers of Southworth's stature received as much as $150 for each serial installment, although the going rate for most writers was considerably lower: basic arithmetic shows that Crawford's five hundred dollar prize for *Winona* works out to less than a third of that amount. Louisa May Alcott's journals reveal that she received payments from Leslie during the 1860s and early 1870s that ranged from $25 to $40 per story (Alcott, *passim*).

Usually priced at six cents per copy, the story papers supplied readers with a dependable diet of threatened maidens, stolid heroes, and duplicitous villains. While setting and genre for their serialized fiction might vary across the gamut of "Indian" tales, sea stories, historical romances, mystery thrillers, and tales of working girls, immigrant boys, labouring men, and socially refined "city life," the basic formula remained constant: abduction and rescue, conspiracy and false identity, extraordinary encounters, coincidences, separations, and ultimate reunion. While violence, or at least its possibility, was almost indispensable, sex was kept off stage within strictly regulated bounds of propriety, and virtue was certain to prevail. As Mary Noel observes, "The counterpoint to evil as a sensation was virtue as a sentiment. The two, in their inevitable story-paper relationship, constituted sentimentality—emotion indulged in for its own sake" (244). The consumers of this fiction were the broad North American reading public: young and old, housewives and college students, clerks and tradesmen, merchants and professionals. These periodicals thrived until the late 1880s, eventually giving way to competition from the Sunday supplements of daily newspapers, the diversification of popular magazines, the rise of the dime novel, the production of inexpensive editions of good literature, the increasing sophistication of readers, and, as Noel suggests, sheer "surfeit." The 1870s may be regarded, in Noel's words, as "the time of the great story-paper flood" (133). *The Hearthstone* was one of several such papers—mostly ephemeral—that flourished briefly and then foundered in Canada. While it existed from May 1870 until December 1872, passing through the hands of three owners, it has survived only in a badly broken run from its final year when it was under George-Édouard Desbarats's control. A typical story paper in almost every respect, it was published in eight folio pages of five columns each, with editorial material confined to page four, brief compendia of "News Items," "Scientific Items," "Farm Items," and "Gems of Thought," a puzzle billed as the "Hearthstone Sphinx," a few poems, and a plethora of serialized novels, novellas, and short stories. Its front page followed the standard format, leading with a brief poem labeled *"For the 'Hearthstone'"* at the top of the first column, followed by the featured serial installment with its attention-grabbing woodcut illustration. The paper's masthead framed its title and subtitle ("Devoted to Choice Literature Romance &") within a partly ornate and partly rustic border of arboreal branches enclosing a panoramic sketch of Montreal, looking from the river towards the mountain. The authors it carried were an eclectic mix of foreign stars and less known Canadians. Among the novels serialized in 1872 were Charles Kingsley's *The Water Babies*, M.E. Braddon's *To the Bitter End*, and Rosanna Leprohon's *The Dead Witness; or, Lillian's Peril*. Crawford's stories "The Hospital Gondola" and "Windale's Souvenir" and her poems "The Departure of Winter" and "The Nightingale and the Lark" appeared in *The Hearthstone* between April and August that year.

During 1872, with the eager Desbarats at its helm, the paper implemented a variety of vigorous marketing strategies, urging readers to "Make Up Your Clubs" and sponsoring a lavish contest for anyone willing to canvass for new subscribers. The "First Grand Premium" for the largest number of new subscriptions sent in by one person before the deadline was to be "A Grand Square 7 octave Piano-Forte, rosewood case, rich mouldings, and of the finest tone," valued at $400.00 ("A Rare Chance"). But these efforts to promote sales were ultimately to no avail. A notice "To Our Subscribers" in the final number, on 28 December 1872, summarized the paper's chequered history by way of offering an explanation for its demise.

According to this valedictory editorial, *The Hearthstone*'s second owner, T.H. Churchill, who had acquired it in September 1870, had devised a seductive means to increase subscriptions to more than 15,000: he reduced the subscription rate from $2.50 to $1.00 per annum "and offered *half a dozen nickel silver teaspoons to each subscriber.*" The point of these italics is quickly made clear: Churchill had failed to deliver this premium to his customers and, in May 1871, he absconded with the subscription funds, "leaving the subscribers and his creditors completely in the lurch." With *The Hearthstone* in such disarray, Desbarats had assumed control, adding it to his small stable of periodicals that included *The Canadian Illustrated News, L'Opinion Publique,* and *L'Étendard National.* Unfortunately, as the editorial takes pains to explain, the new proprietor had been put at an irreconcilable disadvantage by the lingering "bad odium" of his predecessor's larceny, since "we never intended to carry out Mr. Churchill's promise to perform impossibilities in the way of spoons." Given this continuing problem and the resulting decline in subscriptions, Desbarats felt obliged to terminate the troubled story paper, seeking to placate its remaining list of readers with copies of his newly launched weekly, *The Favorite,* for the balance of their subscriptions.

This buccaneering publishing milieu, together with the climate of nationalist sentiment following Confederation, is the context of *Winona*'s origin. It was the era of the Canada First movement, which sought to moderate the country's relation to Great Britain by fostering a national consciousness, and of a flurry of new literary periodicals such as the *Canadian Monthly and National Review,* established in January 1872 with a mandate to "deal with Canadian questions and to call forth Canadian talent" ("Introductory").

Attuned to these cultural initiatives, in late June 1872 *The Hearthstone* began to run a prominent weekly headline on page four: "WANTED!! $1,275 REWARD. TO THE LITERARY MEN AND WOMEN OF CANADA." What followed were details of the sort of competition by which story papers often sought fresh fictional grist for their columns. This contest, however, had at its heart a decidedly nationalistic emphasis:

> We want to become acquainted with you!
> We want to unearth the hidden talent, now buried in our cities and hamlets, inland farms and seaside dwellings, primeval forests and storm-tossed barks.

We crave narratives, novels, sketches penned by vigorous Canadian hands, welling out from fresh and fertile Canadian brains, thrilling with the adventures by sea and land, of Canadian heroes; redolent with the perfume of Canadian fields and forests, soft as our sunshine, noble as our landscapes, grand as our inland seas and foam-girt shores. What inexhaustible fields in the realms of fact and fancy lie open to your industry and genius, women and men of Canada! What oceans of romance! What worlds of poesy! Why then do we see so little worthy of note brought forth in literature by our countrymen and countrywomen? Merely for want of material support and encouragement! That is all.

Now we open a tournament to native talent, and invite all to enter the lists. We ask for novels and stories formed on Canadian history, experience and incident—illustrative of back wood life, fishing, lumbering, farming; taking the reader through our industrious cities, floating palaces, steam-driven factories, ship-building yards, lumbering shanties, fishing shacks, &c, and we offer the following prizes for the best Canadian stories

	1st prize.	2nd prize.
For a story of 100 cols	$500	$300
" 50 "	250	150

For the two best short stories, complete in one number, $50 for the best, $25 for the next best.

We want to have an essentially Canadian paper, and gradually to dispense with selections and foreign contributions, &c.

Stories will be received until the first of October, when the selections will be made and the prizes forwarded at once. Rejected stories will be preserved for three months, and the authors may have them returned on forwarding stamps.

Send along your manuscript now as soon as you please.

This advertisement epitomizes the rhetoric of early literary nationalists who sought to create a hospitable environment for writing in post-Confederation Canada.[1] Lamenting the lack of production but

---

[1] Three years previously, Desbarats had launched his *Canadian Illustrated News* with a similar contest, offering $150 for the best romance "founded on incidents in the history of Canada" ("To Literary Men"). The winning entry was S.J. Watson's *The Peacekiller; or, The Massacre at Lachine*, serialized from 2 July to 27 August 1870.

celebrating the potential of literature in the new Dominion, it appeals to the energies of youth, emphasizing the inspiration to be found in landscape and evoking a pan-Canadian vista of the nation's varied scenes and activities, just as the title of Lighthall's anthology was to do 17 years later. As Diana Theman has shown, the suggestion that the country's intellectual wealth must be cultivated to build up the nation, just as its material resources were being exploited to the same end, is a commonplace of the period, and is frequently accompanied by the trope of "buried treasure." Also noteworthy is the imagery of chivalric romance, which is consistent with the dominant conventions of plot, character, and sentiment in popular fiction at the time, and also, no doubt, with the desire of readers for a glamour that was all too absent from their daily lives. It is pertinent to note how many topics broached in this announcement did, in fact, find their way into *Winona*, where we do indeed encounter primeval forests and seaside dwellings, "back wood life," industrious cities, floating palaces, and lumbering shanties.

The following week, in response to inquiries, *The Hearthstone's* editor, J.A. Phillips, a Montreal writer of some note, stated that stories set partly outside the country would be considered but preference given to "a purely Canadian story." He also observed, rather sharply, that "we do not consider the time at all too short; three months is ample time in which to write stories of the lengths we require" ("Our Prize Stories" 6 July 1872). By November, however, he was more sensitive to the demands of time. Even as he assured competitors that a list of winning titles would be published shortly, he pleaded his own need as judge for further leeway to cope with the large number of submissions received ("Our Prize Stories" 2 November 1872). There can be little doubt that at this point Desbarats and Phillips knew that the paper's survival was in question; in fact, they had already begun to implement a plan to shut it down and reinvent it as *The Favorite*. In any case, *The Hearthstone's* final number (28 December 1872) included, alongside the rationale for its termination, a notice "To Our Contributors":

> By the announcement in to-day's paper the competitors for our prizes for Canadian stories will see one reason why there had been some delay in announcing the awards; the labor of planning and getting up a new paper, added to our editor's illness, made it impossible to complete the labor of reading over *twelve thousand pages* of manuscript as quickly as it

would otherwise have been done. The reading is now very nearly completed, and the announcement of prizes will be made in an early number of *The Favorite*, in which paper the stories will appear.

In fact, no such announcement did appear in *The Favorite* and, if Crawford's experience was typical, the cash prizes were withheld from the rightful winners. How many submissions for the competition found their way into *The Favorite* is uncertain, although the list of prospective contributors published at its debut—a special Christmas issue dated 28 December 1872—may be a clue. A number of authors listed under the heading "Who Will Write for *The Favorite*" had been contributors to *The Hearthstone*, and it is certainly suggestive that Crawford's name heads this list, which also includes Emma N. Crawford, Susanna Moodie, and Mary Muchall. Indeed, this initial issue of *The Favorite* featured Isabella's seasonal story "The Silvers' Christmas Eve" on its front page and also contained Emma's story " 'The Course of True Love,' Et Cetera." It is equally suggestive that the work of both sisters appeared frequently in the paper over the next six months, then abruptly ceased in June 1873, no doubt because, by then, it had become clear to the Crawfords that payment for their work, or at least for Isabella's, was not forthcoming. The sequel to this chain of circumstances took place in Judge Wilson's Peterborough courtroom in October.

Following its inaugural Christmas issue, *The Favorite* appeared every Saturday from 11 January 1873—when the first installment of *Winona* was published—until 27 June 1874. Priced at five cents per copy (or "six cents U.S."), it was offered to subscribers at two dollars per annum. Although it abandoned the usual folio layout for sixteen quarto pages of four columns, in almost every other respect it was *The Hearthstone* reincarnate. Again, one finds three or four serials running concurrently, together with short stories and poems, editorials both serious and humorous, regular compendia of "News Notes," "Family Matters," "Hints for Farmers," and so forth, as well as "Our Puzzler," and the occasional advertisement.

Its prospectus of eminent American and British authors "Who Will Write for *The Favorite*" was more than mere puffery, though entirely typical of story-paper self-promotion and pretense: leading writers like Wilkie Collins, Oliver Wendell Holmes, Mark Twain, and Louisa M. Alcott were promised to readers but were conspicuous by their absence over the course of *The Favorite's* eighteen-month existence. Desbarats operated his papers with a close eye to copyright obligations and tried, within his budgetary limits, to purchase Canadian serial rights simultaneous with book publication elsewhere. His strategy, however, favoured the placement of popular writers in his flagship national paper, *The Canadian Illustrated News*, over its lesser sister, *The Favorite*.

Still, *The Favorite* offered a range of attractive material for hungry readers. There were translations of Pushkin, plenty of ghost stories, and a few pieces—almost certainly pirated—by such stalwarts of the story-paper world as Mary Kyle Dallas, Sylvanus Cobb, Jr., and various Canadians, including a young May Agnes Fleming, Mrs. J.V. [Ellen Vavasour] Noel of Kingston, John Reade, an Irishman living in Montreal, and the paper's editor, J.A. Phillips. The standard fare consisted of serials such as Eliza Winstanley's *Desmoro; or, The Red Hand*, a tale of Australian bushranging, and *Feudal Times; or, Two Soldiers of Fortune: A Romance of Daring and Adventure*, which, readers were apprised, had been "translated especially for the FAVORITE from the French of Paul Duplessis." Its great coup, triumphantly announced in the summer of 1873, was the securing of a new novel by the queen of sensation writers, M.E. Braddon, called *Publicans and Sinners*, which was serialized simultaneously with its publication in three volumes in England. During the paper's final six months, long after Crawford's work had ceased to appear in its columns, its pages were increasingly filled with anonymous prose sketches, stories, and illustrations.

Notwithstanding this large proportion of foreign material and the American spelling of its name, *The Favorite* attempted to position itself as an "essentially Canadian" publication devoted to the same nationalist mission that had been declared in the story contest sponsored by *The Hearthstone*. An advertisement for this "New Canadian Weekly" that appeared in Desbarats's other papers could hardly have been more explicit:

> "THE FAVORITE" MAXIM.—Canada for the Canadians—whether by birth or adoption. Let us help each other, if we aspire to be a Nation. "The Favorite" is a genuine Canadian enterprise,—Canadian in its conception, its plan, its execution,—written, edited, printed by Canadians, on Canadian paper, with Canadian type. GIVE IT YOUR SUPPORT.

Perhaps with a view to prospective American subscribers, an editorial in the initial Christmas issue offered two less aggressively patriotic

28   INTRODUCTION

reasons for the creation of *The Favorite*: "first, a desire to furnish a thoroughly good paper, perfectly moral in its tone and tendencies, to take the place of the trashy publications with which the country is deluged; and, secondly, we have what we conceive to be a very reasonable desire to make a little money by the transaction" ("Our First Bow"). Here, Canadian nationalism is part of a nexus of motives ranging from profit to a commitment to "moral tone." Readers were promised that the content of *The Favorite* would be lively but respectable: "It will be designed especially for the family circle, and may safely be placed in the hands of childhood. The stories we publish, while interesting and full of adventure and incident, will be free from any of the vulgar sensationalism of the day, and will tend to elevate, improve, and instruct as well as humor" ("Our First Bow"). This appeal to family values was typical of contemporary story papers like *Frank Leslie's Chimney Corner*, reflecting their commercial objectives as well as their resolute moral orientation. Nevertheless, this moral posture precluded neither the melodramatic violence that pervaded their fiction nor the outright editorial pride with which *The Favorite* offered up the latest Braddon.

What is of interest in the claim to moral purity is its connection with the paper's nationalist stance. If the source of "the trashy publications with which the country is deluged" went unnamed in this editorial, it was made quite clear a few weeks later in a leader titled "Artistic Filth," which identified New York as the fountainhead of periodical iniquity (see Appendix B). It was reported that *The Favorite's* own agent for the lower provinces had persuaded customs officials at Saint John "to seize a large number of *Police Gazettes*, *Day's Doings*, and other kindred publications." What was needed was a campaign "to drive indecent literature out of Canada." The tabloids singled out for opprobrium here were obviously a moral cut or two below the average story paper, or at any rate they were directed to a specifically "adult male" readership. It is no coincidence, however, that *The Day's Doings* was a Frank Leslie publication, though a relatively ephemeral one. Indeed, it is hard not to detect marketing as well as morality in this polemic. At this period, as throughout Canadian history, the influx of American publications was a daunting economic threat to the survival of domestic publishing. When *The Favorite* announced its demise a year and a half later, a final "Notice" explained with chagrin that the paper had to be terminated because of lack of public support from Canadian readers against the persistent American onslaught.

The ideological and material forces at play in this border environment are important to an appreciation of *Winona* as well as to an understanding of Crawford's career. Readers might well consider whether, or to what extent, her novel inscribes the moral constraints as well as the nationalist agenda of *The Hearthstone* and *The Favorite*. At the same time, the failure of these ambitious papers underscores one of the difficulties that confronted Canadian writers in the era immediately following Confederation. In the aftermath of the story-contest debacle, Crawford's decision to direct her fiction almost exclusively to an American market had a transforming effect on the eventual shape of her oeuvre. Whereas four of her five short stories written "for *The Favorite*" have, like *Winona*, an explicitly Canadian setting, not one of the two dozen stories that she subsequently wrote for Frank Leslie's periodicals does. As a consequence of her decision, and regardless of any distinctions that we may wish to note in considering her potboilers for the story papers and her "real" work as a poet, *Winona* remains, if only by default, her most Canadian work of fiction.

Winona and the Victorian Sensation Novel

If *Winona*'s publishing matrix was distinctively North American, its principal generic model, the sensation novel, has been largely associated with British writers like Wilkie Collins, Mary Elizabeth Braddon, and Ellen (Mrs. Henry) Wood. In the 1860s, these writers had excited controversy by challenging the conventions of the English domestic novel through introducing the stuff of melodrama into the households of ostensibly ordinary middle-class or aristocratic characters. Collins's *The Woman in White* (1860) is usually credited with inaugurating the vogue, which flourished for the better part of the decade and left its mark on writers as diverse as Charles Dickens, Anthony Trollope, and Thomas Hardy. As Deborah Wynne has observed, "the sensation novel was the first middle-class Victorian genre to conspicuously retain aspects of its 'low' origins in melodrama and penny fiction while still appealing widely to 'respectable' readers" (14). The genre was thus well matched with the story paper as vehicle and the serial as format. It is ironic, then, that in August 1872, after announcing its story contest but before choosing *Winona* as a winner, *The Hearthstone* ran an editorial deploring the influence of "Sensation Literature" on contemporary taste and morals.

Among other things, this editorial pointed out, "it was not until serial stories came into fashion, and the cheap weeklies began to make their appearance, that the sensation writers commenced to come out in full force." Wynne makes the related point that "the exigencies of the serial form itself became responsible for many of the distinctive generic features of the sensation novel" (40). No doubt the opening chapters of *Winona*, with their wilderness adventure, threatening "red-skins," and doughty backwoodsmen, have more in common with dime-novel romance than they do with Collins or Braddon, but the lineaments of the sensation novel emerge when the scene shifts to the more "civilized" (and domestic) settings of Toronto, Montreal, and the Frazer estate on the upper St. Lawrence in the Thousand Islands area.

One distinctive feature of the genre is a fast-paced narrative, highlighting mystery, suspense, and surprise, and calculated to sustain the interest of readers—and their willingness to pay up on subscriptions—from week to week. Certainly these elements are prominent in *Winona*, and at times might be considered egregious. Withholding information to prolong the mystery is fair enough where the villain's background is concerned, but withholding Winona's account of what actually happened at Lake Chetowaik until long after she so dramatically reappears at the Harty farmhouse to tell her tale, may annoy readers more than it excites them. Indeed, the circumstances of Androsia Howard's abduction are never adequately clarified: when Winona finally recapitulates this event near the novel's conclusion, details of the affray out on the lake—the part played by the Native youth Jimsy, for example—remain vague. So too the narrative offers little explanation of how Androsia and Winona came to be foster-sisters and how their lives together evolved. Moreover, the preservation of these and other mysteries sometimes seems incongruous with the omniscient narration and instances of outright editorializing on the narrator's part. On the other hand, Crawford's plotting is in many respects shrewd and effective. Individual serial installments conclude with heightened suspense or matter for reflection, and almost invariably they comprise a sequence of chapters that achieves internal coherence through a continuity of character and action or through an instructive contrast of characters and locales. The larger structure of the novel is also well conceived, aligning the main plot concerning Andrew Farmer's machinations with the subplot about Cecil Bertrand's intrigues, and arranging their eventual intersection through the intervention of Valerie Lennox.

Readers of this edition will, of course, encounter the novel in a markedly different form than readers of *The Favorite* did. At that period, as Michael Lund has noted, "installment issue and parts reading … determined the primary shape of literary experience" (9). Reading fiction in serial form amplified the pleasures of savouring individual segments, anticipating what was to follow, and making a particular novel part of the fabric of one's experience over a period of months, or even years (Lund 81-82). In her recent study of sensation novels and Victorian magazines, Deborah Wynne suggests that serials fostered "a 'community of readers'" (12) and she examines ways in which periodicals, and their editors, fashioned contexts that influenced the reception of such fiction. A particular novel's juxtaposition with poems, opinion pieces, and other serials inevitably produced resonance or dissonance among the ideas and values that these texts projected. Moreover, the numerous illustrations that accompanied serialized installments affected their reception through emphasizing certain events and through the visual rendering of characters. The first episode of *Winona* in *The Favorite* is accompanied by a woodcut, over the caption "Archie's Meeting With Androsia," which pictures the young officer being greeted by the maiden in buckskins at the threshold of her father's home while a heavily bearded Andrew Farmer looks on, appraising Archie's demeanour. The romantic attraction of the young couple and the ominous gaze of their antagonist are thus suggested, though it might be noted that Androsia looks far more welcoming in this picture than she is in the text, and that the massive stone portal of Colonel Howard's wilderness domicile looks distinctly more European than it does northern Ontarian.[1] Together with this

---

[1] While the illustrations for *Winona* in *The Favorite* are undoubtedly generic (see "Archie's Meeting with Androsia," frontispiece to Chapter I, and "Winona's Return," Appendix E), they bear some resemblance to the work of Edward Jump (1832-83), an itinerant French artist who had worked for Frank Leslie's publishing firm in New York before coming to Montreal to join Desbarats's staff on the *Canadian Illustrated News* in the early 1870s. It is conceivable that Jump worked on more than one of Debarats's publications, and he may well have been assigned to illustrate the prize serial featured prominently in the latter's new story paper. In particular, there is a suggestion of Jump's gift for caricature in the pictorial rendering of Crawford's comic Irish factotum Mike Murphy. As well, the treatment of scenery and costume in these illustrations bears a resemblance both to an unsigned cover of the *Canadian Illustrated News* for 24 June 1871, titled "A Moonlight Excursion on the St. Lawrence" (see Appendix E), and to various drawings signed by Jump, whose work for Desbarats can be viewed at the website "*Images in the News: Canadian Illustrated News 1869–1883*," Library and Archives Canada, 25 April 2005 [http://www.collectionscanada.ca/cin/index-e.html].

illustration, the opening of *Winona* also shares its page with a poem by *The Favorite*'s editor, J.A. Phillips, titled "The Factory Girl," which protests the degradation of its exploited protagonist in terms that might well put into perspective the privileged if also vulnerable position of the two isolated women in Crawford's novel. While this edition does not aspire to reproduce the experience of reading *Winona* as a serial, readers who are interested in this aspect of the novel may note that headings are included in the text to show where breaks occurred between weekly installments in the original.

Certain conventions of the serialized sensation novel, then, are manifest in *Winona*'s structure. Whether this vogue also bears a relation to the novel's style is a more complex question. The opening pages, in particular, may strike readers as exceedingly overwritten, congealed with adjectives, and prone to clichés such as "trackless solitudes" (81) and archaisms such as "finny tenants of the lake" (81). Such weaknesses can be ascribed in part to Crawford's haste and inexperience but they are also indicative of the genre and the particular contest in which she was participating; ultimately, they prefigure certain aspects of her own developing style, in poetry as well as fiction. Dorothy Farmiloe has defended this style in terms of a general Victorian taste for embellishment (75), but in *Winona* it also has a specifically generic significance. *The Hearthstone*'s editorial on "Sensation Literature" sourly observes that "the sensation reporter must write in the most florid style; he must be an adept at verbal ornamentation, must be prepared to go into ecstacies at a moment's notice, if given a ball or other pleasurable entertainment to 'write up;' or must be gloomy, pathetic or witty if given a murder, or suicide, or elopement." More recently, Lyn Pykett has pointed out that "women sensationalists put the emotional and linguistic excesses of melodrama to new uses" (75) and has proposed that such excesses represent "an irruption into narration of that feeling (particularly the erotic feeling) which is repressed in the narrative" (97). This claim is suggestive in view of the erotically charged language and imagery of Crawford's most characteristic verse. Arguably, the lushness and even the prolixity of her writing in *Winona* contain rudiments of the linguistic richness and power that distinguish her best poetry. Indeed, it is not difficult to find passages in the novel that correspond to specific poems. A description of the evening star's ascent "on quivering pinions of light" (209) unmistakably anticipates the "The Vesper

Star," published in *The Mail* [Toronto] on 24 December 1873. Even more striking are passages that are echoed in work composed at much later stages of Crawford's career: a vision of Indian summer in eastern Ontario (131) clearly anticipates the mythopoeic "South Wind" section in Part 2 of "Malcolm's Katie," and a passage on pioneering (134–35) looks forward to the central "nation-building" passages of both "Malcolm's Katie" and *Hugh and Ion*.

Other staples of the sensation novel that are employed in *Winona* include the family secret, the threatened inheritance, the gentleman criminal, the implacable detective, and the scandal of bigamy (Farmer's intended union with Androsia and Theodore Denville's proposed union with Valerie). It is clear that Crawford was thoroughly, and to some extent ironically, aware that she was working with a fashionable genre; indeed, she introduces the detective Jack Fennel as a figure "written of in novels" (210), while at the opening of Chapter XVII she archly alludes to the sensation genre itself in Ensign Spooner's fascination with reports of violent domestic crime. The amusement with which she describes Spooner's taste for the sensational is also apparent in certain episodes where the melodrama is laid on with a thickness that becomes positively suspicious. No doubt the most spectacular of these is the scene at the Harty farmhouse when Mike Murphy's ghost story is told to the backdrop of a fearsome thunderstorm that reaches its climax simultaneously with the apparition of Winona, lamented and believed to be dead, upon the threshold. Murphy's terrified antics and the intervention of a precocious squirrel leaven this outrageous episode with an indispensable measure of comedy. Such comic, satiric, and even parodic moments indicate that Crawford was well aware that she was testing the credibility of her material as well as the credulity of her audience, and that she enjoyed the literary game that she was playing.

The villain of the tale, Andrew Farmer/Harold Macer/Malcolm Lennox, may appear extravagantly stereotypical to readers today. Nevertheless, he is interesting for his literary pedigree and relevance to Crawford's later work. He becomes a focal character on a par with Winona herself, and he is certainly more central to the narrative than Archie Frazer, who provides the initial (and innocent) point of view. Archie rather resembles the passive heroes of Sir Walter Scott, whose role is to experience the unfamiliar, "savage," and dangerous rather than to take decisive action; contrary to expectation, a climactic confrontation between Archie and

Farmer never occurs, and like the protagonist of Scott's *Waverley* (1814), Archie is physically disabled at a crucial juncture. Moreover, he and Winona both disappear from view for lengthy intervals.

As a result, the sinister gentleman who is introduced as Andrew Farmer moves inexorably to centre stage and remains there on the novel's final page, where the equivalent of a sombre Shakespearean epitaph is conferred upon him. Cultivated, brooding, and with depths of formidable passion, Farmer is the descendant of such philosophizing villains as Edmund in *King Lear*, Satan in *Paradise Lost*, and the Byronic heroes of early nineteenth-century literature, as his own self-conscious choice of literary allusions may suggest. Like them—and like the renegade Sir Reginald Morton in John Richardson's novel *Wacousta* (1832)—he is a disinherited and disappointed aspirant to aristocratic privilege who in his despair renounces aristocratic honour. He also prefigures one of Crawford's most widely discussed characters, the nihilistic interloper Alfred of "Malcolm's Katie." Much like Alfred, he saves a maiden in peril of drowning but throttles any stirrings of remorse as he plots against her family, and he represses volcanic passion beneath an outward appearance of suavity and patience.

Despite his stereotypical features, Farmer does have some of the depth and appeal of his grand precursors and his successor in Crawford's celebrated poem. He has a powerful mind, is loved by the two most remarkable women in the novel, displays urbanity and an aesthetic sensibility (not to mention a mastery of billiards, small talk, and disguise), and might even be said to encompass a tragic dimension in his single-minded consecration to self. In opposition to his professed rationalism, the narrative hints that his cynicism and avarice had their genesis in his early life, when he was deprived of the sort of nurturing family that is represented pre-eminently in the novel by the Frazers, but also by the cozy suburban Fennel home and the rustic Harty household. In a scene that will repay close analysis, at the end of the nineteenth chapter (and seventh serial installment), he arrives at a crisis in his designs against the Frazers and Androsia Howard. Having spent the afternoon half charmed by the affectionate family circle into which he has insinuated himself, he watches the sun set while considering whether to go forward with his scheme. The charged imagery and suggestive allusions in this passage endow his character and motives with complexity and interest, in spite of the patent melodrama.

Among those characters who oppose Farmer, and among the novel's most memorable minor figures, is his nemesis, Jack Fennel, the mild-mannered Toronto detective whom Archie Frazer employs to track down the missing Winona, and who is in all probability one of the first detectives in Canadian fiction. In a pioneering anthology of Canadian detective stories, Michael Richardson claims that the genre arrived in Canada "with James De Mille's fine Victorian mystery, *The Cryptogram* (1871)" (ix), while according to David Skene-Melvin, "[t]he first piece of criminous writing in Canadian literature to utilize Toronto as an identifiable setting is John Dent's 'The Gerrard Street mystery' that appeared in his collection *The Gerrard Street mystery; and other weird tales* published in 1888" (7). *The Cryptogram*, however, is Canadian only by virtue of its author's citizenship: like much of De Mille's fiction, it was published in the United States and has entirely non-Canadian settings and characters. In this context, Crawford's novel of 1873, with a Toronto detective who plies his trade from a home base on north Yonge Street to points east along the rail line to Montreal, is very much in the vanguard.

In her characterization of Fennel, we see Crawford working consciously against a newly-established set of literary conventions. She defines the detective as "one of those useful outgrowths of modern society written of in novels, scoffed at by a thankless public, and working brain and body day and night for a very trifling meed of fame or fortune …" (210). However, her Fennel is "not at all like the recognized type of detective. He wasn't middle-aged, he wasn't grey-headed, he wasn't particularly reserved or quiet" (213). Instead, he is a cheerful young man of slight, military bearing, professional in his approach to his work, happily married to the attractive Gracie, and keenly musical in his tastes. With respect to class, he is positioned between the well-bred Frazers and characters of lower or servant caste such as Mike Murphy. As an urban professional, he is, in fact, a representative of the new Canadian middle class and an image of the future. An independent thinker, he is "courageous as a lion" in a "risky, uncertain business" (217), level-headed, and physically strong. On the job, he is seen in action interrogating witnesses like the station master, Archelaus Simkins, and adopting disguises, first as a drummer and then as an Irish servant near the fictitious town of Scranton (possibly based on Brockville or Gananoque). At the same time, a pleasant domesticity and a love of music characterize his charming home on Yonge Street. The Fennel cottage, with its piano and the intoxicating violin of talented

Uncle Ferdinand (who was "like some old wizard of sweet sounds" [217]), seems a modest Arcadia of healthful repose, a fleeting glimpse perhaps of Crawford's own recipe for "humble" but healthful domestic life. Music there looms very large, "[t]he true panacea for most ills of mind or body" (217), in Uncle Ferdinand's words.

The Woman Question and "The Foster-Sisters"

Recent critics have pointed out that at the heart of the sensation novel, and the sensation that it caused during the 1860s, is its bearing on the so-called "woman question"—the controversy over women's nature and place in society that exercised writers and the reading public in England and North America through most of the century. This debate had accelerated in the decade preceding *Winona*, yielding such notable documents as John Ruskin's "Of Queen's Gardens" (1865), Eliza Lynn Linton's "The Girl of the Period" (1868), and John Stuart Mill's *The Subjection of Women* (1869). In various ways, *Winona* participates in this controversy, and is therefore highly relevant for critics engaged in ongoing debate over the role and significance of the heroine of "Malcolm's Katie." One of the novel's striking features is its number and variety of prominent female characters: in addition to the two "foster-sisters," there are the three Frazer daughters, as well as Valerie Lennox and Cecil Bertrand, and there are also colourful minor figures such as Sal Harty, Grace Fennel, and Rosie, the Irish parlor-maid. Each is characterized with some particularity, and, collectively, they imply a view, at this early stage in Crawford's career, of the situation and possibilities for women in post-Confederation Canada. Admittedly, most of them, especially the three Frazer sisters, are variations on types: Dolly is the vacuous but tender beauty, Sidney the irrepressible "kid sister," and Olla the gracious young woman whose modesty and passivity leave her exposed to disaster when she is made the victim of intrigue. Dolly, in her dazzling physical appearance, and Olla, in terms of her role in the narrative, bear more than passing resemblance—and with a tinge of parody—to that fictional "heroine of old time" whom Sara Jeannette Duncan recalled with gentle ridicule in an article published in the following decade (see Appendix A).

Cecil Bertrand and Valerie Lennox are slightly more dimensioned characters and are obviously positioned as antithetical figures. The latter will be familiar to many readers as one of those wronged and abandoned women who throng Victorian literature. She is introduced at a relatively advanced point in the narrative, sitting by a harp in the Denville drawing room, "as still as the statue of Diana, with bow and crescent, behind her" (224). Her association with the goddess of chastity and protector of young women is apt, for she demonstrates integrity and courage when she intervenes on behalf of the young women threatened by Cecil Bertrand and Andrew Farmer. Unlike Olla, but like Winona, Valerie is prepared to take action in the face of evil, though her methods are dramatically different. The deliberate contrast between her wisdom and compassion on the one hand and Cecil's vanity and egoism on the other is nowhere more striking than in their treatment of Theodore Denville and Percy Grace, their immature cousins who seek to marry them.

Many readers, however, will probably find Cecil, like most antagonists, the livelier and more memorable of the two. While she is clearly a variation on the stock figure of the heartless coquette, she has some of the novel's best lines, and certainly she has the most spectacular rendezvous with destiny. She also embodies types that had achieved currency in the Victorian discourse of womanhood, namely Linton's notorious "Girl of the Period" and that figure's kindred incarnation in the "Fast Young Lady," perhaps not coincidently the subject of a lively article in the *Canadian Illustrated News* in September 1872. Thus, Cecil is set against the ideal of "true womanhood" embodied by Olla and Valerie. Indeed, Crawford introduces her as "one of those daintily 'fast' girls of the period who can venture upon doing almost anything, confident of tripping out of even a shadow of reproach with the most bewitching air of innocence, and supremely blest in never sinning against the 'proprieties' ungracefully" (142). Like Linton's "G.O.P.," she is fundamentally mercenary in her relations with men; in Linton's formulation, "the legal barter of herself for so much money, representing so much dash, so much luxury and pleasure—that is her idea of marriage; the only idea worth entertaining" (340). Cecil is, of course, also ultra feminine in costume, appearance, and appurtenances—at one point she is viewed in bravura coquette mode "sobbing in her chintz nest" (167). However, her outward delicacy is belied by her vulgarity when angered and her lack of discernment regarding others: she successively mistakes, with serious and finally mortal consequences, the characters of Archie Frazer, Theodore Denville, and Percy Grace. As the villain of the novel's subplot, she corresponds to Farmer but lacks his depth and impressiveness, and her own end is bathetic and ironic rather than tragic.

While the positioning of Valerie and Cecil as moral opposites is a highly conventional narrative strategy, the pairing of "the foster-sisters" is more ambiguous. Winona is manifestly a disruptive figure in the novel's representation of womanhood, and her relationship with Androsia Howard is at the centre of its ideological tensions. According to Lyn Pykett, sensation novels written by women in England during the 1860s reproduced a discourse of "the 'proper' or respectable feminine" while simultaneously expressing a fascination with its "suppressed other ... the 'improper' feminine" (16). This is precisely the dynamic that shapes the roles of Crawford's foster-sisters, or of "'Miss Drosia' and her dusky familiar," as Sidney Frazer calls them (180). From the beginning, Winona is portrayed as an outsider capable of the extreme passion, feats of strength, and even violence that are taboo to other women in the novel. Androsia, in the meantime, is transformed from the "Indianized" maiden of the introductory chapter—her father calls her "a complete savage" (92)— to the respectable young matron married to Archie Frazer at the novel's end.

More than any other major character, Androsia appears to function as an allegorical "counter" rather than an individual; indeed, she represents precisely what is at stake in the narrative, in more than one sense. Her physical appearance, like that of all the prominent women characters, is described in detail, but her subjectivity is exceptionally limited. Depicted almost entirely from the perspective of others, she has relatively little dialogue and almost never assumes the narrative point of view: the single passage in which the narrative is fleetingly aligned with her viewpoint reveals her "puzzled and confused" sense that the enamoured Archie's manner towards her has changed (174). Who looks at whom, and how, is an important matter in Crawford's novel, which throws exceptional emphasis on the colour of people's eyes, the quality of their gaze, and the surveillance undertaken by schemers, stalkers, and detectives. When introduced in Chapter I, Androsia is described (in an allusion to Longfellow) as having "magnificent hazel eyes, shadowy and 'burning yet tender'" (85). Once she comes to reside with Archie's family, however, her fiery side is tempered by her "new style of dress" (188), her rapid progress in the "to her, hidden art of reading" (207), and her acquaintance with models of feminine grace and propriety in Mrs. Frazer, her daughters, and Valerie Lennox. Her name has the polysyllabic euphony of the typical romance-heroine names that

Duncan makes fun of (Araminta, Genevieve, Rosabel), and perhaps also implies her psychic duality and its eventual resolution in her marriage. "Andro" connotes a masculine element that makes her, at first, more akin to her foster-sister, but it is an element that is ultimately subsumed in the "ambrosia" that she comes to signify to an adoring husband.

By contrast, Winona is impervious to domestication. When Archie first glimpses her peering from the loft at Colonel Howard's lodge, he sees "a pair of immense dark eyes, burning like stars of fire" (88). She sustains this intensity of gaze throughout the narrative, suggesting an agency and power beyond the pale of proper female conduct and expression. She is also repeatedly described as shadowy and "phantom-like"(187), and thus encodes repressed elements of human nature (especially of the feminine) in Gothic terms that again bring Richardson's *Wacousta* to mind. Like many Gothic protagonists, she is a shape-shifter. At one point, she dresses in a European lady's costume and at another she assumes the disguise of "a lame Indian boy" (222); moreover, when she arrives with her foster-sister at the Frazer estate, we are told that Sidney does not mistake her for Androsia's maid (179). Thus her difference is striking to the discerning, and she unsettles not only codes of gender, but also boundaries of race and class that are otherwise sharply defined in the novel. Her most resonant gesture occurs almost precisely at the mid-point of the narrative when she decides to leave Androsia in the Frazers' care as she departs to track down Farmer and eliminate the threat he represents:

> "I must leave her a gift to remember Winona by," she muttered softly, and gliding to a little stand in the window she lifted from it a pair of scissors, and in a couple of moments her magnificent hair lay in a black mass at her feet. She lifted it, and without a change of countenance, tore a strip from the crêpe veil attached to the hat she carried, and tying it round the heavy raven tresses laid them on the white quilt beside her foster sister. Then she lifted one of the sleeping girl's bright curls, and cautiously severing it from her head, thrust it into her bosom. (185)

While Winona says that she performs this ritual to provide a memento for Androsia, it also contributes to the disguise that she is about to assume, and in a narrative that repeatedly furnishes lavish descriptions of women's hair, it has other meanings as well. On the one hand, it may bring to mind epitomes of beauty such as Dolly Frazer: "a poetic grace about her graceful head, a nameless exaltation shining like a light on her broad, low brow, from which the golden hair rippled back in large soft waves, and, caught in a silky mass behind, fell in great loose curls on her lovely shoulders" (130). On the other hand, it recalls Winona's appearance at the Harty farmhouse with Hawk-eye's scalp dangling from her belt, an episode that certifies not only her "Indian" identity but also her emphatically masculine qualities relative to the other women in the novel.

In the context of her farewell to Androsia, then, Winona's divestiture of her hair suggests her rejection of the conventions of femininity, civilization, and morality represented by the Frazer household. It also implies self-consecration (nun-like and unequivocal) to revenge, and a commitment to self-sacrifice on her foster-sister's behalf. Symbolically, she spares Androsia through assuming the burden of "darkness" for both of them, and leaves behind a sign of that darkness. At the same time, in taking one of Androsia's "bright curls" as a remembrance for herself, she bears away with her a residual trace of Androsia's more normative and much-valued femininity. A few paragraphs later, in a lengthy exposition of the relationship between the foster-sisters, we are told: "Androsia was to her a purer, higher, brighter self" (187). This may be the most troubling instance of a conundrum that persists throughout the novel: the intersection of a moral discourse of light and darkness with a discourse of complexion relating to both race and class that encompasses almost all the major characters and acquires particular emphasis where the women are concerned. The meaning of this semiotic complex should not be reduced to the crude racism that certain characters express. It is complicated, for instance, by the fact that Olla Frazer, one of the most sympathetic characters, has a "brown" colouring (117), whereas Cecil—who includes the epithets "brown, mean thing" (169) and "Miss Black-a-moor" (279) in her lexicon of spite—not only has a complexion of "lucid pearl and rose" (142), but also, ultimately, is remembered in a funeral that is a veritable (and ironic) riot of virginal white. It is similarly complicated by the consistently positive charge of the adjective "bronze" as it is repeatedly applied to Winona.

Nonetheless, modern readers who are more critically aware of racialized discourse than were most nineteenth-century readers may be troubled by a narrative arc that eventually brings the "wild, bronze, Venus" (88) of the opening chapters to her apotheosis in a "life size statue ... hewn in

WINONA; OR, THE FOSTER-SISTERS   41

the purest marble" (285) that gleams "whitely" (286) from the shadows, in the final pages of the novel. In this regard it may be more than a coincidence that both the subtitle and the paired white and Native heroines of *Winona* have a precedent in E.D.E.N. Southworth's novel of the American South, *Virginia and Magdalene; or, The Foster-Sisters* (1852), in which issues of colonialism, race, and gender are made still more problematic by the inclusion of African-American slaves among the characters. In *Dreaming Black/Writing White: The Hagar Myth in American Cultural History*, Janet Gabler-Hover offers a suggestive reading of the ways in which Southworth's novel "hybridizes symbolically white/pure and ethnically other/fallen women" (66). Her central thesis, that white women writers of the American South invoked the Biblical story of Hagar to appropriate the strength and sexuality that they associated with black women, only to reprivilege whiteness through ultimately finding some narrative means to "bleach" or "whitewash" their Hagar figures, would seem to have a parallel in Crawford's treatment of Winona.

Among other things, the contradictions in Crawford's representation of Winona inscribe precisely that ambivalence about "the 'improper' feminine" that Pykett identifies as the hallmark of women's sensation novels of the 1860s. Wynne makes a similar point in observing that "although sensation novelists usually provided conservative solutions at the ends of their novels, their complex depictions of subversive possibilities are prominently placed for most of the narrative, suggesting alternatives without necessarily endorsing them" (149). With its climactic triple wedding, Crawford's novel certainly reinforces the most conservative of "solutions" for women in nineteenth-century Canada and in the world of nineteenth-century fiction.

Nonetheless, the character of Winona clearly raises "subversive possibilities" throughout the narrative. It is her very status as "Indian," of course, that permits her contravention of the normative femininity represented in all the other women, and it is this element of the novel, highlighted in its title, that most demands an adequate critical reading.

"[T]he Indian girl with the romantic name"

What are the provenance and scope of the Native materials that Crawford uses in *Winona*? Her biographers and critics have cited two sources for her knowledge of Native culture, usually in connection with the "South

Wind" passage in "Malcolm's Katie," but also with reference to poems such as "The Wooing of Gheezis: An Indian Idyll" (1874), "The Camp of Souls" (1880), and "The Dark Stag" (1883). Taking their cue from the 1927 biographical sketch by "Antrim," several commentators have claimed that during her early years growing up in Paisley, Crawford came to know the Ojibwa bands living in that area and acquired at first hand a substantial knowledge of their culture and myths (see especially Farmiloe 15–16). There is no way of corroborating or refuting this claim, except to conjecture as to how much contact Isabella, as a young and protected girl, might actually have experienced there. If she had more than a cursory contact with Native peoples, it is more likely to have occurred in Lakefield when as a teenager she may have had more opportunity to make the acquaintance of neighbouring Ojibwa who lived on reservations like Hiawatha on Rice Lake and Curve Lake, located north of the town, and those who still carried on their traditional hunting and fishing in the area. Still, in its paucity of detail about Winona and her heritage, the novel suggests distinct limitations in Crawford's personal knowledge of Native peoples.

At the same time the text reveals the importance to her of a very different source, the American poet Henry Wadsworth Longfellow's popular narrative poem *The Song of Hiawatha* (1855). Indeed, the novel's many allusions not only to *Hiawatha* but also to other poems by Longfellow suggest the general importance of his work to her at this early stage in her career. It is curious, for instance, that Winona, who is introduced as "the daughter of a once celebrated Huron chief" (88), speaks Ojibwa, which is an Algonquian, not an Iroquoian, language. The Huron nation had been irrevocably shattered and dispersed fully two hundred years before the period in which *Winona* is set. A remnant of that nation did find refuge with the Ojibwa of the upper Great Lakes and no doubt had been assimilated by the middle of the nineteenth century, but these circumstances are nowhere delineated in the novel.[1] What is clear is that Crawford found the "Indian" words that she

---

[1]   On the dispersal of the Huron following their conquest by the Iroquois in the seventeenth century, see Trigger 767-840; on their relations with the Ojibwa of the upper Great Lakes, see Schmalz 118. It is conceivable that Crawford took her cue for Winona's lineage from Adam Kidd's *The Huron Chief* (1830), a volume of poems that was allegedly subscribed for publication in an edition of fifteen hundred copies and thus may have had "more than double the recorded sales of any other pre-Confederation literary work" (MacDonald 406). Like Crawford, Kidd locates his Huron chief's people "on Huron's banks" (5) at a period long after their historical expulsion from the area.

needed for her character in the Ojibwa glossary that Longfellow had attached as an appendix to *Hiawatha*, a resource that she would draw upon again, years later, when she came to write "Malcolm's Katie." Ultimately, there is no sign, despite the reference to Winona's lineage, that Crawford has any real interest in differentiating her heroine in terms of a particular tribal identity. Winona speaks simply "in the Indian dialect" (269) and Androsia "in the Indian tongue" (86, 179).

Crawford also drew on Longfellow in naming and, to some degree, in characterizing Winona. For Archie Frazer and for the Ontario public who are canvassed for clues after Winona disappears from the Frazer home, she is "the Indian girl with the romantic name" (194). For many readers in 1873, that "romantic name" would have brought to mind the tragic character of "Wenonah," the "winsome" mother of Hiawatha who, in Longfellow's poem, is courted by the god Mudjekeewis and then cruelly deserted by him, just as Winona is wooed by the compelling Andrew Farmer and then callously dropped by him while he seeks to gain the hand and dowry of her white foster-sister. Even more explicitly, Crawford encourages readers to compare her protagonist to a second figure from Longfellow's poem, Hiawatha's sweetheart, Minnehaha:

> In her brighter moods one could have fancied her an embodiment of Longfellow's ideal Indian maiden, the lovely Minnehaha; but in her frequent hours of gloom and abstraction, she was terrible, ominous and inexplicable. Her intense love of Androsia and the frightful perils she had risked for her, pleaded strongly in her behalf with Archie; but he could seldom look at her without remembering with a faint thrill the fire-lit vision of the terrible-eyed woman standing on Joe Harty's hearth, with the reeking scalp clutched in her extended hand. (176)

In contrast to Longfellow's one-dimensional "Indian maiden," Crawford's heroine combines both the erotic allure and the proclivity for violence that Terry Goldie has analysed as, respectively, feminine and masculine "commodities" in colonial representations of Native peoples. More particularly, she embodies the formidable strength that both fascinated and alarmed women writers of genteel European antecedents, from Frances Brooke through Anna Brownell Jameson to Susanna Moodie, in their depictions of Native women in Canada.

Although she goes beyond Longfellow's depictions of "the ideal Indian maiden," Crawford nonetheless remains within the confines of popular white discourse about Native peoples, framing her protagonist romantically and heroically in the familiar lexicon of colonial representations of the other. Among Winona's stereotypically "Indian" features are her "haughty stoicism" (185) and her "vindictive, revengeful" temperament (191). She is a woman of great strength, dark resolve, and deep passions. In Farmer's authoritative words, she is "certainly the loveliest Indian woman in this part of America, and certainly the most utterly untamable" (88). In terms of emotion, physical power, and presence there is no one in the novel, with the possible exception of Farmer himself, to equal her.

While her beauty and carriage often astound those around her, Winona's "dusky" exterior and dark inner moods indicate a deep divide with white society and culture when, by circumstance, she is forced to come south to Lake Ontario and the St. Lawrence River. Though she can provide dramatic and exotic interest, the Native heroine can find no place in the social drama that the novel develops. Nor, in Winona's case, does she want such a place. Crawford's narrator notes in passing that "her religion did not teach her to hope" (185); hence, when she dies, almost willing her own death despite the best efforts of a white doctor at the Frazer estate, she seems inwardly glad to fly to "the hunting grounds of [her] father [because] the spirits of the white men do not come thither" (270). The narrative urges us to regard Winona as magnificent in her "otherness"—Olla Frazer describes her as "simply unique"(180)—but her characterization appears to have little basis in fact. Rather, it has everything to do with popular stereotypes of "the Indian," as well as with the prevailing requirements of genre as Crawford understood them. In its characterization of its title character, then, as in many other respects, *Winona* is eminently a novel of its period.

One of the first and still one of the most trenchant critiques of the delimiting depiction of Native women in English-Canadian literature was provided by the celebrated part-Mohawk writer Pauline Johnson in her article "A Strong Race Opinion: On the Indian Girl in Modern Fiction," which appeared in 1892 in the *Toronto Sunday Globe*. In Johnson's view, such characters usually served as fictional devices "to lend a dash of vivid coloring to an otherwise tame and sombre colonial life" or as "imaginary makeshifts to help out romances, that would be immeasurably improved by their absence." Casting back over such texts as Richardson's *Wacousta* (1832), G. Mercer Adam and Ethelwyn Wetherald's *An Algonquin Maiden* (1887), Jessie M. Freeland's "Winona's Tryst" (a short tale published in *The Week* in 1891), and Charles Mair's closet drama *Tecumseh* (1886), Johnson saw many reasons to lament the depiction of "the Indian girl": such a heroine was typically "doglike," "fawnlike," "deer-footed," "fire-eyed," "crouching," and "submissive." She came from no identifiable tribe and before the white hero, whose superiority is a given in the scheme of things, she had to grovel even as he (usually) ignored her genuine feelings. When she is finally rejected by the paleface protagonist so that the white lovers can duly pair off, she "secures the time-honored canoe, paddles out into the lake and drowns herself." Johnson identifies a lamentable pattern in which Native heroines are "all fawn eyed, unnatural, unmaidenly idiots" in the face of the indifferent, almost brutal treatment they receive from their "paleface lovers." While Lefroy in Charles Mair's "magnificent drama" breaks the pattern by truly grieving his lost lover Iena, Johnson calls out for more such positive and worthy treatment, identifying the subject as "a chance for Canadian writers."

Because Johnson was apparently unacquainted with Crawford's novel, it is all the more striking that her article designates the stereotyped "Indian Girl" who recurs in English-Canadian literature as "the inevitable 'Winona'": "Once or twice she has borne another appellation, but it always has a 'Winona' sound about it.... We meet her as a Shawnee, as a Sioux, as a Huron, and then, her tribe unnamed, in the vicinity of Brockville." Perhaps this epithet is intended to evoke Longfellow's famous poem, which, as an American work, falls outside Johnson's immediate concern with Canadian literature. Crawford's *Winona* would have appeared in *The Favorite* when Johnson was but twelve years old and, together with the low-grade pulp pages of that short-lived story paper, it likely vanished quickly into the dim past. Even John Garvin and Ethelwyn Wetherald (the same writer who co-authored *An Algonquin Maiden*), who later took a serious interest in Crawford's writing and assembled an edition of her poems at the opening of the twentieth century, seemed unaware of the novel's history and substance. Crawford had been dead for five years when Johnson wrote her essay, and the latter's only known comment on Crawford came later still in a letter to Garvin, when on 24 May 1906 she wrote to thank him for sending her his new edition of Crawford's poetry: "I really knew so little of her heretofore. I think she grows upon one's heart, as one gets into the depths of her work, and I know that as I grow more familiar with her that she will come very close to my heart."

The question that obviously arises in the present context is how far Crawford's Native heroine conforms to the model of "the inevitable Winona" that Johnson deplored. Just as the stereotype requires, Crawford's protagonist has a merely nominal tribal affiliation, is the daughter of a chief, and suffers unrequited love for a white man who rejects her to pursue the white heroine—in this case, her own foster-sister, on whose behalf she exhibits the obligatory virtue of self-sacrifice. As observed above, while Crawford's Winona is not literally suicidal, she does, in the end, embrace death gladly.[1] On the other hand, there are ways in which she breaks the mould that Johnson delineates, notably in her lack of submissiveness, powerful passions, and resolute action, attributes more commonly associated with the image of the "savage" warrior than that of the Indian maiden. Whether these differences would have prompted Johnson to extend her admiration for Crawford's poetry to the latter's youthful novel and its portrait of the Native heroine is open to question. Johnson's own view was that, contrary to the imaginings of the white writers whom she discusses,

---

[1] The ultimate source for the lovelorn and tragic figure that Johnson criticized may be an indigenous legend of the Dakota Sioux. In an early account of this legend (1821), Henry R. Schoolcraft gives the heroine's name as Oola-ita; however, in William H. Keating's version (1824), later included in revised form under the title "The Maiden's Rock" in James Athearn Jones's *Traditions of the North American Indians* (1830), she is named Winona. According to Keating, this Winona was a young woman of the Keoxa band of Dakota near Lake Pepin on the upper Mississippi around the end of the eighteenth century. Her parents are said to have driven away the young hunter whom she loved, insisting that she marry a warrior whom they preferred. On the day that her forced marriage was to occur, she climbed a precipice above the lake, since known as "the Maiden's rock" and, having reproached her people for their unkindness and sung a dirge, dashed herself to the ground below.

The name "Winona" (which in Sioux means "First Born Daughter") was given to a number of towns during the settlement of the American West, while in Canada, shortly after Confederation, it was given to a town near Stoney Creek, Ontario. In his entry on this town in *Place Names of Ontario*, Alan Rayburn refers to what is almost certainly a variation on the tradition recorded by Schoolcraft and Keating, "a legend that the Shawnee chief Tecumseh had a daughter called Winona, who jumped to her death from the Niagara Escarpment in 1812" (378). For adaptations of this story by two nineteenth-century Canadian poets, with the heroine renamed Ta-poo-ka and transferred to the Huron nation, see Adam Kidd's *The Huron Chief* (1830) and Charles Sangster's "Taapookaa—A Huron Legend" (1864).

"the real wild Indian girl ... is the most retiring, reticent, non-committal being in existence!" ("A Strong Race Opinion").

The Use of Dialect and the Irish Presence

Regarding Winona's manner of speech, perhaps the best that can be said is that it is no worse than the prevailing standard for Native characters in North American fiction from Cooper's *The Last of the Mohicans* (1826) to the dime novel Westerns of the 1880s and '90s. At least Crawford makes some effort, however problematic, to endow her protagonist with authenticity through lacing her speech with the Ojibwa words borrowed from Longfellow's glossary. For the most part, however, Winona speaks the stilted English typical of her myriad sisters (and brothers, and fathers) in nineteenth-century fiction by white authors. She tends to eschew first- and second-person pronouns ("Winona must speak ... and her white sister must listen" [271]), and her profusely figurative language draws heavily on the natural imagery of seasons, forests, and animals. While she is largely, and formulaically, taciturn through much of the narrative, her intrinsically poetic disposition and powerful personality are ultimately and most fully (perhaps effusively) realized in the oratorical flourishes and "exquisite minor cadences" (273) of her lengthy deathbed statement to Valerie Lennox.

Crawford also uses dialect, with varying degrees of success, to characterize and vitalize her lower-class white characters. Predictably, while the novel's high-born, city-bred, and military characters typically speak impeccable English, those of lower stature define themselves through their unrefined but colourful use of language. Much of the book's early energy depends on these characters who are, by and large, linked to the backwoods and the wilderness that lies "three hundred miles [from] the outskirts of civilization" (83).

Four of these characters are notable and two of them are defined by conventional racial traits. Bill Montgomery, the kindly young trapper who saved Captain Frazer's life at Sandy Point, is "a splendid specimen of a Canadian backwoods-man" (107). He speaks tersely in what might be called a frontier idiom using words like "varmint," "rustling," "wrathy," "down-right" "darndest," and phrases like "tarnal galoot," "a sight of bad work" (108), and "that ere rifle" (80) in his few conversational interactions. He drops syllables ("well's" [as well as], "'varsal" [universal], "tarnal"

48 INTRODUCTION

[eternal], and "pears" [appears]). An older married trapper, Bill Harty, echoes Montgomery's tendencies.

By contrast, Lumber Pete enacts an Anglicized version of French-Canadian experience. Formerly a Lower Canadian voyageur, he is cast as a trapper in the northern Ontario wilderness who is planning to head out west, like so many men of the time, to try out the newly opened territory of Manitoba. A "dapper and dandified" (110) bachelor of fifty, he is small, spare, flexible, playful, and benignly flirtatious. Inseparable from his "huge violin" (110), which he has affectionately dubbed "Madame," he hums a familiar old voyageur *chanson* and mixes French words with clipped English phrases.

Crawford's creative triumph in terms of dialect is Mike Murphy, a red-haired "son of Erin" drawn from the resilient tradition of the stage Irishman, but individualized within the narrative by his humour, geniality, theatricality, and good-heartedness. The stage Irishman, typically named Paddy or Teague, had been introduced into English literature by dramatists such as the post-Restoration playwright George Farquhar. Paddy was initially a villainous and slippery character, a servant figure who, reflecting English feelings about the Irish, was not to be trusted or admired. Over time that figure evolved increasingly into a comic resource, both in drama and prose. Irish writers were not hesitant to draw on this stock figure themselves but they inevitably sought to make "Paddy" more positive and consequential.

In the novels and stories of popular nineteenth-century Irish writers, among them Samuel Lover, William Carleton and John Banim, and in the plays of Dion Boucicault, the "Paddy" figure became increasingly creative and trustworthy, despite an unsavoury occupation and a poor reputation. Not surprisingly then, Crawford's Mike Murphy is transformed into a largely positive creature ("a red-headed guardian angel" [93]) without losing his dramatic roots. He represents a refreshing validation of Irishness in post-Confederation Canada and is one of the liveliest contemporary characterizations in Canadian fiction of that stock figure. Clearly, he reflects the continuing affection and concern for the land of her birth that Crawford also expressed in poems such as "Erin to Her Grandson, Ned Hanlan" (1879), "A Hungry Day" (1881), and "Erin's Warning" (1881).

Small in stature, big-pawed and broad-shouldered, Crawford's Mike has "a rich voice, redolent of the Isle of Erin" (81) and his native

Connaught. He is initially positioned as a trustworthy and loyal servant figure (he is Colonel Howard's valet) who speaks his mind spontaneously and in comic brogue. Despite nearly two decades in the north, he knows "little or nothing about woodcraft" (135), and prefers the more convivial life he finds in the south. Once out of the woods he finds a new home with the Frazer family, as their "general factotum" (231), and becomes a welcome presence in their lives. In effect, Crawford positions him so as to participate in and comment upon most of the novel's action. Whether in the wilderness or at the Frazers' villa, he develops affectionate, avuncular bonds with the lively young women of the place—Androsia and Winona in the north, and Sidney Frazer on the St. Lawrence.

His amusing blue eyes "twinkle" with "drollery," and his talk is awash in stage Irish tags like "bedad," "wirra," "asthore," "mushee," and "begorra." He shares the hard "A's" of stage Irish pronunciation ("craythur," "aiqual"), the habit of repetition ("at all, at all"), and a penchant for affectionate address (calling Captain Frazer and Colonel Howard "honey," "darling," and "dear"). He mispronounces words and phrases ("alludering to," "indade," "sharkumstanshial") but he is always dutiful and reliable in his good-natured way. His (rac)coon-tail hat serves in various scenes as a comic touchstone of his "quaint" manners (119) and social awkwardness.

Dramatically, Murphy is prone to exaggerated and scene-stealing reactions. Time after time, his Milesian "talk" bubbles over in sheer exuberance. Crawford takes delight in understating Mike's superstitious nature—he was "not altogether the slave of imagination" (151)—only to have him vividly describe his experience of ghosts seen during a stormy night spent at a portage. When Winona and Androsia suddenly reappear after an absence of two months, he breaks into "yowling" (151) and then collapses in a startled faint. His "expressive pantomime" (155) is, as Crawford aptly describes it, both pleasingly stagy and entertaining in the narrative.

Mike Murphy's Canadian roots likely have something to do with James McCarroll's popular journalistic creation, Terry Finnegan, whose comical letters to the Hon. Thomas D'Arcy Magee appeared in various Toronto satiric papers and journals in the early 1860s. Terry's lyrical brogue is echoed in Mike's sprightly and colourful talk while Mike's name, so typically Irish in itself, may have slyly reminded readers of a well-known Toronto tavern keeper who led the city's Hibernian

Society, was actively aligned with Fenian politics, and had Irish-American connections. It is further interesting to note that, along with Patrick Boyle, the editor-owner of *The Irish Canadian*, this actual Michael Murphy had befriended McCarroll during his politically charged troubles after he lost his job as Outdoors Surveyor for the Port of Toronto in 1863. Murphy and Boyle offered to serve as McCarroll's sureties when his previous guarantors deserted him. Moreover, Murphy, who had been arrested as a suspected Fenian operative, had only recently died (1870), shortly after his release from prison. There is, however, no hint of politics in Crawford's Murphy; what counts is the presence in the narrative of the engaging and high-spirited Irishness that made Terry Finnegan so popular among Toronto and Canada West readers in the 1860s.

It is further indicative of the importance of the Irish presence in the novel that the detective Fennel is, in the guise of an Irishman, instrumental in resolving the story. Indeed, it is in his undercover role as Pat, a new hired hand at the Frazer villa, that he proves his versatility and mettle, helping to bring *Winona's* mystery to a conclusion. Adopting a "decidedly Milesian" accent (238)—does that mean more Milesian than Milesian, which is to say stage-Irish?—a flannel shirt, and a toothache in order to gain access to the maid-servant Rosie's good graces, he is able to have a close look at the interior of the Frazer home. Using a story of his Irish grandmother's charms and potions, he is able to confirm Macer's identity and study the villa's interior. He then becomes one of several night-watchers of Macer's movements, and at the crisis of the narrative he confronts the villain. Dropping his Milesian disguise for the showdown, Fennel is "cool, alert, [and] watchful" (266), the able detective completing the plot he has uncovered.

Predictably, however, in tying up her plot's loose ends, Crawford allows no time to Mike Murphy or to Jack Fennel. Her denouement focuses on the three upper-crust Frazer marriages, the completion of Winona's life-size statue, and the final revelations about Malcolm Lennox's past. In fact, the futures of her crucial "Irish" players have already been anticipated. Fennel will return to the pleasant sanctuary of his musical cottage and Mike will attempt to carry out his plan to marry the good but coquettish Rosie, who clearly favours him, despite his age. It is a measure of his own growth, or perhaps of his naturalization to his adopted land, that he has come to "worship at the shrine of the pretty Canadian parlor-maid" rather than continuing to lament his long-severed relationship with a "daughter of Erin" (242–43).

Representing "Kanyda"

Is *Winona* the quintessentially Canadian story that it was judged to be when it won first prize—if not the prize money—in the *Hearthstone* competition? Certainly it met the criteria outlined in the contest rules, and these specifications, with their call for stories "formed on Canadian history, experience and incident," should not be dismissed as simply yielding a miscellany of sensational events enacted in exotic Canadian scenes and settings. The settings are one of the novel's strengths and pleasures. The Toronto chapters are especially striking for their freshness of perception, telling detail, and vivid evocation of the growing city, and the more so when one considers that well into the following century Canadian fiction would be dominated by narrowly-gauged stories of small-town and rural life. While the wilderness provides a scene for adventure, deceit and intrigue, it is *Winona*'s insistence on foregrounding a movement away from the frontier, towards the modern world, that gives it peculiar resonance more than 130 years later. "Wirra," says Mike Murphy, in the opening pages, as he welcomes Archie Frazer to Colonel Howard's forest lodge; "it's a haythenish place is Kanyda" (82). But this verdict is shown to be a function of specific locale as the narrative sweeps southward from its initial northern Lake Huron wilderness into the cities, railway stations, and domesticated countryside where most of the subsequent action takes place. One corollary of this movement is, of course, the death of the title character. As Terry Goldie has observed, this common fate of the indigene in works by writers of European descent in settler colonies such as Canada "reinforces the image of the indigene as passing if not past" (46).

As in the introductory chapter of Richardson's *Wacousta*, the symbolic movement in *Winona* is not westward, not towards the frontier, but eastward. Just as Richardson's description of British North America begins at "the most distant of the north-western settlements of America ... at the head of the lakes Michigan and Huron" (6), then moves through the lower great lakes and down the St. Lawrence to the gulf, so does Crawford's narrative proceed from the remote forest "beyond the Manitoulins" (164), southward to the settlements and cities,

52 INTRODUCTION

and to the cultured homes of the Frazers on the upper St. Lawrence and the Denvilles in Montreal. Similar treatments of an easterly bearing occur in colonial Canadian writing as early as Frances Brooke's novel, *The History of Emily Montague* (1769), and Thomas Cary's long poem, *Abram's Plains* (1789), and they form a counterpoint to the long journey up the St. Lawrence and into the wilderness in immigration narratives such as Catharine Parr Traill's *The Backwoods of Canada* (1836) and Susanna Moodie's *Roughing It in the Bush* (1852). In the works by Brooke, Cary, Richardson, and Crawford, the movement of the narrative, and of the narrator's eye, from the remote west (or north) to the more familiar east (and south) could be interpreted as a metaphor of historical change and thus of a developing colonial or national identity.

This pattern should not be hastily equated with naïve or Eurocentric notions of progress. An even more significant parallel between *Winona* and *Wacousta* occurs when Mike Murphy hands to Captain Frazer "a small package, wrapped in birch-bark and tied round with thongs of fawn skin" (125) that he has brought from the far Manitoulin region to the country house on the upper St. Lawrence. Much to the Captain's astonishment, it contains a "worn morocco case" (125) with a miniature portrait of his dead first wife, the Scottish mother of the lost and embittered son who is about to descend on his household. This moment echoes two closely-linked scenes in *Wacousta*, one in which young Charles de Haldimar is surprised to find a portrait of his long-dead mother among his father's papers at Fort Detroit, and another in which a duplicate of this portrait is used to smuggle a message into the besieged fort:

> After removing several wrappers of bark, each of which was secured by a thong of deer-skin, Colonel de Haldimar, to whom the successful officer had handed his prize, at length came to a small oval case of red morocco, precisely similar, in size and form, to that which had so recently attracted the notice of his son. For a moment he hesitated, and his cheek was observed to turn pale, and his hand to tremble; but quickly subduing his indecision, he hurriedly unfastened the clasp, and disclosed to the astonished view of the officers the portrait of a young and lovely woman, habited in the Highland garb. (387)

While it is not possible to know how consciously Crawford "borrowed" these details from Richardson, it is possible to regard this link between

Wacousta and *Winona* as evidence of an emerging tradition in Canadian fiction, one that reaches its culmination, perhaps, in Margaret Laurence's *The Diviners* (1974). As Crawford composed her "essentially Canadian" story, she recognized, at some level, not only the usefulness of the bark-wrapped, morocco-cased miniature as a plot device, as well as its dramatic (or melodramatic) value, but also its symbolic power. In both *Wacousta* and *Winona*, as this microcosmic image suggests, the wilderness origin of the Canadian narrative gives way to the disclosure of its prior origin in a ruined European romance. The destructive forces that threaten the central characters are in the end not a question of "savagery" pitted against "civilization," but of the complex pressures of past upon present and of the more sinister motions of the heart in this new country. In *Winona*'s repeated emphasis upon the appearance and activity of the human eye, perhaps no passage is quite so suggestive as this description of the lost son who is first introduced as Andrew Farmer, later calls himself Harold Macer, and is eventually exposed as Malcolm Lennox:

> His eyes even were not the regulation villain steel gray or fiery black, but a rich, deep sympathetic blue like the edges of the Mediterranean, with the rosy twilight lingering on them, and they were safe eyes, seldom betraying his thoughts, except rarely by a sudden, curious dullness or a horrible flash, like the leaping of a Damascus blade from its scabbard in the light of a conflagration. (94)

Implicitly, not only his Scottish ancestry, but also all of Europe and more have gone into the making of this dissembling Canadian Ishmael. In view of such passages, a second pronouncement by Mike Murphy seems more satisfactory, if also more nebulous, than his first such statement: "it's a mighty quare counthry this Kenady, any ways" (171).

With her own share of ebullience but a much finer sense of irony than Mike, it is a playful and high-spirited Isabella Valancy Crawford who authors *Winona*. In her "modest tale" (283-84), she self-consciously pursues several fairly ambitious ends. Despite her recognition of what she calls "the sunken reefs and shifting sands of literature" (144), she is forthright and deliberate in her attempt to dramatize a compelling national narrative as required of her by the *Hearthstone* contest. Thus she designates Mike Murphy to be the purveyor of categorical statements about the fledgling country. At the opening of the novel, Mike characterizes Canada as the realm of the new and the fresh, varying his perspective on the dominion just as he varies his enunciation: "this Kanydy," he boasts, "bates all for givin' wan a youthish air!"(82). To amplify this pleasant aspect of the nation, Crawford furnishes her narrative with characters ranging from the robust backwoodsman to the musical French-Canadian trapper to the stylish coquette who, whatever her faults, is "a lovely little creature of the pure Canadian type, a dainty, glowing blonde, fragile and spiritual looking, but rounded and moulded to a perfect symmetry" (141-42).

Such racial and occupational types abound in the novel. These types are offered for consumption rather than questioning, the better to build the national picture in an anticipated way and to hasten the narrative along its chosen paths. But whether it is the "regulation villain," the "Indian maiden," the stage Irishman, or the keen-eyed detective, Crawford resists the pure stereotype through attempting to imbue her version of it with a measure of individuality and humanity. As a matter of course, she announces the stereotype in question as a way of identifying her greater particularity of approach. Thus, as noted above, Andrew Farmer's eyes are not those of "the regulation villain" (94) and Jack Fennel is "not at all like the recognized type of detective" (213). Where minor characters are concerned, comic figures with strongly connotative names clearly delight the author and reveal her satiric propensities. If Fennel suggests the kind of unpretentious herb that promotes fine cottage cookery, Archelaus Simkins is Crawford's starcrossed lover of unregulated temperatures, her Diogenes victimized, as he himself sees it, by "the Lacrosse ball of Fortune" (220). So too she introduces incidental characters with Thackerayesque names such as the florist, "old Bluebell" (147), the dressmaker Madame Frillmeout, the lustful seventy-year old, Mr. Horneyblow, and the feckless military men of the Toronto garrison, Lt. Prancer and Ensign Spooner.

As a writer of serialized fiction, Crawford reveals an acute consciousness of the story paper as a particular kind of publication even as she plays variations on its standard features of the sensational and the melodramatic. While allusions to periodicals in *Winona* are few, appearing only as passing references, they gain a greater significance when considered together, suggesting the author's knowledge of the medium and an attempt to distance herself from its worst elements. In addition to her satirical observations on Spooner's taste for sensational journalism,

Crawford makes several other significant references to the popular press. In referring to books of "heathen mythology," she calls attention to the crude and limiting effect of their "cheap wood-cuts" (161), slyly implying, perhaps, a criticism of the low standard of illustrations that readers will find in *The Favorite* compared to the superior artistic work in competitors like *Frank Leslie's Illustrated Newspaper* where she also had a serialized novel in progress. Again, in a clever drawing-room detail early in the novel, she has Olla Frazer casually reach over her mother's shoulder in the darkening library to take up "an illustrated paper that lay on the table" (133). Olla does not realize that Mrs. Frazer has deftly positioned the paper to cover up the tell-tale miniature case, thus preventing her daughter from becoming curious about the hidden object. "Never mind now, dear," she says and sends Olla off to order tea (133) for the family. Thus the portrait of the first Mrs. Frazer remains literally concealed by an illustrated paper and figuratively shrouded in the kind of mystery that such papers sought to capitalize upon and promote to their audiences. Similarly, Cecil Bertrand's superficiality is sharply pinpointed by her devotion to "the monthly fashions" (fashion magazines), which, Crawford tells us, is the extent of "her literary researches" (144).

These and other passages imply a critique of the medium as well as the conventions in which the author has chosen to write, and show that she regarded the more sensationalist and melodramatic aspects of her exercise in popular fiction with amusement and irony. Nevertheless, at the opening of the novel's final chapter, she counters the predictable objections to her adopted genre through confronting the imagined figures of the censorious Miss Cross-patch and Mr. Singlestick, tiresome critics of "the good old style" (283) of romantic fiction that she now brings to a conclusion. She informs the reader that, regardless of what such critics might think or demand, she chooses "joybells" (283), three marriages, and the "way ... through the sunshine" (286) for her ending. Let us allow for the "sigh of satisfaction" we find in "old romance" (283), she urges. In the voice of a merry prophet rather than an angry one, she banishes Miss Cross-patch and Mr. Singlestick from the stage in favour of the "the dimpled Hebes, the gay young bachelors and the blooming matrons of the land" who delight in happy endings (284)—albeit this one is qualified by a visit to the gravesite of the novel's heroine and a final sombre reference to its villain. As author she will have her way, however inconsistent that way may be.

56   INTRODUCTION

Clearly, Crawford undertook a varied agenda in *Winona*. Even as she penned her robust and wide-ranging national tale, she mixed her inclinations as a romantic storyteller with her satiric impulses and her self-conscious ambivalence as a practitioner of story-paper fiction to suggest and even assert her individuality. There is no apparent consistency in her approach. She is at once nationalist, romancer, melodramatist and satirist. Within the limits of the literary world in which she tried to make her way, she sought to be as diverse, as knowledgeable, as satisfying, and as witty as she could. She knew what the medium required and she delivered her story accordingly.

Works Cited

Alcott, Louisa May. *Journals*. Ed. Joel Myerson and Daniel Shealy, Assoc. Ed. Madeleine B. Stern. Boston: Little Brown and Company, 1989.

"Antrim." "Old Paisley Landmark Once Writer's Home." *London Free Press*, 2 July 1927: 6.

"Artistic Filth." *The Favorite*, 1 February 1873: 56.

"The Assizes." *Peterborough Examiner*, 30 October 1873: [2].

"The Autumn Assizes." *Peterborough Review*, 31 October 1873: [2].

Burpee, Lawrence J. "Isabella Valancy Crawford: A Canadian Poet." *Poet-lore* 13 (1901): 575–86.

Coultrap-McQuin, Susan. *Doing Literary Business: American Women Writers in the Nineteenth Century*. Chapel Hill: U of North Carolina P, 1990.

Crawford, Isabella Valancy. "At the Opera—A Fragment." *Evening Telegram* [Toronto], 27 October 1882: 3.

——. "The Camp of Souls." *Evening Telegram* [Toronto], 9 August 1880: 3.

——. "The Dark Stag." *Evening Telegram* [Toronto], 28 November 1883: 2.

——. "Erin's Warning." *Evening Telegram* [Toronto], 7 March 1881: 4.

——. "Erin to Her Grandson, Ned Hanlan." *Evening Telegram* [Toronto], 25 June 1879: 3.

——. *Hate*. [Serialized] *Frank Leslie's Chimney Corner*, 1 May—11 September 1875.

——. "'He Arose and Went into Another Land.'" *Evening Telegram* [Toronto], 9 February 1883: 3.

——. *Hugh and Ion*. Ed. Glenn Clever. Ottawa: Borealis, 1977.

——. "A Hungry Day." *Evening Telegram* [Toronto], 15 February 1881: 4.

——. *Old Spookses' Pass, Malcolm's Katie, and Other Poems.* Toronto: James Bain, 1884.

——. "Verses." *Evening Telegram* [Toronto], 21 July 1882: 2.

——. "The Vesper Star." *Mail* [Toronto], 24 December 1873: 3.

——. *Winona; or, The Foster-Sisters.* [Serialized] *The Favorite* 11 January—29 March 1873.

——. "The Wooing of Gheezis: An Indian Idyll." *Mail* [Toronto], 18 September 1874: 3.

——. *Wrecked! or, The Rosclerras of Mistree.* [Serialized] *Frank Leslie's Illustrated Newspaper,* 26 October 1872—29 March 1873.

Duncan, Sara Jeannette. "Saunterings." *The Week,* 28 October 1886: 771.

"Editorial Notes." *Arcturus: A Canadian Journal of Literature and Life,* 19 February 1887: 83–84.

Farmiloe, Dorothy. *Isabella Valancy Crawford: The Life and the Legends.* Ottawa: Tecumseh, 1983.

"Fast Young Ladies." *Canadian Illustrated News,* 28 September 1872: 195 [rpt. from the *Liberal Review*].

Gabler-Hover, Janet. *Dreaming Black/Writing White: The Hagar Myth in American Cultural History.* Lexington: UP of Kentucky, 2000.

Galarneau, Claude. "Desbarats, George-Édouard." *Dictionary of Canadian Biography.* Vol. 12. Toronto: U of Toronto P, 1966. 246–50.

Galvin, Elizabeth McNeill. *Isabella Valancy Crawford: We Scarcely Knew Her.* Toronto: Natural Heritage/Natural History, 1994.

Goldie, Terry. *Fear and Temptation: The Image of the Indigene in Canadian, Australian, and New Zealand Literatures.* Kingston, ON: McGill-Queen's UP, 1989.

Hale, Katherine. *Isabella Valancy Crawford.* Toronto: Ryerson, 1923.

Hildreth, Margaret Holbrook. *Harriet Beecher Stowe: A Bibliography.* Hamden, Connecticut: Archon, 1976.

"Introductory." *Canadian Monthly and National Review* (January 1872): 1.

Johnson, E. Pauline. "A Strong Race Opinion: On the Indian Girl in Modern Fiction." *Toronto Sunday Globe,* 22 May 1892: 1.

——. Letter to John Garvin. 24 May [1906]. Canadian Literature Collection, Box 32, file 6, item 1. Queen's University Archives. Kingston, Ontario.

Jones, Rev. Harry. "Railway Notes in the Northwest; or, Dominion of Canada." *Leisure Hour* [London], March 1885: 165.

Jones, James Athearn, comp. and ed. "The Maiden's Rock." *Traditions of the North American Indians*. 2nd rev. ed. 3 vols. 1830; Upper Saddle River, NJ: Literature House/Gregg Press, 1970. 2: 131–40.

Keating, William H. ["the Maiden's rock."] *Narrative of an Expedition to the Source of St. Peter's River, Lake Winnepeek, Lake of the Woods, &c. Performed in the Year 1823*. 2 vols. 1824; Minneapolis: Ross & Haines, 1959. 1: 290–93.

Kidd, Adam. *The Huron Chief*. Ed. D.M.R. Bentley. 1830; London, ON: Canadian Poetry Press, 1987.

"The Library." *Evening Telegram* [Toronto], 12 June 1884: 4.

Lighthall, William Douw. Introduction. *Songs of the Great Dominion: Voices from the Forests and Waters, the Settlements and Cities of Canada*. Ed. W. D. Lighthall. London: Walter Scott, 1889.

Lindsay, Charles. Papers, MU 1923, file 5. Archives of Ontario, Toronto, Canada.

[Linton, Eliza Lynn.] "The Girl of the Period." *Saturday Review* [London], 14 March 1868: 339–40. This article was unsigned when it first appeared in *The Saturday Review*.

Lund, Michael. *America's Continuing Story: An Introduction to Serial Fiction, 1850–1900*. Detroit: Wayne State UP, 1993.

MacDonald, Mary Lu. "Kidd, Adam (1802–31)." *The Oxford Companion to Canadian Literature*. Ed. William Toye. Toronto: Oxford UP, 1983. 406–07.

Martin, Mary F. "The Short Life of Isabella Valancy Crawford." *Dalhousie Review* 52 (1972): 390–401.

McCarroll, James. *The Letters of Terry Finnegan to the Hon. Thomas D'Arcy McGee*. Toronto: 1863.

——. *Madeline, and Other Poems*. New York, Chicago: Belford, Clarke, 1889.

Murray, Heather. *Come, bright Improvement! The Literary Societies of Nineteenth-Century Ontario*. Toronto: U of Toronto P, 2002.

"The New Canadian Weekly." *Hearthstone*, 28 December 1872: 4.

Noel, Mary. *Villains Galore ... The Heyday of the Popular Story Weekly*. New York: Macmillan, 1954.

"Notice." *The Favorite*, 27 June 1874: 410.

"Our First Bow." *The Favorite*, 28 December 1872: 8.

"Our Prize Stories." *Hearthstone*, 6 July 1872: 4.

"Our Prize Stories." *Hearthstone*, 2 November 1872: 4.

Ower, John. "Crawford's Move to Toronto." *Canadian Literature* 90 (1981): 168.

Payne, Alma J. *Louisa May Alcott: A Reference Guide*. Boston: G.K. Hall, 1980.

Peterman, Michael. *James McCarroll, alias Terry Finnegan: Newspapers, Controversy and Literature in Victorian Canada*. Peterborough, ON: Peterborough Historical Society: Occasional Paper 17, 1996.

Petrone, Penny. "In Search of Isabella Valancy Crawford." *The Isabella Valancy Crawford Symposium*. Ed. Frank M. Tierney. Ottawa: U of Ottawa P, 1979.

Pykett, Lyn. *The 'Improper' Feminine: The Women's Sensation Novel and the New Woman Writing*. London: Routledge, 1992.

Ramsay, Ellen L. "Art and Industrial Society: The Role of the Toronto Mechanic's Institute in the Promotion of Art, 1831–1883." *Labour/Le Travail* 43 (1999): 71–103.

"A Rare Chance for Everybody!" *Hearthstone*, 10 February 1872: 8.

Rayburn, Alan. *Place Names of Ontario*. Toronto: U of Toronto P, 1997.

"Recent Poetry and Verse." *National Graphic* [London], 4 April 1885.

Richardson, John. *Wacousta: or, The Prophecy; a Tale of the Canadas*. Ed. Douglas Cronk. 1832; Ottawa: Carleton UP, 1987.

Richardson, Michael. Preface. *Maddened by Mystery: A Casebook of Canadian Detective Fiction*. Toronto: Lester & Orpen Dennys, 1982.

Sangster, Charles. "Taapookaa—A Huron Legend." *Selections from Canadian Poets*. Ed. Edward Hartley Dewart. Montreal: John Lovell, 1864. 243–46.

Schmalz, Peter. *The Ojibwa of Southern Ontario*. Toronto: U of Toronto P, 1991.

Schoolcraft, Henry R. *Narrative Journal of Travels Through the Northwestern Regions of the United States ... in the Year 1820*. 1821. Rpt. Arno Press, 1970. 329–30.

"Sensation Literature." *Hearthstone*, 3 August 1872: 4.

Skene-Melvin, David. Introduction. *Bloody York: Tales of Mayhem, Murder, and Mystery in Toronto*. Toronto: Simon & Pierre, 1996.

Stern, Madeline B. *Louisa May Alcott: A Biography*. New York: Random House, 1996.

Sutherland, Fraser. *The Monthly Epic: A History of Canadian Magazines 1789 – 1989*. Markham, ON: Fitzhenry & Whiteside, 1989.

"A Talented Lady Dead." *Globe* [Toronto], 14 February 1887: 8.

Theman, Diana Lynne. "'Mental Treasures of the Land': The Idea of Literary Resource Development in Nineteenth-Century English Canada." Diss. York U, 1996.

"To Literary Men." *Canadian Illustrated News*, 13 November 1869: 22.

"To Our Contributors." *Hearthstone*, 28 December 1872: 4.

"To Our Subscribers." *Hearthstone*, 28 December 1872: 4.

Trigger, Bruce G. *The Children of Aataentsic: A History of the Huron People to 1660*. Kingston, ON: McGill-Queen's UP, 1987.

The Varsity [Toronto], 23 January 1886: 116.

"Wanted!! $1,275 Reward. To the Literary Men and Women of Canada." *Hearthstone*, 29 June 1872: 4.

Wetherald, Ethelwyn. Introduction. *Collected Poems of Isabella Valancy Crawford*. Ed. J. W. Garvin. 1905. Toronto: U of Toronto P, 1972.

"Who Will Write for *The Favorite*." *The Favorite* 28 December 1872: 8.

Wilson, Adam. Notebooks. Ms. RG 22-390-16, Box 119. Archives of Ontario. Toronto, Canada.

Wilson, Maud Miller. "Isabella Valancy Crawford." *Globe* [Toronto], 15 April 1905: 8; 22 April 1905: 8. Wilson's middle name is mistakenly given as "Wheeler" in the byline to the first installment of this two-part article.

Wynne, Deborah. *The Sensation Novel and the Victorian Family Magazine*. New York: Palgrave, 2001.

Isabella Valancy Crawford: A Brief Chronology

1850　Isabella Valancy Crawford's probable date of birth is 25 December of this year, in Dublin, Ireland; she is the sixth child of thirteen born to Stephen Dennis Crawford and Sidney Scott Crawford.

c. 1855　Seven of the Crawford children perish of "fever," possibly typhus or diphtheria.

c. 1857　Crawford's family immigrates to Canada, settling in Paisley, Canada West, where her father establishes a medical practice.

1861　The Crawfords leave Paisley, possibly because of legal and financial embarrassment arising from Dr. Crawford's questionable stewardship of municipal funds as township treasurer.

c. 1862　The Crawford family settles in Lakefield, in the Kawartha Lakes region.

1869　Dr. Crawford moves his family and practice to Peterborough, Ontario.

1872　On 13 April, Isabella Valancy Crawford's first known publication, a short story titled "The Hospital Gondola," appears in Montreal entrepreneur George-Édouard Desbarats's weekly story paper, *The Hearthstone*. It is followed on 4 May by her earliest known poem, "The Departure of Winter," and in subsequent issues by another poem and a second short story. Her novel *Wrecked! or, The Rosclerras of Mistree* is serialized in a New York weekly, *Frank Leslie's Illustrated Newspaper*, from 26 October 1872 to 29 March 1873. A second novel, *Winona; or, The Foster-Sisters*, wins first prize in a story contest sponsored by *The Hearthstone*.

1873　*Winona* is serialized in *The Favorite*, a new story paper published by Desbarats, from 11 January to 29 March. Five short stories and six poems by Crawford, as well as five stories by her sister Emma Naomi, also appear in this paper. On 27 October Isabella's suit against Desbarats for payment owing for her work is decided in her favour at the Autumn Assizes in Peterborough. On 24 December, a poem, "The Vesper Star," appears in a Toronto daily, *The Mail*, the first of twelve poems by Crawford published in *The Mail* through May 1875.

1874 On 31 October, the short story "River-Lead Cañon" appears in *Frank Leslie's Chimney Corner*, the first of about two dozen stories by Crawford to be published in several of Frank Leslie's periodicals between 1874 and 1885.

1875 Crawford's novel *Hate* is serialized in *Frank Leslie's Chimney Corner*, 1 May to 11 September. Her father dies on 3 July.

1876 On 20 January, Emma Naomi Crawford dies, and in the spring Isabella and her mother move to Toronto, where during the next ten years they live in a series of boarding houses, mostly at addresses on Shuter Street and Adelaide Street West, surviving largely on earnings from her writing. In July 1876 her poem "Where, Love, Art Hid?" appears in *The National*, a Toronto weekly magazine now extant only in a fragmented sequence, and is followed by at least ten more poems through May 1879.

1879 On 25 June, Crawford's poem "Erin to Her Grandson, Ned Hanlan," appears in the *Evening Telegram*, a Toronto daily newspaper, and is followed by more than ninety poems published in this paper over the next seven years, through May 1886.

1884 In May, Crawford's book *Old Spookses' Pass, Malcolm's Katie, and Other Poems* is published in Toronto by James Bain and Son in a run of one thousand copies, of which about fifty are sold.

1885 "Phyllis," the first of Crawford's poems to be published in the Toronto daily *Globe*, appears on 10 October, and is followed by seven more poems through May 1886. Late in the year, she and her mother move to rooms above a grocery shop at 57 John Street, at the corner of King and John.

1886 In January, Crawford's novel *A Little Bacchante; or, Some Black Sheep* is serialized in the Toronto *Evening Globe*. *Old Spookses' Pass, Malcolm's Katie, and Other Poems* is reissued under new covers. On 4 September, a short story, "Extradited," appears in the *Globe*.

1887 In the first week of February, Crawford visits the Toronto offices of a new magazine, *Arcturus*, to look into the possibility of publishing her work in its pages. On 23 February she dies of heart failure at the age of thirty-six, and is buried in Little Lake Cemetery in Peterborough. The following month, what may be her final poem, "Toboggan," appears in the New York sporting and travel magazine *Outing*.

A Note on the Text

Winona; or, The Foster-Sisters was serialized in the Montreal publisher George-Édouard Desbarats's weekly periodical *The Favorite* in twelve installments, from 11 January to 29 March 1873. Each of the first eight parts was accompanied by an unsigned woodcut illustration, and all twelve were introduced by a heading that identified Isabella Valancy Crawford "of Peterboro' Ont." as *Author of "The Silvers' Christmas Eve;" "Wrecked; or, the Rosclerras of Mistree," &c., &c.* The twelve installments appeared in *The Favorite* as follows:

1. Chapters I-II: 11 Jan 1873, pp. 9-11; illustration, "Archie's Meeting with Androsia," p. 9.
2. Chapters III-V: 18 Jan 1873, pp. 25-26; illustration, "Winona's Sacrifice," p. 25.
3. Chapters VI-VIII: 25 Jan 1873, pp. 41-43; illustration, "What Farmer Left Behind Him," p. 41.
4. Chapters IX-XI: 1 Feb 1873, pp. 57-59; illustration, "Winona's Return," p. 57.
5. Chapters XII-XIV: 8 Feb 1873, pp. 73-75; illustration, "Is Thim Kebs?" p. 73.
6. Chapters XV-XVI: 15 Feb 1873, pp. 89-90; illustration, "Winona's Farewell of Androsia," p. 89.
7. Chapters XVII-XIX: 22 Feb 1873, pp. 105-07; illustration, "Sidney's Adventure," p. 105.
8. Chapters XX-XXII: 1 Mar 1873, pp. 121-23; illustration, "Valerie's Telegram," p. 121.
9. Chapters XXIII-XXIV: 8 Mar 1873, pp. 132-33.
10. Chapters XXV-XXVI: 15 Mar 1873, pp. 148-50.
11. Chapters XXVII-XXVIII: 22 Mar 1873, pp. 162-63.
12. Chapters XXIX-XXX: 29 Mar 1873, pp. 186-87.

The serialization of *Winona* is the only known prior text of Crawford's novel, and therefore must serve as the copy text for this edition, which is based on an original copy of *The Favorite* held in the Bibliothèque Nationale du Québec, Montreal. Predictably, the serialized text contains a variety of errors and anomalies that reflect both the haste with which it was composed and the hazards of its production in print. Written to deadline for a publishing house that was in financial difficulty and under editorial stress, the novel had little if any chance to profit from authorial revision or conscientious editing. Imprecise expressions such as "sacrifice myself on the shrine of gratitude" (229) and "tried to tear his grasp from the rudder" (281)—where "altar" and "tiller" would be more exact—are blunders of the sort often made by writers in the rush of composition, as are minor discrepancies of detail, inconsistencies of plot, and improbabilities of action. Does the journey from Lake Chetowaik to Bill Montgomery's cabin take three hours (101) or nine hours (104)? Is Andrew Farmer "of middle height and of a well-knit and graceful frame" (84) or is he "tall" (148) with a "massive chest" (174)? When we are told that Winona's feelings towards Farmer "had changed to unfathomable hate, unquenched even by his death" (187), has Crawford herself forgotten for the moment that Winona (unlike the reader) knows very well that Farmer is alive? And why does Farmer, at the melodramatic climax of the novel, "rush upon" (266) Jack Fennel rather than simply fire his revolver a second time?

Even more disconcerting in the original text are numerous instabilities in the names of places and characters. From Chapters XVI through XIX, the railway stop in the vicinity of the Frazer estate on the upper St. Lawrence is identified as "Brampton." Most Ontarians at the time (and at present) would be perplexed to find Brampton relocated from Peel County, northwest of Toronto, to the Thousand Islands region at a considerable distance northeast of the city, a problem that Crawford may have apprehended, for this place name is altered to "Scranton" in Chapter XXI, and thereafter. As for characters' names, the most notable anomaly involves Cecil Bertrand, who is called "Cecile" in the first two chapters, then becomes "Cecil"—not unusual as a female name prior to the twentieth century—for the balance of the narrative. Similarly, the Harty family is at times styled "Hardy," the name of Cecil's sister changes from "Linda" to "Lina" to "Lena," and Olla Frazer's beau, who is originally referred to as Hubert Denville in Chapter VIII, becomes "Theodore" when he appears in person in Chapter XV.

Whether such problems had their origins in hasty composition, ambiguous handwriting, or lapses in the compositor's room, and what Crawford's preference might have been in cases of contradictory or uncertain details, can only be matter for speculation. We have therefore adopted a conservative policy in intervening in the 1873 text. While we have resolved blatant inconsistencies, such as the variations in proper names, we have not considered ourselves licensed to resolve anomalies such as the question of Farmer's physique, or to correct imprecise phrasing as in the examples cited above. We have also resisted the temptation to modernize syntax and punctuation, only adding commas in a few places where their absence is apt to cause confusion, and substituting question marks for periods where warranted by sentence structure and context.

Chapter headings, the use of single within double quotation marks, and the use of italics for foreign words have been silently regularized, but all other changes to the text published in *The Favorite* are noted in the "Editorial Emendations." As mentioned, many of these involve proper names. Other emendations involve apparent compositor's slips, spelling mistakes and inconsistencies, and erroneous references: for example, the realignment of a questionably formatted passage on page 181, the restoration of Longfellow's "nee-ba-naw-baigs" and Tennyson's "Vivien" to their proper forms, and the correction of "west wind, wabun" to "east wind, Wabun" and of "Quintus" to "Marcus" Curtius. In two instances we have changed "master" to "masther" to render Mike Murphy's Irish brogue a little more uniform. Finally, we have included headings at the beginning of certain chapters to indicate where breaks between installments occur in the serialized text of *Winona*.

Footnotes to the present text of *Winona* identify literary, historical, and geographical references and define words that may be unfamiliar to modern readers. In the preparation of these notes, the following sources have been particularly important: the Bible (King James Version); the *Oxford English Dictionary*, 2nd ed., *OED Online*, Oxford UP, July 2002 [http://www.oed.com]; Joseph Wright, *English Dialect Dictionary*, 6 vols. (London, H. Frowde, 1898-1905); J. Lemprière, *Lemprière's Classical Dictionary* (1788; London: Bracken, 1984); *Concordances of Great Books*, ed. William A. Williams, Jr., July 2002 [http://www.concordance.com]; William Shakespeare, *Complete Works*, ed. Hardin Craig (Chicago: Scott, Foresman, 1961); John Milton, *Complete Poems and Major Prose*, ed. Merrit Y. Hughes (New York: Odyssey, 1957); Thomas Moore, *Poetical Works*, ed. A.D. Godley (London: Oxford UP, 1915); Henry Wadsworth Longfellow, *Poetical Works*, Cambridge Edition, with an appendix of notes by the author including a "Vocabulary" (664-65) of Ojibwa words in *The Song of Hiawatha* (1893; Boston: Houghton Mifflin, 1975); Alfred, Lord Tennyson, *Poems*, ed. Christopher Ricks (Harlow: Longmans, 1969).

Editorial Emendations

In the following list, the reading that appears in the present edition is given first, followed by the reading from *The Favorite*. Locations in the text are indicated by page and line number.

79.13	moccasins] mocassins
79.25	Creek] creek
79.25	Harty] Tomkins
80.10	Tavern] tavern
81.35	Ah, thin] A thin
82.2	to-day?] to-day,
82.8	Captain] captain
82.8	waitin'."] waitin.'"
83.14	Captain] captain
83.20	Cecil] Cecile
84.15	Colonel] Captain
86.17	ankles] ancles
87.17	Cecil] Cecile
87.22	dullness] dulness
88.18	wild,] wild
89.3	hall,] hall
90.7	growled,] growled
91.5	Cecil] Cecile
91.18	rampant] rampant,
92.3	savage?] savage,
92.4	bitterly.] bitterly,
92.17	Cecil] Cecile
92.23	it's] its
92.32	it's] its
93.19	lake,] lake
93.22	background] back-ground
93.23	angel,] angel
95.9	Hawk-eye] Hawkeye
95.37	trapper.] trapper,
96.8	Hawk-eye] Hawkeye
98.21	two lights] two-lights

100.26	occurred?] occurred,
100.28	it?] it.
101.16	trial] 'trial
104.16	weeks'] weeks
106.26	Joe] Jim
107.1	He'd hev] We'd hev'
108.4	Tavern] "Tavern"
108.14	background] back ground
109.1	hev] hev'
109.11	meantime] mean time
110.14	Archie] Archy
110.14	Tavern,] "Tavern,"
110.15	Harty] Hardy
110.35	Harty] Hardy
111.16	trappers.] trappers,
111.21	Harty] Hardy
113.3	red-skin] redskin
117.34	"but] but
118.12	nineteen] nine, ten
119.2	reappear] re-appear
119.6	moccasins] mocassins
120.2	me,] me.
121.3	waked."] waked.'"
122.22	men] man
123.36	masther] master
124.24	coon-tail] coon tail
125.20–21	Mike. Stay] Mike." "Stay
125.31	Grecian] grecian
126.6	meantime] mean time
126.29	Theodore] Hubert
130.30	moonlit] moon lit
132.26	Olla softly,] Olla, softly
134.4	Tavern] 'tavern'
135.15	Captain] captain
135.22	down] down to
136.8	Rembrandt] rembrandt
140.38	night] light
143.27	Ball] ball

144.3	Lina] Linda
144.11	Confucius] Confuscius
144.20–21	out of one] out one
147.17	he?] he,
148.25	Denville] Denville's
149.15	fuchsias] fuschias
149.30	Ball] ball
156.17	colleen] coleen
156.33	outline,] outline.
158.5	Calico Ball] calico ball
158.11	rhythmical] rhymthical
163.17	coon-skin] coonskin
164.4-5	east wind, Wabun] west wind, wabun
169.36	possible,] possible
171.18	Bedad] Dedad
171.30	masther] master
171.36	be] we
172.9	father] father,
174.8	It] I
174.11	previous] precious
177.23	mirage,] mirage
178.20	hope"—] hope—"
178.22	Steward] steward
179.9	it's] its
180.9	[A break has been inserted after line nine.]
180.23	same, as Mike would say,"] same," as Mike would say,
181.18–182.3	[Cecil's letter has been reformatted to reflect the fact that it is read aloud by Olla, as part of the Frazer sisters' dialogue.]
182.23	Archie?] Archie.
185.9	hideous,] hideous
187.30	Scranton] Brampton
190.21	to cast] casting
194.3	Street] street
197.19	Scranton] Brampton
197.22	Scranton] Brampton
203.20	whiled] wiled
204.3	Macer.] Macer
204.11	Macer."] Macer.

WINONA; OR, THE FOSTER-SISTERS   71

205.12	astonishment.] astonishment,
205.27	Scranton] Brampton
205.31	Scranton] Brampton
209.17	day.] day."
210.20	depot] depôt
211.27	exhilaration.] exhilaration,
212.11	little,] little
214.4	depots] depôts
217.18	leant] lent
218.5	Station-Master's] Station Master's
218.18	earth?] earth.
219.9	hospitably; "too] hospitably;" too
219.24	this?"] this?
220.23	red-skins] red skins
220.26	Fennel,] Fennel'
221.22	Jones?] Jones.
228.34	me?] me.
229.22	promise?] promise,
230.6	importance.] importance."
231.14	murphy] Murphy
238.18	hartist,] hartist'
241.18	ridiculous] rediculous
241.18	to leer sentimentally] to her sentimentally
241.34	wood-shed] wood-sheds
243.2	date] dates
244.4	Rosie?] Rosie.
244.32	"Is it] "It is
244.33	alannah?] alannah.
245.6	wood-cuttin'] wood cuttin'
245.30	noisily] noisely
247.9	it's meself] it' meself
247.30	stiffly] stiffily
248.17	juggernaut] juggernant
248.24	innocence,] innocence.
249.5	sweet face] sweet-face
251.4	Cupidon] "Cupidon"
251.8	Cupidon] "Cupidon"
251.12	Cupidon] "Cupidon"

252.10	spake] spoke
252.12	reins] rein
252.13	evermore] ever more
252.24	bell:] bell.
253.8	all."] all.
253.16	vengeance?] vengeance.
253.20	mental] mutual
253.25	weird] wierd
255.20	win,] win.
256.30	falls] fall
257.2–3	your employer] my employers
257.21	Madame] madame
261.28	stepped suddenly, appeared phantom-like] stepped suddenly appeared, phantom-like
262.32	was] has
263.26	Cavalry] Cavalery
265.23	Oh?] Oh!
266.23	pool, stood] pool stood
267.17–18	Archie, summoned home by a telegram the day before,] Archie, (summoned home by a telegram the day before,)
269.33	woman?] woman,
269.35	him?] him.
270.17	and anxiety] of anxiety
272.33	nee-ba-naw-baigs] hee-banaw'-baigs
273.1	Fox] fox
273.3	"When] When
273.3	red-skins] redskins
273.28	foot-fall] foot; fall
276.8	Vivien] Vivian
279.14	Lina] Lena
279.21	Lina] Lena
280.21	Flora had "gone] "Flora had gone
281.18–19	heroically—in] heroically in
282.14	Marcus] Quintus
283.10	Lina] Lena
284.1	and so] an so
285.2–3	you're to put] you're put

WINONA; OR, THE FOSTER-SISTERS 73

Line-end Hyphenated Compounds in the Original Text

[The following words appear as hyphenated compounds broken at the end of lines in the text of *Winona* published in *The Favorite*. Where possible, they have been resolved in the present text, as indicated below, as hyphenated or unhyphenated words (or, in one instance, as two discrete words), on the basis of Crawford's customary usage. Those that occur uniquely have been let stand, in view of Crawford's penchant for hyphenated constructions and in light of precedents found in the *Oxford English Dictionary*, 2nd edition.]

81.10	king-fisher
81.17	water-lilies
82.2	to-day
85.4	city-ward
88.3	bear-skin
88.9	doorway
88.18	reappear
92.17	golden-haired
93.9	straightforward
94.15	far-off
95.30	self-reproach
96.17	fishing-lights
98.14	anything
99.4	jack-lights
101.7	good-hearted
105.24	pine-grove
106.24	red-skins
112.36	rudely-carved
119.4	coon-skin
122.13	self-upbraiding
136.29	undertone
138.30	back-log
139.17	re-seating
143.8	heavily-draped

143.28	to-day
144.1	to-night
150.20	to-day
153.19	master-hand
158.4	button-hole
169.33	queenly-looking
171.5	sherry-cobbler
171.25	peat-bog
172.1	death-bed
173.17	eye-glass
173.29	reappeared
182.11	any one
188.8	household
190.36	self-control
196.23	love-land
211.15	pale-browed
211.24	Wood-racks
216.22	household
223.12	first-rate
223.20	cab-man
223.21	to-night
223.31	flower-crowned
224.18	drawing-room
226.21	warm-hearted
227.30	match-makers
235.36	doorway
237.8	sunlight
237.10	wood-yard
237.29	cedar-hedge
239.10	hand-sleigh
239.12	cedar-hedge
241.34	wood-shed
242.17	trap-door
243.27	goose-berry
244.4	love-charms
244.10	love-charms
246.33	copper-colored
247.21	anything

WINONA; OR, THE FOSTER-SISTERS   75

249.19	time-honored
254.3	cross-bones
254.32	whip-cord
256.6	midnight
260.15	moonlight
264.24	thunderbolt
267.1	headlong
270.9	foster-sister's
272.11	water-courses
273.33	Hawk-eye
277.3	drawing-room
277.7	orange-flowers
278.33	anything
279.7	to-night
279.27	Black-a-moor
283.1	ice-boat
285.29	rose-draped

WINONA;
OR,
THE FOSTER-SISTERS

THE FAVORITE. 9

January 11, 1873.

For the Favorite.

THE FACTORY GIRL.

BY J. A. PHILLIPS.

For the Favorite.

WINONA;
OR,
THE FOSTER-SISTERS.

BY ISABELLA VALANCY CRAWFORD,
OF PETERBORO', ONT.

Author of *"The Silver Christmas Box," "Wrecked; or, the Rosicrucian of Mistere," &c., &c.*

CHAPTER I.

ANDROSIA.

ARCHIE'S MEETING WITH ANDROSIA.

The first page of the serialized text of Winona, with woodcut illustration
"Archie's Meeting with Androsia," from *The Favorite*, 11 January 1873, p. 9,
courtesy National Archives of Canada e002852792.

[PART I—II JANUARY 1873]

CHAPTER I

Androsia

"I guess if we wait a bit someone'll come to take up the traps; but whatever you cumbered yourself with sich a heap of tackle for, I don't see, comin' all this way."

"I've caught more trout with a willer wand, in an hour than you're like to catch in ten with them jointy things, I tell you, Cap'n."

The young man addressed as Captain smiled, showing under his heavy moustache a set of dazzling teeth, and with a light bound, sprang from the canoe to the reedy bank, to the admiration of his two companions, a pair of wide shouldered trappers in doeskin jerkins and moccasins, gay with porcupine quills, for the frail boat hardly rocked as he leaped ashore.

"Guess, Billy, that's like it," remarked the elder of the two approvingly, "the Cap's an active feller and no mistake, guess he'll make Andy Farmer leave that!" this last in an undertone, and with a low chuckle of delight.

"You're about right, old man, an' he'll be just about right pleased to see him too, will Andy."

"Hallo!" cried the subject of their remarks from the bank, "I can't stay here all night, you know, I'll pay you two fellows well, if you'll help me with my things to the Colonel's, it can't be far."

"'Tain't far, sure enough," responded the elder man, "but I guess here's Mike Murphy and Jimsy comin' to take them up, and we've got to be back at Lizard Creek afore sun-down, along of Billy here and Sal Harty."

"You shut up!" retorted Billy, much exasperated and crimsoning to the roots of his curly brown hair. "You ain't got as much sense as an owl; can't you let Sal be?"

"You've no call to get your back up, Billy. You're not the first man on yearth as has meant to get married, eh, Cap?"

"By no means," replied the young man laughing, and as I find such an event is impending, pray, Billy, tell Miss Sally that she has my best wishes as you have also, my friend."

WINONA; OR, THE FOSTER-SISTERS   79

The young trapper extended his huge brown hand, and shook that of the speaker cordially, "you're a down-right good-natured chap," he said, pleasure beaming from every line of his bronzed face, "and if such a thing as a bar would lie in your way, say the word, and Billy Montgomery's the man to show you their tracks. Thar!"

"Thank you," responded the young gentleman smiling, and added, "I have no gift suited to a lady, but here's something may suit you, Billy," and he lifted an elegant rifle from the ground, where it had been carefully laid.

"I have not forgotten," he said, with a grave smile, "my adventure at Sandy-Point Tavern or your interference in my behalf."

Billy's dark eyes flashed as he glanced at the rifle, its silver mountings, and beautifully marked twist barrel gleaming in the sun, but he shook his head.

"Couldn't fix it nohow, Cap," he said, still fondly eyeing the rifle. "The fact is Hawk-eye is just one of them 'varsal terrors as a man owes it to his country to squash when he gets the chance, no matter whether they're red or white. I guess he'll keep snug now for a time, the tarnal galoot!"

"There ain't much of a doubt of it," said the elder trapper with a wide grin of intensest enjoyment. "You mashed him into apple sass, Bill Montgomery." Bill laughed good-humouredly, and by a dexterous shove with the paddle sent the canoe several feet from the shore, rustling through a bed of rice.

"I guess I'd best make tracks away from that ere rifle," he called back, "it's powerful tempting, Cap, but I'm not the mean beggar to take pay for standing up for a friend. Mind you give Sal and me a call when you're comin' down the rapids."

Captain Archie Frazer of the 19th Blues[1] looked disappointed at having his grateful intentions frustrated by the generous spirit of the trapper, but remembering that he would see him again shortly, when he would insist on carrying out his design, he returned the parting signals of his quondam guides, and leaning on the rejected rifle watched them as they shot out into the little lake, that lay like a solitaire diamond

---

[1] The most famous military unit known as "the Blues" is the British Royal Regiment of Horse Guards (the nickname refers to its uniform, blue with scarlet facings); however, there is no record of this regiment having been stationed in Canada. While it is possible that Crawford had in mind a unit of Canadian militia such as the 19th Lincoln Battalion, organized in 1863 and called out during the Fenian raid of 1866, the name of Archie Frazer's detachment may be purely fictitious.

gleaming in the eye of the sun. It was completely surrounded with dense forest, except where a narrow opening let its limpid waters leap out into a narrow channel, which widened gradually into a fine river, running for many miles through trackless solitudes, and towards this liquid gateway the trappers shot, leaving a track of wavering gold on the calm bosom of the lake. A heron sailed slowly across the cloudless sky, and here and there a widening circle, or a heavy splash showed that the finny tenants of the lake were disporting themselves in the cool of the approaching evening. A couple of cranes were stepping daintily along a little sandy reach farther up, and a gorgeous king-fisher, wheeled his shy flight to his reedy bower on the opposite shore. A couple of tiny islets rose like twin emeralds from the lake, and were mirrored in its bosom with a fidelity that did not forget the faintest fern spray, or the slenderest vine that clambered up their sides. The melancholy cry of a hidden loon came plaintively across the water, and the tap, tap of a woodpecker, came with startling distinctness from the woods behind. A flotilla of water-lilies gleamed like huge pearls in the shadow of a group of graceful willows bending from the bank on which Captain Frazer had landed, and the rice bed waved softly in the light breeze. There was a kind of cathedral quiet, mingled with a vernal cheerfulness reigning over the spot. Nature rejoiced in her solitary place, and at this bright hour, the minor undertone that perpetually sighs through the forests of America was almost hushed. A rosy mist was creeping over the lake, and the lucid shadows were stealing out on the amber waters, deepening them near the shore to bronze, gradually merging into gold and mellow purple where the light had fuller sway.

There was nothing very striking in this little bit of woodland scenery, no telling effects of frowning rocks or whirling rapids, but it was perfect in its way, and Captain Frazer became so absorbed in contemplating it that he quite forgot the approach of Mike Murphy and Jimsy, until a rich voice, redolent of the Isle of Erin, and close at his ear, brought him round with a start, to face a little man with comical blue eyes and a tall gaunt Indian lad of about nineteen, who stood like a bronze statue, while Mr. Murphy introduced himself to the Captain.

"Ah, thin, Captain, for it's him you'll be, I'm judging, it's Mike Murphy that's deloighted to see a Christian gintleman who hasn't been through a tannery, in these parts; for barrin the Masther an' Miss Drosia, the craythur, a white face hasn't gladdened my eyes for a matter of two months and ten days. Wirra,[1] it's a haythenish place is Kanyda, any ways."

"Did Colonel Howard know I was coming to-day?" inquired Frazer, as Mr. Murphy paused in his speech of welcome, and scanned him with his twinkling eyes which overflowed with drollery.

"Well, now, mebbe he did, but it wor Miss Drosia as made ye out down by the Portage yonder, and sent me and Jimsy there to carry up yer traps. Here, Jimsy, lend a hand wid the things, can't ye, and don't be kapin' the Captain waitin'."

Jimsy moved haughtily forward, and swung the heavy portmanteau on his shoulder as though it had been a feather, without deigning a glance at Frazer, while Mr. Murphy loaded himself with the baize-covered fishing-tackle and the rifle, and preceded by the young Indian, guided Frazer up the bank into a footpath leading through the forest, and apparently kept with some degree of care, for it was quite free of underbrush and fallen timber. It was almost dark in this leafy lane, so closely were the trees interwoven above it; but here and there a ruby shaft of sunlight fell athwart the narrow path, or a slight opening in the umbrageous roof let a space of azure sky be visible, with rosy patches of clouds drifting across it from the sunset. The path was just wide enough for two to walk abreast, and while Jimsy strode noiselessly on in advance, Captain Frazer and Murphy walked side by side.

"Well, now!" remarked Mr. Murphy, after a moment's sharp scrutiny of his companion, "it's mighty quare, but this Kanydy bates all for givin' wan a youthish air! Who'd be afther thinkin' that yer honor served in the same regiment wid the ould masther nigh forty years back! Wirra, but ye carries yer years light, Captain, honey!"

Archie Frazer laughed. "Why, Mike, I think I look my age; but I see how it is. Colonel Howard, of course, expects my father; but I was obliged to come in his place, as he is quite unable to leave home. How is the Colonel, Mike?"

"Bedad, yer honor, he's fine and cross, and that last's a good sign in an ould man, and if it wasn't for Miss Drosia there'd be no standin' him at all, at all. Bad luck to them spalpeens[2] that it's owin' to!"

Archie looked curiously at Mike Murphy's face. He felt anxious to learn something of his host's affairs, as he had many reasons for feeling keenly interested in the old commander of his father's regiment; but he

---

[1] An exclamation of sorrow or lament (Irish).

[2] Rascals (Irish).

82   ISABELLA VALANCY CRAWFORD

felt that there would be a want of delicacy in questioning the Colonel's domestics on such matters, and while he was quite willing to allow Mike's eloquence to proceed unchecked, he did not wish to appear inquisitive. Mr. Murphy, however, caught his interested glance, and instantly assumed an expression of intense simplicity.

"It's the muskitties I'm alludering to, yer honor," he said, looking Archie full in the eye; "they're in fine voice about now, and many's the male's meat they're beholden to the masther for, the dirty spalpeens!"

Jimsy was listening intently, as Archie could see by the position of his head, as he strode like a dark shadow before them, and nodding towards him Mr. Murphy wagged his red head with expressive pantomime, as if he would say, "be cautious," and then went on: "Och, murther, but it's a quare life to lade, isn't it, now, shut up in the woods? It's Miss Drosia'll be glad to see you, Captain, an' no mistake."

"I hope so," responded Archie, carelessly. He was not prepared to feel a very keen interest in this wild young girl, who had never been within three hundred miles of the outskirts of civilization, added to which there was a glowing face pictured on his heart, the owner of which was his betrothed wife; and even as he walked along the narrow path and listened to Mr. Murphy's remarks, the sylph-like figure and golden head of Cecil Bertrand flitted before him, and he heard her soft laughter in the waving boughs. Mr. Murphy remained silent for a few moments, until a thinning of the trees and sudden burst of rosy light proclaimed that they were nearing a clearing, and turning a little curve in the path, they found themselves at the foot of a gently rising hill, one shoulder of which sloped into the lucid waters of the lake. The hill was partially cleared, so as to give a view of the lake; and detached masses of plumy maples cast tracts of trembling shade on the emerald turf. Midway up the hill, on a natural terrace facing the lake, stood a large, rambling log house, built in the rudest style of architecture, of great trees with the bronze bark clinging like armor to their sides, but which at this time of year were hardly visible, as a vast grape vine flung its verdant banners even over the sloping roof, and fluttered in long streamers from the rude chimneys of unhewn stone.

There were some fields on the crest of the hill under a rough kind of cultivation, with blackened stumps bristling up amid the ripening wheat; and here and there a rampike[1] cutting the sky like a lance of jet. A dilap-

---

[1]   A standing dead tree or stump, especially one that has been burnt.

idated log barn stood behind the house, and two monstrous elms waved their great boughs over its ruinous roof. A flock of pigeons wheeled in the air, or daintily dropped on their rosy feet in search of food, and the lowing of kine came from a distant pasture. As they approached the house four or five lanky deer-hounds came bounding from its interior to welcome them, followed by a man of middle height and of a well-knit and graceful frame, who came forward to meet Archie and his guides.

"It's Andy Farmer," muttered Mike in Archie's ear. "Oh, won't he be the proud man to see you this day!"

Farmer had the air and address of a gentleman. Yet he started and his brow lowered as he looked at Archie, but he controlled himself with an effort.

"This is hardly Captain Frazer?" he said inquiringly, and with what Archie instantly resented as a suspicious and rather insolent gaze. "There must be some mistake. However, sir, I am sure Colonel Howard will make you welcome for the night. May I inquire if you belong to Captain Frazer's party?"

"I am Captain Frazer," returned Archie, looking full into the dark blue flashing eyes of Mr. Farmer. "My business is with Colonel Howard, and any explanations must be made to him."

"Oh, certainly," replied Farmer, readily; "but Colonel Howard led us to expect in Captain Frazer a gentleman of his own years, and really, you must pardon my seeming mystification."

Archie was too good-humored to be proof against the cordial tone and extended hand of Farmer, and he gave his readily.

"Well," he exclaimed, " I certainly am Captain Frazer, and yet I can lay no claim to being the Captain Frazer expected by Colonel Howard. The fact is, my father is quite incapable of leaving home; and I obtained a three months' furlough to act as his deputy. I hope I shall prove of some use to him."

"I hope so," replied Farmer. "Here, Jimsy, carry in Captain Frazer's traps, and tell the Colonel and Miss Androsia that he is here."

Jimsy obeyed with a smile and lighting up of his bronze face as the other spoke, and hurried into the house with his long noiseless stride, while Farmer led Archie towards a long bench running along the front of the house, and canopied by the luxuriant vine.

"Sit down here," he said, "and take a smoke. It's intolerable in the house; but here there is a cool wind from the lake, very refreshing after the heat of the day. You smoke, of course?"

"Oh, of course," said Archie, lighting his cigar. "It's a pleasant change up here, after the glare and heat of Toronto."

"It's four years since I bent my steps city-ward," said Farmer, smiling. He was a handsome man of about thirty, bronzed and bearded. A rippling beard of russet brown, with golden lights in it that fell to the middle of his broad chest. His eyes were intensely, darkly blue, rather restless and flashing, but undeniable in shape and color; and his hair, cut close to his well-shaped head, was of a rich, dark, auburn very rarely seen out of old Italian paintings. He was dressed well, even carefully, in the picturesque doeskin jerkin and gaily embroidered leggings and moccasins of a trapper, but all were of the best and most elaborate description.

Archie Frazer looked at him compassionately. A world where billiards and croquet, dancing and flirtation were not, was certainly not in the young fellow's way. Farmer saw the glance and smiled oddly. He looked at Archie with a strange, eager, measuring glance, and the smile deepened to one of satisfaction.

"You could not exist here," he said, in answer to Archie's glance. "The silken throng of the gay city is necessary to you. You would die here of *ennui* in a month."

"No," said Archie, quietly, "I wouldn't; but certainly I like the society of, well, plenty of people, you know. I think there must be something odd about a fellow who deliberately retreats from the world."

"Like our host, for instance. Well, it *is* odd, or rather must seem so to men of your stamp."

There was a faint, covert, sneering inflection on the words "your stamp," but light as it was Archie caught it, and his dark face flushed. Mr. Farmer was caressing a huge hound, whose head lay upon his knee, and he did not observe the effect his words produced, or he might have altered his hurried estimates of the young man's character.

Further conversation between the two young men was prevented by the sound of a light step behind them, and Archie turned and rose from the bench as his gaze encountered that of the young girl who had paused on the threshold, and was regarding him with a grave and oddly penetrating glance. She was a tall, willowy creature of, perhaps, nineteen, with magnificent hazel eyes, shadowy and "burning yet tender."[1] Her face was

---

[1] Longfellow, "The Skeleton in Armor" (1841) 60.

a delicate oval, and the nose daintily aquiline, with transparent nostrils, fine and slightly dilated. The silky eyebrows formed a straight line across the purely white brow, shaping what is termed the "bar of Michael Angelo,"[1] and gave a look of strange power to the sweetly girlish face, the lovely mouth of which was softly curved and scarlet as that of a child. A warm crimson glowed through the lucid bronze of the delicately rounded cheeks, but the throat was round and white as a pillar of marble. The slightly parted lips showed glimpses of a row of somewhat uneven but beautifully white and small teeth, and the wide shoulders were thrown back with a poise that lent a certain untutored dignity to the slender form. Her hair, of a rich warm brown, with tints of molten yellow flickering through it, was cut close to the small, yet nobly shaped head, over which it curled in a close mass of glittering rings and waves that caught the light, and seemed to surround her head with a species of nimbus, such as one sees in old paintings of saints. She was clad in the full dress of a squaw, but of the finest materials, and daintiest finish. A doeskin tunic gaily embroidered fell nearly to her ankles, and her beautiful feet were encased in moccasins brilliant with porcupine quills. Archie returned her grave searching look with a rather prolonged gaze of surprise and admiration, and a slightly amused smile, for her costume impressed him with the idea that she was in masquerade for his benefit. A slight frown contracted her brows as she caught the laughter sparkling in his dark eyes, and turning to Farmer she said something in the Indian tongue, in a singularly sonorous and musical voice, accompanying her words with a slight gesture expressive of disdain. Farmer's blue eyes flashed with suppressed delight as he turned to Archie, who stood with his soft felt hat in his hand, and remarked, "Captain Frazer, allow me to present you to Miss Androsia Howard. Miss Howard, Captain Frazer." Androsia extended her slender, brown hand and said in English, "You are very welcome here, sir."

She spoke in a curiously formal voice and manner, very unlike the rich mellow tones in which he had just heard her address Farmer, and as one unfamiliar with the language. He took her hand and pressed it cordially, wondering inly if the old recluse had brought up this

---

[1]   See Tennyson, *In Memoriam* (1850) lxxxvii.39–40: "And over those ethereal eyes / The bar of Michael Angelo." Tennyson subsequently explained that his friend Arthur Hallam, whose death inspired *In Memoriam*, had, like Michelangelo, a "broad bar of frontal bone over the eyes" (Hallam Lord Tennyson, *Alfred Lord Tennyson: A Memoir by His Son*, vol. 1[London: Macmillan, 1897] 38).

dazzlingly beautiful creature in almost complete ignorance of the language and customs of her land, or whether she was enjoying a little amusement at his expense.

"I thank you," he said in answer to her words of welcome, "but I fear Colonel Howard will feel disappointed when he learns how impossible it was for my father to comply with his request. He is altogether an invalid I regret to say."

She listened to him earnestly, and appeared to comprehend in part what he said, for she sighed and placed her hand on her bosom with a pained look in her lovely eyes.

"Mine too," she said in the same, even monotonous voice, "very sick, very bad often. Die soon perhaps." She paled and shuddered as she spoke, and Farmer bit his nether lip, as he observed the sudden interest that sprang into Archie's eyes as he looked at her.

"Oh, I hope not!" said Archie hopefully, admiring the pensive beauty of her expressive face, and despite the recollection of Cecil Bertrand's azure eyes, full of love and laughter, he thought the shadowy hazel orbs, gazing so earnestly into his were the most beautiful objects his had ever beheld.

Farmer was not slow to read his hardly defined thoughts, and he set his lips in an iron line hidden partially by his drooping moustache, and his eyes suddenly assumed a curious opacity and dullness, which, to those who knew him, boded no good.

"My father sleeps," said Androsia, after a moment's pause, "but there is bread for you within. Come." She extended her hand graciously to the young officer, and, nothing loth, Archie clasped the pretty brown, soft fingers in his, but Farmer said something rapidly in the Indian tongue, which covered her from neck to brow with a hot blush, and with flashing eyes she withdrew her hand, and with the air of a princess turned and walked into the house.

"She thinks your manner a thought too demonstrative," said Farmer with a quiet sneering smile, "but come in, supper must be ready, and the Colonel is probably awake." Angry, he hardly knew why, distrustful, at once and without being able to define a cause for the feeling, Captain Frazer followed Farmer into a rude hall, hung from rafter to floor with trophies and implements of the chase. Huge antlers bore powder flasks by the score and rifles of every make sufficient to stock a small arsenal. Spears for jack-fishing, trolling-bait, snow-shoes, rude bows and arrows hung against the walls in "orderly disorder,"[1] mingled with paddles of all shapes, dyed and carved in the most approved Indian fashion. Some magnificent wolf-skins and a mighty bear-skin lay upon the rough floor in lieu of mats, and every species of trap known to the backwoods trapper hung from strong iron hooks in the dingy rafters of red cedar, which gave through their ribs a dim view of a shadowy loft, partially floored with unplaned pine planks, which formed a kind of ceiling half across the great hall. Archie glanced round him with some interest, as he followed Farmer towards a doorway hung with deer-skins at the further end, and as he looked up at the empty space, where the planking on the rafters ceased, a pair of immense dark eyes, burning like stars of fire in a dusky face, shrouded by a pall of raven hair, met his, peering at him from the upper gloom. There was something so weird and unearthly in their piercing gaze that involuntarily he paused, but even as he did so the dimly seen face disappeared like a shadow, and Farmer turned to ascertain what kept him. Archie, with a rather bewildered air, was gazing up at the loft, wondering if the burning eyes would reappear, or whether the wild, beautiful, shadowy face was a creation of his own fancy, but he was unwilling to betray his uncertainty to Farmer, and walked forward as the other turned towards him. Farmer looked sharply at him, in a covert way peculiar to him, from under his heavy bronze eye-lashes, and a faint smile played coldly over his perfect face. He looked like a man who had suddenly acquired an idea.

"You have seen our wild, bronze, Venus," he said laughing. "Winona is certainly the loveliest Indian woman in this part of America, and certainly the most utterly untamable."

"Winona!" said Captain Frazer inquiringly, "who is she?"

"The daughter of a once celebrated Huron chief, and Miss Howard's foster-sister," replied Farmer drawing back the deer-skins which shrouded the door-way. "Ah, Colonel, I see you are awake at last. May we enter?"

"Oh, by all means," responded a growling voice from the interior, and Archie with some slight feeling of trepidation found himself in the presence of the friend and benefactor of his father's youth.

---

[1] Most likely proverbial; but see Ben Jonson, *The Masque of Blacknesse* (1605), preface: "that orderly disorder which is common in nature"; and Edward Dicey, *Six Months in the Federal States*, vol. 2 (London: Macmillan, 1863) 7: "the orderly disorder of a Zouave march."

CHAPTER II

The Recluse

Like the hall, the apartment in which Archie found himself was uncarpeted, save for fox and wolf-skins scattered here and there over the dingy and loosely fitting floor, and a narrow bed, a huge bath full of water and a couple of rough wooden benches standing against the unplastered walls was the only furniture the room contained; but a lofty window gave a beautiful view of the now shadowed lake and wide stretching forests. Just aroused from his slumber Colonel Howard sat upon the side of the bed, from which he rose as he caught sight of Archie just within the threshold. He was a tall old man, of a lion-like port, and with great ragged masses of white hair descending on his broad breast. Small, flashing eyes, whether black or not it was impossible to say, gleamed from under eyebrows making the same straight line as those of Androsia, and giving a look of fierce determination to his rugged features. He was an ugly man, but the dome of his head and his general air would have befitted a Charlemagne.[1] The expression of his face, though not malignant was haughty, sour, and stern, but at the same time candid and straightforward. His glance softened strangely as it rested on the gallant figure and manly face of the young soldier, and quick to read the welcome of eye and extended hand Archie advanced and grasped that of the old man heartily and warmly, while his face flushed with pleasure at a welcome somewhat different from that which he had anticipated, for his father had warned him of the eccentricities of his old comrade. There are some people, the grasp of whose hand is almost electrical, seeming to convey something of their own nature, for the instant, into those whom they salute, and a slow smile, passed like wintry light across Colonel Howard's face, as Archie's nervous, muscular, fingers closed round his gnarled and withered hand.

"Next to your father you are welcome," he said sitting down again on the bed-side, and Archie observed that his voice and movements were alike strangely feeble. He pointed to one of the wooden benches, on which Archie seated himself facing the bed and its occupant.

---

[1]   Charles the Great (742–814) was the King of the Franks in Germany and later rose, as Charles I, to become the emperor of the Holy Roman Empire from 800 to 814.

After a second's hesitation, Farmer quietly left the room, and Archie felt a sensation of relief of which he was instantly ashamed, and he was not a little surprised to observe a gleam of satisfaction pass over Colonel Howard's face as the deer-skin curtain flapped behind the tall, stately form; but it passed in a moment, and the air of bitter gloom descended on the old man's face again.

"Well young sir," he growled, suddenly turning on Archie. "What brought you to my lodge in the wilderness? I did not send for you."

Had he not had the recollection of his welcome fresh in his mind, Archie would have been angry, and as it was his cheek flushed slightly as he answered—

"I have a letter with me from my father, explaining my intrusion on your privacy, sir. He thought that perhaps you might make me useful in some way, as he could not come himself."

"Pshaw, pshaw," exclaimed the Colonel brusquely. "What use can I make of a boy? There! don't redden, one day you'll be old enough in all probability, old enough to have outlived even friendship as I have done. Time was when I held Dick Frazer incapable of slighting the dying request of a friend."

"If you will read this letter, you will find how you mistake him," said Archie, with an air of great dignity that sat well on him, "my father has never walked without the aid of crutches during three years."

"Worse than me," said the Colonel eagerly, "why I can paddle my sixty miles a day, and walk thirty, or at least," he added with a sudden change of countenance, "I could until this cough attacked me. It's wearing me out fast. But he's worse than me, worse than me, Jolly Dick Frazer."

Archie glanced round the desolate room, and a vivid picture rose before him of the pretty, bright home on the St. Lawrence, where the old officer lived with his wife and three pretty daughters, and had his pain lightened and his tedium cheered by their affection and tender care, and mentally disagreed very strongly with his host; but he was too compassionate to remind the old recluse of this and remained silent, until the latter spoke again. He raised his huge, leonine head, and looked at Archie with a grim smile.

"Come," he said, "I will tell you why I say that. He is happiest in dying who has least to regret. I have nothing. My old comrade doubtless fancies he has much to bind him to earth. It was ever his way to gather so many into his brave, foolish, generous heart. Bah! I found only one to love in the world, and she was not worth a sigh." His countenance darkened to such a deadly gloom that Archie who had never encountered anything out of the commonplace expression of every day feelings, became exquisitely uncomfortable, and wished himself back at Toronto where his regiment was quartered, and where Cecil Bertrand had her "local habitation."[1] There was such a dead silence in the room that he felt obliged to break it, so seizing his courage *à deux mains*,[2] he burst out—

"Why, there's Miss Howard, Colonel, and you say you have nothing in the world to regret leaving."

A look of tenderness for a brief second softened the old man's face, but it was gone almost before defined.

"She is little to me," he said coldly, "but yet it is for her sake that I entreated my old friend to visit me. As I go down into the dark valley a fear begins to oppress me that I have acted towards her mistakenly, and yet I can truly say that I thought by separating her nearly altogether from her kind I was bestowing on her the greatest boon in my power— ignorance, blessed ignorance of the rampant wickedness of the world. But now I fear, I fear."

Having found the world for six-and-twenty years a very kindly, jolly, pleasant place in its way, Captain Frazer made a faint protest in its favor. "I can't see it myself," he said, "of course a fellow gets hanged now and then, or blows open a safe, or runs off with the dividends or something, but there are lots of good fellows all about, if you don't overlook them purposely you know."

"Dick Frazer all over," muttered the Colonel, looking fixedly at Archie's dark, glowing face, "body and mind, heart and soul. He was always looking for the pleasant side of things. Have you seen my daughter?" he added sharply.

"Yes," said Archie concisely. He was not at all certain of his ground and thought it better to allow the Colonel to continue.

"What do you think of her?"

---

[1]   See Shakespeare, *A Midsummer Night's Dream* V.i.14–17:
    And as imagination bodies forth
    The forms of things unknown, the poet's pen
    Turns them to shapes and gives to airy nothing
    A local habitation and a name.

[2]   With both hands.

"I really don't know," responded Archie a little startled by the question. "She is uncommonly lovely."

"Do you know that she is a complete savage?" inquired the Colonel, bitterly. "I have secluded her from knowledge as you hide a pearl from the light. She is uncultivated as her foster-mother, and now that I am dying I leave her to fall unprotected into the hands of the Philistines. Come closer," he said eagerly. He glanced cautiously about the room as Archie rose and approached the bed, and drawing the young man down beside him he placed his lips at his ear and in a hurried whisper went on. "I betrothed her a year since to that man who has just left us, because I thought he would guard her well. His mind and mine seemed thoroughly in unison, except that he seemed to have a nobler, more generous nature than ever I could boast, but of late distrust of him has shaken my very soul. It has come whence I know not, but it will not depart, and as the shadows close, I feel that I have doomed her to a life of misery."

"Doesn't Miss Howard like the fellow?" inquired Archie with more eagerness than golden-haired Cecil would have liked to have heard.

"Bedad an' it's herself the craythur, that doesn't," remarked a confidential voice close behind Archie, and to the astonishment of the latter, Mr. Murphy was visible leaning familiarly against the bed-post. "Now be aisy, Colonel," he continued in a whisper, "Andy Farmer's ear's cocked not a mile from that windy, the left-handed blessins' of the saints be about him! and Miss Drosia has yer suppers ready in the hall, an' it's famishin' you'll be Captain dear, after your day's journey."

To Archie's surprise the Colonel seemed startled when he heard of the proximity of Farmer, nor did he appear to resent Mike Murphy's intrusion into the confidential conversation between himself and his guest, nor was Mike's manner even bordering on disrespectful.

"I will see you again in private," said the old man hurriedly, "go now, and remember, keep fair with Andrew Farmer."

"Wouldn't you be afther tidying yourself up a bit, Colonel darlin'?" queried Mike coaxingly, "sure it's yerself is the born image of King Nebuchodnezzar,[1] the misfortunate craythur! an' it's not every day we've quality visitors. There's yer coat an' it's well you look in it, sir."

---

[1] A ruler of Babylon (6th century BCE), Nebuchadnezzar is a prominent figure in the Old Testament. See Daniel 4.33: "The same hour was the thing fulfilled upon Nebuchadnezzar: and he was driven from men, and did eat grass as oxen, and his body was wet with the dew of heaven, till his hairs were grown like eagles' feathers, and his nails like birds' claws."

Mike was evidently the old man's valet, and while the Colonel growled discontentedly, Mr. Murphy inducted him into a thread-bare and ruinous coat with an air of careful kindliness that was not thrown away upon Archie's observation, a quality in which he was by no means deficient, although his careless good-natured bearing was apt to lead others to imagine that he was shallow and superficial, a mistake as we have seen already made by Farmer who was a clever man, after a wily, scheming fashion. Such men frequently fail just in this way. They cannot understand a perfectly candid straightforward character. There is nothing worthy of admiration in their eyes but a talent for intrigue.

Machiavelli[1] wins their homage where a Newton[2] or a George Stephenson[3] is considered hardly worthy a thought, and Farmer failed utterly to see beneath the youthful gaiety and careless good humor of Captain Frazer, the earnest soul and powerful mind which only required the spur of circumstances to waken into full life and power.

"A commonplace military fop and athlete," was his sentence on Archie, and it remained for time alone to shew him his fatal mistake.

Presently he came sauntering into the hall where a deal table guiltless of a cloth was spread with rosy trout, fresh and curdy from the lake, and smoking potatoes in a huge wooden bowl, golden butter and huge tin cans of milk, at which repast was seated the Colonel with Archie on his right hand, and Mr. Murphy hovering in the background like a red-headed guardian angel, and three or four lanky hounds rested their forepaws on the edge of the table, while with moist black noses they sniffed inquiringly at the steaming dishes just an inch or two beyond their reach.

Mr. Farmer was much indebted to mother nature for the physique with which she had endowed him, and under cover of which he had committed a very fair share of cold-blooded villainy during his thirty-three years of life. He had a noble brow, a benevolent dome to his scheming head, and an upright carriage and chivalrous air worthy of a Bayard.[4]

---

[1] Nicolas di Bernardo Machiavelli (1469–1527) was an Italian statesman, political philosopher, and author. His famous treatise, *The Prince*, argues that, in politics, expediency takes precedence over moral issues.

[2] Sir Issac Newton (1642–1727) was an English philosopher and mathematician. Among his many theories and accomplishments, he formulated the law of gravitation.

[3] George Stephenson (1781–1848) was an English engineer and the key figure in the development of the locomotive and railway.

[4] A model of chivalrous honour and courage, after the French soldier Pierre Terrail, seigneur de Bayard (1473–1524).

His eyes even were not the regulation villain steel gray or fiery black, but a rich, deep sympathetic blue like the edges of the Mediterranean, with the rosy twilight lingering on them, and they were safe eyes, seldom betraying his thoughts, except rarely by a sudden, curious dullness or a horrible flash, like the leaping of a Damascus blade[1] from its scabbard in the light of a conflagration. People worshipped him for a short time, and when they found him out, which they sometimes did in his schemes and plots, they held generally a regretful and mournful memory of him, and were much inclined to lay the blame of any transaction in which they had suffered at his hands, on any shoulders other than those of the handsome, noble-looking Bayard who had robbed them or jilted them as the case might be. He was less popular amongst the rough men of the woods, for just as what man is pleased to term creatures of the lower creation are possessed of immeasurably keener senses and finer instincts than ours, so those to whom the civilization of cities is a far-off dream, have a natural insight or instinct which pierces through the exterior show and reveals the real man, as a conventionally educated man or woman of society could only do, in nine cases out of ten, by the long and painful process of experience.

"Where is Androsia?" were his first words as he advanced to the table, over which fell a wavering tide of crimson light from a pine-torch stuck into the crevice of the log wall. The open door behind him gave a lovely glimpse of the moonlit lake and the dark, mysterious stretches of woodland tipped and crested with silver.

"I don't know," responded the Colonel, briefly, and turning to Archie he resumed the conversation which the entrance of Farmer had interrupted. His manner was almost rude, but Farmer did not appear to notice it, but seated himself at the table, with his usual air of stately indolence, and Mike advanced to attend upon him.

"Is it Miss Drosia yer askin' for?" he said, in what he pretended was meant for a confidential whisper but which was loud enough to reach even the dulled hearing of the Colonel, "why she's gone this half hour spearing on the lake for maskinonge wid Winona and Jimsy. She went whilst ye wor sittin' on the settle nigh by the masther's windy Mr. Farmer, sur. There's her light nigh half-ways across the lake."

Archie glanced out and in the silver distance saw a light like a great

---

[1] Damascus, the capital of Syria, was famous for its tempered steel.

lurid star moving slowly across the water, but the forms of the girl and her companions were invisible.

Farmer returned no answer to Mike, but turned and looked earnestly out over the lake, where a second light was now visible slowly approaching the other from an opposite direction.

"Did they take two canoes?" he inquired, as he perceived the advancing light, and he helped himself to some curdy trout, and commenced his supper with much gusto.

"Not they," responded Mike, "but I'm thinking that's Hawk-eye that's out, I see him schaming round in that black canoe of his just at dusk."

Farmer rose from the table and pushed back his tin plate. He went to one of the rough stands and taking down a paddle, threw it over his shoulder and without a word or a glance at his companions rushed out into the moonlight. Colonel Howard turned almost savagely on Mike who was leering after the retreating figure of Farmer with indescribable humor.

"Why did you let the girl out with that scoundrel prowling round?" he said, in a voice hoarse with rage, and shaking his trembling hand at Mike.

"Be aisy now, Colonel," replied Mr. Murphy, "it's meself didn't see the red rascal at all, at all, sure it was only jokin' Mr. Farmer I was. A brisk paddle on a wild goose chase'll do the craythur good and kape him out of ear shot whilst yer honor spakes what was on yer mind to the Captain here, an' to make sure I'll just run to the landing an' help him out with the canoe," and Mr. Murphy disappeared through the open door.

"A clever ruse," said the Colonel turning to Archie with a grim and bitter smile, "that man haunts me day and night, and I cannot rid myself of him. Had you stayed for weeks I might not have found an opportunity of unfolding my wishes to you. Now we can speak without interruption."

Archie bowed in silent bewilderment, and with an expression of almost anguished self-reproach the old man continued. "It is indeed a bitter hour in which I see my daughter, the descendent of a proud house, and my heiress placed between the diabolical schemes of a penniless adventurer and the love of an untutored savage such as Hawk-eye—ha, you know the name, I see."

"Yes," said Archie quietly, "a week since, he would have murdered me at Sandy-Point Tavern, but for the intervention of one of my guides, Bill Montgomery the trapper. I bear the mark yet," and he touched a long, newly healed scar on his right temple.

WINONA; OR, THE FOSTER-SISTERS   95

"The cowardly dog!" exclaimed the Colonel, "how did it happen?"

"Very simply," replied Captain Frazer, "I detected him a few days previously in an attempt to purloin our supply of powder, and I'm sorry to say I knocked him down. He must have followed our trail to the Sandy-Point Portage, for he stole on me while I was asleep, and had not Montgomery been awake at the moment I would have been a dead man."

"As it is I would not give much for your chance of life, if you remain here," replied the Colonel earnestly. "Hawk-eye is a combination of the evil qualities of both races, without a touch of remorse in his composition. He is a snake deadly venomous and cowardly."

"Oh, I'll look out for the fellow," said Archie contemptuously, "but to return to your affairs, sir?"

"Yes," said the Colonel, with a heavy sigh, "but what is that?"

The loud report of a rifle came sharply to their ears followed by another and another, and mingled with the sharp explosion, the distant and piercing cries of female voices. Archie rushed to the door in time to see the fishing-lights suddenly extinguished. "Something has happened," he cried and dashed down the hill towards the lake, followed by the trembling steps of the Colonel.

[PART 2—18 JANUARY 1873]

CHAPTER III

Winona's Sacrifice

Archie rushed down the moonlit hill, and into the arms of Mike who was rushing up, terror in his eyes and blanched face.

"What is the matter?" cried Archie, as Murphy gasped for breath, "speak man!"

"Yes, speak," thundered the voice of the Colonel. "What has happened?"

"Oh wirra! it's meself doesn't know, but there's bad work out yonder," replied Mike in a voice shaking with emotion. "Here Captain, run up to the house and bring a rifle or two from the stands, while the masther an' me brings out a canoe. Oh run, man, if you've any sinse in your head."

Archie turned and fled up the hill without a word, his heart bounding with wildest excitement, and Mike dragged the Colonel towards a small hut of logs where the canoes were kept.

"Come, rouse yerself," he cried, somewhat terrified at the stony expression of the old man's rugged face. "My name's not Mike Murphy or that tanned rascal has carried off Miss Drosia; but it'll be quare if me an' you, an' the Captain an' Andy Farmer, don't get her back. The apple of me eye that she is!"

While he spoke he had got out a large bark canoe, and now turned to glance over the lake as he placed the light thing on the water that rippled at his feet, while the Colonel stood like a figure of grey granite in the moonlight.

Though the moonlight was excessively brilliant it was almost impossible to discern any object on the wavering, dazzling sheet of water, and as a profound silence now reigned, and the fishing lights had disappeared, the lake appeared deserted, but that a trained eye might have discovered about a quarter of a mile out some dark specks floating idly on the water; but Mike's sight was not good and they escaped his observation. He held the canoe and pointed to the Colonel to enter it, but a sudden faintness appeared to overcome the old man, and just as Archie came rushing back with the rifles and paddles, he sank down on a large boulder standing on the margin.

"You must go without me," he said slowly, "but bring me back my daughter."

"It's best so," said Mike, motioning Archie into the canoe, "he's so wakely. Now, Captain, steady an' let her have it."

Like many even city-bred Canadians, Archie was a magnificent canoe man, and casting a look of compassion on the dreary form of the old man sitting on the rock, his paddle flashed through the molten silver of the lake, and steered by Mike the shore rapidly receded behind them. For the first time Archie had an opportunity of questioning Mike, and as the canoe flew over the water he called out—

"What has occurred? Did you see anything?"

"Bedad I did," responded Mike in a voice of mingled grief and excitement. "I helped Andy Farmer out with his canoe, laughing to meself at the fool's arrand I wor sendin' him on, and thinkin' the second jack-light was belonging to an Indian camp that's pitched below the narrow portage yonder,[1] and then I stood watchin' him as he paddled off like fury, for he hates Hawk-eye like poison, and when he got quite nigh to the two lights, I heard Miss Androsia scream out, an' thin Winona an' the crack! crack of two rifles or mebbe more, and then the lights went out, an' the lake was as quiet as a churchyard. The saints be good to us!"

---

[1] The setting that Crawford describes here bears a strong resemblance to the landscape of the Lakefield area in the 1860s. While there was "nothing very striking in this bit of woodland scenery" (81) as Crawford puts it, the lake where Colonel Howard's lodge in the wilderness is located suggests Lake Katchewanook, a widening of the Otonabee River between Lakefield and Young's Point, Ontario. Its several islands and extensive beds of wild rice disguise a southward-flowing current that leads to a dangerous narrowing of the lake and a twenty-foot waterfall at the "Narrows Portage" just below the town of Lakefield. Wandering Indian families often camped at the lake's southern end. Below those falls the Otonabee races southward over many rapids as it drops another 140 feet in covering the ten miles it takes to reach Peterborough, where it widens into Little Lake, forming a route that offers a popular challenge to area canoeists. Archie Frazer makes just such a harrowing canoe trip in Chapter IV; once he completes the trip, however, Crawford deftly shifts the scene, having the river empty into the immensity of Lake Huron rather than the modest body of Little Lake. Given her relative youth when she left Paisley, it makes sense that she would draw on waterways with which she was more familiar in describing Archie's canoeing adventure.

"Didn't you see anything?" asked Archie, "to give us a clue should we want one."

"Yes, just that they wor red-skins as wor in the second canoe, but no more, for the jack-lights went out in a wink and my eye-sight's but wake," replied Mike, guiding the canoe towards the spot where the jack-lights had disappeared.

Archie's stalwart frame quivered with excitement, and at this moment a faint cry came from the spot towards which they were paddling, and the canoe absolutely bounded through the water, as they wielded their paddles with redoubled energy. In another moment they reached the spot and in an instant discovered the position of affairs. Farmer's canoe floated bottom up on the lake, and at a little distance floated that which had contained Androsia and her companions, and clinging to its side with one bare arm, while her pall of raven hair floated out on the shimmering water, was Winona, her dark eyes burning like wells of fire, and the blood pouring in a stream from a gun-shot wound in her bronze shoulder. Of Androsia or Farmer, or the Indian boy there was not a single sign, and it was evident that the Indians who had attacked the party must have succeeded in escaping behind the shelter of one of the two little islands, one of which rose not far from the spot where Archie and Mike now found themselves. Dumb with dismay Mike paused with uplifted paddle, and gazed over the lonely sheet of water; but Archie accustomed to prompt action brought the canoe alongside that to which Winona was clinging, and prepared to take her into the frail bark, as he saw that her strength was ebbing fast, for the water was turning crimson around her. As Mike perceived his purpose he roused himself from his momentary stupor and while Archie endeavoured to maintain the balance of the canoe he leant over and grasped Winona's arm to draw her closer. "Ah, thin, Winona, asthore,[1] where's Miss Drosia?" he exclaimed, "sure it's not murdhered the colleen is! spake, girl, and don't be smilin' in that deadly way!"

Winona drew back from his grasp, and in a voice that already sounded faint, she exclaimed—

"Linger not here! The opposite shore, quick before she is lost to you for ever."

"We can't leave you here to die," said Archie, in terrible perplexity, "come let me draw you into the canoe, quick."

---

[1] My treasure, or darling (Irish).

Winona waved her beautiful arm with a gesture of determination and authority. She looked Archie fearlessly in the face.

"Squaw must die in few minutes, squaw not afraid to die now. Hurry on the trail and say to my white sister when you take her back to the lodge of her father, that the spirit of Winona will be ever at her side. She loved me."

Before Archie or Mike could guess at her purpose, the girl relaxed her hold on the canoe, and, with a single radiant upward look, the dusky head and lovely face disappeared beneath the waters of the lake, and she had vanished from before them like a dream.

Mike uttered a cry of grief and Archie nearly upset the canoe as he involuntarily half rose from his knees, intending to dive after the heroic girl, who had thus removed the only obstacle to their immediate pursuit of Androsia; but with a powerful stroke of the paddle Mike sent the canoe flying towards the head of the island, which they would be obliged to round before making for the opposite shore.

"She's gone," he said, in a low voice, "but as sure as my name's Mike Murphy, I'll be death of the man that done it. Captain dear, see if them rifles is ready."

Archie obeyed eagerly, and ascertaining that they were ready for instant use he seized his paddle, and the canoe leaped on her way hardly leaving a track on the shining waters. He was obliged to keep silent for a moment to collect his scattered thoughts, and then he looked at Mike on whose usually laughing countenance a stern and gloomy air had settled down.

"Can you imagine what has occurred?" he inquired. "Certainly it is plain that Miss Howard has been carried off, but who has done the deed?"

"Hawk-eye," responded Mike, "who else was to do it?"

"But Jimsy and Farmer?" said Archie, "where are they?"

"At the bottom of the lake," said Mike quietly, "them two shots finished them complete, an' no mistake. Och, why didn't Winona, the poor craythur, last long enough to tell us all about it!"

"They can't be far ahead of us," said Archie, straining his eyes towards the opposite shore as they rounded the head of the islet; but there was nothing visible but a stretch of rippling silver with the solemn shade of the forest on the bank stretching blackly over it. The fugitives must already have reached this protecting shadow, for as far as Captain Frazer's keen gaze could reach there was neither canoe or Indians in sight.

He conveyed this disheartening intelligence to Mike, who listened in silence, and then turned the head of the canoe back towards the shore they had left.

"It's no use pursuing them," he said, "you nor I knows little of them woods, Captain; but before three hours is over there'll be a party on their trail as'll make them hear reason. To think of the purty colleen as is in their dirty paws, the rascally spalpeens! and the good-hearted girleen they've put under the lake. The heavens be her bed this night."

"The blood-thirsty crew," said Archie, whose breast boiled with rage at the idea of leaving Androsia in their clutches even for an hour, but who saw his present inability to compass her deliverance, from his insufficient knowledge of wood-craft.

"They have a heavy account to pay. Three murders to answer for: Winona, Jimsy, poor lad, and Farmer!"

"That same last is what Father Delaney in his prachments used to call a trial wid a blessin' in it," replied Mike with intense philosophy, "if that wor all the Injuns did this night it's not Mike Murphy 'ud be afthur callin' them hard names, the craythurs. But, och wirra! to think of Miss Drosia an' Winona, an' the ould masther we've got to face wid the news."

Archie could hardly repress a shudder as they swept over the spot where Winona had disappeared, and Mike turned away his head, as he paddled on with, if possible, redoubled speed. The current set rather strongly down the lake at this spot, and it had already swept the empty canoes a considerable distance from the place where Winona had so nobly sacrificed her chance of life in the vain hope of serving her beloved foster-sister. As they paddled towards the landing it was decided that Mike should remain with the old Colonel, while Captain Frazer returned to Sandy Point and procured the assistance of his guides of the morning, and as many experienced hands as they could muster to join in the pursuit and rescue of Androsia, and merely pausing to let Mike spring to shore, Archie turned the canoe towards the abode of Bill Montgomery, which lay at a distance of some fourteen miles from the lodge of the old recluse.

CHAPTER IV

Bill Montgomery, the Trapper

As Archie sped along through the lonely moonlight, the rapidly follow-ing events which had marked this first day of his abode beneath the roof of Colonel Howard, flitted through his brain over and over again until as if under the influence of some weird dream. The solemn stillness of the cloudless night, the extraordinary effect of the fathomless purple sky, with its golden hosts reflected in the now motionless bosom of the lake, conveying a sensation as though he swung in some measureless space, where stars revolved beneath, above and around him, added to the unreality that seemed to invest all things. The dazzling yet pensive face of Androsia as he had seen her for a few brief moments, flashed on him from the white mists that curled on the banks, where swamps or morasses stretched back from the lake, and amongst the reflected stars over which his canoe rushed, the burning eyes of the noble Indian girl flashed up at him, or the perfect face of Farmer went drifting by in the unfathomable purple abyss beneath the prow, with dead, wide-open eyes, and golden beard swayed by some unseen influence, and a mock-ing smile carved on his ivory lips. The forest rose up like a huge black wall on every hand, threaded by myriads of fireflies emitting a pale, phosphorescent light; and so intense was the silence, that Archie hailed with delight the distant sound of the rapids at the Narrows Portage, as the waters of the lake rushed tumultuously down a slight and rocky incline, ere they settled into the channel of the river which ran through some ten miles of wild and magnificent scenery before emptying itself into one of our mighty inland seas. The sound restored his mental balance at once, and he braced himself for the arduous task he had before him. He had to carry his canoe unassisted over a portage some mile and a half in length, and through a dense wilderness of which he was almost ignorant; but it was not the physical exertion or the personal risk he ran of becoming inextricably involved in the dark woods through which he would have to make his way, that sent the blood rushing to his heart in almost suffocating waves, it was the knowledge that if any misadventure befell him, Androsia would be beyond any hope of succor long before a party could start on the trail of her captors.

His hair clung to his brow in damp masses, and every muscle ached again, as he leaped ashore at some distance above the rapids, and drew his canoe up the mossy bank, slippery with dew, and dark as Erebus[1] from overhanging trees; but without a moment's pause, he lifted the light vessel of bark on his shoulders, and carrying his paddle and rifle in his hand, he pushed boldly into the impenetrable darkness of the faintly defined track he had to follow. For two hours he labored on through a darkness that might almost be felt, dashing himself against the fallen timber, climbing over huge decayed logs, bursting by sheer physical force through thickets of underbrush, struggling through marshy holes, but keeping the roar of the river close to his right hand. This sound was his only guide, for he had almost immediately wandered from the merely nominal path over which he had come in the morning. He was nearly exhausted with his tramp, laden, as he was, with canoe and rifle, when through the damp night air there came the spicy perfume of a pine wood, and with a feeling of inexpressible relief, he knew that the wearisome Portage was passed. He remembered the grove of kingly pines at the foot of the rapids, and pushing his way to the margin of the river, in a few minutes he was seated in the canoe, which fortunately had sustained no injury in its rough transit, and simply using his paddle as a rudder, was being borne rapidly towards his destination on the resistless current of the broad river. In place of walls of sombre foliage, great crags loomed through the shadows, for, during his passage of the Portage, the moon had disappeared, and it was not yet dawn. Vast, uncouth shapes of granite, bare of shrub or verdure, opening ghastly gleaming gateways into the shades beyond, or rising from the foaming waters like the walls of mammoth cathedrals, or meeting across the channel like shadowy bridges, spanning the hideous torrent of an Acheron,[2] sped away to the right and left as the resistless current bore him easily forward. He was glad of the rest, and was content, as he knew that he was proceeding even faster than if dependent on his own exertions, and he glanced anxiously at the sky in an effort to calculate how long he had been upon his journey. The motionless darkness which precedes dawn hung upon the heavens, but even as he looked a sudden rose tint stole up the sky, and slowly, slowly rippled over the dark dome. In another five minutes a bar of fire ran along the jagged peaks overhanging the west bank of the river.

[1]   The underworld or land of the dead in Greek mythology.
[2]   A river of hell in Greek mythology.

The ruby tint slowly paled to a faint tender gold, and as the sun rose, the night rolled away like a purple scroll on which her story had been written in countless hosts of stars. An eagle rose screaming from his eyrie close at hand, and turned his flight towards the sun, mounting until he faded into the radiance of the morning. Never was daylight less welcome, for Captain Frazer felt that despite his exertions nearly seven hours had passed since Androsia had disappeared, and two more must elapse ere he would reach the shanty of Bill Montgomery. He knew that the cleverest trappers and guides of the region would assemble promptly to avenge an outrage as daring as it was extraordinary at this period of Canadian history, when the red man and the white join in a not altogether hollow fellowship, and when war-paint and scalping-knives are romances of the past, at least so far as regards the greater portion of our vast territory. He knew this, but who could tell whether or no success would crown their efforts to recover her. It seemed as though his three weeks' absence from Toronto had extended into a score of years, and the faces of the friends he had left there appeared like the phantoms of a dream. Even Cecil Bertrand's starry eyes were dim and far off, but close to him, radiant, vivid, absorbing, was the face of Androsia Howard, whom he had seen but for five little moments, in the gloaming of the previous evening, and whom in all probability his eyes would never rest on again. He felt almost angry at the persistency with which the girl's face haunted him, and endeavored in a score of ways to banish the vision, but in vain, for fix his mind on what he would, above all rose the lustrous eyes, and snowy brow, with its halo of rich hair. A fresher, keener air warned him that he was nearing the mouth of the river, and approaching the vast sheet of water on the shore of which stood the shanty of Bill Montgomery, and in another half hour he had rounded the right bank, and was out on the lake, over which a faint ripple was running, just sufficiently strong to cover the sapphire waters with a dainty lace-work of snowy foam. He had half a mile of coasting to do before reaching the residence of the young trapper, but the tiny shanty was plainly visible standing under a grove of dark pines, on a promontory ahead of a peculiarly bold and magnificent character. A vast cliff, four hundred feet in height, rose like a wall of alabaster from the lake, and towards the land declined in a majestic sweep until it met the emerald bank, and its jagged summit was crowned by a few gigantic and gnarled pines, which shewed against the liquid blue of the cloudless sky like swarthy giants plumed and crested with jet. A tiny beach like a fairy ring of gold surrounded the cliff. In the distance, like a beautiful and shadowy mirage, loomed one of the great Manitoulin group of islands,[1] and on the horizon the dingy sails of a lake schooner caught the slanting sunbeams.

Far or near the only visible links with man, were the brown shanty in its shady eyrie amongst the pines, and the schooner fading dream-like into the blue distance.

Archie's keen eyes detected a wreath of smoke rising from the shanty, and a couple of canoes turned bottom up on the strip of beach in the frowning shadow of the cliff, and he judged correctly that Bill was at home. He had felt rather uneasy on this point, as he had feared that the young trapper might have remained over-night at the home of the parents of the girl he was to marry, some ten miles farther down the coast, and whom, as we have seen, he intended to visit the previous evening.

In a few moments he had sprung on the crisp yellow strand, and drawing his canoe out of the water, commenced the ascent of the cliff by a rude, ladder-like path hewn in its precipitous side partly by dame nature and partially by the muscular hands of the trapper. The ascent would have been formidable to a light head or unaccustomed limbs, but Archie arrived at the top with his dark face in a glow, and with that sense of exultation which a man experiences when he has scaled an eminence either mental or natural.

He dashed into the spicy shadow of the pine-grove, and found the shanty door swinging open, and a savory odor of cooking puffing out from its dim recesses. A semi-circle of lank deer-hounds, hairy terriers and grotesque otter-hounds was ranged closely round the rude thresh-old, so intent on the culinary operations going on within that they hardly observed his approach, and he stepped into the shanty before Bill Montgomery, who was leaning over the hearth, perceived that he had a visitor. Archie's quick tread on the earthen floor, brought the young trapper round from his task of grilling the rich slices of a lake salmon, over the embers, and he eyed Archie in silent astonishment, as he reared

---

[1] The Manitoulins are an archipelago in Lake Huron, northwest of Georgian Bay, consist-ing of three large islands and several smaller ones. They were, and still are, mainly inhab-ited by Native peoples, primarily Ottawa, Potawatomi, and Ojibwa. Manitoulin Island has the distinction of being the world's largest lake island. The other large islands are Drummond and Cockburn.

his lofty form, until his curly head nearly disappeared amid the rude rafters of the shanty. Captain Frazer was in his shirt-sleeves, and his passage of the Portage, had not only torn his clothes into huge rents, but his face and hands were literally covered with scratches, several of which had bled profusely. He had long since lost his hat, and altogether his appearance was startling in the extreme to the trapper who, some few hours previously, had seen him in the unexceptional get-up of a modern tourist, point-device,[1] indeed, for our Archie was not above being somewhat particular in his toilet.

"Wal, I'm bet!" was Bill's first ejaculation as Archie flung himself on a primitive seat, formed of a log sawn across and elevated on end, "what's up, Capt'n?"

In a few words Archie explained his presence at the shanty, interrupted by ejaculations of indignation from the trapper, whose brown eyes gathered ominous fire as he listened. When Archie concluded he brought one mighty hand down on the other like a sledge hammer, as he exclaimed—

"By ginger! it's the darndest owdacious trick I ever heerd on. The tarnal galoots! but they'll suffer, you bet!"

Bill was a man of prompt action, and after snatching a hasty meal, the two young men, entered the trapper's canoe, and turned her head in the direction of the Sandy-Point Tavern some ten miles farther down the coast.

"It's not a mite of use follerin them red-skins without two or three men along," remarked the trapper as the birch bark flew like a thing of life over the gently swelling lake, "an' I left Joe Harty and Lumber Pete, down to the tavern last night, they're nigh about the best men in the woods you'd happen on in quite a while."

"It's a pity we've lost so many hours," said Captain Frazer, who, greatly invigorated by the hospitality of the young trapper, was using his paddle with nervous energy as he thought of Androsia and her wretched and despairing father.

"Wal, you see they've taken to the woods," replied the trapper thoughtfully, "an' they can't make much tracks until we're up with them. I guess Lumber Pete'll be able to give us a short cut way to catch up with them. It's the darndest good piece of luck that he hadn't taken

---

[1] Perfectly correct.

up his stakes for Manitoba.[1] He'd hev been off there next week. There's a providence in the way things happens."

"Do schooners often come up this way?" inquired Captain Frazer whose eye had been caught by the white sails of the vessel he had seen some three quarters of an hour previously, as she glided now suddenly between them and the shadowy Manitoulin, evidently making in shore.

The trapper glanced at the distant vessel a little curiously.

"Why no, they're off and on at the Copper Mines[2] a good sight farther down, but they don't come nigh here often. A fishing smack I bet, a little out of her grounds."

Of course Bill agreed with Mike's idea that Hawk-eye was the abductor of Androsia, and Winona's melancholy fate, not to mention the murder of Farmer and the Indian lad, "filled him," as he expressed it, "chock full of burnin' rage." He was a splendid specimen of a Canadian backwoods-man, an honest, simple fellow with a heart as tender as his muscles were tough, and about as learned in the ways of the outside world as the huge hound which lay at his feet in the canoe, and was his confidential friend, the very prince of canine deer-slayers, and wiser, in the eyes of his master, than any sage who swept the stars, or read the history of the creation in pre-adamite formation and old red sand-stone, as though they were primers especially gotten up for his delectation. Wherever Bill Montgomery loomed upon the vision, the deep chest, long fine ears and wistful eyes of old Put were surely to be seen, and he lay now in the bottom of the canoe, with his huge head upon his paws dozing and blinking lazily in the hot sunshine that poured broadly over the lake, as the sun rose higher in the sky. Bill was shrewd too, but the life of solitary adventure he led had not tended to sharpen his faculties, as communion with his kind would have done, and it rarely happened that events occurred to put his natural "social

---

[1] With the opening of the Canadian west and the vast territory that would become the Province of Manitoba in 1870, many young men set out from Ontario to make their fortunes. Youths from Lakefield and Peterborough were no exception. Crawford knew both Willie (William) and Walter Traill, Catharine Parr Traill's youngest sons, who went west in the 1860s to take up Hudson Bay Company appointments. Many others set out to take advantage of the free land that was being made available to opportunistic settlers.

[2] Crawford likely refers to the Bruce Mines on the north shore of Lake Huron in the Algoma region. First opened in 1846, the Huron and St. Mary's Copper Company spawned a company town (Bruce Mines) in 1847 and attracted many miners, especially from the Cornish area of England. Operations struggled during the 1850s and 1860s but flourished with further development in the 1870s.

keenness," to coin an expression, into play; when they did he was generally equal to the emergency.

Archie learned from him that Hawk-eye had not been seen round the Tavern for some days, indeed since his *rencontre* with Captain Frazer, and the conclusion they arrived at was that he had been engaged in elaborating the plot which had resulted in the abduction of Androsia. The fact of the passion with which the girl had inspired the wild and daring half-breed being well known to the scattered dwellers in that lonely region.

"Here we be," said Bill, as after a couple of hours steady pulling, he ran his canoe on a sandy tongue of land, jutting a little distance into the lake. A tangled shrubbery of low lying cedar bushes grew rankly over it, but on the mainland the familiar vision of an orderly, square log farmhouse, standing in a trim orchard, that reposing in turn in a setting of golden wheat fields, and all thrown picturesquely out by a background of dense green woods, proclaimed that some solitary settler had battled with, and wrested from the mighty forest, a precious freehold.

The trapper stepped ashore, followed by Archie, while Put yawned and stretched himself on the level sand, and throwing their paddles over their shoulders, the two young men pushed through a narrow path amid the cedars, and made for the Tavern, as this cheerful, cultivated oasis in the wilderness was termed. The door stood open, shaded by a huge vine of hops, its tassels and leaves dancing in the wind, and the drowsy bir-r-r of a spinning wheel came from the interior. A rosy matron in a black, quilted petticoat and loose cotton jacket stood in the doorway feeding a troop of chickens like balls of yellow animated floss, and she looked up as she heard the steps of the two men. She recognized the trapper and Captain Frazer, and her fresh, comely face assumed an expression of some concern as she observed the troubled looks on their countenances. She stepped down to meet them, surrendering the pan of cold mush an undisputed prey to the chickens.

"What's the matter?" she said anxiously. "Bill, has anything happened along of the old man?"

"I hain't seen the old man since last night," replied the trapper, "I guess he's all right, but there's been a sight of bad work up to Lake Chetowaik.[1] Hawk-eye, well's we can make out, has carried off Miss Drosia and killed

---

[1]   This place is fictitious. Crawford probably found "chetowaik," Ojibwa for "plover," in Longfellow; see *The Song of Hiawatha* (1855), Introduction 32, and "Vocabulary" 664.

that there Farmer, poor Winona and Jimsy, and the Capt'n and me hev come for your old man and Lumber Pete to track the snake."

"Harty's been out trolling since dawn," replied Mrs. Harty, "I thought you'd a met him, but Lumber Pete's inside talkin' to Sally. Come right in."

With a face pale with horror the good woman led Frazer and Bill into the great square room, where pretty Sally stood at her spinning wheel, as rosy, fair and arch, as the "Puritan Maiden Priscilla,"[1] and lounging on a wooden settle against the wall was the form of Lumber Pete, admiring her through clouds of tobacco smoke.

In the meantime the schooner was tacking towards the shore, from the shelter of the Island.

CHAPTER V

Lumber Pete

Sally paused in her demure walk to and fro before the spinning-wheel; and Lumber Pete sat upright on the settle, as Mrs. Harty ushered in the new-comers. Sally's roses deepened as the form of the trapper darkened the narrow doorway, but faded again as she observed the dark and stern expression of his usually laughing countenance, and the unexpected presence of Captain Frazer.

Her bright hazel eyes asked a thousand questions her tongue would not summon courage to form before the stranger, added to which the consciousness that she had been rather encouraging the playful gallantries of Lumber Pete in the absence of her betrothed, kept her silent.

She was a lithe, rosy creature, brown and dimpled, active as a fawn, and her pretty round face lighted by a pair of the archest, shyest, frankest eyes that were ever placed in a woman's head. She could handle a rifle or spear a trout with considerable dexterity, and had never seen a white woman with the exception of her mother, and occasionally Androsia, in her life of eighteen years.

Lumber Pete was a Lower Canadian *voyageur*, turned trapper. He was

---

[1] Priscilla is the heroine of Longfellow's *The Courtship of Miles Standish* (1858); see I.85–86: "Letters ... / Full of the name and the fame of the Puritan maiden Priscilla!"

about fifty years of age, of a dapper and dandified aspect, and much esteemed for his social qualities as well as his great skill in woodcraft. He was small, spare and active, with a droll, old, wrinkled face completely bare of moustache or whiskers, which made him look like an elderly boy. In his hours of social relaxation he was inseparable from a huge violin, of a brown and antique appearance, and which he invariably spoke of as "Madame." It lay beside him on the settle, with the bow lying across it, and he had evidently been regaling Sally with tender melodies while she spun.

Bill Montgomery was too pre-occupied to feel even a pang of jealousy, though at other times the position of affairs would have made him what he called "wrathy," and, with a kindly nod to Sally he turned to Lumber Pete, and, in a few terse sentences explained the errand which had brought himself and Archie to the Tavern, while Sally and Mrs. Harty listened with faces of dismay and horror.

Lumber Pete listened in silence, absently patting "Madame" fondly, while his small, grey eyes snapped and sparkled in the cool shadow of the "keeping-room"[1] like points of fire. He set his little thin lips into an iron line, and as Bill concluded he rose to his feet and tightened the leathern belt round his slim figure, feeling to ascertain if his sharp hunting knife was in its sheath.

He settled his coon-skin cap tightly on his head, and lifted the violin tenderly from the bench.

"Mam'selle," he said, turning to Sally, who was crying beside the spinning-wheel, "behold Madame, from whom circumstances obliges me to part for a period; to thy care I commit her."

"Bother your old fiddle!" retorted Sally, ungratefully, emerging from behind her blue check apron, in a burst of indignant tears, "you mindin' your fiddle, and Winona shot and Miss Drosia carried off. Oh, you—"

Speech failed to convey her indignation, but she shot looks of fire at him, and retired, sobbing behind her apron.

"Ingrate!" murmured Lumber Pete, in tender reproach; "Madame, who has so often warbled a thousand things to thee, to be thus despised!"

As he spoke he was tying the thongs of his moccasins.

"Don't you mind her," said Mrs. Harty, comfortingly, "I'll see to it for you. Here's your rifle and powder pouch."

---

[1]   Parlour in common use; family room.

"*Merci*. Now, behold! I am ready. Madame, adieu! Adieu to thee, Sarah, *ma petite*."

"Get out!" said Sally, enraged at Bill witnessing the result of her coquetry with her elderly adorer, and tossing her pretty head she rushed out of the front door, followed by Bill, who wanted a word with his pretty sweetheart before he departed on his perilous expedition.

Archie chafed under the unavoidable delay that had taken place, and with a hasty adieu to Mrs. Harty, he retraced his steps towards the canoe, followed by Lumber Pete singing in a debonair manner:

"*En roulant ma boule roulant,*
En roulant ma boule,"

the refrain of a *chanson* familiar to every *voyageur* on the St. Lawrence.[1]

Bill lingered for a moment whispering to Sally in the inadequate shade of a neighboring corn-patch, and thus it happened that the three men wound their way through the cedar bushes in Indian file, Archie very much in advance of the two trappers. Each moment added to his impatience to be gone, to be actively employed in the effort to recover the lost girl.

Bill overtook Lumber Pete, and the two men hurried their steps to reach Captain Frazer, who had disappeared amid the bushes ahead.

"I left word with Mrs. Harty to send the old man along after us," said Bill; "and I guess us three will be able to fix that varmint Hawk-eye. Thar's old Put rustlin' among them bushes. Queer he'd leave the canoe anyways!"

At this moment a sharp cry came from the bushes ahead, amongst which Archie had disappeared, and at the same moment a fierce, yelping bark and deep growl from old Put.

The trappers ran forward, Bill breaking down the tough bushes as he plunged through them, and paused with a cry of horror as they nearly fell over the prostrate body of Captain Frazer, who lay on the sand, his right arm pinned to his side with a long, slender arrow, and the blood, in a stream slender and slow, trickling over the glittering sand like a crimson thread.

---

[1]   *Chansons* were the songs of the *voyageurs*, French Canadian and Métis paddlers who plied canoes for the fur trade in eighteenth- and nineteenth-century British North America. "En roulant ma boule" might be translated as "While rolling my ball."

Bill Montgomery's bronzed face turned livid in the bright sunlight, and hardly waiting to see if Archie still breathed, he shouted to the hound which stood near by growling in a low, savage key, with bared fangs and glittering eyes.

"Hi, at him, old boy, at him!"

"*Ciel!* Is the young man dead?" exclaimed Lumber Pete, stooping over Archie's white and rigid face, as the hound flung himself with a headlong rush into the bushes on the right, cheered on by Bill's loud cry.

"'Pears to me it's so," said the young trapper, ruefully, gazing down at the motionless form; "it seems to me as if the devil was hoofin' it mighty spry through this here location these times! 'Er! if that ain't Put settin' his fangs in some feller's carcass!"

A savage growl of triumph came through the bushes to them, and died suddenly into dead silence.

"He's got the devil, whosomever he be's!" cried Bill, triumphantly. "Now, Pete, you look after the Captain, and let me at him."

To judge from the expression of the young trapper's face, it would be but a short shrift the slayer of Archie Frazer had to expect at his hands; and while Lumber Pete sought for some sign of life in the prostrate form, Bill Montgomery, guided by the last growl of the hound, pushed through the bushes with Lumber Pete's rifle in his hand at full cock. His eyes were almost savage in their deadliness of purpose, and his strong, white teeth showed between his parted lips, clenched so rigidly as to alter the outline of his jaw.

He beat back the bushes in his impetuous course until he had nearly crossed the narrow tongue of land, and the sparkling waters laughed through the lace-like, aromatic boughs of the cedars. In another moment he stood on the little margin of beach, and a single glance sent the fiery blood leaping like a flame over his face.

Almost in the lapping water lay the huge, white body of Put, with a shining knife plunged deep into his faithful breast, and the water beyond dyed a deep crimson by the blood pouring from the wound; but over the wide lake or along the wooded shore, there was not a single sign or token of Archie Frazer's slayer. Bill gazed vacantly at the body of his dog, and then he stooped and plucked the knife from the gaping wound. As his eye rested on the rudely-carved handle, a look of bewildered recognition swept across his face, succeeded by an expression of deadly hate.

"Hawk-eye!" he said slowly to himself; "but how's he about here, the red blood-sucker? Well, Miss Drosia can't be far off, that's one thing. Put, my old chap, the red-skin that killed you's did a dark day's work for himself."

In the meantime the schooner had nearly disappeared round a slight curve in the coast, in the direction whence poor Archie Frazer had come in the early morning.

[PART 3—25 JANUARY 1873]

CHAPTER VI

The Captain's Quarters

It stood on one of the banks of the St. Lawrence, neither above or below the Thousand Islands; but just about midway through that fairy scene, where the great silver riband is garnished most thickly with the tiny emeralds nature has so lavishly decked it with. It was a large, low house, with deep eaves and great verandas surrounding it on every side, on which lofty French windows opened; where huge pyramids of brilliant geraniums bloomed in the liquid shade. Its walls of rough white plaster, were mellowed to a golden grey by time and weather; and its peaked roof and fantastic chimneys gave it a picturesque effect, very frequently wanting in the country houses scattered through Canada and the States. A vast vine of Virginia creeper shrouded the whole building in a fluttering tapestry of ruby-tinted foliage, and it had crept up the sloping roof, fastened its tendrils round the rough stones of the chimneys, and waved ruddy banners of triumph out on the hazy autumn air. A dainty lawn, yet green as velvet, bright with vases of scarlet geraniums, and shaded by some half-dozen bowery maples and murmuring beeches, stretched nearly to the water's edge, where a tiny boathouse peeped from a low shrubbery of cedar bushes. Behind the house loomed a grove of lofty pines, with here and there a maple rising like a fountain of flame, amongst their sombre green in its fall robe of scarlet, or like a tree of gold from some Aladdin's land,[1] standing crisply out perfect in every leaf, as a lovely Hindoo widow decks herself in her gayest attire to perish on the funeral pile of her dead lord. A croquet set lay upon the lawn, long lace curtains fluttered out of the open windows, a fresh young voice was practising one of Claribel's sentimentalisms[2] within, and a group of three persons was seated on the veranda enjoying the balmy air and the lovely scene of

---

[1] Aladdin is the hero of a well-known tale of marvels from *The Thousand and One Nights*.
[2] "Claribel" was the pen name used by Charlotte Alington Barnard (1830–69), English composer of songs such as "Come Back to Erin," popular in the mid and later nineteenth century.

the river below. A steamboat was slowly winding up the stream, bearing the latest summer tourists from their resorts at Murray Bay and Tadousac,[1] threading her way slowly in and out amongst the islands in order that her passengers might fully enjoy the beauty of the sunset-lighted stream. A couple of late rafts went sailing by with the current, the voyageurs idly lounging against the cabooses, the smoke from which proclaimed that their evening meal was in progress. On one a man in a scarlet blouse was singing one of the merry songs peculiar to the Lower Canadian French, and on the other, two young fellows were dancing to the sound of a fiddle played by a comrade. A faint rose dyed the majestic stream, and the track of the pretty steamer lay like a riband of lace and pearl, twisting in and out amongst the islets. Her upper and lower decks were crowded with groups, whose laughter came faintly to the ears of the group seated on the veranda.

A pretty, dark-eyed girl, in a white muslin, sat on the steps leading down to the lawn, watching the boat as it steamed slowly past, and talking to a lovely old lady, and a pleasant faced though rather rugged featured man of some sixty years, beside whose wheeled easy chair there lay a pair of crutches, proclaiming him a confirmed cripple.

"Papa," said the young lady, suddenly, "do lend me your glass. I could almost feel certain that I see Cecil Bertrand on the upper deck of the steamer. See! she is waving her handkerchief to us."

"Your eyes are almost as sharp as Archie's would be under the same circumstances," said the old gentleman laughing, as he handed her the glass.

"Is it Cecil?" inquired the elder lady, after the girl had examined the steamer with the aid of the glass.

"Yes, mamma," replied the young girl quietly, putting down the glass, and turning away her eyes from the river.

---

[1] From about the middle of the nineteenth century, Murray Bay and Tadousac (or Tadoussac) were popular summer resorts on the north side of the St. Lawrence River east of Quebec City. Small Charlevoix villages, they boasted waterfront hotels of various size and status (for example, the Manor Richelieu in Murray Bay) built to serve wealthy American and Canadian vacationers and excursionists who could readily travel there by steamer from points west along the St. Lawrence River and the Great Lakes. An 1870 article on "Tadousac" observed: "The air here is more fresh and invigorating than anywhere on the Lower St. Lawrence, and this with the combined attractions of bathing, fishing, and boating, serve to make Tadousac, next to Murray Bay, the favourite resort of the tourist, the city man, and the invalid" (*Canadian Illustrated News*, 23 July 1870: 51).

"Who are her companions, Viola?" asked Mrs. Frazer. She was a *petite* woman, who showed her lofty French descent in every tone of her still musical voice, and every gesture or movement. Her eyes were yet extremely brilliant, of a deep intense blue, and her cheeks retained much of the delicate bloom of her youth. There was an unconscious stateliness about her, and one invariably found oneself thinking of old point[1] and court trains[2] in her society, though she might be clad in the simplest morning cap and gown a Canadian matron could wear. Her eyes were cordial, frank, radiant, and her lips parted readily in a smile, that was all things to all men, witty, tender, grave as the case might be, but over and above all, lighted by a lovely kindliness that made her absolutely beautiful. Her hair had been blonde, but now was a peculiarly bright and soft silver. She was at once the proudest and the humblest of women, and never for a moment did she forget that she was the grand-daughter of a French nobleman, who had laid down his life in a vain attempt to save Marie Antoinette[3] from the scaffold. She had never for an hour left the shores of Canada, but she was as perfect a type of a courtly French Dame, as though she had flourished in the palmy days of the Faubourg St. Germain.[4]

Viola made a pretence of looking again at the receding vessel through the glass before answering her mother's question.

"I'm not quite certain, mamma; but I think the gentleman she is with is Mr. Denville."

"Humph," ejaculated Captain Frazer, dryly, "sits the wind in that quarter! I'm afraid Miss Cecil is a sly little pussie. Eh, Desirée?"

"I am afraid she is hardly worthy of Archie," replied Mrs. Frazer, a little coldly. "I think it is rather heartless of her to display her coquetry so openly, when she knows our anxiety about him."

"Oh, mamma," cried Viola, "pray don't think so hardly of Cecil, and I'm sure Mr. Denville has not the least intention of flirting with her.

---

1   Needle-point lace.

2   A court train is a length of fabric falling from the waist or shoulders of a lady's formal gown, designed to trail behind.

3   Daughter of the Holy Roman Emperor Francis I and the Archduchess of Austria Maria Theresa, Marie Antoinette (1755–93) was the wife of Louis XVI, and Queen of France after 1774. Famously contemptuous of the masses of French society, she was executed during the French Revolution.

4   Located in Paris, France on the left bank of the Seine, the Faubourg St. Germain was home to an impressive array of French aristocrats who lived behind the high walls that characterized the area. Visiting writers like Henry James were struck by the exclusiveness and grandeur of the district.

He told me he intended visiting some friends in Toronto this fall, and that was long before he met Cecil."

"Ah, Olla," said Captain Frazer, smiling, "has Denville's little tour in that direction, anything to do with your dutiful pilgrimage to aunt Ursula's next week? I thought it was odd all those pretty dresses being got for old auntie's delectation."

"They are very gay in Toronto, papa," returned Olla, turning her smiling brown eyes on her father, "and dear old auntie has a pretty taste in colors. You know too I shall be staying with Cecil part of the time, and the Bertrands go out so much."

Olla was like her father and Archie, but a soft and pretty likeness of both. She had a lucid brown skin, a soft-featured oval face, lighted by dazzling brown eyes, tenderly radiant, and a quantity of rich black hair, rolled away from her forehead over a low cushion, and hanging in large curls nearly to her slim waist. She was far from being regularly beautiful, but her face grew upon you until you found it one of the loveliest in the world. She was ordinarily pale, but the slightest emotion sent waves of rose, like flying clouds of dainty color across her cheeks, and her lips were of a rich deep scarlet.

"Didn't Cecil write that she and this Mr. Denville, had some thrilling adventure at Murray Bay?" went on the Captain, "saved her life in fact."

"So he did," replied Olla, her eyes flashing and the sudden lovely rose flying across her cheeks; "he risked his in the noblest way to save her. She says she would certainly have been drowned, had it not been for his exertions."

"I knew his mother when I was a girl in Montreal," said Mrs. Frazer; "she and I were educated in the same establishment. I have not met her since both our marriages, however. She married a very wealthy Montreal merchant."

"I wish we heard from Archie," said Olla, after a moment's pause; "it seems so strange that he has never written to us during an absence of three months."

"I do feel very uneasy about the boy," confessed the Captain; "but then we must remember that he is quite beyond the pale of civilization and mail bags, up behind the Manitoulins."

Mrs. Frazer sighed deeply, and a shade crept over Captain Frazer's open countenance. Archie was their only son and his silence troubled them not a little. Olla's bright face grew very pensive in the fading light. Her brother was the hero whom she worshipped, the embodied ideal of her imaginings, pure, chivalrous, honest and true; not a lofty, moral, colossus walking on distant mountain tops of impossible virtue, but kindly, generous, strong-handed, and with the basis of character and intellect time would only ennoble and expand. How seldom a girl says to herself, "If ever I marry, it shall be just such a man as my brother I will choose;" but this had ever been Olla's feelings towards Archie, and it may here be mentioned in strict confidence to the reader, that the hero of Murray Bay strongly resembled him both physically and morally. Olla was the next in age to the young officer, and there were yet two younger girls, aged respectively nineteen and sixteen, slim, erect young creatures with clouds of golden hair, tied back from their blooming pretty faces, and with their mother's brilliant deeply blue eyes, and high-bred air.

"I would have liked to have gone to poor Howard, myself," remarked Captain Frazer, after a moment's pause, "but that was impossible," and he looked at his crutches a little ruefully. Mrs. Frazer placed her beautiful hand fondly on her husband's, and was about to answer, when a sunny head appeared between the floating curtains of one of the open French windows, and a dazzling white throat, with a blue riband tied round it.

"Madame Mamma, Monsieur Le Capitaine and Olla, tea is ready," said a sweet girlish voice; "and oh! papa, there is a wonderful man in the kitchen who wants to see you. An Irish party, Olla, with a voice exactly like Mr. Denville's."

"Sidney, you monkey, behave yourself! What does the man want?"

"You, papa, he says he has a message for you."

Sidney came dancing into full view from her lurking place behind the curtains, made a dash at a great spray of scarlet geranium on one of the stands, tucked it under the blue riband tying back her radiant hair, executed a step or two of a galop before her father's chair, and then folded her white hands and became demure.

"What are your commands, sir?" she inquired, "Is Mr. Denville's double to be introduced on the scene or not? He has a sweet novelty in the *chapeau* line, Olla, that might furnish that person you know, with an idea for a winter head-gear."

"Send the man here, Miss," replied the Captain, smiling with very allowable pride on the lovely sparkling face before him. "I will see him before we go to tea."

"I am gone!" said Sidney, theatrically, waving her rosy hand and disappearing through the open window, to reappear presently round the corner of the veranda, followed by a short man with a shock of red hair, surmounted by a coon-skin cap, with the tail of the animal hanging down on his shoulders, and swinging like a pendulum as he advanced. A greasy doeskin jerkin and well-worn moccasins, with trousers of coarsest Canadian frieze, completed his costume. He carried a large leather wallet in his hand, and his naturally merry countenance looked careworn and fatigued.

"Good evening," said the Captain, courteously; "I hear you have a message for me?"

"That same's thrue, yer honer, if yer yerself an' no one else, Captain Frazer."

"I am Captain Frazer," replied the old gentleman, suppressing a smile at the quaint figure and address of his visitor, while Sidney stole behind him more closely to inspect his head-gear, daintily touching the swaying tail with her mischievous fingers, watched in alarm by her mother and Olla, who were tenacious to a degree where another's feelings were in the case, and dreaded lest the man should discover and feel hurt at the occupation of the sixteen-year old sprite; but he was too much preoccupied to observe her.

"Well, Captain, it's myself is disthressed this day," said the owner of the coon-tail, "shure it's dead he is, Captain, an' no mistake about, glory be about him."

"What do you mean!" cried the Captain, with a look of terror, while Mrs. Frazer and Olla turned deadly white. "Has anything happened to my son?"

"He wor skewered up as nate as a Christmas turkey wid an arrow through him, an' it's dyin' we thought he wor for a matter of six weeks; but mushee,[1] he's gettin' bravely over it, the stout young gentleman that he is; it's the Colonel's dead, an' the heart ov me's broke intirely, intirely," and Mike Murphy sighed profoundly, and putting back his hand, brought the coon-tail round and wiped his eyes with it.

"Has my son been in danger, my friend?" said Mrs. Frazer still very pale, and Mike, remembering his manners, lugged his head-gear off by the tail, and ducked his head in the direction of his questioner.

---

[1] If so it be; therefore (Irish).

"Bedad he has, ma'am, but he's gettin' finely over it, though he's too wake to come home yet awhile. So says he to me, 'Mike, the best you can do is to go right down to my father wid the pore Colonel's will, and give him a clear discount of the way matters has gone here as ye can. Mind an' be sharkumstanshial,' says he, 'so as he'll understand ye.'"

"Sit down," said Captain Frazer, pointing to one of the pretty rustic chairs that furnished the veranda, "and tell me as plainly as possible what has occurred."

Mike seated himself as requested, laying the coon-skin cap carefully at his feet, and Sidney stole to Olla and seated herself quietly beside her, softly stealing one of the slender, brown hands into her own. Archie had been in danger, and the girl's pallid cheeks and dilated eyes showed how deep was the soul over which played so continual a ripple of sunshine, baffling the sight in its effort to penetrate to the depths below, by its glitter and radiance. It is in the shadow of the hanging alders that one sees most clearly into the bosom of the laughing rivulet.

Captain Frazer listened with astonishment, dismay and grief to the tale Mike proceeded to relate, emotions in which Mrs. Frazer and her daughters fully shared.

That the search for Androsia had proved utterly unavailing, though prosecuted with the utmost vigor and skill by Lumber Pete and Bill, with a strong party to assist, was a matter of the most serious moment, as it left her fate in terrible uncertainty.

The old Captain's face flushed deeply with emotion, as he listened to Mike's simple account of the death of his old commanding officer and early friend. He had lingered for a couple of days after the disappearance of Androsia, busily employed in writing during most of the time, and on the evening of the third day had slept, and sleeping, died.

"The last words he sez to me, wor, 'Mike if ye wants me to stay wherever I be's goin' to, take that writin' down to the sittlements to me ould friend Captain Frazer, an' don't be afther givin' it into any one's hands bud his own, do ye hear me!' 'Och, wirra, Colonel darlin' ' sez I, 'it wouldn't be for the likes ov me to be wantin' ye to stay anywheres ye mightn't be comfortable, but hopin' an' trustin' it'll be other ways wid ye, I'll take the papurs. An' a good man to the poor an' a heart ov gold to them as wanted ye've ever had. God be good to ye, sur, this day!' Wid that he took my hand in them long, white claws ov his, wid a shadowy kind ov smile. 'Good-bye, my good friend Mike,' he said, 'the night

120   ISABELLA VALANCY CRAWFORD

is fallin' that there is no mornin' to. Look for my daughter.' He turned his head round on the pillow and lay lookin' at the sunset until he fell off aslape, but he never waked."

Mike was so affected by the remembrance, that he lifted the coonskin cap suddenly by the tail and applied it to his eyes. After a pause he proceeded to give an account of Archie's unlucky *rencontre* with Hawkeye and its disastrous results, and it is needless to say that he was listened to with breathless interest by the little group. As he concluded, Mrs. Frazer rose and walked quietly into the house. She was too much overcome with emotions of gratitude and a sickening sense of what might have been, to remain. Olla and Sidney followed her, and Captain Frazer and Mike were left *tête-à-tête*.

"Have you the papers left by my old friend?" inquired the former, after a pause of painful meditation.

"Yis, sur," responded Mike, proceeding to open the beforementioned leathern wallet. "Here they is. Och! bud it's a wake scrawl anyways."

The package he handed Captain Frazer was indeed directed in a hardly legible hand, to "My old friend and fellow-officer, Captain Richard Frazer, of the — Blues."

"Here, Mike," said Captain Frazer, "push open that door at the end of the veranda, and wheel me into the library. Thank you. That will do. Go back to the kitchen and tell them to make you comfortable. I shall have much to say to you in the morning. Tell them also, that I do not wish to be disturbed for some hours."

Mike glanced in awed admiration round the pretty room, only a library by merest courtesy, with its chintz lounging chairs, pearl and rose carpet, covered with tangled bronze reeds and moss, its book-shelves of bird's-eye maple, and gleaming busts, and its pretty little organ, the pipes gleaming mellowly in the cool shadows, and withdrew, leaving the Captain to a solitude he seldom coveted.

CHAPTER VII

News of Archie

In the unusual solitude of the library Captain Frazer opened the dying communication of his old friend. There was a long letter addressed to himself, and a smaller package labelled "my last will and testament," unsealed in order that Captain Frazer might peruse its contents, which he proceeded to do, not, however, until he had made himself acquainted thoroughly with the accompanying epistle.

The letter, written in a faint but legible hand, commenced by recalling their olden friendship to mind. It touched on Archie's arrival, and then on the subject of Androsia's disappearance, and here it seemed to warm into the expression of something like love for the missing girl; but above all there ran a current of bitter self-upbraiding for the fatal mistake he had made in secluding her so completely from the world. It then went on to give an account of the arrival of Farmer on the scene, and the unsuspected influence he had gained over his entertainer. "Where I was weakest I boasted of my strength," went on the letter. "I deemed myself so completely removed from danger by a total disregard of all kindly interest in mankind, and an impregnable armor of Timonism,[1] that I suffered him to abide in my lovely home day after day. Hour by hour he read my thoughts, and built himself a fictitious character on the basis afforded by them. Where I gathered men and their vices in one strong hatred, he towered over me from the Divine height that can abhor the sin and love the sinner. In all ways he showed himself above and altogether beyond me in generosity of soul, in greatness of heart. I hated the world, he would purify and ennoble it. I could not fail of gradually admiring a character so uncommon, and I began to observe his growing love for Androsia with pleasure. When he begged her of me I readily consented to their betrothal. 'Take her,' I said, 'her mind is an empty page to be written upon. It is to such a man as you I would entrust the task. I had never hoped to meet a heart and soul like yours, and I feel assured that together, in this wilderness, you will found a purer and loftier life. Take her and write your mind upon her soul.' Thus I

---

[1]   Misanthropy, or hatred of the human race, so called after an Athenian citizen of the 5th century BCE who is best known as the protagonist of Shakespeare's tragedy *Timon of Athens*.

betrothed them careless that Androsia, with what appeared to me senseless obstinacy, rebelled and struggled against the yoke I imposed upon her. I made a will in which I left Androsia my sole heiress on condition that she married Farmer, and this ill-advised testament I committed to his keeping. He must have concealed it with jealous care, for after his death the strictest search failed to discover it amongst his effects. Gradually, after I had placed such a tie between us, I began to feel rather than see a change in him. The lovely mirage of his assumed character began imperceptibly to fade away, and the bare, repulsive, true nature revealed itself instead. Hardly in perceptible signs, but, perhaps, as I began to loose my hold on earth, my mental vision became clearer. It was then I wrote to you, old friend, hoping in your counsels to find some means of escape from the toils I had so carefully spun round myself and my child, but a higher ordinance than that of the human will interfered. I have as you will see, left your son Archie my sole legatee, should he recover from his wound and no trace of Androsia be discovered. I pray, if the burning longing of a soul can be called prayer, that she is dead, but something tells me that it is not so. Farmer is dead, and therein is a gleam of comfort. He had a powerful mind and some of those minor virtues, which frequently float like a bridge of cobwebs over the poisonous and remorseless current of natures such as his. Wo to the foot that is betrayed to such a foothold." There was much more, and the letter closed with an earnest commendation of Androsia to the care of his old friends, if she should ever be discovered. On reading the will Captain Frazer found that Colonel Howard had died worth some five hundred thousand dollars, invested principally in English securities, all of which Archie was to possess if Androsia remained undiscovered for a term of five years. The will was clearly and succinctly worded, and was witnessed by Mike and Lumber Pete, so that its legality was unimpeachable. Curiously enough there was not the least clue in either of the documents to show what or whom Farmer had really been, and when the old Captain applied to Mike Murphy for information on the subject, Mike pleaded profound ignorance.

"He kem one day wid a couple of guides, on a hunting tower, he called it, and got a night's lodging at the ould place, an' it fell out that the ould masther took a mighty fancy to him, an' he stayed on an' on, bad luck to him, a matter of three years come October. Och! he wor the bad sight to the house, he wor."

"Did he never send or receive letters?" inquired the Captain, who wished if possible to obtain some clue to his friends, if he possessed any, in order to communicate to them the tidings of his untimely end.

"Divil a wan, yer honer. It's my belafe, savin' yor presence, sur, that he'd no need to write to his friends. Sure what med him aiqual to throwin' dust in the ould masther's eyes in the ways he did, if he hadn't his best friend at his elbow ever an' always? Bud it's not me as'll make bowld to put a name to the gintleman. The saints be betwane us an' harrum, this day! an' thin Winona, the poor darlint!"

"What of her, and who is she?" inquired the Captain.

"Miss Drosia's foster-sister, sur. They wor as fond of aich other as two wild doves, but fond as she was of Miss Drosia, she worshipped the flure undhur the feet of Farmer, she'd have drawn a knife across her purty brown throat any day he told her."

"Did he make love to her, then?" asked the Captain.

"Bedad, yer honer, ther's coortin' and coortin', an' in his way he did it strong enough, but quiet an' sly so as not to come round to the Colonel an' Miss Drosia; but it's meself ever an' always had uncommon foine eyesight where anything of that sort wor handy. Whin I wor a bye in Connaught[1] sure the girleens christened me 'Mike the Mouser,' considherin' the scent of me for that sort. Och! bud that's a long time ago. It is."

Here Mike sighed retrospectively and shook his red head mournfully. He felt at the back of his neck for the coon-tail, but it was not there, and this brought him back to the present.

Captain Frazer shook his head gravely. "I am afraid that the man was altogether bad," he said. "Where is the girl now?"

"In the bosom of the saints if ever a craythur wor," responded Mike, with emotion, and he proceeded to give the Captain an account of her heroic death, to which the old soldier listened with a kind of reverent admiration. "The heroism of Jeanne d'Arc had the enthusiasm of wondering thousands of friends and foes to sustain it," he mused, "but

---

[1] One of the five ancient kingdoms of Ireland, Connaught is a large province in the northwest part of the Republic of Ireland, comprising the counties of Galway, Mayo, Sligo, Roscommon and Leitrim. Stretching from the Shannon River estuary in the south to Sligo Bay in the north, the province was among the poorest in the country, but was a centre of Celtic culture and resistance to English control. Crawford's fellow Irish immigrant and likely mentor James McCarroll was from the Leitrim area and set some of his writings in Connaught and especially in Roscommon and Leitrim.

this simple act of self-denying devotion, has a finer courage in it, than that of the woman warrior of France.[1] What a noble nature the poor creature must have had!"

During this brief reverie Mr. Murphy was searching diligently in the capacious pockets or pouches of his doeskin jerkin, from one of which he presently produced a small package, wrapped in birch-bark and tied round with thongs of fawn skin. This he proceeded to open, and having done so handed it to Captain Frazer.

"It's about the only thing of Andy Farmer's I brought wid me," he remarked; "indade he didn't lave much behind him, nothin' but this, barrin' a trifle of clothes. By the looks of things misther Andy didn't wait to come up to us to larn the meanin' of swatheart. A purty craythur, Captain dear!"

Captain Frazer opened the worn morocco case and turned his chair to the window to catch the light, and thus it was that Mike did not see the expression on the rugged face as he looked at the portrait, though he heard the slight exclamation which burst from his lips.

"What did ye plase to say, sur?" inquired Mike, stepping forward; "do ye want the blind lifted?"

"No, no," replied Captain Frazer hurriedly, "you may go now, Mike. Stay," he continued as Mr. Murphy tip-toed towards the door, "tell me was Farmer like this portrait, in the least?"

"As like as two pase," replied Mike decidedly, "barring the look in the eyes. Perhaps afther all it might be a sister an' not a swatheart, yer honer?"

"Perhaps," returned the Captain absently.

Mike went out closing the door, and the Captain turned his pallid face back to the picture.

He looked at it long and earnestly, his hands trembling like leaves in a strong wind, and yet it was but a girl's face that smiled up at him from the dusk. A sweet, fair face, framed in short curls of gold, with straight, Grecian features, and eyes of the deepest blue. A pathetic face despite the smile, and the roses blooming on the delicately rounded cheeks. The deep eyes had a prophetic, visionary glance, and she looked like some seeress sitting in the sunshine of a complete present happiness, but looking onward to a hugely looming shadow. Though the case

---

[1] Saint Joan of Arc (c. 1412–31), French national heroine and martyr, inspired the French in their ultimately successful effort to expel the English from France during the Hundred Years War.

was worn and stained, the miniature was vividly fresh, the colors brilliant as ever.

For fully an hour, long after darkness had fallen on the room, the old officer sat motionless with the case in his hand, and then hearing some one at the door he pressed it to his lips, and thrust it into his bosom.

In the meantime Mrs. Frazer had been reading a few faintly penned lines that Archie had made almost superhuman efforts to send by Mike. They were not many, but they were all things to her.

"My darling mother:
I am all right again. Will be home in October. Love to all.
ARCHIE."

"Isn't it funny, Olla," said Sidney meditatively, "that he doesn't mention Cecil?"

"No, dear, how could he? see how faintly his name is written, I do wish we had him back at once, mamma!"

"So do I, Olla," returned Mrs. Frazer anxiously, "but all in good time, my darling."

And with the echo of her words we close this chapter.

CHAPTER VIII

Mourning for the Dead

Mrs. Frazer and the three girls looked at the Captain in astonishment almost too deep for words. That he should feel the death of his old friend and benefactor acutely, was to be expected; it was not altogether unreasonable that he should have ever sat up all night alone in the library with the door locked, thinking of and mourning him; but that he should request his wife and daughters to wear mourning for a man they had never seen, and one not even remotely connected with the family, was rather startling. Olla's face grew pensive as she thought of her rose-colored grenadine and dark-eyed Theodore Denville, for whose especial bewitchment it had been purchased; and Sidney, who invariably did exactly as seemed best in her eyes, broke into instant mutiny.

"Now, papa, that's what I call cruel, when you know you had promised Dolly and I new blue velveteens for the winter and grebe caps and muffs, to want us to wear hideous crêpe cloth and dowdy old black astrachans![1] Oh, papa, I'm ashamed of you, sir!"

In her moods of excitement golden-haired Sid was rather apt to be a little wild in her punctuation, and even spiritual looking Dolly, with her Clytie-like head[2] and saintly face, seemed a little disturbed. The Captain, who was merely pretending to breakfast, pushed away his coffee cup and leant back, with a strangely worn look, in his chair.

"Well, well!" he said, "I won't press the point, but consider how warmly my poor friend must have thought of us all to leave your brother his heir."

"Oh, of course, papa," said Sidney, practically; "but then consider that Androsia may appear any day, and I'm sure, poor dear, I hope she will."

"Still, if you wish it, dear, of course I'll go into town and order our mourning at once," said Mrs. Frazer, looking at the Captain almost curiously. His present mood puzzled her. His worn face and hollow eyes spoke of a depth of emotion that she had not expected to have seen called forth by the death of one not tied to him by blood.

The Captain looked at her, and meeting her clear steadfast eyes, turned his face abruptly towards the French window, which was thrown open, though a bright wood fire burned cheerfully on the hearth. One of the early frosts during the night had left a bracing keenness in the golden air, but the warmer breath of the noon was mellowing it again to a pleasant warmth. The vine rustled in the breeze, and from a musk plant on the green wire stand between the long windows of the dining room, a spicy incense floated through the room. Outside on the lawn the maples flaunted their flaming banners of fire and gold in the sun, and the knots of furbelowed dahlias and variegated chrysanthemums burned and glowed like gems from the soft green of the emerald turf.

---

[1] "Grebe caps" were ladies' hats trimmed with the silky down or plumage of the waterfowl of that name, while astrachan (or astrakhan) garments were made of lambskin from Astrakhan, Russia, or of inferior woollen fabric imitating this material.

[2] In Roman mythology, Clytie, a maiden in love with the sun god Helios, was changed to a sunflower. Crawford's description of Dolly refers to a well-known piece of Roman sculpture, "the Clytie bust," part of a collection assembled by the antiquarian Charles Townley (1737–1805) and acquired by the British Museum early in the nineteenth century. The bust is of a young woman with classical features and closely waved hair growing low on the forehead and parted in the middle. See Appendix E, and compare the description of the protagonist in Oliver Wendell Holmes's novel *Elsie Venner*: "... a low forehead, as low as that of Clytie in the Townley bust ..." (vol. 1 [Boston: Ticknor and Fields, 1861] 104).

A few truant leaves fluttered like brilliant-winged birds across the lawn, and across the river sailed a stork, his long legs streaming out behind him like pennants. A peacock strutted in the sun, through the vines shot an arrow of light across the dainty table, with its old silver and brilliant china, and its central bouquet of autumn berries, gorgeous leaves, and rich mosaics of gravely tinted lichens, their cool greys dotted with infinitissimal rubies, paly browns and golds, shading into softest green, and sprays of fern from the dim shades of the woods. Captain Frazer's gaze took note of none of those things, but wandered across the St. Lawrence, and lost itself in the distance, the hazy, dreamy, unutterably lovely distance of a Canadian sky, in the fall of the year.

"Oh, mamma!" ejaculated Sidney, in dismay at her mother's words, and she looked piteously from Dolly to Olla, the latter of whom had remained silent because she wished to gratify her father in his extraordinary freak. Indeed, had he entreated her to appear in a toilet of last year's fashions, she would have braved the sarcasm of her bosom friends and done so unmurmuringly. Dolly didn't speak, because she had nothing to say; the normal condition of the pensive young beauty, whom nature had gifted with the inestimable boon of a deeply spiritual expression and a kind of rapt air, which veiled the simple fact that she possessed but one idea and was capable of but one emotion. The idea was a supreme consciousness of the beauty of her exquisite face, the emotion an intense affection for her own immediate family circle. She waltzed the slow, dreamy German waltzes to a marvel, but no one had known her during the season in which she had been in society to flash through the eddying whirls of a galop, join a snow-shoeing party, or do one thing likely to accelerate the motion of the cool ruby fluid flowing through her beautiful form or disarrange the lovely Greek coiffure that suited her Clytie head so admiringly. When Roderick Armor, the clever, rising, kindly young lawyer, with a good practice and many friends, had asked her in broken tones of strong emotions of hope and fear, to grace his pretty home in Montreal, she had said "yes" very sweetly and coolly, and wondered vaguely why his voice should tremble and his dark eyes burn as he asked her. They were to be married in the coming spring, and already Mrs. Frazer and Olla were busy with dainty embroideries for the pretty trousseau, while Sid assisted the lovely bride elect in the composition of her replies to Roderick Armor's love letters; and if that hardworking young fellow, pondering over those violet-perfumed epistles in his chambers in Montreal, pounced eagerly on some tiny sentence that seemed to echo back something of the murmur of the strong tide of love that rolled through his large, honest heart, it was to Sid's imagination that he was indebted for the boon. Sid said it was "splendid practice," and Dolly was grateful for the aid, and vaguely admired Sid's powers of composition. "It's so nice," she used to say in her tender expressive voice, "for you know, mamma, I really should not know in the least what to say to Mr. Armor." He was "Roderick" to her mother and Olla, and "Roddy" to pert Sid, but to her he was "Mr. Armor," who had given her a very pretty engagement ring, and whom she was to marry in the spring. Her gaze never penetrated into the matrimonial future beyond a hazy vision of her name and his on white enamelled cards, tied together with dainty bows of white satin riband.

"Oh, mamma," said Sid, and at that piteous exclamation Captain Frazer wrenched his gaze from the blue distance and looked at his youngest daughter, who sat facing him, radiant as a young Flora,[1] in a fashionable blue and white morning dress; despite her distress, faint dimples flickering round her rosy mouth and a lurking smile ready to break in her wide, bright eyes. Her young, unclouded beauty seemed to strike him with fresh force, and he said softly, "Yes, it would be a pity to cast a shadow on you, my bright Sid."

"Papa," cried Sid, suddenly repentant, and flying round the table to catch him round the neck with her slender pink-tinted arms. "I'll cut off my hair and wear a widow's cap, if you like. It was only my nonsense; and, after all, when one has a good complexion one needn't mind wearing black, and it need only be complimentary—white dresses trimmed with black until the winter sets in, you know."

Despite his evident melancholy, Captain Frazer laughed heartily.

"It was rather a grotesque piece of folly on my part to expect you to fall very readily in with the idea, you monkey," he said, pulling her long bright hair; "and for a man you had never seen. There, make your mind easy, you shan't be called upon to mourn even complimentarily for him."

"I'm sure, papa," said Olla, "if you wish it we—"

"I don't wish it, dear; I see the incongruity of the thing plainly," said Captain Frazer, a little sadly. "There, Sid, be off and tell Mike I'll require to see him by-and-bye."

---

[1] In Roman mythology, Flora is the goddess of flowers and the spring.

"Sidney," said Dolly plaintively, "don't forget, dear, that you promised to think of something for me to write about to Mr. Armor to-day."

"Why you have all about poor Archie and Miss Howard to tell him, and then," continued Sid, meditatively, "you'd better say something about wishing so much to see him, and that you look at his photograph very often."

"But you know I don't, Sidney," said Dolly, raising her heavenly eyes from the ham on her plate; "I think I lost it last week."

"But," retorted Sidney, frowning, "you know you ought to have looked at it. All engaged people, in stories, always do. Why, there's Olla, she isn't quite engaged to Mr. Denville, and the album opens directly of its own accord at the place where his vignette is."

"I don't think Mr. Armor is quite as nice looking as Mr. Denville," said Dolly, vaguely. "Dear me, Olla, what a pretty color you have this morning; when shall you be ready to help me, Sid?"

"When I have given papa's message to Mike and got him to help me to tie up the dahlias. But, Dolly, you might have the letter dated, and write my darling Roderick, and that will take you until I'm ready."

Sidney tripped off, and Mrs. Frazer set the example of rising from the table. Dolly rose, tall, slight, elegant, a poetic grace about her graceful head, a nameless exaltation shining like a light on her broad, low brow, from which the golden hair rippled back in large soft waves, and, caught in a silky mass behind, fell in great loose curls on her lovely shoulders. Her blue eyes shone tenderly under their heavy lashes of bronze; the petal of the maiden blush rose was not more softly pink than her lovely cheek. Her pensively smiling lips of richest coral shewed teeth like pearls, she might have just descended in a cloud of misty pink and gold, from some far off starry world, for all there seemed of this gross earth about her. Her white draperies fell round her like a silvery mist clinging to a tall lily in a moonlit garden. Her one idea moved her to turn first to the mirror over the fire-place, her one emotion sent her to drop a gentle kiss on the Captain's bald forehead, before she moved like a silent vision of some dying martyr's ecstacy into the library to write to "Darling Roderick." Olla was graceful, pretty, charming; Sidney undeniably beautiful; but Dolly moved serene in a loveliness all her own.

There was nothing more said about mourning, but on Sunday the Captain appeared with a deep band of crêpe round his white hat, whereat Sidney remarked jealously to Olla and Dolly—

"Papa couldn't do more if it were for one of us, Archie for instance; and do you know, girls, he seems not to have recovered the old creature's death yet; I can hardly wring a laugh from him, and if it were not for Mike Murphy, I'd get a fit of low spirits."

Dolly was gracefully silent, and Olla could not but acknowledge that the house was unusually gloomy just now. Mrs. Frazer seemed to share in some degree her husband's melancholy, and the girl began to dislike the idea of leaving home until the cloud had passed. Her aunt wrote to her urging her to come to her pleasant home in Toronto, and though her own heart passionately seconded the entreaty, she deferred her departure day after day until a fortnight had elapsed from the date which she had fixed for her visit. The weather became damp and lowering, the leaves fell in cascades on the lawn, and the crimson vine dropped away from the lattice work of the verandas. The river wound past like a stream of lead, and the nightly frosts seared the turf and deadened its soft green. In all probability there would be the usual burst of glorious October weather, and perhaps an Indian summer stretching its mysterious and beautiful arms into the heart of November, to wrest a treasure of days of weird beauty from the iron winter, to string them like beads of red gold on the chaplet of the dead summer; but now all was grey and mournful. The wind sobbed amongst the swaying pines, the rain dashed in blinding slants against the windows, and every object and individual about the Captain's household, except Dolly, succumbed to the grey influence. Dolly sat by the crimson fire, like a holy presence, working with slender fingers a pair of gorgeous slippers, commenced at Sid's suggestion, as a token of the warmth of her sentiments towards Mr. Armor, sorting her bright wools and thinking of nothing, with an air of devout reverie. She was equally content that the sun should shine or the rain should pour. She troubled not her soul with thoughts. She was a beautiful picture, but it was not to her Olla could turn for exhilaration. Mike had persisted in setting out again for the spot where Archie still remained, "intending," he said, "to bag a trifle of Injuns or find out Miss Drosia." Sid lamented his departure pathetically. She and Mr. Murphy had formed a decided friendship for each other. He had talked of Androsia and Winona to her until it seemed as though she must have known the ill-fated girls all her life. He had taught her to paddle on the river, and use a rifle, and she had alarmed and scandalized Mrs. Frazer by firing in the early dawn from her bed-room window at the croquet balls on the lawn. The refined and stately old lady was secretly rejoiced at his departure, for she had some indefinite idea that Miss Sid would become perfectly untameable should he remain much longer.

Olla had her own secret cause of disquietude, and October loomed gloomily enough on the house. The brightening of the sombre tints was the anticipated return of Archie.

Captain Frazer directed Mike to collect all Farmer's effects and send them down by Archie, "in case," he said, "we ascertain anything about his friends."

"He didn't lave many defects behind him," said Mike, scratching his head; "bedad it's my belafe that he took them wid him, Captain."

"Surely that was strange," said the Captain, in some surprise.

"Now Captain, dear," returned Mike in a tone of expostulation. "How would he be afther laving them afther him, I'd like to know?"

"And why not, may I ask?"

"Is it lave his defects behind, yer honer?"

"His effects, Mike, his property," said the Captain, smiling, "not his failings, poor fellow."

"I comprihend, sur. I'll do it for sure and good luck to you, Captain, an' yer lady, sur, and the young ladies and Miss Sid, the blessin's of the Just be about her purty head for a swate, spirited girleen that she is."

Mr. Murphy drank the glass of wine the Captain had poured out for him as a kind of stirrup cup, and pulling the coon-skin cap over his eyes, shook the old soldier's hand in a mighty grasp and took his way back to the woody haunts from which he had emerged.

"Mamma what are you doing?" said Olla softly, that evening, coming behind her mother's chair and laying her slender, brown hands on the shoulders of the latter who was leaning over a small table in the library, drawn near the window so as to catch the light.

"Your papa wishes to erect a monument to the memory of Colonel Howard and Mr. Farmer," replied Mrs. Frazer, bending more closely over her work, "and I offered to make a suitable design. Do you like it, my dear?"

"Yes, mamma, it's lovely," said Olla, thoughtfully looking at it over her mother's shoulder. "What an interest papa appears to take in everything connected with Colonel Howard! Is the face of the angel holding the scroll a fancy face?[1] It is very pretty."

---

[1] That is, an imaginary face.

"Yes, very pretty," said Mrs. Frazer, in a low voice.

Olla stretched out her hand to take an illustrated paper that lay on the table. She had come to the room for it, but Mrs. Frazer detained her hand. "Never mind now, dear," she said. "I want you to go and order tea. This will keep me busy until dark."

Olla bent and kissed her mother, and singing softly to herself, went away.

As soon as the door was closed behind her, Mrs. Frazer lifted up the paper and took from under it the miniature case that had been found amidst Farmer's effects. She compared the face in the drawing with the painting, critically. "I have copied it faithfully," she murmured, "but I must keep the original concealed. Richard would hardly like the girls to know the truth just yet."

She placed the miniature in a secret drawer of her own writing table, and quietly resumed her drawing.

Before the first snow fell, there rose in a little grove of pines on one side of the lawn, a graceful monumental stone of purest marble, representing an angel holding a scroll, bearing the records of the deaths of Colonel Howard and Andrew Farmer, and the face of the angel shining in the dim shadows of the kingly trees, was that of the miniature which had so strangely affected Captain Frazer.

[PART 4—1 FEBRUARY 1873]

CHAPTER IX

Mr. Murphy's Experience

Mr. Murphy presented himself at the Tavern on the eve of the day on which Archie had decided on venturing to commence his homeward journey. He found Captain Frazer recovering rapidly from his dangerous wound, carefully nursed by pretty Sally and her mother. Bill Montgomery and Lumber Pete had started for the country lying yet further back on a fall hunt, and "Madame" hung in her green baize cover on a peg beside the dresser, dumb in the absence of her owner. It was understood that while the chasing of the antlered deer was the ostensible object of the expedition of the two trappers, they were to keep a sharp watch for any traces of the lost girl and her captors. Archie had promised them a most munificent reward in case of success, a reward that opened to the mental vision of Bill the fair prospect of a mighty clearing and a roomy farm-house, close by his future father-in-law's, where he could combine the profits of agriculture with those of trapping, and see rosy Sally the proud mistress of flocks and herds and smiling cornfields, and he set his brown determined face towards the dark, mysterious forest, resolved to wring the secret of the girl's hiding place from it, if it lay in the power of man to do so. Nor was Lumber Pete less earnest in his airy way. He too had his *Château en Espagne*,[1] rising from the glittering foundation of the promised reward. A "shanty" of his own back in the mighty treasure-houses of the untrodden forests, from which at dawn his own axemen would issue with their teams of mighty oxen, and send unusual thunder bellowing through the vast arcades, as the great sovereigns of the shady places toppled and crashed to the earth under the blows of their heavy axes; his own "logs," to float in great armies on tiny creeks, whirl on broader rivers, and at length out on the vast lake, to float as mighty rafts down the broad highway of waters, past farms, villages, growing towns and fair cities, to the great timber yards of

---

[1]   Castle in Spain; that is, a cherished hope, or daydream.

some Montreal or Quebec lumber merchant, and thence, the precious freight of navies, east, west, north, south, from shore to shore of the Old World and the New.

Certainly, if skill, patience and utter fearlessness could compass her deliverance, Hawk-eye, the half-breed, would not long retain her in his possession.

Mike's face fell when he heard that the trappers had departed without waiting for him, but on reflection he candidly endorsed the frankly avowed opinion of Joe Harty, pretty Sally's father, that he "didn't just think he was much of a loss to them," as he knew little or nothing of woodcraft, and would inevitably have marred their plans with his misdirected zeal.

Archie endeavoured to persuade him to return with him to the settlements, but to this Mike would by no means agree.

"Is it have the ould masther 'walkin', ye'd be, Captain?" he inquired, with melancholy sarcasm. "An' it's meself knows he'd think as little of comin' out of his comfortable coffin to look to things himself than I'd think ov a pinch ov snuff, if he dreamt it wor in me to lave the ould place an' its rightful misthress wantin', the heavens be good to her, the maid ov me heart."

So Archie forbore to press the matter for the present.

Joe Harty had agreed to paddle him down Lake Huron as far as the little village of Saugeen, lying behind Chantry Island;[1] and as the lake now often showed a heavy sea tumbling against the crags, under the lashing of the fall winds, it behoved them to start without unnecessary delay, as they expected to be nearly a fortnight on the way. At Saugeen a lake steamer touched occasionally, and schooners resorted there daily during the season, so the rest of his route would present but little difficulty.

Archie gave Mike clear directions as to the steps he was to take in case of the restoration of Androsia. He was to leave immediately with her for his father's residence and not lose sight of her until she was safe under the care of the old officer and his family.

"Do you understand me thoroughly, Mike?" he inquired, after a pretty exhaustive conversation on the subject.

---

[1] Now the town of Southampton, Ontario, the community of Saugeen was founded in the 1850s on the eastern shore of Lake Huron at the mouth of the Saugeen River, about twenty-six miles (forty-three kilometers) downstream from the village of Paisley where Crawford's family lived from 1857 to 1862. Chantry Island is just offshore.

"Indade an' I do, Captin," replied Mr. Murphy, who was certainly anything but deficient in intelligence; "bud I'm misdoubtin' somehow that we ever clap eyes on the girleen again. It's a warnin' I've had, shure enough."

"A what?" said Archie, looking at him in astonishment. "What do you mean?"

A noble fire was leaping up the cavernous chimney, throwing a Rembrandt[1] warmth and richness of coloring over the homely kitchen, lighted alone by its generous crimson. Joe Harty, by its glow, was cleaning his trusty rifle, and the toils of the day over, Sally was burning her round cheeks to deep damask, as she leant her fair curly head close to the flame, in order that she might lift a dropped stitch in the huge indigo blue stocking of homespun yarn that her nimble brown fingers were knitting for the stout legs of the stalwart Joe. She looked up with rounded eyes at Mike's last words, and her comely mother turned from the table at which she was "setting a sponge," and eyed Mike in astonishment, her plump arms up to the elbows in the white dough.

Mike glanced round on his companions and shook his red head dismally, with a lengthening of his comic visage that was somewhat startling. He had been in very fair spirits since his arrival at noon, but as night drew on, with a howling wind and driving battalions of inky clouds, a very unusual depression had crept over him which at last found audible expression in the words we have related. Joe Harty, a silent and phlegmatic fellow, with a round, honest face, slowly laid down his rifle and stared at Mike, who stared into the fire.

The wind howled and yelled across the Lake, and through the uncurtained window there came a spectral glimpse of Alps of water thundering, in the ghastly light of an uncertain moon, against the crags and belts of golden beach. The unutterable sadness of the undertone of the swaying tracts of forests mingled with the wild bellowing of the tempest, like the breathings of a mighty Æolian harp;[2] and, snugly sheltered as was the farm-house, by its maples and oaks, a constant swirl of surf dashed against the windows, torn in flying masses of snowy foam from the advancing breakers. The wind tore down the chimney and hurried away again with

---

[1] Suggesting the characteristic effect of light and shadow, as well as the "warmth and richness of coloring," in paintings by the renowned Dutch artist Rembrandt Harmens van Rijn (1606–69).

[2] A harp designed to produce musical sounds under the influence of the wind.

an army of flying rubies and carbuncles in its train, torn from the swaying mass of richly-hued flames writhing serpent-like round the huge back-log. The dark rafters of oak intersecting the low, white-washed ceiling glowed ruddily, and the tins and delf on the dresser of white pine twinkled comfortably in the cheerful light. The faint low of an animal disturbed in the comfortable shed by the raging storm, mingled with its thunders and relieved, by its every day sound, the oppressive sense of the vast solitudes of wave and wood over which the tempest rushed. Tomorrow there would be prostrate trees, with up-torn roots like vast claws marking its path, and perhaps the battered hull of more than one tight little schooner drifting across the sullen waste of grey waters, or speared on some needle-like crag guarding the lonely coast.

A squirrel, black as jet, with eyes like stars, round and luminous, sat like a familiar spirit on Joe Harty's broad shoulder, daintily cracking hazel nuts under the embowering shadow of his plumy tail, and eyeing the fire sideways with a meditative air, and directly at the guide's feet lay a white deerhound dreaming, with his nose on his paws. The Great Manitou[1] might be walking through the outside night, shod with thunder, and followed by the shouting of the winds and waves, but inside the very spirit of domestic peace and untroubled calm brooded by the hospitable hearth of the Canadian guide.

A wooden clock with a great, white face, hung against the snowy wall, and its large black hands pointed to the hour of eight.

Mike looked into the fire and shook his head with a slight groan before he answered Archie's interrogation, and the wondering looks of Joe Harty and his family. The casements rattled in the wind, and it seemed as if spirit hands were touching the wooden latch of the heavy door.

Mike drew his chair a shade closer to the fire, and rubbed up his red hair until it stood out round his head like a flaming furze bush,—an operation that he invariably seemed to consider necessary to any considerable degree of mental brilliancy.

"Now, it's not after belaving me ye'll be, I'm afeard," he said, appealingly; "but it's Gospel truth I'm goin' to tell ye, ivery word ov it. —The Heavens be our safety this night!"

---

[1] The "Great Spirit" of North American native peoples, who figures prominently as "Gitche Manito, the mighty, / ... Master of Life" (I.3–4) in Longfellow's *The Song of Hiawatha* (1855).

This exclamation was wrung from Mr. Murphy by a sudden clap of thunder bursting directly over the house with the sharp, metallic crash it frequently assumes in the neighborhood of cliffs and crags. It was followed by the thundering of rain upon the roof, beating like a deluge of molten lead upon the shingles, and coming in vast sheets against the windows. The din was deafening, and nearly five minutes elapsed before Mike could make his voice audible above the roar and brawling of the storm. The wind seemed, like that which smote the four corners of the house where the sons of Job were feasting, to gather from all points of the compass and culminate in a mad vortex round the farm-house;[1] but the stout timbers stood it well, and the gust died howling away in the distance.

"That beats!" said Joe Harty, slowly. "Listen to it howling off in the woods like a pack of hungry wolves scared from a deer."

"Magnificent!" said Captain Frazer, his dark face lighting up. "I never heard anything to touch the roar of that sudden burst. The storm seemed to leap on us like a wild beast on its prey."

Mrs. Harty and Sally were well accustomed to the commotion of the elements round their lonely habitation; but the healthy bloom had faded a little in their comely faces at the unusual fury of the hurricane. Mike sat leaning his chin on his hands and his elbows on his knees, listening intently to the lingering wail of the dying wind. As it fell, he sprang to his feet with such energy that the squirrel made a sudden leap from Joe's shoulder, and rushing up the rough wall, clung to one of the rafters, whence it eyed Mr. Murphy with terrified suspicion, its black eyes sparkling like diamonds from its shadowy elevation.

"Bedad!" ejaculated Mike, "afther that yowl it's time for me to be spakin. Shure now I know what the warnin' was for. Joe, ye mind Dead Man's Bay, now?"

"Sartinly, Mike," said Joe, kicking the back-log until it deluged the room with light, and gazing earnestly into the excited countenance of Mr. Murphy, who was, indeed, devoured by the eyes of all present, Archie included.

"Well, now, it's there I camped last night, more betoken clear agin me will; bud the night was down on me, like a hawk on a chicken, and I ran

---

[1] See Job 1.19: "and, behold, there came a great wind from the wilderness, and smote the four corners of the house, and it fell upon the young men, and they are dead; and I only am escaped alone to tell thee."

138   ISABELLA VALANCY CRAWFORD

the canoe into the bay, thinkin' that the night wor perhaps a thrifle stormy for ghosts. The wather in the mite of a bay wor as heavy as lead and as black as ink; the red lightning curlin' an' twistin' over it like fiery sarpints, and the wind came groanin' and sighin' like a Banshee[1] from the lake beyant, through them high rocks that makes the gateway loike into the bay. Outside, the white caps was commencin' to pop up an' down in the moon-light, loike the 'good people' from a fairy rath,[2] but it wor like oil inside the rocks. The moon had a weeny bit ov sky to herself, all blue and clear, bud every inch ov the rest was full ov black clouds wid bright edges, all tumblin' an drivin' over an' thro' aich other, like a faction fight at a fair, an' the lightning twistin' in an' out in sheets an' tongues an' great chains, that looked as if some one was forging thim white hot above, an' throwin' them slap into the lake. There wor no thunder, bud a shakin' in the air that showed it wor trampin' up in the distance; an' the dhry leaves on the trees rustled as if skeletons wor shakin' them. The Saints be good to us! Captin, what's the matther wid you?"

"I beg your pardon, Mike," said Archie, re-seating himself in the chair from which he had suddenly risen; "but I really fancied I saw a face pressed against the window. It must have been the merest juggling of fancy."

"Thar ain't no creetur about this night," said Joe. "I guess, Cap'n, it wor Sally's shadder. Cut along, Mike, old man."

Mike's teeth chattered, but he turned his back carefully on the window, and resumed his narrative.

"Well, Joe, you know there ain't much of a campin' ground at Dead Man's Bay, by raison ov the trees that grow sheer into the wather, an' it wor a while afore I settled down for the night on a bit ov baich no bigger than the table beyant. I propt the canoe up on one side and wrapt meself in me Mackinaw, and was aslape afore ye'd say Jack Robinson, for I'd paddled me forty mile since dawn. It worn't much thought I took ov them three trappers as had been murthered there years ago for the sake ov their piles ov peltries, an' I slaped on quite heavy until the middle of the night, when I waked up on the suddint, as wide awake as the squirrel there, the dawshy[3] thafe! and as quiet as a corp. Now, in

---

[1] In Irish folklore, a female spirit whose unearthly scream portends a death in the family of anyone who hears it.

[2] Irish fairies, often referred to as "the good people," were supposed to inhabit abandoned raths, ancient hilltop forts found throughout Ireland.

[3] Silly (Irish).

gin'ral, it's no thrifle ov time it takes me to git me head straight in the mornin's, but there I wor as bright as a new pin, an' me starin' out from undher the canoe in the darkness. Saints alive! I felt the marrow melt in the bones of me. Agin the yallow blackness of the sky I could see a figure standin' within hand's grasp ov me, bud whether man or woman, it warn't in me power to say. 'Shpecthers, Mike,' says I to myself, for I could see another a little ways off, 'make yer sowl, me boy,' an' I fell to pattherin' an Ave as loud as I could. Well, at this same moment there came a flash of white lightning, an' by it I saw"—Mike paused, and with a face blanched by the remembrance, looked round the excited little group of his listeners.

Archie laughed as Mike's eye caught his, for he felt certain that Mike was relating the experiences of a nightmare.

"The skeleton forms of one of the trappers and his murderer, I suppose," he said, stooping over the flame to light his cigar.

"The face of Winona," uttered Mike, in a tone of such deep awe that Archie gazed at him in astonishment, "the eyes ov her lookin' into mine, an' her long, black hair drippin' wet all round her, just as you an' me seed her last, an' behind her—Sally! what's come to the child? Spake, asthore. Mrs. Harty, ma'am, spake till her, for it's dazed she is!"

Sally had risen from the low settle in the chimney corner on which she had been seated, and was gazing past Mike with such blank horror in her dilated eyes, such stony terror in her fixed face, that her fresh young beauty had given way to the wanness and lines of old age. At the same moment a sudden hurricane filled the room, the fire leaped up in lurid splendor, the rain and surf dashed coldly on the faces of the startled group, as the heavy door dashed back against the wall.

"Look!" came from Sally's blue lips, and in the act of raising her arm she fell straight along the hearth.

Joe's love was for his daughter, and before he turned his pale face to look, she was in his arms, with her white face lying like a lily on his broad breast. He turned, and for the first time in his life his heart melted like water. Mike, Archie and Mrs. Harty stood motionless, as though carved in stone, facing the open door; and on the threshold, her length of black hair torn by the wind, her bronze face and starry eyes lighted by the red billows of light from the fire, stood the lofty form of the Indian girl, Winona, and behind her a shadow that crouched from the glow that swept out into the murky night.

Mike Murphy dropped on his knees, his hair rustling as it rose on his head; and Mrs. Harty threw her blue apron over her face to shut out the spectral form.

Archie recovered his mental poise at once and sprang forward, determined to solve the mystery at any risk.

At the same moment Winona glided into the apartment.

CHAPTER X

Mr. Macer

"So extremely unkind of dear Olla," murmured Cecil Bertrand with infinite pathos, folding up a closely-written sheet of pink paper with a dainty monogram, all pale purple and gold at the top, and raising her speaking eyes to the watchful face of Mr. Denville, who strode at her side, looking down at her curiously.

They had come from the Post-office and were strolling up King Street at the fashionable hour, about half-past four in the afternoon. She had met him down town, and he had joined her, a proceeding to which she was by no means averse.

Miss Cecil was in her glory. There was a soft, bracing breeze blowing, just sufficient to deepen the delicate tints in her cheeks, and stir to a more bewitching "fluffiness" the fantastic but perfectly enchanting "waves, frizzes and curls" of sunny hair that was the envy of every woman she met. There was the pink shade in the afternoon sunlight Parisian milliners recommend to all complexions in their artistic toilettes. Her fall suit had three more frills and a more gracefully draped "panier"[1] than that of any to be seen the whole bright length of King Street, and her light blue velvet "toque," set jauntily somewhere on the top of the puffs and King Charles curls, she felt was the greatest success of the season; the pheasant's wing in the left side, she was proudly certain, being fully three inches taller than any she had seen during her promenade. She was a lovely little creature of the pure Canadian type, a dainty, glowing blonde, fragile and spiritual looking, but rounded and

---

[1] A frame made of whalebone or wire designed to puff out the skirt of a woman's dress at the hips.

moulded to a perfect symmetry. The blonde hair was bronze but where the light touched it; the eyes deeply blue, with the archest lights flickering in them, or wells of deepest tenderness, as occasion required. There were the merest shadows of dimples playing round her mouth, and on the upper lip, to the left, was a jet black mole about the size of the head of a pin, and which Cecil regarded as a treasure beyond all price, for if anything could have heightened the lucid pearl and rose of her matchless skin, that mole was decidedly the thing. She was one of those daintily "fast" girls of the period[1] who can venture upon doing almost anything, confident of tripping out of even a shadow of reproach with the most bewitching air of innocence, and supremely blest in never sinning against the "proprieties" ungracefully. The men raved about her, flung as many bouquets under her kid "bottines"[2] as though she were Patti[3] or Nilsson,[4] lost incalculable amounts of Jouvin's gloves to her in insane bets,[5] and filled her music-rack with new music, with which she

---

[1] Crawford conflates two phrases familiar in contemporary debates about women. See Eliza Lynn Linton, "The Girl of the Period" *Saturday Review*, 14 March 1868: 339–40, and "Fast Young Ladies" [rpt. from the *Liberal Review*] *Canadian Illustrated News*, 28 September 1872: 195, both included in Appendix A.

[2] Ankle-boots.

[3] Adelina Patti (1843–1919) was an Italian coloratura soprano and the preeminent opera diva of the nineteenth century; early in her career, in 1853 and 1860, she appeared at the St. Lawrence Hall in Toronto.

[4] Christine Nilsson (1843–1921) was a Swedish coloratura soprano; she gave a "Farewell Concert" at the Music Hall in Toronto on 31 May 1871.

[5] In 1834, Xavier Jouvin (1801–44), of Grenoble, France, invented a cutting die for the manufacture of precisely fitted gloves. Crawford refers to gloves simply as "Jouvins" several times in her stories, and in "The Perfect Number Seven" (*Frank Leslie's Chimney Corner*, 6 November 1880: 403–407) she again portrays an eligible young woman who makes wagers for gloves. According to an unsigned article reprinted from the *Liberal Review* in the *Canadian Illustrated News* for 28 September 1872 (see Appendix A), one of the attributes of "Fast Young Ladies" is that they "understand betting, and, unlike most gamblers, win a good deal more than they lose. Fortunately, however, their wagers are confined to such trifles as gloves and feminine articles generally" (195). For a near precedent in fiction, see William Makepeace Thackeray, *The History of Pendennis* (1850), in which "sportive bets" are proposed to the novel's leading coquette Blanche Amory by "a number of dandies, and men of a certain fashion" when she attends the Derby (London: Oxford UP, 1908, 752); as Michael Flavin notes, Blanche is interested in betting purely as "a form of flirtation" (*Gambling in the Nineteenth-Century English Novel: 'A Leprosy is o'er the Land'* [Brighton: Sussex Academic Press, 2003], 119). See also Thackeray's novel *Vanity Fair* (1848), in which we are told that two of Becky Sharp's admirers "purchased her gloves and flowers, went in debt for opera-boxes for her, and made themselves amiable in a thousand ways" (New York: Modern Library, 1950, 520). There are numerous echoes of Thackeray in Crawford's satirical treatment of the young officers who vie for Cecil Bertrand's favours.

charmed their rivals in her melting little voice, that was just loud enough to be confidentially audible to some happy wight turning the pages for her in a shadowy corner of the drawing-room.

She was one of the fortunate few who retained alike the favor of the military and civilian *partis*, and dispensed her smiles with great exactness between the red coats and the black coats. If Lieutenant Prancer had the privilege of "sitting out" a quadrille with her in some shady retreat in a conservatory or heavily-draped bow window, young Briefless was pretty certain to whirl her off in the next galop after supper, so she kept the balance pretty well poised. She made it a point to be "engaged" to a new man every six months or so, and Archie Frazer was her ninth victim. Him she had made up her mind to marry if "she could not do better," and as Mr. Denville was "better" financially, she was spreading a net as fine as those invisible cobwebs most fatal to flydom for his capture.

"What, may I ask, is your friend guilty of to call such a complaint from you?" said Mr. Denville.

He was a good fellow, and if any one had called him a "flirt" he would have been in a very honest rage; but he had melting black eyes, a deep baritone voice, and a dangerous habit of accenting personal pronouns and quoting Tennyson. He was deeply in love with Olla Frazer, but as he glanced down into Cecil's face, one would have thought his happiness was dependent on her smiles alone.

Cecil flashed a tiny smile and gracious bow to a group of young officers on the opposite side of the street, and then sighed slightly.

"It's so provoking," she said. "I quite reckoned on taking Olla with us to-night to the Calico Ball.[1] Every one is to be there, and though she had promised to be in Toronto to-day, here she writes me not to expect her for an indefinite period. Too bad, isn't it?"

"I suppose so," returned Mr. Denville, with an air of supreme indifference that delighted Cecil, who was far from guessing what the effort

---

[1] Sometimes held as charitable fund-raisers, Calico Balls were fashionable events in the social calendars of towns and cities in Canada and the United States during the second half of the nineteenth century. Because ladies who attended were obliged to dress in cotton gowns rather than fine silk, these events had an ostensibly egalitarian air as well as a benevolent purpose. However, a report in *The Irish Canadian* of 29 December 1869 of a Calico Ball held in Toronto to benefit the Protestant Orphans' Home offers a distinctly critical view of the affair, satirizing the local elite who used the occasion to don "the trappings of the commoner" by dressing in "plain gingham and bandanas" and "unbleached homespun."

of self-control cost him. "You will show to-night, of course, Miss Bertrand. Do give me the first galop, please."

"Oh, of course, mamma, Lina and I are going; but as to the first galop, I'm so sorry, but—."

"Exactly! engaged, of course; well, tell me at what hour of the evening I may approach your throne."

"You may have the first slow waltz after supper; my card is full up to that."

"Thanks. I shan't require to 'make a note of it,' like the famous Captain Cuttle,[1] I assure you, Miss Bertrand."

Cecil smiled sweetly. The compliment she understood, but whether Captain Cuttle was a nautical contemporary of Confucius,[2] or an officer in the new regiment ordered to Toronto, she was in total ignorance, as her literary researches extended not beyond the monthly fashions and the Sunday lessons in church. When conversation came dangerously near the sunken reefs and shifting sands of literature, it was droll to observe how skilfully she "tacked" until she caught a favoring gale in her rosy sails, and danced lightly away on the foam of flirtation from the uncanny neighborhood, fit only, in her estimation, for strong-minded sirens of an uncertain age, in spectacles and some one else's chignons, certainly not for a creature who looked as though she had just stepped daintily out of one of Watteau's artificial Arcadias,[3] or floated on butterfly wings from some fairy-land where the forests were of myrtle and roses, and the chief end of woman was to dance and do "shopping" after some Celestial fashion, or "catch" the most eligible Fairy Prince of the season.

"Olla says," she said, dashing into conversation, lest Denville, who was rather literary, should talk "books," "that she does not like to leave home until her brother's return from—what's the name of the place— Man—something or other."

"Manitoba," suggested Denville.

---

[1]   Edward Cuttle, a retired mariner in Charles Dickens's novel *Dombey and Son*, habitually embellishes his speech with quotations and enjoins listeners to "overhaul the book it's in, and thereof make a note" (1848; Toronto: Penguin, 1985, 549).

[2]   Confucius was a Chinese teacher and philosopher of the 5th and 6th centuries BCE. His wisdom, coined in the form of sayings and later published as his "Analects," has held great fascination for centuries. "Confucius says" is the phrasing by which his various sayings are initiated.

[3]   Jean Antoine Watteau (1684–1721) was a popular French painter and admirer of Rubens. He gained considerable fame for his highly decorative Arcadian or pastoral scenes based on classical mythology.

"It's islands," said Miss Bertrand; "but the name doesn't sound quite right."

"Manitoulin, up beyond the Georgian Bay."

"Oh, that's it, thank you. Do you know Captain Frazer had a most romantic adventure up there! Got shot by an Indian with an arrow. It was so nice it wasn't a gun, because, of course, it couldn't be so dangerous, and it's so much more common, and there was something about a young woman in it."

"Oh!" said Mr. Denville thoughtfully, with a sudden lightening of his face, "that is Olla's reason for postponing her visit, is it?"

He called her Olla in a tone that was unmistakable to Miss Bertrand's practised ears, and she hastened to add:

"I think dear Olla has some other reason for not caring to come to Toronto just now. Do you know young Armor of Montreal?"

"Slightly. What of him, pray?"

Cecil laughed and blushed prettily, toyed with the tassel of her glove, and turned away her face ever so little from her companion, who was watching her with darkening brow, and eyes full of the shadow of her coming words.

"I am to be bride's-maid in the spring," she said, laughing merrily, "and I do so enjoy the idea. Do you know I never was one before, and a wedding is such jolly fun; don't you think so?"

"No," said Mr. Denville, with a countenance worthy of Othello.[1] "I must say *au revoir*. I have some business up town."

"Don't forget to-night," said Cecil, giving him her soft little hand, and smiling up in his face dangerously.

Denville strutted away with his nose in the air and his heart like an old red sandstone under his unexceptional waistcoat. He loathed the smiling, rustling, bowing crowd he wended his way through, and, like Mr. Longfellow's very uncomfortable friend in the light toilet of bones,—

"Hateful to him were men,
The sunlight hateful!"[2]

---

[1] That is, dark with anger and jealousy, in reference to the protagonist of Shakespeare's tragedy *Othello*.

[2] See Longfellow, "The Skeleton in Armor" (1841) 147–48: "'Hateful to me were men, / The sunlight hateful!'" The protagonist of this poem is a skeleton—hence his "toilet" or costume of bones—who appears, clad in "rude armor," to tell his tale of love and death.

Ha! he had been trifled with, his heart had been ripped up by a faithless coquette whose shy smiles had meant nothing! He had—but was there no remedy? Hope, the dulcet charmer! sought to murmur in his ear, but Reason gave such loud denial that Hope, fragile child of mist and sun, faded and died. He glared straight ahead, and thought grimly of "La Trappe," of Peter the Hermit, of St. Senamis, of Robinson Crusoe,[1] of some land where women, and consequently falsehood, were unknown, of suicide as fashionable amongst the Japanese, and then he pulled up the flying steeds of wrath and despair that were running away with him, and became majestic and philosophic, and politely cynical for a little. He smiled loftily at his burst of rage and pain, and asked himself, "Was there a woman worth a second thought on the face of the earth?" and he answered, "Not one" with infinite readiness; and then he was in the middle of the whirlpool of disappointment and lacerated affection again, tossed to and fro as madly as ever, and feeling curiously stunned and bruised and light-headed. In this mood he turned into a billiard saloon off Yonge Street, much frequented by the upper tendom of Toronto,[2] and found a number of men there he knew, with three or four officers, young fellows possessed of fine animal spirits and illimitable ideas on the subject of "chaff."

"Hilloa! Denville, so you're entered for the Bertrand," shouted Lieutenant Prancer, as Denville walked up to the table. "I say, old fellow, is it your cue to cut Frazer out in that quarter? Confound that ball! say I."

The Lieutenant missed his stroke, and swore gently for a minute or two.

"You'd better leave that game alone," said another. "Archie Frazer is a Tartar, I tell you, once he's roused."

"What are you talking such nonsense for?" said Denville angrily. "Miss Bertrand is a mere acquaintance. Be good enough to leave her name out of our discussions."

---

[1] All four names are associated with isolation from the world, and the first three with vows of chastity and the rejection of women: La Trappe is the abbey of the Trappist monks located northwest of Paris; Peter the Hermit (c.1050–1115) founded an Augustinian monastery near Lièges; the Irish missionary St. Senan or Senames (c. 488–544) founded a monastery on Scattery Island in the river Shannon where women were forbidden to set foot (see Thomas Moore's poem "St. Senanus and the Lady" [1835]); Crusoe, the hero of Daniel Defoe's novel *Robinson Crusoe* (1719), is marooned on a remote island for twenty-eight years.

[2] That is, upper ten, or elite.

"As if we didn't meet you as spooney as Romeo and Juliet,"[1] cried Ensign Spooner, "not twenty minutes ago! But it's *fin contre fin*[2] there, let me tell you, my boy, if flirting's your ticket."

Ensign Spooner, in complexion and physique, bore a startling resemblance to the copies of humanity in gingerbread sold by elderly ladies under the peaceful shade of calico umbrellas at fairs and street corners, and chastely decorated with gilding. An immense eye-glass went about with him, with which he was ever engaged in a spirited but fruitless struggle to make it stick in his eye with the proper air (his eye was like the current optics gracing the before-mentioned works of culinary art), and the glass invariably remained master of the field.

Denville cast a withering look at the Ensign. He turned to Prancer. "Come," he said, "will you play?"

"Thanks, no more just now," said Prancer; and then, lowering his voice a little, "regularly cleaned out by that fellow with his chin in a black muff. You should see him play."

"Who is he?" said Denville, turning and looking at the man indicated by a slight nod of Prancer's head.

"Don't know, I'm sure," returned the Lieutenant, yawning dismally. "Going to the Calico affair to-night?"

"Yes, and after that all you fellows come back with me to the Rossin,[3] and we'll have a champagne supper in my rooms."

"Thanks." The Lieutenant drew out his watch. " I must be off to old Bluebell's to order a bouquet for La Bertrand for to-night. She lives such a deuce of a way out of town that I'll just have time to canter out there and back before dinner. *Adio, mio amico*," and with a wave of his hand Lieutenant Prancer took leave of the company, and was quickly

---

[1]   These are the famous "star-cross'd lovers," protagonists of Shakespeare's tragedy *Romeo and Juliet*.

[2]   Spooner alludes to a French saying, *fin contre fin n'est bon à faire doublure*, that is, "two materials of the same sort don't go well together," or perhaps more proverbially (in English), "two of a trade never agree."

[3]   The Rossin House was one of Toronto's leading hotels in the 1850s and a gathering place for both military personnel and visitors to the city. After a fire levelled the hotel in 1864, it was rebuilt on the corner of York and King Streets, complete with merchants' room, bar, billiard room, a spacious and well-lit dining room, a state-of-the-art steam-heating system, and a flat of shops opening on to King Street. Reopening in 1867, the (new) Rossin House, under the management of G.P. Shears, was regarded in the 1870s as the city's premier hotel.

followed by Spooner and the other officer, a ponderous young man with a red head, and an upper lip projecting like a bracket.

The room was nearly deserted, and Denville walked up and down once or twice impatiently. He would have given a thousand dollars for some means of drowning remembrance of Olla's deceit, even for a moment, for each instant the memory was becoming more intolerable to him. Once or twice he felt tempted to rush to some bar-room and drown all thought in wine, but he was not a weak man, and rejected the idea the instant it formed itself in his mind. He had, as the French term it, too much "respect of himself in the presence of himself"[1] to venture on such a debasing expedient, the last and ruinous resort of a coward.

"The man with his chin in the muff," as Prancer had happily described him, stood by an empty table, knocking the balls about in an idle, desultory fashion, but with a style and skill that would have delighted Dion.[2] He was a tall, stalwart-looking man, with a face bronzed almost to the hue of that of an Indian, jet black hair and immense beard and whiskers, flowing in an ebon tide on his chest. He sauntered quietly round the table, glancing occasionally at Denville, and exchanging a word or two with the billiard marker. In his present vein, Denville was on the *qui vive* for something, no matter how trifling, to distract his attention, and after standing for a few moments, watching the skilful caroms made by the stranger, he approached the table, and, after a remark or two, proposed a game, to which the other readily assented. On the stranger's proposal, they played merely for "tables," and though his play was far superior to that of Denville, the latter soon saw that his opponent was not giving his undivided attention to the game. He seemed greatly more inclined to talk than play, and, a rather uncommon gift, he spoke well. He had a trite fashion of moulding his sentences, and a clear, low, incisive voice, that dropped every word like the single soft stroke of a bell on the ear. He had seen a great deal, and drew more than one short, grim laugh from Denville by a droll anecdote or two of his personal experience of the gaming tables of Homburg and Baden, and the *rouge-et-noir* of Paris.[3] An hour's

---

[1] That is, *respect de soi*, or, perhaps, *amour propre*.

[2] Cyrille Dion (1843–78), a French-Canadian billiard player, won championships in Montreal and New York City in the 1860s and early 1870s.

[3] Homburg and Baden-Baden were European spas well known for their elite and luxurious gambling establishments. The many-roomed gambling casino in Baden-Baden was designed by a Parisian named Edouard Benazet and became a site of fascination for the

conversation with him left Denville under the impression that his companion was a gentleman by birth and education, possibly a *roué* and blackleg[1] by profession, certainly untroubled by too dainty a code of honor, a thought cynical, one who concealed strong and long claws under *pattes de velours*[2] of conventional refinement; in fact, a man with whom parents would hardly care for their sons to associate. He won of course, for Denville played only a tolerable game at the best, and finding that he also was staying at the Rossin House, Denville and he strolled slowly thither in company, as dinner hour was approaching. As they turned a corner, into a quiet but fashionable thoroughfare, a pretty little "bit," in art parlance, met their eyes. A light spring wagon, freshly painted green, and drawn by the most demure, roundest and brownest cob that ever trotted between the shafts of a vehicle. The cart was a moving bank of bloom and emerald foliage, scarlet geraniums, rose camelias, oleanders, roses wagging their luxuriant heads in the breeze, fuchsias vibrating their graceful bells of scarlet and purple, every blossom that the skill of a florist could force to bloom at that season, and great plumes of ferns waving over all. A pretty, soft-eyed girl was standing on the step of a florist's shop, watching the wagon move away, and she moved aside as Denville drew his companion into the store, and walked behind the marble counter, flecked here and there with scarlet petals blown from the plants in the window.

"What can I do for you, sir?" she said, as the young man looked round the dainty bower of this mercantile Flora.

"You make up bouquets here, of course," he said, while the stranger looked on with amused interest in his dark eyes.

"Oh, certainly," she said, smiling. She was very pretty, and smiles became her. A great damask rose in a hanging basket touched her jetty hair, and an oleander tree behind her tossed a fountain of pink blossoms above her head.

"I wish you to make me up a bouquet for a lady for the Calico Ball to-night," said Denville, impatiently tapping the marble slab with his

---

general public. A popular game of the time was *rouge-et-noir*, in which two rows of cards were dealt and players could bet either on the colour of the cards (red or black) or on which row had a count of colours closest to a predetermined number. By the 1840s the game of roulette had ousted card games like *rouge-et-noir* from their earlier dominance; interestingly, Crawford's allusion does not take account of this change.

[1]   Swindler, especially a crooked gambler.

[2]   Velvet paws.

cane, for he felt that he was doing a foolish thing. "Make it as large and as brilliant and as expensive as you possibly can," he added.

"For a brunette, then, of course, sir?" said Flora suggestively.

"Not at all; the lady is a small blonde, but I fancy she doesn't care much about flowers unless they cost a great deal."

"For a blonde, I should recommend white camelias, a spray or two of scarlet geranium, cape jessamine, daphne and tube-roses. Shall I also send for the coiffure? Flowers will be mostly worn this evening with the calico toilettes."

"Oh, certainly. Can you send them to the house of the lady?"

"The boy has just driven flowers for the decoration of the tables to the hall, but on his return he shall take them right away. The name, please?"

"Miss Cecil Bertrand, at Maple Villa, a little beyond the Asylum.[1] Be kind enough to place this with them."

He tore a leaf out of his note-book, and wrote in pencil, "With Mr. Denville's compliments," and handed it to Flora, who read it with a little twitching of her cherry lips.

"I wonder who he is," she mused, as she slipped the crisp notes he had handed to her into the dainty rosewood till; "rich, that's plain. That's the sixth bouquet I made up to-day for that little minx. She's safe to wear his though, for it cost the most. Won't that Prancer be in a jolly rage."

Miss Flora came in for curious little bits of the great drama played by the puppets of the Paphian boy,[2] in her leafy bower on the busy street.

The stranger stood in the hall of the Rossin looking after Denville as he disappeared to his rooms to prepare for dinner.

"I think I see my way to something I want," he said; "but I must be careful. Well! I seldom am anything but that, and yet how Fate has gone against me of late. *Patienza, mio amico.*"

"What say, sah?" said a waiter skipping up, with a napkin dangling from his sable fingers.

"I say bring me a sherry cobbler to my room, and to-day's paper, and be quick, my friend."

---

[1] Located at 999 Queen Street West, the Provincial Lunatic Asylum was built in 1850. Under the able leadership of its first superintendent, Joseph Workman, it was seen as a leading institution of its kind. Its pastoral grounds were to the west of the city proper where villas such as Cecil Bertrand's were few and no doubt somewhat exclusive.

[2] Cupid, god of love in Roman mythology, is the son of Venus or Paphia, goddess of love and beauty.

"Cern'ly, sah. Jim! sherry-cobbler and paper to No. 8. Nice gemman No. 8! Golly! what a beard he got. Wunner whar he cum from."

CHAPTER XI

Winona's Return

Mr. Murphy bounded from his knees, and, with the spring of a grasshopper, bounded towards the back-door. Of all the powers of earth arrayed, rank and file, against him, his Milesian[1] heart knew not fear, but the appearance of Winona's "Fetch,"[2] heralded by such tempestuous turmoil, opened the flood-gates of superstitious terror, and with a "whoop" of exceeding mental anguish, he sought safety in flight. Mrs. Harty had taken the precaution of fastening the latch with a cord early in the evening, and Mike found his retreat in that direction cut off.

He kicked the door violently, roaring in a voice that out-howled the tempest:

"Let me out, yer sowls, let me out for the love of glory! Och! me shirt's burnin' into holes on me back wid the eyes of her! Stand betune us, Captin dear, and spake her fair. It's yerself has the larnin', an' sure wanst they're a corp it's only the Latin they mind. *De profundis osculum,*[3] an' get out wid ye!"

"Leave go of that yowling," roared out Joe Harty, as Mike beat on the door in the energy of despair, and groaned in mortal terror. "Can't ye make use of yer eyes, Mike?"

"Is it an' have the eye-balls ov me melted clane out? Isn't her eyes scrapin' the flesh ov me this minnit like red-hot claws. Captin, Captin, out wid the Latinity, or we're lost enthirely."

Mr. Murphy was not altogether the slave of imagination. The squirrel had dropped in an agony of terror from his eyrie on the rafter to Mike's back, and, confused by the turmoil, was rushing up and down the broad expanse of his shoulders, making free use of his sharp claws to the extreme detriment of the linen and epidermis of the latter.

---

[1] Irish.
[2] Spectre or apparition.
[3] Mike's garbled "Latinity" translates roughly as "from the depths of the kiss."

"Mike," cried Archie Frazer, in a voice that rang like a clarion, "look! see who Winona has brought to us. Oh, man, look round!"

There was such a thrill of joy in the young officer's voice that Mike was encouraged to turn his terror-stricken countenance over his shoulder, still, however, clutching the unyielding latch.

The entrance door had closed with a loud crash, and Winona stood in the full blaze of the fire-light, watching Mike with eyes that scintillated in the red glow, the leaping scarlet touching the rich bronze of her lofty face, and finding a dead reflection in the masses of dripping ebon hair that hung dankly to her knees. One rounded arm supported a rifle over her shoulder, the other was clasped closely round the form of Androsia Howard, who, nearly unconscious, leant against the vigorous form of the Indian girl, the clear outlines of her marble features sharply defined against the dark figure of her companion. The garments of both the girls were rent and torn, and Androsia's delicate feet were bruised and bleeding. Her head was uncovered, and the dusky gold of her hair, clinging to her white throat and shoulders in damp, uncurled masses, caught red pencillings of light from the fire. Her garments, sodden with rain, clung to her limbs, and her large eyes were half-open and glazed like those of a corpse. Instead of being reassured by the appearance of his beloved Miss Drosia, Mike's terror was exactly doubled, but, fortunately, its effects now were simply those of complete paralysis, and, his stout legs giving way under him, he slipped to the floor in a sitting posture, propped up against the door, his eyes as round as buttons, and fixed on the little group with an unwinking steadiness that threatened to force them from their sockets.

A wooden bench ran along the wall beside the fire-place, and without a word Archie took Androsia from the Indian girl, and carried her towards it; but Mrs. Harty, recovered from her panic, pushed a low, cushioned rocker before the direct warmth of the fire, and bade him place her in it, as she began to show slight signs of returning animation.

Winona advanced with her usual supple, majestic, noiseless tread to the hearth, and leaning with clasped hands on the rifle, watched Mrs. Harty and Sally, who had recovered almost instantly from her brief swoon, as they busied themselves about Androsia, wringing the water from her hair and clothes, and issuing shrill directions to honest Joe to pile on more wood and "keep hisself out of a body's way."

The honest fellow was so absorbed in staring at Winona that he was found to be quite impervious to lingual remonstrances, and, to keep him at all "out of the road," as Mrs. Harty expressed it, the good woman was fain to resort to free use of her stout elbows, and Joe was hustled hither and thither, being apparently quite unable to remove his eyes from the Indian girl.

The water was running in little streams from her hair and clothing, and lay in the tiny hollows of the roughly-hewn hearthstone, like pools of blood in the rich red light, and, from the shadow of her falling night of hair, her large eyes burned with a smouldering heat and fire like the reflection of a conflagration on the dark tarns of a wilderness on a moonless midnight. She stood voiceless, her black shadow flickering vast and spectrally across the floor and white-washed wall, a statue of bronze such as it is alone in the power of the Indian to become, motionless as though sculptured from some firm and dusky cliff. Her steady gaze was fixed on the pallid face of her foster-sister, gaining a faint rose in the warmth of the apartment.

Archie stood leaning on the back of one of the heavy wooden chairs, with all a man's incapacity for assisting in such an emergency, his eyes also fastened on the lovely face shining out from the scarlet flannel cushion fastened to the back of the rocker like some rare cameo traced in lines of perfect, pallid beauty by some master-hand.

The moment had not yet arrived for explanations to be either given or demanded, though it must be confessed his soul burned with impatience for light to evolve from the mystery of the sudden appearance of the two girls.

He felt a heavy hand laid on his arm, and looked up to find Joe at his side, still eyeing Winona, to whom he directed Archie's attention in a guttural whisper:

"Corn-shucks! Cap'n, look at what she's got slung to her wampum. I'm bet, that's all, Cap."

Archie glanced at Winona and back at Joe.

"I see she's got a bunch of dirty-looking horse-hair slung to her belt," he said, "but what of that?"

Joe drew his brown fore-finger in a circle round the top of his grizzled head with a slow gesture of great significance.

"I'm darned, an' blowed, an' busted," he whispered, "ef 't ain't a SCELP. Whar upon airth hev the young catamount made the raise on it?"

"Eh! What?" cried Archie in very natural dismay, "what are you talking such rubbish for, Joe?"

"You bet I ain't," responded Joe confidently; "it's a scelp, an' fresh raised, or I never seed or teched one when I war a youngster on the Rocky Mountains."

"Yes," said Winona, speaking suddenly in English and turning her great eyes slowly on the two men; "yes, behold, it is the scalp of the enemy of my sister, the scalp of the lover of my sister. He fell but two suns ago under the hand of Winona. The leaves rustle on the body of Hawk-eye! The crows clamor in the air above him!"

She showed her white teeth in a dazzling smile of triumph; but reading the expression of horror in the countenances of her listeners, she darkened into added gloom, with a touch of lofty scorn in it, as she looked at them.

Androsia turned her brightening eyes on her foster-sister, and held out her arms to her appealingly. The latter understood the significance of the gesture, and, compressing her lips, tore the ghastly relic from her belt, and flung it upon the crimson cavern of the fire.

"It is done!" she said. "Winona kept it but to show that her tongue was not the tongue of a liar."

Androsia's face flushed with joy as the flames licked up the last fibre of the scalp, but the inbred instincts of the Indian girl had been fully aroused, and she stared with sullen regret at the vanishing trophy she had sacrificed to the wishes of Androsia.

Androsia looked round her as one awakening from a dream, and, with a sudden yell of joy, Mr. Murphy bounded from his sitting posture and executed what her Majesty of glorious memory, Elizabeth of England, was wont to describe as "a merrie volte."[1]

"Och, be japers! it's herself it is, an' no spechther, at all, at all. Miss Drosia, acushla,[2] it's me heart's broke wid joy to see ye, an' it's mended it'll be sure if yez can only say that it's not the widdy of Hawk-eye ye be. Winona, yer sowl, whin war it ye picked off the honest gintleman so purty? An' how cem it he kep yez so snug, an' so menny out afther yez for this two months an' more?"

---

[1] This passage alludes to the reaction of Elizabeth I to unwelcome news brought by the Scottish emissary Sir James Melville that her rival, Mary, Queen of Scots, had given birth to a son. Elizabeth's nineteenth-century biographer Agnes Strickland cites Melville's report that agents informed him the queen had been advised to conceal her chagrin: "However, she rather overacted her part, if Melville bears true witness, since, at his introduction, he says, 'She welcomed me with a merry volt,' which certainly must mean, that she cut a caper at the sight of him" (*Lives of the Queens of England* 6 [London: Henry Colburn, 1843] 266).

[2] Darling, dear heart (Irish).

154   ISABELLA VALANCY CRAWFORD

Winona turned on the excited Mr. Murphy and looked at him. "An' besides," ejaculated Mike, retiring suddenly, "it's dead I seed ye meself, an' Captin Frazer here! Oh, begorra, is it come for a dacent berrein' ye are, afther all?"

Mr. Murphy retreated suddenly to the other side of the chair occupied by Androsia, as his superstitious terrors revived, and in expressive pantomime besought of Archie to question the supposed "fetch;" but anxious as Archie was to do so, he could not help agreeing with Mrs. Harty that Androsia should at once be placed in bed, as she appeared utterly exhausted and incapable of uttering a word. Under the good woman's directions, he carried her into an inner room, and, laying her on the clean patchwork covered bed, stole out again, leaving her to the kindly ministrations of Sally and her mother.

He found Winona wringing the heavy masses of her hair, and drying her doeskin tunic at the fire, watched by Joe from the midst of a cloud of blue tobacco smoke, and by Mike, who, apparently, was slowly regaining confidence, from a shadowy recess behind the glittering dresser, from which he peered cautiously at the dusky form and beautiful face of his former pet and *protégé*, but who, now wrapped in gloomy musings, seemed unconscious of his presence. She turned abruptly and faced Archie as his light step sounded on the boards, and her dark eyes roved inquisitively over his face and figure, both of which bore traces of his recent severe illness. Mike came cautiously from his lair, and placed himself near Captain Frazer, who, with a cordial grace, pushed the rocker towards Winona.

"Sit down," he said gently; "you seem greatly fatigued. Mike, put down more wood; it grows colder every moment."

So certain had he been of Winona's death that it seemed a curious dream, her dark presence in that homely room; and his voice sounded unfamiliar to himself as he uttered these commonplace words to one, the mystery of whose appearance amongst the living was yet unexplained. Up to this moment he had had no leisure to feel anything but the pleasure of the restoration of Androsia, but now there was a pause, and other emotions filled his heart. He did not now wonder so much at Mike's display of terror, for despite education and a tolerable share of common sense, he was conscious of a kind of mental shiver as he looked at the weird beauty of the dusky countenance brooding over the flame. There was profound silence in the room, during which she seemed to read his inner soul with her stern eyes. Her face relaxed as she looked at him, and with a smile she sank wearily into the low chair. Did any doubts as to her earthly condition remain in Mike's mind, her first words dispelled them once and for ever.

"Food," she said. "Winona is hungry. Winona is like the wolf when the snow lies softly in the woods."

Joe's pipe smashed as it fell to the ground, and in less time than it takes to relate he had placed before the half-famished girl cold meat and bread in abundance, with the laconic, but hearty exclamation, "Pitch in."

With every mouthful the girl devoured, in the manner of one who had nearly died of lack of food, Mike drew a pace nearer, eyeing her proceedings with exquisite pleasure, and when, at length, she concluded her repast, he rushed up and took her long, slender hand in his brown, hairy paw.

"Shure it's the wholesome, comfortable appetite ye have, acushla, the heavens be praised for that same! an' it were bether than bell, book or cannle[1] to see the cowld pork goin' into that purty mouth of yer own, me darlint! Shure it's yer own ghost I wor afther takin' ye for, ma colleen d'has.[2] The divil a wan ov me bud did."

Winona smiled gravely, and seemed pleased at Mike's evident joy at her restoration; but suddenly she started and looked searchingly at him.

"Did Hawk-eye utter the words of truth? He shrieked it in the ear of Winona that the father of her white sister had journeyed to the hunting-grounds of the spirits of his people."

"The truth it war, honey," responded Mike, much affected. "Thim hands," and he extended his brawny paws, "nailed him down in as comfortable an' tidy a coffin as ye'd care to see, and laid the daisy quilt over him, his sowl to glory an' his name to grace! Bud how in the name of wonder did ye come across Miss Drosia an' that owdacious haythen wiggler, Hawk-eye?"

A terrible light leaped like a flaming sword from the dusk eyes, and inspired by the memory of her dangers, Winona rose, tall and divinely terrible, as some dark avenging power. Her form seemed actually to dilate and become shadowy in its outline,

---

[1] "Bell, book and candle" is a phrase associated with ritual excommunication in the Roman Catholic Church, and, more broadly, with the portentous trappings of religious ceremony.
[2] Pretty girl (Irish).

"Inwardly brightening
With sullen heat,
As a storm-cloud lurid with lightning."[1]

Her explanations we must leave for another chapter.

---

[1] Longfellow, *The Golden Legend* (1851), "Epilogue: The Two Recording Angels Ascending" 60–62.

[PART 5—8 FEBRUARY 1873]

CHAPTER XII

Is Thim Kebs?

Denville, with a moss-rose bud in his button-hole, and the green-eyed monster rearing his crested head in his bosom, went to the Calico Ball. The rooms were full when he arrived, and dancing had been in progress for some time, and making his way to a quiet corner, he seated himself in the shadow of a draped Union Jack, near the orchestra, partly because he did not feel disposed to be in the least sociable, and partly to observe the gay crowd whirling past. The band was playing one of those galops that would animate a marble Minerva,[1] and the peculiar rhythmical tripping of satin-shod feet mingled pleasantly with the measured, intoxicating strains of the instruments. Presently came the flash of a scarlet coat and the glimmer of a golden head shining against it, and Cecil drifted past with Prancer, in a wonderful toilette that might have been from the looms of Persia, but was in reality a blue and white striped print. Cecil lent a dainty grace to any fabric she deigned to wear, and she had never looked lovelier than she did to-night. Denville saw with a kind of cynical satisfaction that it was his camelias that shone, starlike, in the golden mist of her hair and in her bouquet-holder, though it was tolerably plain that, unconscious of his presence, she was doing her most bewitching best to bring affairs with the lieutenant to what she was wont to term "something decided," otherwise a formal proposal. She was somewhat on her mettle about this devoted but wary sub,[2] who sported round her dainty hook and yet managed to keep clear of that "something decided," without which the soul of Cecil was disquieted within her. She liked to keep her matrimonial accounts in the simplest manner possible, and had no mind to enter Prancer on the list of men who did not "come to the point," and, to do Prancer justice, he was fully up to all her little schemes on his behalf, being a gentleman

---

[1] Goddess of wisdom in Roman mythology.
[2] Subaltern.

158 ISABELLA VALANCY CRAWFORD

of a delightfully astute and calculating kind, and, in the choice language of those sportive youths, his fellow officers, "up to no end of dodges!" Miss Cecil's amongst the number.

Denville danced with some half a score of houris,[1] and seemed, like Tennyson's prince,

"To move amongst a world of ghosts,
And feel himself the shadow of a dream."[2]

He simpered, and complimented their pretty dresses, looked at the moon with the sentimental from the conservatory, laughed with the lively over ices and tea in corridors and refreshment rooms, and behaved like the other men present externally, while mentally a mist clouded his brain, and a kind of numbness deadened his senses. Wherever he looked rose the face of Olla Frazer, the deep brown eyes searching his, the pure brow calm and serene as that of some pictured saint. It was the only real thing in that floating crowd of brilliant shadows circling round him. He thought of it persistently, and was as wretched as any human being could well be, with a kind of vagueness in the pang. When it was the good old custom in the good old times to break the bones of criminals, stretched on the wheel, one after the other, with an iron bar, it was asserted that after the first blow or two they felt no pain; yet we cannot suppose them to have felt anything but intensely uncomfortable, and the first stages of a man's mind after some severe shock resembles not a little the probable sensations of the broken-alive criminal, a dull insensibility quivering on the edge of keenest agony.

After supper he had his slow waltz with Cecil, and, after a turn or two, Cecil found it so warm that there was nothing for it but the conservatory, and thither he led her, carrying her fan and bouquet, and bending his dark head to catch her laughter-lit chatter. She laughed delightfully, like a peal of silver joy-bells, and her velvet cheeks were vivid as roses, her blue eyes dazzling, and her small, fine lips like dewy coral; and presently they were seated on a cushioned bench, behind a great bank of gorgeous bloom, with the moonlight streaming over

---

[1] Beautiful virgins who are believed to await the devout Muslim in Paradise.

[2] See Tennyson, *The Princess* (1847) I. 17–18: "I seemed to move among a world of ghosts, / And feel myself the shadow of a dream."

them, and her little head very near his coat-sleeve. This was a *tête-à-tête* after Cecil's own heart. They had the conservatory to themselves; there were flowers, moonlight, softened music, all the adjuncts of sentimental flirtation, and an eligible *parti* to angle for. Cecil was a scientific flirt. She dashed into the thing *con amore*,[1] and with a zest that never tired.

> "The pleasant'st angling is to see the fish
> Cut with his golden oars the silver stream,
> And greedily devour the treacherous bait."[2]

So Shakespeare said, but Cecil enjoyed the sport more thoroughly when some trifling obstacle rendered the prey less certain. What, to the thorough sportsman, would be the enjoyment of a "burst" across country without the hedges and ditches which try the mettle of himself and his steed? Cecil had some uphill work before her, such as a trifle of treachery towards her bosom friend, a few ready inventions, and her vivid loveliness, she felt, would inevitably surmount, and when she joined her mamma, some hour later, her face was brilliant with triumph, and Denville, walking home with Prancer and Spooner to the Rossin, carried in his note-book a camelia bud he had a shadowy remembrance of begging from her, with some sentimental commonplace that he had not attached even the shadow of meaning to.

He laughed absently at Spooner's "chaff" on the subject of his flirtation, and Prancer's keener little shafts of lazy cynicism fell blunted from the shield his dulled sensitiveness presented. He had looked upon Olla as tacitly but assuredly his own, to claim when he would, and perhaps had not held her so inestimably precious in that lordly certainty of possession. Now that she was altogether removed beyond his reach, that no vows or protestations could ever bind her to him, he was stunned and cruelly unjust to her under the blow. She must have known that he loved her! and what right had she to turn from him to another? Who had given her the privilege of crushing his heart beneath her careless feet? She was his, in that he had loved her beyond and above every earthly thing. It was a vile treachery on her part that she had bound

---

[1] With delight or zeal (Italian, "with love").

[2] See Shakespeare, *Much Ado About Nothing* III.i.26–28: "The pleasant'st angling is to see the fish / Cut with her golden oars the silver stream, / And greedily devour the treacherous bait …"

herself to another. That he had led her through paths that, if pleasant, were involved in shifting mists of painful doubt and uncertainty of him and his affection, he never allowed himself to remember. The treachery was hers, all hers, the pain his alone.

Mr. Macer, the pleasant acquaintance he had made at the billiard room, made one of the party collected in his room, and under his quiet manipulation, the usual rather jovial and noisy characteristics of a gentleman's supper party gave place to two or three quiet groups of men at cosy little card tables, on which shone little piles of gold, that changed hands frequently. Mr. Macer had formed a select party for himself, consisting of Denville, Spooner and an elderly young man, with a bald head, a chronic weakness pervading his brain and his knees, and a plethoric purse. They had all, with the exception of Macer, poured out generous libations to the vine-garlanded god of champagne suppers, and while Macer's bronzed face was as undisturbed as that of a statue, Denville's was deeply flushed, the elderly young man developed a remarkable tendency to break into sudden warblings of amatory odes, and Spooner's countenance assumed exactly that expression bestowed on the bird of Minerva,[1] as pictured in cheap wood-cuts of the heathen mythology. When the dawn struggled in through the curtains, the party broke up, a gentle melancholy on the faces of Spooner and the elderly young man, and a cold smile glittering in flashes across the face of Mr. Macer, as he shot covert and derisive glances at them from the corners of his treacherous-looking eyes. The elderly young man was put by a sleepy waiter into a cab, and departed through the dawn to the address, viciously given by Prancer, of two old maiden aunts, from whom he had "expectations," and in whose porch the maid-servant found him, propped against the hall-door, snoring peacefully, with his hat jammed over his eyes, and his necktie twisted suggestively in a knot under his left ear.

The wine Denville had drank had excited him considerably, and, after his guests had departed, he changed his coat and, lighting a cigar, sought the brisk morning air, for his head was aching violently. As he passed Macer's room, the door of which stood slightly ajar, the latter came out, apparently bound on the same errand as himself, and they strolled through the empty, shadowy streets in the cool grey of the morning, enjoying the

---

[1] Owl.

virginal freshness of the growing dawn. The spires of the churches glittered up into the misty sky like shafts of faintly gleaming silver, and a star or two flickered in the vapory rose through which the moon, like a globe of pearl, sank slowly westward. Flights of pigeons wheeled from roofs and pigeon houses, and dropped on their rosy feet on the dewy ground, softly cooing, and rustling their variegated feathers.

Wherever a large body of water exists, the feet of aimless pedestrians turn instinctively towards it, and without giving the matter a thought, the two men strolled towards the lake through the quiet streets. Macer glanced frequently at the moody countenance of his silent companion, for Denville was little inclined for conversation, and, indeed, would have preferred the companionship of his own thoughts to that of his new acquaintance, for whom, despite his pre-occupation, he was conscious of perceiving a growing distaste. Denville was but one-and-twenty, and at that age one is morely likely to like or dislike from instinct than by any of those rules of reason and experience that control our likings in after-life. At thirty an honest man may like a rogue, because he may judge him from a false basis of presumed honesty, but at twenty, as a rule, there is instinct, that experience has not warped, and instinct is truthful.

Macer was content to stroll on in silence. By and by he had one or two items of information to obtain, he hoped, from Denville, but he had plenty of time before him, and lazily enjoyed his cheroot, undisturbed by the taciturnity of his companion, and reflecting pleasantly on the, to him, profitable pleasures of the past night. He had won considerable sums from Spooner and the elderly young man, and was at ease concerning his board for a few weeks to come, for his finances had been at a very low ebb, and he had not seen his way very clearly towards replenishing them.

"There's a steamer coming in, I see," he said as they found themselves on one of the wharves. A few cabs were waiting about, and one or two hotel busses to receive passengers. Some porters were seated, waiting to manipulate the luggage, and enjoyed their breakfasts out of cheerfully tinted pocket handkerchiefs of scarlet and yellow.

"Yes," answered Denville, looking over the lake; "she'll be in in about ten minutes. Suppose we wait. She is a neat-looking vessel."

So she was. Floating towards them in the spreading rose and gold of dawn, like a white bower rising from the purple lake, slowly brightening to amethyst, flecked with long ridges of swaying scarlet as the mists faded from its waters. A long band of ebon smoke floated into the shadows from her lofty funnel, and her great paddle-wheels dashed the spray into cascades of carbuncles and diamonds. Suddenly the sun lifted itself into the shadowy world, and a tract of quivering gold ran along the lake. The porters began to bestir themselves, and to one of them Macer turned.

"What is the name of the steamer?" he said, offering the man a cigar.

"She's the *Lake Queen*, from Windsor," replied the man civilly. "She seems pretty full this morning."

The decks were sprinkled with groups making ready to land, and in a few moments they were pouring over the gangway, and the wharf was a lively scene of bustle and confusion.

"Ah thin, now, is thim kebs, yer honor?" said a voice close in Denville's ear, so close, indeed, that the speaker's red head was thrust between him and Macer, bringing the latter round with something like a start by its sudden proximity.

Denville turned, and beheld a short, stout man in a doeskin jerkin and a coon-skin cap, regarding him with an affable smile on his broad countenance, and pointing one gnarled brown finger at the row of cabs.

"Yes, they're cabs," said Denville, smiling a little at the man's simplicity. "Do you want one?"

"Well now, no, yer honor, I can't say but that I'm aiquel to walkin'. It's for the Captin an' Miss Drosia I'm wantin' one."

Denville signalled to one of the file, who drove up as a gentleman and two ladies, clad in deep mourning and closely veiled, hastily advanced to the gangway, and his face flushed deeply as he recognized Captain Frazer. One of the ladies was about the height and figure of Olla, and dreading to catch a glimpse of her sweet face, Denville turned hastily to leave the wharf, a mist before his eyes and twenty million little bells ringing in his ears, but Archie saw and recognized him.

"Hallo, Denville!" he called out in his frank, clear voice, "you are about the last man I expected to see in these parts. Here, Mike, put that bag into the cab! Now, Winona, take care of the wheel; there, you're all right." Archie placed the taller of the two ladies in the vehicle, and turned to assist her whom Denville half-suspected to be Olla in, when a sudden puff of wind tore the heavy crêpe veil from her face and blew it to Macer's feet, who was leaning against a capstan, surveying the party through a double eye-glass he constantly used. He lifted it, and with a deep bow restored it to its owner, who stared at him with a shy bewilderment, as though uncertain how to acknowledge the courtesy, and Denville saw with a mixture of pleasure and disappointment that she was not Olla.

Archie's eyes smiled as he watched her for a second, gazing shyly at Macer, the morning light glorifying her beautiful face, and the "east wind, Wabun,"[1] stirring the bronze tresses of her hair, and then he relieved her perplexity by a word of thanks to Macer, who drew back with a bow and smile to his former position, while Archie handed her into the cab.

"Wait a moment, Denville," he called out as he closed the door; "I'll walk up town with you. Drive to the Rossin," he said to the cabman; "and, Mike, remember there are rooms taken there for Miss Howard and Winona. I'll be there directly myself."

"Divil a doubt of that same!" replied Mike, clambering to a seat beside the cabman, with a broad grin of contentment, and the vehicle whirled off, leaving the three men on the wharf.

Archie slipped his arm through Denville's.

"You look as cheerful as a Scotch mist," he said, regarding the latter laughingly. "Who's your friend?" he inquired, as, lifting his wide felt hat, Macer strolled slowly away, evidently surmising that he might be *de trop*.[2]

"He's a mere acquaintance I picked up yesterday," replied Denville. "But how is it that you're in by the steamer? I heard you were up at the Manitoulins, and Miss Bertrand told me something of a dangerous wound you received, and some knight-errantry that you were engaged in."

Archie's face fell just a shade at mention of Cecil's name.

"I was beyond the Manitoulins," he said, "but I was obliged to come all the way down by water on account of my companions, who did not like the idea of land-travel. We have been a considerable time on the way, as they had to stop at one of the lake towns to make some purchases. I had to stop at headquarters to get an extension of leave, or we should have gone straight on to my father's at once. By the way, how is it you are up here just now?"

Denville saw that he did not care to be questioned about his adventures, and indeed the former was too much engrossed with his own troubles to feel much interest in anything else.

"I had business affairs in Toronto," he said, unwillingly, "and I

---

[1]   See Longfellow, *The Song of Hiawatha* (1855) II.79, and "Vocabulary" 665.
[2]   In the way.

accompanied Miss Bertrand's party up from Murray Bay. I am going down again to-morrow."

"Come with us," said Archie, who had a dim idea that Olla and Denville rather liked each other, "and I daresay that the girls can spare time from making wedding finery to amuse you for a few days."

Denville nearly choked with jealous rage, and his dark face grew so strangely lowering that Archie was perplexed inexpressibly.

"Thank you," he answered stiffly, "but it's quite impossible."

"I feel as though I had been out of the world for years," said Archie, after a moment's silence, "and come back to find things strangely unfamiliar. You are changed, and it would hardly surprise me to find Spooner with a moustache, and Prancer with flowing locks of silver. I can fancy myself almost a modern Rip Van Winkle.[1] Where are you staying?"

"Here;" they were opposite the Rossin. "By the way, I think I'll leave for Montreal to-day. I sail for Europe next week, and there are some little matters I must see to before I leave. So I bid you good-bye, old fellow."

"I hope nothing unpleasant has occurred," said Archie, concernedly. "You are changed, and in a way I don't like."

"I was up all night," answered Denville, looking away from Captain Frazer's searching, kindly dark eyes, "and found the champagne rather too heady, that's all."

Twenty-four hours had made a startling change in his appearance. His dark face looked old, worn and haggard in the morning light, and his eyes were fiery and bloodshot. If Archie could only have guessed the cause!

They parted with mutual promises of writing, and in the course of a couple of hours Denville was on his way to Montreal.

As Archie passed into the reading-room, he ran against Mr. Macer, who was coming out. He apologized, and was answered in Mr. Macer's most urbane manner. As the latter walked away, whistling softly, Archie turned and stared after him.

"I could almost swear that I have seen that fellow before; but, on my life, I can't recall the time or place. Fortunately, it's not of much consequence."

Archie's time was fully occupied during his brief stay in Toronto, and as he did not see Mr. Macer again, the remembrance of him slipped completely from his memory.

---

[1]   The protagonist of Washington Irving's tale "Rip Van Winkle" (1820) sleeps for twenty years and awakes to find the world profoundly changed.

CHAPTER XIII

Miss Bertrand Makes a Mistake

Cecil put her handkerchief to her eyes, and as a faint sob issued from behind its filmy folds, it was only fair to suppose that she was crying. The scene was a pretty little chintz drawing-room, in a tiny, fantastically-gabled villa beyond the Asylum, smothered earlier in the year in the milky bloom of acacias.

Archie Frazer, with a countenance in which anger, embarrassment, and a faint flicker of amusement struggled for mastery, leant over the back of a prie-Dieu and watched the golden head so prettily lighted by a stray fleck of quivering sunlight, and the nymph-like grace of the slender form bending slightly, as though Cecil were overcome with poignant grief.

Archie had conscientiously endeavored, according to the advice of the old saying, "To be off with the old love before he was on with the new;"[1] but he had just sufficient of the older sentiment lingering in his heart to make his daily increasing adoration of Androsia exquisitely painful to him. There was, too, the faint dread that perhaps Cecil was really sincere in her affection for him, in which case he would have relentlessly trampled his own chance of happiness under foot and fulfilled his engagement to her. Fortunately, Fate and Cecil were determined that he should not be called upon to make so tremendous a sacrifice.

"Oh, dear me!" sobbed Cecil, in quivering tones of intense anguish. "I didn't think you could have been so false! But it's just the way women are sure to be treated! Ma always said you didn't, didn't care for me," and Cecil's sobs grew louder.

---

[1] This "old saying" was a favourite with the Victorian novelist Anthony Trollope, appearing in *Barchester Towers* (1857), *Doctor Thorne* (1858), *The Eustace Diamonds* (1873), and *Ayala's Angel* (1881); see, for example, *The Eustace Diamonds*, initially published as a serial in the British *Fortnightly Review* from July 1871 to February 1873, and the American periodical *Galaxy*, from September 1871 to January 1873, at the time that Crawford was writing *Winona*: "We know the dear old rhyme:

> It is good to be merry and wise,
> It is good to be honest and true;
> It is good to be off with the old love
> Before you are on with the new."
>
> (*Galaxy* 14 [May 1872] 635)

"Will you hear reason, Cecil?" exclaimed Archie. "How could I avoid taking care of a helpless girl suddenly and cruelly orphaned, and thrown on my protection? Surely, Cecil, you are fearfully unreasonable."

"Yes, now abuse me like a savage," moaned Cecil. "I won't submit to it! Didn't you say she is the loveliest woman you ever saw? Was that because she is an orphan, sir?"

Archie looked excessively uncomfortable. He dreaded giving his pretty betrothed the faintest hint of the change in his sentiments towards her, and he felt like some crime-dyed monster, as he watched Cecil sobbing in her chintz nest. That she had ever cared particularly for him, he had not fooled himself into believing, but he had thought his own love strong, deep, wide enough to fill the chasm between them. Now he was slowly awakening to the disagreeable fact that while his love had vanished, she appeared to be very much in earnest.

"Now, Cecil," he began; but with a pathetic shake of the bright head Miss Bertrand whimpered from behind the handkerchief, through which she was quietly watching every speaking change of his dark, expressive face.

"No, don't, it's no use. You've behaved shamefully, but I mean to forgive you all the same. Go and marry your white squaw, and when I'm dead or married or something, you'll be quite happy! I wouldn't marry you now, not if you were Prince Arthur,[1] and asked me on your knees with your crown in your hands. No, I wouldn't, you great deceitful thing!"

"All this because I was obliged to take charge for a few days of a lady left as a solemn charge to my father," ejaculated Archie, in a tone of injured innocence, but nevertheless feeling horribly guilty. "Dear Cecil, think how unjust you are to—to think I could behave so badly towards you."

It was well the room was dark, or the hue of Archie's tell-tale countenance as he spoke would have betrayed him.

"My heart is broken," wailed Cecil, "and my eyes will be so red that I will be a perfect fright to-night at the Brignoli[2] concert, and my nose swollen perhaps. But I know my duty, and I won't submit to being treated badly. You never cared for me!"

---

[1] Arthur William Patrick Albert (1850–1942), later duke of Connaught and Strathearn, was the third and favourite son of Queen Victoria.

[2] Pasquale Brignoli (1824–84), an Italian tenor domiciled in the United States, was a distinguished concert and opera singer; he appeared to great acclaim at the Music Hall in Toronto in 1867, 1870, and 1871.

"Cecil, you know that I did!" And indeed he had.

"Now insult me because I've no one but ma and Lina to take my part, and say I tell stories, do," sobbed Cecil. "Oh, it's just what ma said I might expect."

To do Mrs. Bertrand justice, she never even hinted at such a possibility.

Had Archie still continued to care for Cecil, this scene would have driven him through twenty different moods of anger, resentment, wounded affection and so on; but feeling guiltily that she was partially right, he was very patient with her childish display of jealousy. His cheeks burned at her last words, but he came and sat down beside her, and tried to take her snow-flake of a hand in his.

"My dear girl," he said, "what has made you take this fancy into that little head of yours?"

"Let my hand go, and there, take your ring back, perhaps it'll fit your Miss Howard; and I wish I were dead! And there's Madame Frillmeout's girl coming in at the gate with my new dress, and my eyes in such a state. It's all over between us, you cruel, cruel, strong-hearted thing!" and Cecil buried her head in the great pillow of her sleepy-hollow chair,[1] and looked like a crushed lily.

"Cecil," said Archie, in a very low tone, "look at me and say whether you are truly in earnest or not."

"I won't look at you, and I'm quite in earnest, and I wish you'd go away," returned Cecil, in a tone that left no doubt as to her intention on the subject.

Archie turned his face away for a second, and a great change passed over his face. He saw plainly that his dread of crushing Cecil's affection was quite unnecessary, and that she had seized on the most flimsy pretext for breaking off their engagement. He experienced a sudden and delicious sense of freedom, and for the first time his heart answered with a joyful bound of hope as the soul-lit face of Androsia Howard rose before him. He stood up and took his hat and gloves, and then looked down with sparkling eyes at the little figure that had truly once been very dear to him.

"Good-bye, Cecil," he said, "let us part friends."

"Oh, I've no objection," murmured Cecil, still from the pillow, and stretching out her hand, which Archie held for a moment in his. "I'm

---

[1]   A large, upholstered armchair with a hollowed seat and high back.

sure I'll try and get over it, and if I don't— There, go away, please, I can't keep the girl waiting, and Frillmeout is so fussy. Good-bye."

And so Archie Frazer strode out through the leafless acacias, a free man, with a happy light in his honest eyes, and a heart on which there lingered no shadow of self-reproach.

Cecil listened until the gate swung to behind his retreating form, and then bounded into the middle of the room, where she executed an airy *pas seul* of triumph, and then darted to the mirror, supported by gilt Cupids.

"Cecil Bertrand," she soliloquised, "you're in luck, my child! He's too great a muff to go about saying I treated him badly, and Denville's safe to pop directly. The great donkey! he did really and truly think I was crying."

"Cecil," said Lina, a promising young coquette of sixteen, tripping into the room, "do you know what Kitty Duncan told me coming from school?"

"No, of course I don't, you little stupid. I don't suppose it's of much consequence, anyway."

"Yes, it is, my lady. She went to see her brother off by an early train, and they met Mr. Denville at the depot; and he said that he was to sail for Europe next week. He went away on the train with George Duncan to Montreal."

"I don't believe a word of it," said Cecil, turning deathly white, and sitting down trembling in every limb. Was this what she had discarded Archie Frazer for!

"It's true," said Lina, "and I guess, miss, you've been too clever by half this time. Oh, won't ma be jolly mad."

"You spiteful, malicious, brown, mean thing!" cried Cecil, and forthwith went into unfeigned and perfectly audible hysterics.

Archie was for the present fully avenged.

He reported himself at headquarters, received a short extension of leave, and the following morning found him, Androsia, Winona and Mike, *en route* for Captain Frazer's residence.

Few would have recognized in the queenly-looking creature in her sweeping robes of heavy black, the wild wood nymph who had first flashed on his sight some three short months before.

There was, if possible, a more marked change in the appearance of Winona, and wherever they appeared the two girls attracted considerable attention and remark.

CHAPTER XIV

Entering on a New Life

Mr. Macer was easily cordial with his inferiors, or at least those whom fate had placed "below the salt," at the table of life. "*Noblesse oblige*," was the motto of his manners, and his low, carefully modulated voice and courteous polish did not vary whether he commanded "Billy," the errand boy, to call a cab for him, or whether he entered into conversation with those who were apparently his equals. He had a kind of fancy for the study of character, he amused his cynicism with the grotesque distortions that mar the symmetry of the most perfect, and had a happy knack of discovering latent vices and impalpable shadows dulling the brilliancy of the brightest. He was one of a numerous class who believe with illimitable faith in the dominion of universal evil, but bring an overpowering force of cynicism and what they term cool, reasoning power to bear against the existence of virtue. If they discover a man whose character and virtues are of the loftiest, whose talents, guided by those bright guardians, have placed him foremost in the ranks of the great benefactors of mankind, they console themselves under the weight of evidence in his favor by shrugging their shoulders and assuming that there must needs be the skeleton of vice, though there be such a fair superstructure of seeming virtue. Alas for such cynics! Let the roses of life bloom in a perennial beauty and fragrance under their feet, for them indeed beyond all mankind—

"The trail of the serpent is over them all!"[1]

For in faith, whether the higher Divine Faith, the special gift to the Christian, or the faith that rests secure in the virtue and love of man, is certainly the greatest happiness. Where can content be, where faith in God or man is not?

---

[1]   See Thomas Moore, "Paradise and the Peri" 204–207, in *Lalla Rookh* (1817):

> 'Poor race of men!' said the pitying Spirit,
> Dearly ye pay for your primal Fall—
> Some flow'rets of Eden ye still inherit,
> But the trail of the Serpent is over them all!'
> (*Poetical Works of Thomas Moore*, ed. A.D. Godley [London: Oxford UP, 1915] 397)

Mike's comic face and droll eyes had attracted Macer's attention on the wharf, and he whiled away an hour or two in making a study of the quaint peculiarities of the former. Mr. Murphy being of a sociable disposition was by no means loath to respond to his advances. Macer "treated" him in the bar to a sherry-cobbler that filled his soul with a mellow tide of kindliness towards his new acquaintance, and loosened the strings of his nimble tongue. "Well! well!" he said, laying down the tumbler with lingering fondness, when he had drained the last drop of the golden fluid, "it's a mighty quare counthry this Kenady, any ways. It's mighty tough pickin' a cobbler 'ud be in ould Oireland."

Mike grinned approvingly at the empty tumbler, and Macer ordered a second, which Mr. Murphy drank with infinite gusto, watched curiously by his companion, who stroked his long jetty beard softly with his slender brown fingers.

"Cities is great places intirely," said Mike with a gentle sigh of pleasure as for the second time he set down the empty vessel; "it's not the likes of that I'd be afther tastin' in the gay spot I've just shewed the back sames ov me stockins to. Bedad it isn't!"

"You've been travelling through the back settlements, I suppose," said Macer, smiling.

"Oh, begorra, not a wan!" replied Mike vivaciously, "unless ye call bullfrogs lowin' like dacent, respectable cows, and woods as tangly as a tow-wig, settlements! Not to make minshun ov muskitties that had the grip ov a bull-dog, the rapscallions. And the sight ov a strange face as rare as a four-laved clover in a peat-bog!"

"You're not fond of solitude, then," said Macer with one of his slow smiles.

"Faix I'm not," responded Mr. Murphy decidedly. "If it hadn't been that Molley McCarthy giv' me the hard word thirty years come next Michaelmas, an' I picked up wid the ould masther, glory be his bed! and stuck by him ever since, by rayson ov the likin' I had for him an' his, I'd have took a short stick in me hand an' gone to Australy where the very wool ov the shape is gilded, or close upon it."

"Surely you haven't been thirty years in the backwoods of Canada?" asked Macer curiously

"No, it'll be nineteen next summer since the ould gintleman berried his purty wife, an' took Miss Drosia, the dawny craythur, not two months old, up among them snakes an' Injuns, an' sorry he wor for that same on his death-bed, the poor ould gintleman." Mike heaved a tributary sigh to the memory of his master.

"Is he dead then?" inquired Macer filling his meerschaum carefully. He was a very epicure in his smoking, and had a scientific method based on profound knowledge of the subject, of even performing that simple operation.

"As a dure nail," said Mike with a melancholy shake of his head; "bedad he only held out long enough after them spalpeens made off wid Miss Drosia to write to Captain Frazer's father (that's the young gintleman ye seed on the wharf this mornin') an' send him his will. Oh! it'ud have been a light in his eyes if he'd seen Miss Drosia an' Winona back safe an' sound out ov the durty paws ov them that took the colleen. The cowardly spalpeens!"

"Those are the young ladies above stairs, I presume?" said Macer, looking largely interested in the little family history Mike was treating him to. "May I ask how, and under what circumstances they were abducted, such an unusual occurrence at this time of the world, you know!"

Mike suddenly remembered that Archie had entreated him to preserve a strict silence as to the events of the last few months, and he felt a thrill of something like dismay as he reflected that he had been confiding everything to what he would have termed a "black stranger." To get out of the conversation as gracefully and speedily as possible was now his object. His eye fell on the clock and he started melodramatically.

"Now look at that!" he exclaimed. "Och, won't Miss Drosia be in a way! There it's goin' five, and it's meself that promised to do an arrand for her at four! Faix, I wouldn't be afther vexin' the poor, lovely colleen for the wide wurruld!"

"I suppose they are proceeding to Captain Frazer's home?" said Macer strolling beside Mike to the door, a track of pale blue smoke wreathing around and behind him as he puffed at his meerschaum.

"Where else 'ud they be goin'?" said Mike a little shortly, "relations ain't as thick as pine-stumps for Miss Drosia in this counthry. More betoken there's raysons that she should be taken good care ov, with the sight ov money the ould Colonel had hoarded for her."

Macer saw an acquaintance in the street, and as Mike turned up the corridor, he went out into the sunlight with the intention of joining him, but paused outside the hotel door and fell into a reverie instead. His thoughts lent no expression of themselves to his imperturbable countenance, but he was so utterly lost to the outside world in their hidden labyrinths that Spooner came up and addressed him twice by his name before, with a start, he emerged from his reverie.

At present Spooner's object in this life was the attainment of a decent skill in billiards, from which art a stern fate, leagued with a relentless grandmother and the authorities at Sandhurst,[1] had hitherto debarred him; but now he was free, grandmother and tutors were of the shadowy past, and during the pauses of his studies of the science of the warrior, he played billiards, talked billiards and dreamt billiards. His mission now was to secure Macer for a game, but Macer was not in the humor.

"My dear fellow," he said with benign patronage, while Spooner sucked his cane, and skirmished with his eye-glass, "it's very natural at your time of life to be eager in the pursuit of pleasure, flies she in the shape of billiards or beauty. Men at my years require pleasure to come to them. *Voilà tout!*"[2]

"It's not such a deuce of a journey to the billiard-room," grumbled Spooner, trying to stare at a pretty nurse-maid through the eye-glass, and giving himself something of the appearance of a weak-minded Cyclops with a glass eye in the effort, "and you play such a jolly good game." Spooner had certainly a right to know, as his "riches made to themselves wings,"[3] and took flight with undeviating regularity towards the pockets of Macer, when the latter was his antagonist. Macer was not to be moved.

"Can't positively," he said laughing in his low, velvety tones. "Thanks though for your compliment." He went back into the hotel, and ascended to his own eyrie. He flung himself on a chair by the window, and then got up again and locked the door. The level sunlight was rolling through the curtains, and he paced up and down the golden track it made along the carpet until it faded into dusk, into deeper blackness, and then after a brief interval reappeared in a wave of spectral silver from the crescent moon, jewelling the purple vault. Be a man never so much a cynic, be his heart and his conscience alike torpid, there are moments when his eyes turn back on his soul, when something that is not of himself lays an iron hand on his mental volition, and he is compelled to

---

[1] Located southwest of London, Sandhurst is the home of the British Royal Military Academy.

[2] That's all!

[3] See Proverbs 23.5: "Wilt thou set thine eyes upon that which is not? For riches certainly make themselves wings; They fly away as an eagle toward heaven."

"see himself."[1] To dig the skeletons of past deeds of wickedness from the charnel house of his memory, to follow the consequences of each evil deed with a gaze that for a moment sees and understands the widening circles of baleful influence that have emanated from each and every act that has stained his soul. To stand for the brief moment convicted before himself and the awful Unseen, the reality of whose being is for that instant of time as undisputed by his nimble cynicism as his own individuality. The mood fades and leaves no influence behind. It awakes neither heart nor conscience, and is looked back upon with a smile of incredulity that ever it could have existed.

Whatever Macer's previous history might have been, it was evident that memory was busy with him to-night. He disregarded the various summonses to meals, and his footsteps echoed monotonously as he paced to and fro across the narrow limits of his apartment; his dark eyes flashing sombrely through the gloom, and his arms folded across his massive chest. The moon sank, and ghostly shadows filled the room. The night reached its black arms, bejewelled with stars, across the city, and silence fell upon the house and street. Then the dewy breath of morning stole freshly through the open window. The sun sparkled on the hoar-frost that lay like diamond dust on the streets and bare boughs of the trees. Railway whistles shrieked goblin-like, and factory bells rang clearly calling the mighty army of workers to their toil at glowing furnace or whirring lathe. Two little girls on shaggy Lower Canadian ponies, cantered swiftly past for an early "constitutional," their cheeks crimson with the bracing air through which they rode.

The hotel awoke to life, and after breakfasting in Androsia's sitting-room, Archie escorted the two girls to a cab waiting at the door to convey them to the steamer. Mike was already on the box smoking sedately at a short villainously black clay pipe that was Mr. Murphy's chiefest treasure.

Androsia was more than usually silent. There was something in Captain Frazer's manner that puzzled and confused her beyond expression, yet that certainly did not displease her. What could be more courtly and tender than his care of her and Winona? was there word, look, or act that she could wish altered? and yet his presence this morning tied

---

[1] Possibly an allusion to Robert Burns's "To a Louse" (1786): "O wad some Pow'r the giftie gie us / To see oursels as others see us!" (43–44).

her tongue in chains of silence. What was altered, was he kinder now than he had heretofore been? That was impossible. She could only feel that there had suddenly stolen some great change over him. Winona's sombre eyes, of late full of unfathomable and infinite meaning, and a fire that smouldered ready to burst into devouring flame, took cognizance of the alteration. In the lore of the feelings this dusk browed Indian girl's soul was wise, and while Androsia only felt the change, she saw and comprehended. For the first time during their knowledge of each other, Archie saw a smile of grave pleasure on her lofty face. Regarding Androsia with a fervent and devoted tenderness, Winona seemed particularly tenacious where she was concerned, and in her grave, meditative way had made a quiet study of Captain Frazer during the time they had been thrown together. That he had loved her foster-sister from the first, she had at once divined, but there had been an air of uneasiness and constraint marking his intercourse with Androsia that had rendered her doubly watchful of him. The change that the last few hours had produced in him was simply that this constraint had disappeared from his manner. Of course neither she nor Androsia knew of his engagement to Cecil and its, to him, fortunate termination, which had left him free to look in Androsia's eyes without trembling lest she should guess his secret, free to dream that she might yet be his!

Winona stood gazing listlessly at a flight of snowy pigeons circling in the pale blue of the morning sky, while Archie placed Androsia in the cab. They flew over the hotel roof fluttering and whirring, and she turned and looked up at them with a longing, mournful gaze such as he of the olden time[1] might have worn, when to the sounding of his harp rose up the cry, "O, that I had wings like a dove, for then would I flee away and be at rest."[2] The gleaming wings disappeared, and letting her listless glance wander over the front of the building, she was about to turn away when her gaze became suddenly rivetted on an upper window that stood open, with the curtains fluttering out and flapping on the wind.

"Come, Winona," called out Mike, in a mild roar, "don't ye persave that it's twist the Captain has spoke to ye to get into the keb."

---

[1] The Old Testament hero David, who is represented as a harpist and as the composer of many of the Psalms.

[2] See Psalms 55.6: "And I said, Oh that I had wings like a dove! For then would I fly away, and be at rest."

Winona turned round, and with a hasty movement drew the heavy folds of her veil over her face.

Without touching Archie's extended hand she sprang into the cab, and as it whirled from the door she flung herself back into her corner and gave herself up to one of those dumb moods which of late distinguished her.

Archie was so fully occupied in watching the play of Androsia's features and listening to her naive remarks and exclamations of fresh delight at every object they passed on their way to the wharf, that he never once thought of Winona. Indeed, he had become so accustomed to her wayward moods that had he noticed her present silence he would not have given it a second thought.

It was Winona's own wish to assume the every day garb of the nineteenth century, and it was marvellous with what ready grace she adapted herself to her new surroundings.

In her brighter moods one could have fancied her an embodiment of Longfellow's ideal Indian maiden, the lovely Minnehaha;[1] but in her frequent hours of gloom and abstraction, she was terrible, ominous and inexplicable. Her intense love of Androsia and the frightful perils she had risked for her, pleaded strongly in her behalf with Archie; but he could seldom look at her without remembering with a faint thrill the fire-lit vision of the terrible-eyed woman standing on Joe Harty's hearth, with the reeking scalp clutched in her extended hand.

It was an anomaly that he could not comprehend that this wild, dusky child of the woods should at once evince so decided a determination to exchange the unquestioned freedom of her former life for the restraints of civilization, and he could not help speculating curiously as to her future fate, dowered as she was with a dusky beauty that was almost marvellous.

That Androsia should at once feel at home in her new position was no matter of wonder; in her case it was simply a resumption of the habits of her people; but Winona was issuing from the dark recesses of many ages of custom and superstition, laying prostrate at her feet the traditions of her savage ancestors.

---

[1] "Laughing Water," the wife of Hiawatha; see Longfellow, *The Song of Hiawatha* (1855) X.88, and "Vocabulary" 664.

[PART 6—15 FEBRUARY 1873]

CHAPTER XV

Androsia's Welcome

Androsia's heart quivered with fear and uncertainty as she learned from Archie that a few hours would introduce her to the home in which she was to find her dwelling-place. She knew absolutely nothing of what she was to meet on the threshold of her new life, and she clung to Winona as though she dreaded being separated from her familiar presence even for a moment; but her foster-sister was plunged into one of her dark reveries, and sat dumbly on the deck of the steamer, her dusky eyes looking straight forward, her slender hands clasped rigidly on her lap, not in the idle folding that denotes a pleasant rearing of *Châteaux en Espagne*, but the fingers interlaced like bands of steel, the muscles tense and rigid.

Archie was considerably annoyed at this arrangement, for as Androsia would not leave Winona, and Winona would not leave the deck, both girls were exposed to a sharp, biting wind, with the first breath of winter in it, that came whistling amongst the Islands, brown, bare and melancholy under the low hanging sky of a dull grey. Androsia too had developed a sudden shyness of him that nearly drove him wild, and sent him to pacing the upper deck, trying to find soothing in a cigar. He felt a little fearful that he had betrayed his secret, and had frightened her into this sudden timidity, and he made many resolves to be extremely careful for the future. Ah, that lovely mirage, the future! which we see veiled in delightful mists across the arid sands of the present; but never reach, or haply reaching, find barren rocks and tracts as hard and dewless as bricks of old Egypt.

Mike made himself very happy in the company of the Steward in whom he had discovered a fellow Emerald-Islander, and in that gentleman's private den amongst festoons of tea-cups that looked like a grove of crockery they exchanged reminiscences of the "ould counthry," over tumblers of some compound that at least was not tea.

There were few passengers on board, and those were of a class not likely to interest themselves in the little group on the fore-deck, and so the two girls were undisturbed save when Archie descended to inquire were they cold! or hungry! or tired? which he did on an average every ten minutes, and was always answered in low negatives by Androsia; Winona dumb as some figure of bronze, neither heeding nor answering him. She kept her arm closely clasped round Androsia, yet she did not speak even to her, but sat in the prow of the vessel looking forward, her brows contracted into a frown, her lips tightened over her clenched teeth, her long, black hair, which she had not yet learned the art of coiffuring properly, streaming over her in long masses of lustreless gloom.

The sun was declining when the steamer stopped at the wharf of the pretty little village near which lay Captain Frazer's home, and Archie's eyes sparkled as he observed his father's pretty little "Democrat"[1] with its pair of spirited Lower Canadian ponies, drawn up near the platform. An erect little figure, with a great mass of yellow hair dashed about it by the frolicsome wind, and the jauntiest velvet cap on its bright head, held the reins of the lively ponies in slender gauntleted hands, that were firm at their task, and this little form waved its hand to Archie as he leant smiling over the side of the vessel. He pointed her out to Androsia.

"That's my mad cap sister Sidney," he said; "look at her, Miss Howard, I sincerely hope"—what he hoped was left unsaid on account of an interruption in the voice of Mr. Murphy, who after an affectionate parting with his friend the Steward, had issued from the shade of the crockery grove.

"Miss Drosia, asthore," said Mike, indicating Sid and her restless steeds, with affectionate interest, "that same's the purty little lady, I tould ye of. Look well at her, honey, an' see if ye like her, for there's much in what's done by the first peep ov the eye."

Mike was sincerely desirous that Androsia should be at once prepossessed in favor of her new friends, and while she looked shyly at Sidney, he took off the coon-skin cap by the tail and executed a bow that was more remarkable for its profundity than grace. Sidney laughed and waved her whip in answer, and for the first time a faint smile grew in Androsia's eyes as she watched the young girl. She turned to Winona who leant in an attitude of singular grace against the railing watching the scene with something that was half pleasure and half pain in her fine eyes.

---

[1] A four-wheeled cart with seats one behind the other, usually drawn by two horses, in common use in the United States and Canada in the later nineteenth century.

"She looks like the sunlight on a dancing stream, my sister," said Androsia, speaking in the Indian tongue, which fell like softly sonorous music from her lips.

"My sister speaks the thing that is," responded Winona, taking Androsia's hand in hers, "she will be happy with these strange faces before another moon has passed."

"Divil a doubt ov it," remarked Mike who, though he understood the language of the red man, scorned to speak it, "an' moreover, an' no offense meant, it's nathural that she'd take to them as wears the same colored skin as her own purty self."

"You are right," said Winona in English, which she spoke better than did Androsia, and her face was full of a tremulous shadow nearly akin to tears, but yet with an inner light of gladness shining through it. She drew Androsia's arm closely to her side, and the next moment the party had landed.

Sidney received Archie with a joyous outburst, and for a few minutes had neither ears nor eyes for his companions.

"You dear old boy," she exclaimed, "I scandalized the whole family by insisting on coming for you myself, so that I might have the first glimpse, and there wasn't room for Spinks, I drove Prance and Friskey down myself. How well you're looking. Oh what a fright we were in about you when we heard of your being shot. Archie dear, I'm so, so glad to see you," and two bright tears rolled slowly down Sid's face, that was all dimpled with quivering smiles and glowing with excitement.

Archie, despite the loungers and loafers on the wharf, caught her in a warm embrace as she leant down to him from the vehicle, and then directed her attention to Androsia and Winona. Winona had pulled her heavy veil down, and stood a little apart wrapped in her black mantle, but Androsia was looking very earnestly at Sid, and as the latter turned towards her, she put out her hand and laid it in the young girl's with a smile that was singularly expressive.

"I'm very glad to see you, Miss Howard," said Sid much taken by the sweet face, framed in its short bronze curls, "and so will they all at home be. Is that your friend?"

It never entered Sidney's head to say "your maid," of the majestic, shrouded form standing with such a haughty poise of the slender figure a little apart.

"My sister Winona," explained Androsia, simply. Sidney looked speculatively at Winona, and extended her hand which the other just touched. Deeply veiled as she was, Sidney recoiled a little before the eyes that burned out on her from behind the gloom of the heavy crêpe; but her attention was at this moment called to Mike, and while Archie placed Androsia in the vehicle, she was so engaged talking to Mr. Murphy that she did not observe how intently the Indian girl was scrutinizing her every glance and movement. Winona was endeavoring to infer from this first specimen of those with whom Androsia's lot was to be cast, what chances of happiness the lonely girl would have.

★ ★ ★ ★ ★ ★

"Girls," said Sid, "what do you think of 'Miss Drosia' and her dusky familiar?"

Sidney was seated on the hearth-rug before a blazing fire, her arms embracing her knees on which her dimpled chin rested. Dolly, like one of Correggio's Angels,[1] in a flowing white peignoir, was brushing her blonde hair, as though it were some religious exercise, and Olla, with her eyes shaded by her little, brown hand, was gazing into the glowing caverns of the fire.

"I don't know, I'm sure, dear," said Dolly, "she doesn't do her back hair nicely at all."

"They seem beautiful and interesting, though in widely different ways," said Olla, gently, "and I think Androsia will rapidly acquire more than common style and grace. Winona, of course, is simply unique."

"And it's meself is glad of that same, as Mike would say," laughed Sid. "Her eyes blaze in the dark like furnaces and she walks about with that long, silent, shadowy step that one reads of in novels, and when she sits thinking she shows her white teeth like a wolf."

"I thought she was drowned or something," said Dolly, vaguely. "Mike said she was, you know."

"We shall hear her adventures to-morrow; I suppose," remarked Sid, "it will be as good, no, a great deal better than a novel. Won't it, Olla?"

"Perhaps so," said Olla; "she looks as though she had suffered a great deal both mentally and physically."

"Do you know what I think," continued Sid, leaning her head back

---

[1] Antonio Allegri Correggio (1489–1534) was an Italian painter. His angels, as seen in paintings such as "Madonna with St. George" and "Adoration of the Shepherds," are typically blond, cherubic, and adoring children protectively swathed in diaphanous cloth. The same simile is subsequently applied to Cecil Bertrand, p. 227.

on her elder sister's knee, who sat in a dimity covered arm-chair behind her. "I think it's a thousand pities that Archie should be engaged to Cecil Bertrand, when it would be so much nicer for him to marry Androsia and get so much money, and I know Cecil doesn't care for him one bit. She as much as said so once. I wish Archie were free. There Ol! you nearly jerked my head off!"

Olla had risen suddenly and gone over to the toilette table, where she was apparently searching for something. She came back to the fire presently with a pink letter smelling of heliotrope in her hand, but she did not resume her seat, and stood leaning against the mantle-piece where her face was a little in the shadow.

"I am not betraying confidence," she said, "when I tell you that Archie is free to do as he likes. Cecil has given him up."

Sid sprang to her feet; and even Dolly let her brush fall, and turned a face of surprise on Olla.

"Olla," demanded Sid, "was that what grieved you so much the other day in Cecil's letter?"

"I will read it for you," replied Olla, evasively, "at least the passage that concerns Archie, listen: 'Mr. Denville was at the ball, and he was so attentive and delightful! What lovely eyes he has, and his moustache is just beautiful, and he waltzes so well, and that brings me to a little secret I have to tell you. Theodore, I mean Mr. Denville, insisted on taking me into the conservatory after supper, and there he asked me something, and I said, "yes," and you know what that means, my dear. I am awfully sorry for poor Archie, but I've been examining my heart and find I really don't love him the least bit. I hope he won't be worried and go about saying I jilted him for a richer man, for I'm sure there never was a less mercenary little thing than I am. I couldn't help Theodore being rich, could I? I think love in a cottage[1] would be just perfectly lovely, but one can't help one's heart, you know, love.'"

"Her heart!" said Sid, and was silent.

Olla continued, "'I'm sure you'll try and make everything pleasant, won't you, dear? for Denville is so particular that there's no knowing

---

[1] A familiar saying, frequently treated ironically in nineteenth-century literature, signifying "marriage for love without sufficient means to maintain one's social status" (Ivor H. Evans, ed., *Brewer's Dictionary of Phrase and Fable*, 14th ed. [New York: Harper & Row, 1989] 680). The phrase also appears in Eliza Lynn Linton's essay "The Girl of the Period" and the anonymous article "Fast Young Ladies," both included in Appendix A.

what might happen if he heard I treated Captain Frazer badly. I'm awfully done up after the excitement of last night, and so with love to darling Dolly and Sid, I am your own devoted, Cecil Bertrand.'"

"Olla," said Sid, solemnly, "the worst I can wish Theodore Denville, is that she won't jilt him if she has been telling the truth."

"Why should you suspect the reverse?" said Olla, a little eagerly, "tell me, dear."

"I'm not a goose, thank goodness," retorted Sid, her blue eyes flashing whole volumes of determination, "and if I don't find out Miss Cecil's tricks and expose her stories, I'll hide my head in the sand like an ostrich, and never look any one in the face again. Olla! how can you be so silly?"

"What do you mean, little one?" said Olla, a faint blush stealing into her cheeks, while her fingers nervously twisted the letter she still held, and her little foot tapped the carpet. Dolly, with an air of high-souled melancholy, was braiding her massive locks in glimmering gold about her Psyche head,[1] vaguely conscious that Archie would probably be very miserable, and lamenting over it in her own fashion. Her home affections were strong, if nature had denied her more than a very slender modicum of intellect.

"Oh, you, goose," cried Sid, flinging her arms round Olla, and laying her rosy cheek against her sister's, "didn't the man love you, and what could make him turn from you to her, and when he knew that she was engaged to Archie? Oh, wait and see what you shall see!"

"Listen to me, Sid," said Olla, tremulously, "you must promise me not to interfere in any way with this affair. Probably we were mistaken, and you know he never absolutely said anything of that kind to me. Promise me, Sid."

"I won't, Olla," replied Sid, resolutely, "I am not likely to have a chance, but if I should I'll try and expose that monkey, if it were only for the good of society!"

"Sidney, dear, you don't know so much of the world as I do; Mr. Denville was perfectly at liberty to change his mind." Her voice quivered a little, but she smiled across at Dolly, who got up and glided to her.

"I'm so glad you don't care, dear," she said, laying her beautiful arm round Olla's neck; "and after all, he wore such hideous neck-ties! Quite

---

[1] A maiden beloved by Cupid in Roman mythology, Psyche is identified with the soul and has been much depicted in art.

frightful, Olla dear," and Dolly leant over Olla like some guardian angel, sent to comfort and console, her pensive eyes humid, a look of melancholy retrospect on her pure face as she thought of the neck-ties.

The touch about Theodore Denville's depraved taste in neck-ties came just at the right moment, for despite herself, Olla was quivering through all her being with suppressed emotion. Dolly's simple remark turned the tide, and in a moment she had subdued the rising grief that she would not have had mortal eye look upon. Sidney, however, was not deceived, and though she said no more, her resolve deepened and strengthened to come at the secret of Denville's sudden change.

"There's one comfort," she said, "Archie doesn't seem to be much grieved. Has he told you anything about it yet, Olla?"

"No," answered Olla, thoughtfully; "but he seems quite cheerful. I daresay he will mention it in time."

Sidney and Dolly were soon asleep in the white curtained beds at the other side of the room, but for hours Olla sat beside the dying fire thinking and suffering, and making her grief familiar to herself. She heard the clock strike two before she prepared to seek her couch, and she roused herself to find her limbs stiff with cold, and to hear a dull rain beating drearily against the windows.

The house was quiet as the grave, but her long vigil had left the girl in a state of trembling nervousness. No matter how mentally and physically courageous one is, there are times that a black horror of we know not what seizes us, and we rise and flee from the spot we are in, although the sunlight may be pouring its cheerful tide over us. A sudden terror, inexplicable and fearful, of solitude, seizes us, and we rush to seek the presence of our kind, to laugh and wonder at our sudden fear of nothing.

The regular breathing of the sleepers made the loneliness more intolerable, and with hearing strained to the utmost, as though expectant of some ghostly sound to break the stillness, Olla, hastily and shivering, prepared to seek her couch.

It seemed to her as though through the rain there came faint sounds, rather suggestions of noise than the thing itself, and sitting on the side of her bed, she listened intently. If any there had been, it was not repeated, and convincing herself that she had been mistaken, she crept into bed, and worn out with emotion and fatigue, was soon asleep.

In the meantime a very different scene was taking place in a distant part of the house.

CHAPTER XVI

Winona's Departure

The silvery chime of the drawing-room clock rang through the silent house, dropping one mellow peal through the quiet. The dismal sound of quiet, monotonous rain beating against the windows and dripping from the eaves and verandas, and the faint rustling of the bare branches were the only sounds audible after the prolonged reverberation of the sounding hour had died away. A faint, ghostly light from the lobby windows stole greyly in, for there was a moon, though hidden by a pall of sombre clouds. The illumination was, however, sufficient to guide Winona, who, a few moments after the hour had struck, softly opened the door of her apartment, and after listening intently, emerged from the room, closing the door softly behind her. Like a black shadow in the uncertain light, she glided along the narrow passage and laid her hand softly on the door of the chamber occupied by Androsia, and which adjoined her own.

She turned it softly, and pushing the door slightly open, peered in through the gloom, and, satisfied that Androsia was buried in profound sleep, glided into the apartment. The window curtains were not closed, and the room was full of a shadowy light, by which every object was dimly visible.

Closing the door behind her, the Indian girl glided to the bedside of her foster-sister, which stood directly in the light falling across the floor from the window, and stood motionless, gazing down upon the sleeper, whose face was plainly discernible. Winona was completely dressed in her European costume, and she carried on her arm a long mantle and a hat with a veil attached to it. Her long hair fell unbound nearly to her knees, and the spectral light fell weirdly on her dusky face and burning eyes.

For nearly half an hour she stood motionless, gazing down at the lovely face smiling in sleep, the rosy lips parted and showing the dainty white teeth, and the mass of short curls streaming out over the pillow. The face expressed perfect happiness and repose; and as Winona looked a lofty satisfaction stole over her dark face. She knew that Androsia was happy, and her residence of a few days under the roof of her foster-sister's guardian had convinced her that she need not fear for the continuance and growth of Androsia's pleasure and content. Had it been otherwise she would almost have persuaded herself to relinquish her present design in order to keep watch and ward over one whom she was about taking a last farewell of. She knew as she stood in the melancholy midnight gloom that she would never look upon her face again in this world; and her religion did not teach her to hope for a meeting with a daughter of the pale-faces in a future state. She might look back, but it was not given her to look forward in this case. Androsia's life and hers had been so closely interwoven that an earthly future that did not hold the girl for her was simply a hideous, blank, darkness, from which her soul recoiled, but which contained in its black bosom one mighty thing that was powerful enough to lure her on her present path, one lurid fire that lightened with its burning tide the horrid blackness.

She felt that the success she hungered for in her present plans would place an insurmountable barrier between herself and the innocent girl she loved, but she was content that it should be so. Androsia's life would be no loveless blank now, of that she felt assured, for she had read Archie's heart with keen eyes and found him worthy, and she knew that Androsia loved him.

It was not to engage in a mental struggle with herself that she now sought Androsia's side. Her plans were fixed; the conflict with herself was over, and it was merely to satisfy her lonely soul with a last glance at the sleeping face that she had come.

"I must leave her a gift to remember Winona by," she muttered softly, and gliding to a little stand in the window she lifted from it a pair of scissors, and in a couple of moments her magnificent hair lay in a black mass at her feet. She lifted it, and without a change of countenance, tore a strip from the crêpe veil attached to the hat she carried, and tying it round the heavy raven tresses laid them on the white quilt beside her foster-sister. Then she lifted one of the sleeping girl's bright curls, and cautiously severing it from her head, thrust it into her bosom. Her countenance during all this never varied by so much as the quiver of an eyelid. She was showing all the haughty stoicism of her race.

She leant closely over Androsia as though to embrace her, but the girl stirred slightly and she slipped back into the shadow, and waited until she had sunken again into profound slumber.

The wind was rising, sobbing in low dismal wailings round the house, and the intense chill that precedes dawn increased the coldness of the atmosphere.

With a footstep as noiseless as thistle-down Winona stole from the room without venturing a second time to approach the bed. As she closed the door her footsteps faltered for a second, and her hand lingered on the handle, as though at the last moment her resolution was giving way, but in a moment she had risen triumphant over the passing weakness, and shutting the door softly stole down the passage.

At the head of the stairs she paused and looked over the balustrade into the hall beneath. It was empty and ghostly in the deadened light that forced itself through the stained glass that surrounded the hall door, and flitting down the stairs that barely creaked under her feet, Winona reached the large square hall and paused for a second glancing into the drawing-room, the door of which stood open.

The Venetian blinds were closed; but she knew where to lay her hand on what she wanted, and disappearing into the intense gloom of the room, she reappeared almost instantly with something that glittered bluely in the uncertain light of the hall, in her hand. She thrust it into the bosom of her dress and reascended the stairs as noiselessly as she had descended, gaining her own chamber without having disturbed any of the sleeping household. Once in its shelter she locked and bolted the door, and approaching the window, raised the sash cautiously. The window opened on the roof of a side veranda, and without a moment's hesitation she sprang out into the driving rain, and with the agility of a panther slipped down the lattice-work and reached the soaked ground as easily as she would have run along a level path. She crept cautiously under the dripping trees, until she found herself on the front lawn, and then for a moment she paused and looked steadily back at the dark outlines of the house she was leaving, taking care to remain under the dark shadows of the maples that were rattling their skeleton arms in the sobbing wind, lest any one should chance to look from the windows and catch a glimpse of the desolate figure standing in the drifting rain.

The wind, in its rising strength, had torn the sullen clouds into great rifts, edged with silver by the still hidden moon, and as she stood looking back, like a shining bark parting from a clinging mist, the moon rode suddenly into a narrow space of star-gemmed blue, and threw a lovely, but melancholy, light over the whole scene. It paled, faded, and died, as the fleecy edges of a hurrying bank of clouds received her, and all was darker than before.

Neither moon or stars or the eye of man looked on Winona, as, with a mute gesture of farewell, she turned and fled into the black shadows of the pine-grove, where the white angel guarded with folded pinions the memorial stone of Colonel Howard and the unfortunate Farmer.

For a few moments she paused, looking earnestly at the face gleaming whitely on her from the darkness. It was a delicate and spiritual likeness of him who had won all the love of her wild heart, and vowed her his in return. It was one of the strangest anomalies of this strange nature that, though Farmer had turned from her dusky beauty to win and wear,[1] if possible, her foster-sister, that though her feelings towards him had changed to unfathomable hate, unquenched even by his death, her love for Androsia had never for an instant wavered in its strength and fidelity. Androsia was to her a purer, higher, brighter self. Part of Androsia's seemingly unfounded dislike of the husband chosen for her by her father was owing to a vague consciousness of the hidden treachery of his conduct towards Winona, who, however, had disdained to lay bare the cruel wound to any human eye. She could suffer this as, in the same way, she would have chaunted her own death-song at the stake, and smiled defiance as the flames licked her tender skin; but a woman can feel where she cannot plainly see, and Androsia's nature was singularly sympathetic.

The great drops fell through the pines to the sodden ground in a ceaseless patter, and a stronger wind began to sway their dark crests. With the step of her race, long, panther-like and noiseless, Winona glided to the river's edge, and disappeared among the darkness. A desolate phantom-like form, flitting into the mysterious mists that rose from the mighty stream that flowed, silent in its vastness, through leagues of shadows, like some gigantic vision of a solemn and inexplicable dream.

It was Archie's last morning at home, and the household was early astir in order that he might catch the early train for Toronto at the next town, which we will call Scranton.

It was intensely cold, with icicles half-a-yard long hanging, like crystal spears in an enchanted armory, from the eaves, and the trees glistening in a coat of ice like warriors arrayed in mail of diamonds. The sun was brilliant, and the sky that unapproachable blue seen alone in American skies, especially during the winter.

A great fire of dry beech and maple roared on the hearth of the

---

[1] To obtain and possess, especially as one's wife.

breakfast room, for winter was truly laying his icy claw on the land, and Mrs. Frazer, with a look of gravity that her face of late had constantly worn, was making breakfast. The table gleamed in the sunlight and firelight with heavy, old-fashioned silver, and the flower-stands were banks of bloom and perfume. Brown-eyed Olla, serene and gracious, like Werther's Charlotte, was cutting bread and butter,[1] and Dolly was looking out of the window, twisting her white fingers in the cord of her white morning-dress. Sidney, like a household Flora, was busy amongst the plants, her lovely head rising from the flowers radiant in the glancing sunlight.

Archie was in the library with his father, and Androsia and Winona had not yet appeared.

They were unusually silent, and for once Sid forgot to sing at her fragrant task, which, I must confess, was the only household industry that ever threw its chains round her.

"Ah, here's Androsia, mamma," she said, as the door opened and Miss Howard came in, looking anxiously round the apartment as she paused on the threshold. Her tall, willowy figure showed to great advantage in her new style of dress, and she had not lost that shy grace that had distinguished her always. Her color varied as she looked from one to another.

"Where is Winona?" she said abruptly. "See what I found on my bed this morning! Where is Winona?" There was a ring of alarm in her voice, and the color came and went like a flame blown by the wind. The sunlight flashed in her deep eyes as they glanced from one to the other of the group.

Sid came from amongst the flowers and Dolly turned from the window.

"My dear," said Mrs. Frazer, turning very pale, "what is that, and what do you mean?" She laid her hand on the table as though to steady herself, and looked at Androsia with some underlying terror in her eyes. Androsia's eyes, shining and dilated, turned and held hers.

---

[1] In Johann Wolfgang von Goethe's novel *The Sufferings of Young Werther* (1774), the young woman with whom the protagonist falls in love is first seen among a group of children, "holding a loaf of dark bread, cutting for each of the little ones about her a slice in proportion to his age and appetite …" (trans. Harry Steinhauer [New York: W.W. Norton, 1970] 13); see the first stanza of William Makepeace Thackeray's burlesque, "Sorrows of Werther," cited in Steinhauer's "Afterword" 107:

> Werther had a love for Charlotte,
> Such as words could never utter,
> Would you know how first he met her?
> She was cutting bread and butter.

She tried to speak, but the cords of her tongue seemed stiffened, and she stood looking dumbly at Mrs. Frazer.

Olla went to her and drew her into the room. She quietly opened her clenched hand, and took from it the object that had drawn Mrs. Frazer's attention.

"Mamma," she said, in a tone of surprise and alarm, "what can this mean? This is a mass of long black hair tied with a torn piece of crêpe."

"I think I can guess what it means," ejaculated Sidney. "Winona's gone! She was like a caged creature while she was here."

Her words electrified Androsia. Her temples crimsoned. Her eyes became dark and stormy.

"Winona gone!" she said with superb disdain. "No. Sidney speaks foolishness. Why should Winona leave her sister? She is abroad, but she will return."

Even as she spoke, the inborn knowledge that her words were merely words broke her voice into a low wail of terror. She slipped on her knees, and pressed the raven tresses of Winona convulsively to her heart. Then she sprang to her feet and rushed to the door, a new idea lending her a momentary hope.

"He will find her for me," she cried, with her hand on the door. Already she had learned to turn to Archie in her trouble.

Mrs. Frazer detained her with a hand that trembled.

"My child," she said, "you have not told us what is really the matter. Perhaps you are alarming yourself needlessly."

"Winona is gone," replied Androsia, shaking off the slender hand. "I must find her!"

Mrs. Frazer looked imploringly at her eldest daughter, and in a moment Olla's round arm was clasped firmly round the waist of the terrified and excited creature.

"Listen to me, dear," she said, calming her at once by her magnetic touch and glance, "if Winona is really missing, you know her too well to doubt that she will return to you, you whom she loves so entirely. But it is not certain that she is gone. What makes you think that she is not out for a ramble?"

Tears, like great diamonds were pouring silently down Androsia's face. She looked in Olla's face and shook her head.

"I feel it," she answered in a tone of perfect conviction. "She left me this that she might dwell in my heart, when I should see her no more."

Sidney was much distressed at Androsia's grief, and Dolly looked on with eyes like humid violets.

Mrs. Frazer had quietly left the apartment, signing to Olla to detain Androsia. She crossed the hall quickly and entered the library, closing the door behind her.

Captain Frazer and Archie were seated at a small table, conversing with faces of considerable thoughtfulness. The former looked up quickly as his wife entered. Her eyes were fixed on him with an expression of deep tenderness and holy pity, and he was not slow to read something unusual in their glance. Archie rose from his chair as his mother entered and came gaily up to her, but his face changed as he looked down into hers. She clasped her fingers round his strong hand but gazed past him at her husband, whose rugged face looked old and care-worn in the morning light. Startled too as his eyes read hers. His lips moved as though to speak and he leant forward, his muscular hands grasping the arms of his invalid chair.

"It is as we dreaded, Richard," she said, quickly, and keeping one hand on the door as though to prevent intrusion, "Winona is gone!"

Had a thunderbolt fallen at the feet of the old officer, he would not probably have shown the agitation that he now evinced. He bounded in the chair as though he were about to cast aside his infirmity and spring erect, and his dark face changed to an awful ashen hue. Great drops of perspiration rolled down his forehead, and his dark eyes flashed with horror. Inexpressibly surprised and shocked at his appearance, Archie hastened to him, his mother still holding his hand as though the contact gave her strength.

"Open the window!" gasped Captain Frazer, "I am suffocating."

Archie dashed open the window, and the exhilarating, frosty air pouring in, revived the old man almost instantaneously.

"My dear Richard," said his wife in a tone of infinite compassion, laying her hand in his, which closed over it in a tense grasp.

"How do you know, when did it happen?" he said hoarsely, and in a few words Mrs. Frazer explained what had occurred.

Archie listened in amazement, not so much at the event itself, as at its reception by his father, whom he knew as a man reticent though cordial, and possessed of almost complete self-control. The flight of the Indian girl was certainly not a home-sorrow darkening their hearth, and a thing not altogether unanticipated by him. Androsia would grieve, of that there was little doubt, but on the whole he felt a somewhat selfish pleasure in her flight. Androsia would be more his very own.

"Why, father," he said, by way of suggesting something, as a dead pause followed, during which Captain Frazer leant his brow on his hands, and Mrs. Frazer stood looking at him, her hand resting on his shoulder, "she will probably return when she is tired of rambling through the woods. Recollect her race!"

"I do," murmured the old man, looking at him, "and therein lies my grief. Vindictive, revengeful, sure and swift on the trail of an enemy as a sleuth-hound. Relentless as fire or pestilence."

A new light broke on Archie and something of the old untamed spirit of his Celtic ancestors blazed in his eyes.

"By Jove, sir," he exclaimed, starting to his feet, "if you think that is her errand, I wish her every success. If I met him myself I would feel my fingers tingle to choke the life out of his cowardly carcase."

Archie's fine face fired, and his form seemed actually to dilate in his anger. He clenched his strong hands, and stretched out his long arms as though he saw an abhorred enemy standing in his path. His mother ran to him and laid her hand on his mouth.

"Hush," she cried, in a voice shaking with horror. "Oh, hush!"

Captain Frazer turned his ghastly face with a look that sent the blood in cold waves back to his son's heart.

"Do you know that you are calling for the blood of your brother?" he said, in a low intense voice. "Worthy of death he may be, but neither by your hand or will."

"My brother!" echoed Archie, and then there was a dead silence in the room, broken only by the sound of a bird singing in a cage, and the embers dropping on the hearth.

[PART 7—22 FEBRUARY 1873]

CHAPTER XVII

Miss Bertrand's New Conquest

"Glad to see you, I'm sure," said Spooner, kindling into a faint animation, as Archie strode into the reading room of the Rossin, where he was improving his mind with a relishing murder case from one of the English papers. All Spooner's predilections and ideas were of the faintest kind; but by a strange anomaly his soul panted for the most gory and hair-raising literature that could be procured. He would not willingly have injured a kitten, but his heart sang within him when he lighted on such pleasing domestic tragedies as young agricultural gentlemen of acquisitive idiosyncrasies smashing the heads of their venerable bedridden relatives, in order to possess themselves of the sum of "two bob and a tanner,"[1] as one youth playfully mentioned it in his last speech and confession.

Engrossed as Spooner was in a spicy account of the murder of a whole family of promising children by their affectionate father, he flung down the paper and got up to welcome Archie, who was a great favorite with his brother officers. Faint rumors of Archie's adventures in the wilds were rife amongst his set in Toronto, and as it had got about that Cecil Bertrand had "sold" herself about him, he returned to find himself a man of some note. Cecil was reported to be "down no end of a pit" about the affair; and as there were heavy bets pending as to whether she'd "hook" him again or not, his presence was very much required.

"Jove, sir!" said Spooner, shaking hands with him, "I'm glad you're back. It's no end of dull work here just now; nothing but gurls (he was not long from school), and a fellah gets bored to death with the way a fellah's hunted up, you know. Eh? you know."

"I understand," laughed Archie. "How are you all getting on? How's the charming Flora?"

Flora was the pretty presiding deity at the flower shop, about whom Spooner was always in a state of profound despair. He bought stacks of

---

[1] Two shillings and sixpence.

192   ISABELLA VALANCY CRAWFORD

flowers and lingered in the perfumed neighborhood of her bower at all hours, sucking his cane and adoring her through the eye-glass, watched grimly from the opposite side of the road by young Damask, the upholsterer, who was "engaged" to the pretty Flora, and who had been known to utter dark and malign speeches concerning the precarious hold Ensign Spooner would have on this life "if he caught him at it!"

"It's a deuce of a shame, you know, the way she treats a fellah," replied Spooner, sentimentally; "I've nearly ruined myself buying flowers from her. Why, there's not a book at my rooms but is full of them pressed, and I have to keep giving them away to other gurls, and then they fancy a fellah means something, you know. She's the star of my existence; and whatever sinister view my grandmother and aunts may take of me and call me a young fool, which they have not hesitated to do before this, I'll make her the bride of a soldier and carve out a fortune for her on the battle-field; besides which, you know, my uncle Joe allows me a hundred a year. She's a regular downright angel, you know, and I can't live without her."

Spooner's juvenile affection, to do him justice, was an honest sentiment, such as it was, and very ardent for the time.

"Well, with that little affair on your hands, you can't find it so dull," remarked Archie, smiling.

Every one liked Spooner, and with Archie, who had a natural affinity to everything that tended towards the best and purest, the honest, simple-minded boy was a great favorite, and in return, he was the confidant of Spooner's love troubles.

"Oh, well," said Spooner, ruefully, "you see you can't manage to call in more than once a day, and then it gashes one's feelings most awfully to find her most likely behind the oleander bushes talking to that Damask, the red-headed beast! Billiards are all very well, but they don't seem much when your existence is a howling wilderness, only inhabited by a grandmother and aunts who are always down on a fellah with tracts and wholesome advice if a fellah's letter home only smells of a cigar. Macer was a bit of excitement, but he's gone."

"Macer," said Archie, thoughtfully. "I remember I met him with Denville. Man with a great black beard, wasn't he?"

"Yes," said Spooner, "and played a jolly good game. He left here the morning after you passed through. Going home to Scotland, he said."

Archie nodded. Macer's face was vividly before him, though he had seen him only twice, for a brief instant each time, but how often have we all seen faces flitting past in a crowd that haunt us for years, with no volition of our own in the matter? Rising like a spectre and so departing.

Archie and Spooner strolled up King Street, and then the former left him and went to the offices of the two principal papers[1] and left with each a copy of an advertisement, to appear in their daily issues. It contained an accurate description of Winona, and offered a handsome reward to any one who would bring intelligence of her to the advertiser. Archie did not stop here, for against the evening the dead walls and fences were alive with small posters containing a repetition of the advertisement. It was placed in bar-rooms, saloons, close to churches, on the wharves, headed by the magic word in large capitals, "Reward." In order to avoid question and remark, the two dailies appeared as the advertisers, and none suspected how nearly Archie was connected with the mysterious placards that excited no little comment and curiosity amongst those who have time to be curious in the hurry and bustle of a Canadian city.

It was, in the course of a week, scattered broadcast over Upper and Lower Canada, and copied into every paper along the front,[2] but for some time there came not the slightest clue to the missing girl.

Archie developed a restlessness, and at times an irritability quite foreign to his usual even and cordial nature; and people remarked on it in various ways. Some said the breaking off of his engagement with Miss Bertrand was the cause; but as that young lady allowed him to see that he could easily remedy that if he were so minded, the gossips were at fault as to the cause of the change in him. When off duty he haunted the depots and the wharves; but of course no one dreamed of connecting the disappearance of the Indian girl with the romantic name and Archie's disquietude.

He kept out of Cecil's way carefully, for he had not the faintest desire to renew the old tie between them; and the gossip of the city soon informed him as to Miss Bertrand's true reason for casting him off.

He laughed to himself good-humoredly at the manner in which the little coquette had dug a pit for her own dainty feet, and thanked his

---

[1] Toronto had numerous weekly and daily newspapers in the 1860s. George Brown's *Globe* (c. 1849) vied with James Beaty's *Daily Leader* as the most influential and successful of the dailies. The *Globe* was Brown's mouthpiece for "representation by population," Scottish interests, and conservative finances, while the *Daily Leader*, which spoke to the Irish sympathies of its owner, began as a liberal paper but later favoured John A. Macdonald and his policies. Both papers sold between 10,000 and 15,000 copies a day. The *Daily Leader* faded in importance in the early 1870s.

[2] That is, in settlements bordering upon the St. Lawrence River and the lower Great Lakes.

194   ISABELLA VALANCY CRAWFORD

good angel that had led him out of her toils in time. It would have been as bitter, nay, immeasurably more so, than death itself, had he married Cecil before his eyes were open to her true character, and as yet he did not know what a dark shadow her falsehood had thrown across the light of his gentle sister's life. He had received no hint from Olla that Cecil had written announcing her engagement to Theodore Denville. Had he known this, how many bitter hours it might have spared poor Olla!

People found him, Archie, exceedingly reticent concerning his adventures, and no amount of "chaff" drew an enlightening retort from him. He let them speculate to their hearts' content, and extraordinary were the romances that grew out of faint inklings of truth and strong touches of the imagination.

Cecil was in, not despair, she was too young and pretty for that, but she found she had placed herself in a dilemma, from which it would take all her tact to extricate herself. Lovely as she was, men who knew the story of the Frazer-Denville affair, though they flirted as of yore, avoided sentiment, and, what was a great deal more injurious to her "matrimonial chances," people laughed at her discomfiture. A woman may, and often does, ride triumphant over a tempest of hate, slander and malice, but show me the woman who does not succumb to the shafts of ridicule!

Any hope of bringing Prancer up "to the point" had faded into thin air, and Cecil, for the first time during her society life found herself without a betrothal ring blazing forth her triumphs on her pretty finger. Flirting was all very well, but she liked a seasoning of serious matter, and *pro tem.* she spread her shining net for a cousin of her own, a tall, slight, shy boy, who had emerged from the silent forest in which he had been born and bred, to study at the University.

She "read up" with dismal yawns Tennyson and Mrs. Barrett Browning for his benefit, and sentimentalized until she had him bound to her chariot wheels. Above all, she patronized him. She revolutionized his neck-ties, she taught him to dance, she told him what tailor to employ. She swept his foolish young head clear of every dream of fame, fortune or ambition, and filled it with her own seductive image. She was like some lovely young vampire of society drawing the heart-blood of some tender and appetizing young victim, while she fanned him asleep with her gay wings. People watched the affair with a rather sober interest. Percy Grace was just one of those who, when once they love, surrender reason, prudence, nay, even religion, and live but in the light of the meteor they pursue. Some men, happily by far the greater number, find in love the exquisite and gentle light that cheers them on through the hard struggle of practical life; it is a flower they wear on their breasts, delighting in its all-pervading fragrance and beauty. While their hands are clinging to the ladder of wealth and fame, their gaze is fixed on the shining heights towards which they labor. When the laurel or bay is won, love shines amid the garland, the chiefest ornament, the most beloved, because only for its cheering presence, the sturdy heart had oftimes failed, the onward step faltered. To such men love is an inciter to noble deeds, greater and purer than any other, the tender and holy light cast upon the way; not the meteor that absorbs, dazzles, chains the powers of mind and body in a rapt worship, and disappearing, leaves a horrid blackness, a void and death of the soul that seeks for peace in a sister death of the body.

Percy Grace could be but one. He knew nothing of that nature, in the possession of which, the higher and vaster his love, the greater power to do and dare amongst his fellow-men developes. A student, he had known no life beyond his books; a lover, the dream of fame was forgotten, and he lived but in his love. He might, as a soldier, a statesman, even an artist, have risen on the wings of fiery enthusiasm, but he could not entertain in his soul a second guest.

Had his steps not strayed into the golden mists and fragrant paths of rose-bordered love-land, whence he had no power to emerge, his life would have known nothing of its sweet influence.

To do Cecil justice, her ideas of love represented merely a state in which the sterner sex became decidedly "soft," and developed a pleasing tendency to bestow gifts on the objects of their affections. Of the great life of the heart she was totally ignorant; of the tragic possibilities or lovely hopes that the potent wizard, love, might trace on the web of life, she neither knew nor cared, and according to her light so she must be judged.

He was a handsome lad, innately elegant and refined, and it pleased her vanity that he should grace her triumph. She had no vision of her chariot wheels crimsoning themselves in his blood. Archie and she bowed when they met and passed on smiling, but if ever Cecil knew a real, substantial sentiment, it was a keen desire to revenge the failure of her plans on him whom she had deliberately cast off. As for Archie, occasionally he felt a little ashamed that, like Romeo, he had so speedily lost all memory of his love for Rosaline[1] in the present power of his affection for Juliet.

And so the first snow fell, and the fetters of ice were cast upon the mighty waters of the land!

CHAPTER XVIII

Sidney's Adventure

The air was full of life that nipped your blood until it danced through your veins glowing and tingling. The sky was a real Canadian winter sky, cloudless and intensely blue, with a sun rolling through it like an orb of lustrous gold. The solemn pines were crested with snow, and the limbs of every tree, the outline of every object open to the weather were traced in the pearly shower, that drifted before the frolicsome wind, like a fine vapor, in wreaths that caught a diamond glitter from the morning sun.

It was a morning to walk or drive fast, to think hopefully of leaden troubles, to feel an exhilaration of the brain and heart that no breath of summer ever brought, a morning on which it was impossible to fold the hands and say "I despair." It was intensely cold, cold enough to whiten the black beard and moustache of a gentleman walking briskly along the Scranton road, and cold enough to have formed ice half a foot deep on currentless pools and still waters, though the St. Lawrence still rolled proudly free, soon however to succumb to the breath of King Frost.

The Scranton road was a quiet country highway, not lacking a few hundred acres of dense forest, for a part of its length, a cedar swamp unavailable for culture, smelling spicily in the clear air, and making a densely green avenue paved this morning with virgin snow, and as dazzling in the sunlight as an enchanted road of burnished silver.

Up this radiant white path the solitary pedestrian strode, admiring nature through a pair of blue-tinted spectacles, and whistling merrily as he faced the wind; a tall, black form in the universal brightness, occasionally standing aside, as a gay cutter whirled past, all jingling silver bells and waving fox-skins, or a wood or wheat sleigh glided past, the owner

---

[1]   In Shakespeare's *Romeo and Juliet*, Rosaline is Romeo's previous inamorata, whom he instantly forgets when he falls in love with Juliet.

perched aloft cracking his long whip, serenely content as he carried his honestly toiled-for wealth to a secure market.

Emerging from the swamp, he came on a deep pool by the roadside, coated with lucid ice, and shining amid the snow like a diamond laid on ivory. Fringed daintily with low, feathery cedars, their dark green flecked with snow, and guarded by a mighty pine, that reared its dark spire into the cloudless blue; every branch and clinging cone, defined blackly as though carved in jet, against its dazzling background.

·A snake-fence railed it from the road, and the gentleman paused by it for a moment and looked through his blue spectacles at the glittering pool.

Two young girls were flying hither and thither over it like gorgeously-plumed curlews, their skates flashing in the sun as they swept in eddying circles, meeting and parting as two butterflies dance over a rose, throwing themselves into the thing with a graceful abandon, born of the keen air and perfect mastery of the art, wedded to excellent health, and youth, which is the life of all things.

The ice cracked and groaned under their light weight, but was apparently quite safe, and he of the tinted glasses stood looking at the pretty scene admiringly, despite the keen wind.

"What a lovely creature that graceful child is," he thought as he caught a nearer view of a rosy, radiant face, gleaming from a tossing tempest of billowy golden hair. "I wonder what the other is like!"

He was too well-bred to risk annoying them by a prolonged stare, so he walked on slowly, watching them, however, as he went.

He lingered for an instant looking back as the road swept round a sudden curve; someway that pure, young face had attracted him strangely.

He turned away slowly, with a shadow on his face that had not been on it a moment previously, and the pool was instantly lost to his sight, though he could hear their laughter ringing clearly on the frosty air.

"Isn't it Jean Jacques Rousseau, who says, *Quand l'homme commence à raisonner il cesse de sentir*,"[1] he said, laughing to himself, a little bitterly. "Pshaw! no man can build up a rule to embrace every mind. I have made dame Reason my sole deity, and yet I find there is a touch of nature left. But why should that child's innocent face be the first thing

---

[1]   This aphorism ("When man begins to reason, he ceases to feel") was attributed to Rousseau in conversation by his friend Jacques-Henri Bernardin de Saint-Pierre. See the latter's *Études de la Nature* ["Étude Première"], 1784; troisieme éd., tom. 1 (Bruxelles: B. Le Francq, 1788) 22.

to force the unpleasant fact on me that I have some human sympathies left? I have seen scores of pretty children without one of them suggesting that hackneyed tableau of Lucifer, looking up with longing eyes to the shining doors, closed against him by an eternal sentence.[1] But actually as her eyes met mine I felt uncomfortable suggestions of a cloven-foot and that graceful appendage with which a high-toned superstition graces his Satanic Majesty!"

He laughed at this and so resumed his easy cheerfulness, as the merry wind rushed in his face from the open country, dashing a wreath of smoky drift against him, as though brisky frost elves were abroad and at high revel.

At this point the road diverged into forks and he paused to consider which he should pursue. As he did so, a shrill scream from the direction of the pool, followed by a second and a third, smote his ear, accompanied by the sharp cracking of ice, and before he had formed a thought in connection with the sounds, he was speeding back to the spot.

As he came in sight of the little pool one glance showed him what had occurred. The young girl who had so attracted him had broken through the ice towards the centre of the pond, and though hardly in danger of drowning was very unpleasantly situated. The bitingly cold water rose above her shoulders, and wherever she grasped the ice, it broke away in her hands. The screams proceeded from her companion, who was trying in vain to reach her, but was forced to keep back as the ice now began to give way in every direction. The great danger was, that the young girl's strength should give way, and that she should fall and so be drowned. Her long, bright hair floated out on the water, and her pretty face was pallid, but self-possessed.

"Stand back, Olla," she cried, peremptorily, as the other made a futile attempt to reach her, "here is some one coming."

"Don't be alarmed," said the mellow voice of the new comer, "the young lady is in no danger, I assure you."

With a great sigh of relief, Olla sank against the fence, and with anxious eyes watched the efforts of the stranger to relieve Sidney from her predicament. He saw that it would be useless to attempt to draw her on the ice, so he divested himself of his furred great-coat, and with an air of perfect *sang-froid* leaped into the water, and lifting her in his

---

[1] See Milton, *Paradise Lost* III.523–25: "The Stairs were then let down, whether to dare / The Fiend by easy ascent, or aggravate / His sad exclusion from the doors of Bliss."

strong arms, waded towards the shore, breaking the brittle ice before him as he advanced, and in a few moments Sidney was on shore, her teeth chattering like castanets, and her dress rapidly turning to a garment of ice. Olla poured out an incoherent flood of thanks to Sid's rescuer, who with a silent bow, lifted his coat and wrapped it round the shivering girl, who seemed in more danger of freezing to death than she had been of drowning. She seemed quite unable to speak and Olla burst into tears of alarm and distress, as she looked at her.

"I don't know what I shall do!" she said, turning to the spectacled stranger. "Papa is quite close, but I cannot leave her, while I run for him."

"Certainly not," he answered decisively, "and I can only suggest—" He did not say what, but he lifted Sid's little figure in his arms, and looked at Olla.

"Come," he said, cheerfully, "will you be my guide? We ought not to linger a moment. The frost is very keen."

Strong as he seemed to be, Sidney, her clothes and hair saturated and frozen into a solid mass was a tolerably severe strain on his powers, and despite the numbing cold, he was soon in a glow of heat; but he walked swiftly on, and never paused until he stood in the hall of Captain Frazer's residence, which was, as Olla had said, close at hand. Had it been otherwise Sidney would in all probability have been severely frozen.

The drawing-room door stood open, and as he followed Olla into the hall with his burthen, he saw a pretty group of Dolly and Androsia Howard, working by the glittering steel grate, while Mrs. Frazer read aloud to them.

"Mamma," cried Olla, running in, while he paused uncertain whether to follow or not, in the hall, looking into the bright, pretty room and holding Sidney still in his arms, "don't be frightened, please, there is nothing serious the matter. Sidney broke through the ice at the swamp pool, and this gentleman got her out."

Dolly let her work fall, and Mrs. Frazer and Androsia sprang up, the former trembling as her eyes rested on Sidney's figure, motionless in the arms of the stranger; but her fears were at once set at rest by the young lady herself.

"Don't be alarmed, mamma," she called out, "I'm a little damp, that's all, and owing to my skates and being frozen into an icicle, I can't stand. Put me down, please."

In obedience to this request the stranger placed her on one of the hall chairs, and stood aside smiling quietly, while Androsia and Mrs. Frazer embraced and questioned her, the former busying herself in removing her drenched wraps, while Dolly and Olla cried heartily in the drawing-room, the latter overcome by excitement and the former from sympathy. Sidney herself with her golden locks dripping like a naiad's, laughed at her perils, though a shade of deep feeling stole over her expressive face, as she looked from her mother to the stranger.

"Mamma," she said; but Mrs. Frazer had turned to him, and in her sweet, high-bred way was thanking him with great feeling for the service he had rendered.

"Captain Frazer must see and thank you himself," she said; "but in the meantime let me suggest a change of raiment. I think," she added, turning to Olla who had joined them, "that there is a suit of Archie's clothes in his wardrobe. Tell Mike to lay them out."

The stranger looked at Mrs. Frazer curiously. "Is it possible that it is Miss Frazer to whom I have been fortunate enough to render this trifling service?" he asked in a tone of considerable interest. He spoke with a kind of curious impediment in his speech, very trifling in itself but sufficient to render his voice rather peculiar.

"My youngest daughter," answered Mrs. Frazer, looking more attentively at him than she had hitherto done.

"I am very fortunate!" he remarked in his slow, low voice. "It is a curious coincidence that I should be on my way to wait on Captain Frazer on a trifling matter of business, when I had the happiness of assisting your daughter."

Mrs. Frazer looked at him inquiringly, and he continued:

"I am in a position to give Captain Frazer some trifling information on a certain subject in which he is interested, and which I lighted on by the merest accident; but in the meantime allow me to introduce myself. My name is Harold Macer."

"My husband will be happy to see you as soon as you have changed your clothes," said Mrs. Frazer, glancing in dismay at Mr. Macer's garments, which, thawed by the heat of the hall, gave him the appearance of a dripping river-god.

"How dreadfully tanned he is!" breathed Dolly in a tone of saintly compassion in Androsia's ear, against whom she was leaning, and Androsia turned and looked at him, meeting his eyes through the blue spectacles.

He was studying the beautiful group the two girls made in the tinted sunlight pouring through the stained glass, Dolly's angelic loveliness so well set off by the more vivid coloring of Androsia, whose lovely face and brilliant eyes seemed all the more radiant from the sombre hue of her heavy black dress, which swept with such perfect grace round her lofty, pliant form.

Androsia blushed and turned away, the lucid white of her throat and temples crimsoning under his earnest gaze, and she drew Dolly into the drawing-room and closed the door.

"I do not like him," she said, in her measured way, folding her hands and looking inexpressibly haughty, rearing her head like a young Semiramis.[1]

"Don't you, dear?" said Dolly, resignedly, taking up one of the "token of affection" slippers which were yet in progress. "Why?"

Dolly's golden hair gleamed like an aureole round her as she sank into her low-chair, and she looked at the slippers as Lady Jane Grey might have glanced at an offer of pardon on recantation of her religion.[2]

"Because," began Androsia frowning, then paused, and added, "I do not know why."

"Perhaps," said Dolly, considering, "it is the spectacles. Blue spectacles are so unbecoming. Or the tan; perhaps it is the tan, dear."

Androsia shook her graceful head impatiently, and her eyes sparkled angrily as she looked at the fire.

"He looked at me," she ejaculated indignantly, "his eyes burned my skin!"

"Of course, he looked at you," assented Dolly. "Mr. Armor looks at me a great deal when we are together, but I don't mind it much. Indeed I forget that he is in the room half the time. Would you put a white or purple pansie here, Androsia?"

But Androsia was not as yet sufficiently civilized to curb her restless mind at a moment's notice to the consideration of worsted work. She sat down and leant her damask cheek on her slender hand

---

[1] A legendary queen of Assyria (9th century BCE), Semiramis is often cited as a type of female grandeur and power, as in Crawford's poem "Lines: On the picture of Semiramis receiving news of a revolt in Babylon," *Evening Telegram* [Toronto] 6 October 1879: 3.

[2] An English noblewoman of royal blood, Lady Jane Grey (1537–54) became a pawn in the power struggle following the death of Edward VI, at a time of vicious rivalry between Protestant and Roman Catholic factions for the rule of England. Set up as queen for nine days in July 1553, she was deposed by the Catholic Mary Tudor's supporters and eventually executed for high treason, maintaining her ardent Protestant faith to the end.

"Androsia does not wish to speak more," she said, decisively, and Dolly whose great talent was for silence, sat idly looking at her, a brooding pensiveness in her violet eyes that was inexpressibly lovely, and the gorgeous mass of colors heaped on her lap, what time she vaguely wondered about Mr. Macer, his blue spectacles and his bronzed skin.

CHAPTER XIX

News of Winona

"Comfortable," thought Mr. Macer glancing round the pretty library, where he was waiting, pending his interview with Captain Frazer, "and ornamental! One can almost fancy oneself gifted with a sudden virtuous love of domesticity in such a room. Nothing of the conventional library about it, but that walnut escritoire in the corner, and even that is cheerful and graceful. I wonder if it is really as massive and secure as it looks. Modern furniture is seldom anything but a sham."

He looked at it with the air of a connoisseur, admiring the fanciful carvings of wreaths of maple leaves, squirrels and beavers that decorated it, and the exquisite polish and grain of the wood. He saw that though of modern make it was massive and solid, and the unusual peculiarity distinguished it, that no lock or keyhole was visible.

He was by nature observant even of trifles, and he whiled away a few minutes pleasantly, speculating as to how and where the elaborate front opened, and then he sauntered about the room looking at the photographs and engravings on the wall. Good all of them, and two or three even valuable. Where all the sunlight fell broadly upon it there hung an old portrait in oils of Marie Antoinette, in the days of her beauty and power. It had been a gift from herself to the grandfather of Mrs. Frazer, and was an heir-loom of price to the family. It was at this Macer was looking when the door opened and Mike wheeled Captain Frazer into the room.

He turned with a smile on his face and nodded good-humoredly to Mr. Murphy, whose face expressed no little astonishment as he recognized him.

"It's himself," ejaculated Mike, pausing and surveying him without much favor. "Humph! so it's yerself, Mr. Macer, is it?"

WINONA; OR, THE FOSTER-SISTERS   203

He remembered with a slight twinge his loquacity at their meeting in Toronto, and he was not too well pleased to be reminded of it by the appearance of Mr. Macer.

"In proper person, my friend," laughed the other, and then he turned and introduced himself to Captain Frazer, in an easy, dignified way that showed him well acquainted with the manners of society.

"I shall not make any stereotyped excuses for intruding on you, Captain Frazer," he said, smiling. "I might have done so, indeed, and considered that perhaps my business was scarcely sufficient warrant for such a course, had not fate willed that I should in any case introduce myself to you. My name is Harold Macer."

Captain Frazer extended his hand and clasped Mr. Macer's warmly, while he surveyed him with kindly interest.

"I can't express to you," he said, earnestly, "how grateful I am to you for your service of this morning. It might have proved a dark day, indeed, to us, only for you."

Captain Frazer's rugged countenance expressed far more than his words, and Mr. Macer felt really gratified.

"It was nearly altogether riskless on my part," he said; "but there is no doubt that a prolonged immersion would have been fatal to Miss Frazer; but pray, don't make me fancy myself a hero!" He laughed pleasantly, and drew a chair opposite that occupied by his host, and looked at Mike, who was lingering under pretence of replenishing the fire, eyeing Mr. Macer curiously.

"You did not expect to meet me again so soon when we parted so abruptly in Toronto?" he said.

"Faix no," answered Mike, concisely, and was silent.

"You may go, Mike," said Captain Frazer, and Mike went, leaving the two men alone.

Captain Frazer waited curiously for Mr. Macer to unfold his errand and the nature of his business. He swept his glance back and forth over his memory, but could not recall any recollections connected with his guest. The name even he had never heard before, the face was unfamiliar. The low, melodious voice separated from the peculiarity of articulation struck him as one he had heard in some far-off time that he could not recall, but that was only an idea. He faced the window and Mr. Macer, and though the handsome dark head was sharply defined against the light, the features were indistinct, indeed almost indistinguishable.

He did not seem in haste to unfold his errand, but he seemed to do everything slowly and deliberately as he spoke, and so Captain Frazer waited courteously the pleasure of his guest.

"I am afraid," said the latter at last, leaning his arm on the table beside him, and tapping the dark green cloth slowly with his finger-tips as he looked at Captain Frazer, "that you will hardly exonerate me from the charge of a seeming want of delicacy in intruding myself into an affair that apparently it was your desire not to appear in; I allude to an advertisement which met my eye, concerning the disappearance of an Indian girl, named, I think, Winona!"

"What of her?" exclaimed Captain Frazer, regarding the speaker with unconcealed astonishment. "Have you any information to give me concerning her?"

"Or I had not been here," replied the other. "Of course," he added hastily and with the air of one wishing not to raise too secure a hope by his words, "I may be mistaken in her identity, but the description was so accurate that I could hardly have been misled in my recognition of her."

Captain Frazer's face expressed great agitation. It was evidently with a strong effort that he succeeded in steadying his voice to ask:

"Have the kindness to explain yourself; the disappearance of this girl has been a source of great uneasiness to a member of my family and to myself," he added slowly.

Mr. Macer looked at him curiously through the blue glasses, and his fingers ceased tapping the cloth.

"It is a trifling clue, I fear," he answered; "but if followed up may lead to her discovery. I met a girl answering her description in every particular on a crowded platform half-way between Scranton and Toronto, and attracted by her singular beauty, I watched her. She bought a ticket for Toronto and vanished. It was night, and something about her, an air as though she wished to avoid observation, fastened her in my memory. When I got out at Scranton I saw the advertisement, which a boy was just posting up, and then it suddenly struck me that I had seen her before." Mr. Macer paused for a second and then went on. "After some thought I recalled the time and place, and remembered that I had caught a passing glimpse of her in Toronto in company with your son and a young lady."

"But," said Captain Frazer, with an accent and manner of keen disappointment, "this must be nearly a fortnight ago now."

"It is, indeed," replied Mr. Macer, in a tone of grave concern, "but had I only thought of you as interested in the girl it should not have so happened. As it was, the whole affair slipped from my mind, and I proceeded down to Montreal, where I had important business to transact, and it was only when I found myself passing this neighbourhood on my way back and saw the advertisements still up, that the idea flashed on me that the girl had likely fled from your protection. So much time had been lost that I came directly to you rather than lose any more in writing to the offices named, at the risk, I am afraid, of being justly considered intrusive."

"If I had but known this at once," said the Captain hoarsely, and in a tone of such keen pain that for the moment Mr. Macer's well-bred calm gave place to an air of considerable astonishment. "You cannot guess," continued the old gentleman, "how much depends on securing the girl before she—" He closed his lips and his brown face turned grey as ashes.

"Insane, I presume," said Mr. Macer sympathizingly, "a terrible affliction. I sincerely hope you may secure her."

"She is not mad," said the Captain quietly, but passing his handkerchief across his brow, damp with agitation. "Oh, anything but mad. But I fear all will be of no avail."

"If I could be of any assistance," suggested Macer, with an air of courtly deference, "I am going Toronto-wards, and if—"

"I can't see what to do," said the Captain. "I've had detectives employed, but with no avail, and your news confirms my worst fears. I must write to my son at once."

"I would take my leave," said Macer, with a half smile, as he glanced at his dress, "but I am indebted to your son for a portion of his wardrobe while my own clothes are drying."

"Don't think of such a thing," said Captain Frazer, hurriedly, "you must not think of leaving us to-night."

Macer hesitated.

"I should not intrude on your hospitality," he said; "but the fact is, I am not altogether recovered from a sharp attack of rheumatic fever, and I dread the consequences of further exposure to-day. I shall rest your guest gratefully for to-night."

Mr. Macer spent a quiet day, that never left his memory, in Captain Frazer's drawing-room, gloomed on by Androsia from a shadowy corner, where she ensconced herself with a book, which she knitted her straight brows over without gaining much knowledge from its pages. She was rapidly acquiring the, to her, hidden art of reading; and Captain Frazer, who was her delighted tutor, spoke of her as one rarely gifted in mind as well as person. She sat canopied by the chintz and lace curtains in the window, behind a flower-stand, her lovely head rising above the blossoms, like that of some regal spirit rising from an ocean of bloom, and perused Mr. Macer, as he chatted with the others, with a more fixed attention than she did her book. On his part, he politely ignored her scrutiny, and loitered beside Dolly's chair, talking in his pleasant, half-serious way, while Sidney lingered listening eagerly to his every word, with a pleasure that would have charmed Macer, had he been a vain man, which he was not, or Sidney a little older.

He was by no means brilliant, but all he said, told, and he talked about things that girls like, operas, paintings, travels, prima donnas, music, touching every subject brightly, and with a kindly hand, evidently enjoying himself, and drawing Sidney into animated descriptions of Canadian life, of which he said he knew very little, having been only a few months out from Scotland. He seemed much attracted by Sidney, and studied her rosy face with a thoughtful and sometimes puzzled look. Of Olla he saw little, for, like Desdemona—

"Still the house affairs would draw her thence"[1]

but he felt the charm of her exquisite gentleness and sweet graciousness to the full.

He was introduced to Sidney's terrier, "Mop," and advised Dolly in her worsted work, and watched all their graceful ways and dainty belongings, as men do to whom the home-life has hitherto been but a name, and at that, infrequent in their ears. Despite his apparent carelessness of her, he cast many a glance at the dark-robed beauty behind her fortress of flowers, but the glasses jealously hid the expression of his eyes, and his calm, dark face was not very readable.

Perhaps he was a little annoyed at her haughty avoidance of him, contrasting strongly with the evident pleasure the pretty sisters took in his society, and the pleasant cordiality extended to him by Mrs. Frazer, or only amused, but he seemed rather relieved when after dinner she disappeared and did not return till after tea was served.

---

[1] Desdemona is the wife of Othello in Shakespeare's play; see *Othello* I.iii.147.

When she had gone he asked one or two questions about her, carelessly enough, and playing with "Mop" while he spoke, seemingly but little interested in the answers Sidney gave him, praising Androsia volubly, and flying off into an account of Winona, and speculations about her flight and possible return.

"I don't think she liked her new dresses," said Dolly pensively, "though her mourning was exactly the same as Androsia's, and she looked lovely in it. She used to seem quite unhappy and miserable, poor thing!"

"A strange instance of the pervading feminine passion in the untutored child of the forest," said Macer, elevating his black brows and smiling.

"Dolly," said Sidney, reproachfully, "how can you say such things! Vexed about her dress! Oh, Mr. Macer, I'm sure it was not that. If you could only have seen her sitting in a dark corner; her eyes, like two dull fires and her teeth grinding, and her fingers twisting round each other, you'd have felt frightened. She looked as if she saw some one in the distance that she was going to tear to pieces presently. I couldn't help feeling sorry for Androsia, but oh, I was glad when she ran away, I can tell you."

"I daresay," replied Mr. Macer, laughingly; "a rather uncomfortable kind of guest." He paused a moment, pondering, and allowing his face to express that he would have found her anything but an agreeable companion; and Sidney went on speculatively:

"I shouldn't wonder that she'd come back as suddenly as she went, for you see, she is wonderfully fond of Androsia, and every time I look out at night I fancy I see her gliding back from amongst the pines in her shadowy way. Oh, I think she'll come back."

"Perhaps so," said Macer, musingly. He got up from the low ottoman on which he had been sitting and walked away to the window that looked out on the pine-grove. It looked like some vast temple, darkly roofed with sombrest green and floored with pearl, barred with the ruby shafts of sunset. The memorial stone gleamed whitely in its bosom, and stretching round it lay a fairy landscape of snow and rose, and trembling shadows stretching far out across the land as the sun drove his fire-and-gold-maned steeds swiftly westward. There was the utter calm of a fair winter's evening over the lovely scene. The St. Lawrence,

"Silent, majestical and slow,"[1]

---

[1] Longfellow, *The Golden Legend* (1851) V. [v] "The Inn at Genoa" 4.

flowed, dark as a stream of jet between banks of pearl, bridged here and there with crimson light and flashes of spectral gold across its dark waters. The scene was fair enough to chain Macer at the window, until in a dying blaze of crimson, fire and gold, the sun flung his parting benison over the still landscape, and while the glow faded to a silvery rose, through which a great star rose on quivering pinions of light and hung over the gloomy crests of the pines, tremulous in the clear evening air.

Dolly and Sidney had left the room, but he seemed unaware of their absence, and leant against the window frame with folded arms, looking out, his dark face like that of a bronze statue, as fixed and motionless.

At the hour of twilight the robes of man's guardian angel gleam whitely from the shadows. The blessed and ineffable repose and calm of nature finds voice and sings in low harmonies of peace and purity. At this hour, more than any other, the soul inclines, like the flame of a lamp blown by a gentle and invisible wind, towards the pure and holy, and no longer can man say, "Evil, be thou my good!"[1] as in the unhaunted hours of the busy day.

"I could almost feel it in my heart to depart from this innocent roof and never more be seen," soliloquized Macer, watching the climbing star, that sealed the blue vault, like the herald of the starry host; "my vivid imagination and a lucky chance bore me triumphantly into the dove-cot, but kite that I am, I am not altogether and at all times remorseless. Shall I go?"

A light fell into the room, now full of shadow; and looking up, he saw Androsia passing slowly up the hall carrying a lamp.

> "Her step was royal—queen-like—and her face
> As beautiful as a saint's in Paradise."[2]

"Behold my answer," murmured Macer. "Fate, stoop again to my beck, and desert me not."

---

[1] This avowal is made by Satan in Milton's *Paradise Lost* IV.110.
[2] Longfellow, *The Spanish Student* (1843) I.i.29–30.

[PART 8—1 MARCH 1873]

CHAPTER XX

Mr. Fennel

"A telegram for you, sir."

Archie wrote his name in the book, and the messenger departed at a run, clattering down stairs with that rush and tumult that is only known to boys, and Archie stood for a moment looking at the printed envelope as men do look at an unexpected telegram.

It is a curious fact that one never for a moment presupposes that the winged words can have any but a dire meaning. There is a proverb to hand down the fact that "ill news travels fast," but it hardly says much for human nature that joyous tidings generally lag along the road, and is so bemauled and ill-treated by envious tongues upon the way that half its gay plumage is gone before it flutters into our bosoms.

One is never too anxious to end one's suspense by reading the words that may be so terrible, and Archie opened the envelope very slowly, stopping in the operation to wonder and speculate concerning its contents. At length it was spread open, and he read as follows:

"A Mr. Harold Macer called to-day with intelligence of Winona. He saw her on the night of the—, at the depot, purchasing a ticket for Toronto. Take this to Fennel, and telegraph if any clue arises."

Archie's face expressed relief and surprise.

"Macer," he thought, "why that must be Spooner's friend. The name is almost unique so far as I know. How on earth did the fellow find his way down there?"

He kept wondering about Macer as he strode away to look for Fennel, who was one of those useful growths of modern society written of in novels, scoffed at by a thankless public, and working brain and body day and night for a very trifling meed of fame or fortune, in other words, a detective.

Fennel was not to be found in his usual places of resort, and from a taciturn policeman, in charge of an elderly gentleman afflicted with quite a painful mania for instructing himself as to the flight of the rosy hours by the aid of other people's gold repeaters, playfully abstracted from their pockets, he learned that Fennel had gone home early, as there was "nothing on hand much just at present," and so Archie walked off to a certain cottage on a quiet part of Yonge Street, where dwelt Fennel amid his humble Lares and Penates.[1]

Archie walked briskly, as the evening was cold, a biting wind blowing from the lake, and the early stars glittering as they only do in the winter. He met crowds of pedestrians. Business men hurrying home to dinner; enthusiasts in skating, with pink cheeks and dazzling eyes, tripping home from the rinks, dainty in richest furs and velvet, their cavaliers gallantly carrying skates that might have been used in Fairy Land, if that enchanted clime had been favorable to the production of glare ice; laboring men striding along with cheerful faces, and eyes that were not dull with famine, to snug homes where there was peace and plenty; pale-browed mechanics, with thoughtful, but not careworn, faces, quickening their steps as the fresh wind dashed against them, and lent an edge to the anticipation of the cheerful meal and welcome for the part awaiting them.

The first snow had fallen the night before, and the silvery jingle of the sleigh-bells made the crisp air alive, as sleighs, cutters, carioles dashed past in endless succession, heaped up with costly furs, and drawn by steeds that seemed to scorn the ground, as, with tossing heads and steaming nostrils, their hoofs dashed up the powdery snow as they flew past. Wood-racks went creaking past, great wheat sleighs drawn by noble teams of stout farm horses, and bands of rosy light streamed across the white road from cheerful windows, aglow with fire and lamplight.

The whole air was full of life and exhilaration. Wretched little boys with toboggans whooped and yelled in by-streets as they took advantage of every little declivity to rush pell-mell under the runners of vehicles, greeted emphatically but not cordially by the hurried drivers; and the frozen gutters were covered with other youths in party-colored comforters and fur caps pulled over their chubby heads, skating and sliding and yelling after the time-honored custom of boys.

Archie ascended the steps of a small white brick house, with a brass knocker as bright as a planet, and a bow-window with a crimson damask curtain looped back from it inside, giving a glimpse of a flower-stand

---

[1]   Household gods in Roman mythology.

bright with blossoms, and a plain, cheerful little room, with a tea-table set in the glow of the fire, and a pretty young woman in a rocking-chair, swaying softly to and fro, and smiling at some invisible person, whose shadow danced, misty and gigantic, on the wall and ceiling.

Archie knocked, and presently a breath of warm, perfumed air rushed out, as the door opened and a young man appeared on the threshold.

The light from the hall-lamp fell on the face of the visitor, and he recognized him at once.

"Ah, good evening, Captain Frazer," he said in a tone of some surprise; "come in, pray."

"I missed you down town," explained Archie, coming into the little, warm, matted hall, with its pretty hat-rack and umbrella-stand of bird's-eye maple, and a warmly tinted chromo of one of Landseer's subjects,[1] "and I was obliged to look you up here."

Mr. Fennel, a young, middle-sized man, with dark eyes and a plain, pleasant, refined face, looked a trifle chagrined.

"So you've got the first clue, I suppose," he said, pushing open the door. "Please step in. We boast only one sitting-room," and with a pleasant smile he ushered Archie into the apartment with the bow-window.

"My dear," said Mr. Fennel, looking at the young lady in the rocking-chair, who was very pretty and wore a very new and bright plain gold ring on her wedding finger. "My dear, this gentleman has called on business. Would you mind lending us your apartment for a little?"

Mrs. Fennel didn't in the least, and with a pretty, gracious little bow and smile, she opened a door that gave a peep into a tiny gem of a kitchen, a galaxy of shining pans, a shrine, dainty and neat, of the culinary art, and closing it behind her, left the two men alone.

There was a cottage piano[2] in the room, with music on it, a sewing-machine, and a neat bookcase and escritoire in one. An ingrain carpet and cane furniture of maple, and some pretty engravings, amongst which was the "Black Brunswicker,"[3] and the bow-window was full

---

[1] Sir Edwin Henry Landseer (1802–73) was an English painter who by mid-career had become famous for his depictions of dogs, horses and stags. Among his most famous canvasses are "Alexander and Diogenes" (1848) and "The Monarch of the Glen" (1851). Few English painters in his time excelled him in popularity though he was accused on occasion of sentimental renderings of his animal subjects, particularly in his later work.

[2] A small, upright piano.

[3] "The Black Brunswicker" (1860, oil on canvas, Lady Lever Art Gallery, Liverpool, England), by the English Pre-Raphaelite artist John Everett Millais, depicts a German officer

of blossoms and foliage. To be sure you could smell the biscuits baking for tea in the next room quite distinctly, and the perfume of the musk plant mingled with the odor of sausages, that could be heard faintly fizzing in the same apartment, but for all that there was a light about the place that did not alone proceed from lamp or fire.

"Well, now," said Mr. Fennel, placing a chair for Archie, "let me hear your news, for of course you have some, or you would not be here."

"Not much," said Archie, seating himself, "I don't build on it at all, still it may serve as a slight clue. Read for yourself."

He handed the telegram to Fennel, who sat down beside the lamp on the tea-table and read it carefully.

To tell the truth, Mr. Fennel was not at all like the recognized type of detective. He wasn't middle-aged, he wasn't grey-headed, he wasn't particularly reserved or quiet. He had a cheerful face, with a frank and cordial smile, and on the whole he resembled somewhat a young French *militaire* of the present day. His eyes were large, bright and pleasing, his manners graceful and self-possessed, his dress carefully attended to.

A song for a tenor voice lay open on the piano, and a mellow-looking violin rested on the music-rack.

It was curious to observe, as Archie did, how his face concentrated as he read the telegram. His dark brows fell over his eyes until the latter lurked brightly in a deep shadow. His features grew sharper, his lips became thinner and more compressed. In an instant of time he looked older by a half-score of years.

"This Mr. Macer," he said, looking up, "is he a friend of yours?"

"Not at all," replied Archie. "I recollect seeing him, in passing, at the Rossin about a fortnight since. I believe he was staying in town for a short time."

"He was," said Mr. Fennel quietly. "I have the honor to be slightly acquainted with him. Great at billiards, eh?"

"Yes, so I understand," said Archie, calling to mind Spooner's remarks on the subject.

"I don't profess to understand this turn of affairs," remarked Fennel, folding up the telegram and looking at Archie from under his dark

---

taking leave of his beloved before the Battle of Quatre Bras (1815) during the Waterloo Campaign. In the course of this battle, the French force under Marshal Ney decimated a contingent of black-uniformed troops led by the Duke of Brunswick. Millais's picture was widely popular as an engraving in the later nineteenth century; see Appendix E.

brows. "Here Macer said the girl bought a ticket for Toronto. Now, why did she not use it?"

"You think she didn't?"

"I'm certain of it. I've had all the depots closely watched, and most assuredly she never reached the city by rail, or any other means, I believe," asserted Mr. Fennel quietly; "ergo, she must have changed her mind and gone in a different direction. That, perhaps, is not unlikely." He looked intently at Captain Frazer, who, to a certain extent, had let him work on completely in the dark as to the probable reason of Winona's flight, merely telling him it was of vital importance that she should be discovered.

"That is not likely," replied Archie, decidedly. "I am convinced that nothing would turn her from endeavoring to return whence she came, and she was not sufficiently civilized to map out any very perfect plan of eluding pursuit. I am afraid she escaped the observation of your men."

Mr. Fennel looked pityingly at the young officer.

"My dear sir," he said, "that is almost an impossibility; but the time has now arrived, when I claim it as my due, that you should be perfectly candid with me concerning this affair. You see," he continued, as Archie rose in some agitation and walked to the fire, thus hiding his face from his observation, though the bright eyes of the other watched him curiously, "you have placed me at a signal disadvantage. I am in the position of a mole, working in the dark."

"It can't be helped," said Archie, almost brusquely. "I have given you all the information that is necessary to your object."

The words sounded almost rudely and Mr. Fennel's face expressed some slight accession of curiosity. He never lost his temper. His profession led him chiefly amongst persons and scenes that were not apt to be too suave and polished. A man smarting under some exquisite piece of roguery, or the victim of a daring robbery, spends little time on turning his sentences politely.

"Very well," replied Mr. Fennel, promptly, "I must decline having anything further to do with the business. In justice to myself, you understand, Captain Frazer."

Archie glanced at him and saw at once that he was quite in earnest. At the same time he knew that Fennel was highly thought of in his calling, in which he was remarkably successful, and he rapidly weighed in his mind the risk of taking him thoroughly into his confidence. "Were I not tolerably certain that she had passed through Toronto and escaped quite beyond our reach into her native forests, I should have no objection to confiding in you," he said, "of course under a promise of inviolable secrecy."

"That is understood," said Fennel, smiling a little; "but on my part I feel convinced that she never reached Toronto. Toronto is not Paris, New York, or London, and she is of too remarkable an appearance to have escaped us."

He seemed thoroughly convinced of the truth of what he said, and Archie was silent for a moment, endeavoring to bring his mind to some decisive course. Mr. Fennel sat looking at the fire quite aware of the struggle going on in the breast of his visitor, and speculating as to how it would terminate. Keen-sighted as he was, his thoughts had wronged Archie considerably about the affair, and he was prepared for some disclosure that would certainly not redound much to his credit. People were not generally, so anxious to conceal matters wherein they held themselves blameless, and this inexplicable flight of the beautiful Indian girl, and Archie's keen anxiety for her discovery bore, in his mind, but one construction.

"Well, Mr. Fennel," said Archie, at length, "if you cannot proceed without it, I must, I suppose, take on me the responsibility of telling you as much of the history of the affair as you require."

Fennel bowed.

"Are we secure from intrusion here?" asked Captain Frazer, thinking of pretty Mrs. Fennel, in the kitchen beyond.

"Perfectly," replied the detective, and going to the door he addressed a few words to his wife, and then came back to his seat, and turned to Archie with an air of expectation.

About half an hour afterwards, he ushered Archie out, and coming back, went to the escritoire, pulled out a time-table and examined it attentively. Then consulted his watch, and putting it back in his pocket, opened the kitchen door and called, "Grace!" and Mrs. Fennel tripped in a little flushed with the cooking of sausages, but exceedingly pretty and pleasant to look upon notwithstanding.

The detective put his arm round her slender waist. "It's too bad, Grace, pet," he said, lugubriously, "but I've just half an hour to eat my supper and bid you good night."

"And you only came home yesterday from Ottawa, Jack!" said Grace, with the faintest little quiver of voice and lip, and then her housewifely instincts told her to think of his supper, and presently the biscuits and sausages were steaming on the round table beside the fire, and Grace was looking with sober, brown eyes at her husband as he ate his hurried meal.

"When shall you be home, dear?" she said, as she poured him out his tea.

"To-morrow, I hope, love," said Fennel, "Gracie, another woman would not say, when will you be home? but, where are you going?" and he laughed, as he looked at her, a short laugh of extremest pleasure.

"I don't care to know anything, Jack, but just that," said Gracie, softly, "when you are away I keep thinking about your being at home again, and I don't feel lonely."

"You won't be lonesome to-night," said Fennel, "uncle Ferdinand is sure to drop in, and he's jolly company. Now I'm off, my precious pet."

So he was presently, and when she had watched his dark form disappear down the white road, Gracie Fennel went back to her solitary fireside, and stood looking down into the cheerful blaze for a few minutes.

"What a cold night it must be!" she said, with a strong shudder. "I feel chilled to the heart. Someway, I feel strangely about my boy going away to-night. My heart is cold and flutters."

But presently, moving to and fro, washing and arranging the tea things in the little kitchen, she was her own bright self again, and being a resolute little woman, when her household cares were over, she sat down at the piano for what she called "a good practice;" but strangely enough, she found herself playing sad old airs, and her fingers straying into weird, wailing chords, that might have been the voices of ghostly shades flitting by the banks of the Styx.[1] Finding out this, with something like terror, she selected one of Beethoven's knottiest sonatas, and resolutely set herself to interpreting the melody, but though her mind and fingers were fully occupied with its intricacies the same chill, and third sense as it were, clung about her and would not be "banished."[2] She closed the instrument, and went back to her rocking-chair by the fire; and for the first time during

---

[1] The river across which the souls of the dead are ferried to the underworld, in Greek mythology.

[2] Perhaps an allusion to Longfellow, "The Day is Done" (1844):

Come, read to me some poem,
Some simple and heartfelt lay,
That shall soothe this restless feeling,
And banish the thoughts of day. (13–16)

216 ISABELLA VALANCY CRAWFORD

her brief married life, felt thoroughly miserable, in the cosy solitude of her pretty room; and when uncle Ferdinand rapped at the door, a little shrivelled old gentleman escorting a portly violin in a green-baize cover, her heart leaped for joy, and she welcomed him almost rapturously.

"So Jack's away, is he?" said uncle Ferdinand, "dear me, I thought we'd have got a chance to-night at that trio of Bach's. I never felt in better play, Gracie, as firm as a rock and full of fire."

"He'll be back to-morrow," said Grace, confidently, "and then uncle, we shall have a pleasant evening."

"I hope so," said uncle Ferdinand. "What a pity such a fine fellow as Jack, should be at such a risky, uncertain business. Dangerous too, for the most part I've heard, but he's as courageous as a lion, I will say, though he is my nephew."

"Uncle," said Gracie, sitting up and looking at him with a face like one of the snow-wreaths without, "I never heard you say so before. Why do you speak so to-night? Do you know of any danger threatening him?"

"Bless the child," ejaculated uncle Ferdinand, "How should I know anything about him. Gracie! are you going to faint?" for Grace leant back with closed eyes in her chair.

"Bless me, I'd better play her something," ejaculated the old gentleman, much disturbed, and seizing his violin, he began to play, looking at her round the instrument with much anxiety to observe the effects of his novel remedy upon her.

Gracie opened her eyes and smiled, and delighted beyond expression uncle Ferdinand nodded gaily, winding up with rapturous thrilling and quivering of the strings, that was like the audible dancing of a thousand butterflies.

"The true panacea for most ills of mind or body is music," he said. "If I were wealthy I should certainly endow an hospital to be called the 'Ferdinand Music-cure.' Ah! what a loss to mankind it is that the originators of vast ideas such as mine, should almost be as poor as Job. Are you quite well now, Gracie, my dear?"

"Quite well, uncle," she said, soberly; but her rare gravity clung to her all the evening, though uncle Ferdinand, sitting by the fire like some old wizard of sweet sounds, played in his best style, and wandered intoxicated with melody, through a maze that separated him, for the time, from the natural world, and led his feet close to the borders of radiant spheres, whence celestial harmonies answered his magic strains.

He was a rare musician, one of those gems that lie hidden in most cities, either not confident enough to issue from their retirement, or so absorbed in their art as to forget all beside.

CHAPTER XXI

The Station-Master's Story

"No such person passed through on that, or any other night," said the station-master, positively, "of that I'm perfectly sure."

His questioner was Mr. Fennel, and the two men were standing in the grey dawn on the platform of the little depot of —— on the morning following the departure of the latter from Toronto.

It was an insignificant stopping-place where the trains merely paused for wood and water, and such passengers as might possibly wish to embark; and the station-master was a young man who suffered fearful things from *ennui*, and was delighted at an opportunity of a chat with a well-dressed stranger.

"You must be a smart fellow," remarked Mr. Fennel, in a tone of admiration, "to be able to speak so positively on such a subject. How do you do it, on earth?"

A smile of conscious superiority flickered on the rubicund countenance of his interlocutor, and he looked approvingly at the detective.

"I don't do it," he said, patronisingly, "It's a—a talent, you know. I can remember any face I've ever seen."

"A gift shared by most great men," said Mr. Fennel, hiding his sparkling eyes in a cloud of cigar smoke. "Wasn't it Alexander the Great[1] who knew the faces of all the soldiers in his great army? Have a cigar?"

"Don't care if I do," said the other, graciously. "Come into the office. How did you manage to get left behind?"

"Foolishly enough. I got out of the cars to stretch my limbs, and thinking that the stoppage time was twenty minutes I wandered too far, and was left behind. What time does the next down train[2] pass?"

"At 9.20. Guess we'll be froze if we don't get under cover. Come

---

[1] Alexander the Great (356–323 BCE) was the King of Macedonia (336–323 BCE), but gained his fame as the conqueror of the Greek city-states and the Persian Empire.

[2] The down train runs east to Montreal. The up train goes to Toronto and points west.

218 ISABELLA VALANCY CRAWFORD

right in."

He pushed open the door of his den, an eight-by-seven apartment, lighted by a smoky coal-oil lamp, with a brisk fire burning in the rusty box-stove; and making for the wood-box, he thrust more fuel into the fire and pulled forward two wooden arm-chairs, for the accommodation of himself and his guest. A coffee-pot was simmering fragrantly on the damper of the stove; and the change from the keen air of early morning without, was pleasant in the extreme.

"Sit right down," he said hospitably; "too bad you missed your train."

"Oh, I don't know," replied Fennel, flinging off his great coat. "I'm in no great hurry, and it looks first-rate here. So that I get into Montreal to-night, I guess our folks won't grumble."

"I'd trade situations any day," said the station-master, discontentedly. "You drummers have good times of it flying around the country. How would you like to be boxed up here week after week, roused from your Christian sleep every hour or two by the howling of them hungry engines. I'd as lief join a circus to tend the lions."

"It must be awfully stupid for a young fellow of spirit," said Fennel, sympathisingly. "How do you get along at all?"

"In the summer I raise prize tomatoes and cabbages in flower-pots," replied his host. "They don't ever take any prizes, but it's something to look forward to, you know."

"And in the winter, now?" suggested Mr. Fennel, "what do you do in such weather as this?"

"I study physiognomy," replied the youthful station-master, with a grim smile. "I make myself acquainted, sir, with the worst emotions of our very unpleasant nature, as written, sir, upon the human countenances of the passengers, up and down."

"Then you are a thinker?" remarked Mr. Fennel, looking respectfully at the skull development of his new acquaintance, which closely resembled what old-country housewives were wont to term a "skillet," otherwise, a small, round pot.[1]

"I am proud to say I am. My name, sir, is Archelaus[2] Simkins. You

---

[1] Like Archelaus Simkins's interest in physiognomy, popular interest in phrenology continued into the 1870s. This "science" purported to link the cranial structure of an individual to the development and position of organs belonging to the various mental faculties.

[2] An Athenian philosopher of this name (5th century BCE) held that the fundamental principles of the cosmos are heat and cold.

have probably studied classic lore, sir?"

"Well, yes, when I was a boy," replied Mr. Fennel, modestly.

"Well, sir, in classic lore there is, as you are aware, mentioned an elderly person of an uncertain temper, who felt the hollowness and vanity of all human things, profoundly, sir, and shewed his contempt of the world by residing in a common domestic washing-tub. Effective, sir, but trying to the spine, I should say."

"Decidedly," assented Fennel. "I presume you allude to Diogenes."[1]

"Sir, you apprehend me correctly, sir. In me you behold a second Diogenes! I am at two with the world and the times, though, perhaps, you would not suspect it from my appearance?"

"No, certainly not," said Fennel, surveying his chubby countenance with twinkling eyes.

Mr. Simkins smiled sardonically, and waved his hand round his limited apartment.

"Of course, I could not call upon you to believe that the room in which we are now seated, is actually a tub, but, sir, Diogenes had every right to be a balmy philanthropist compared with me, I assure you."

"How is that, may I ask?" inquired Fennel.

"You may, sir. In me you behold the Lacrosse ball of Fortune," replied Mr. Simkins in a tone of profound melancholy. "A malign fate pursues me, even amongst my tomatoes and cabbages and your inquiries, sir, about the lovely child of the red-skins, who has so unkindly fled from the protection of your venerable grandmother opens afresh, a wound, sir, that is not yet done bleeding."

"I'm very sorry, I'm sure," said Mr. Fennel, suddenly, bending his brows over his brilliant eyes, and "concentrating" his glance on his companion from the shade of that pent-house. "Would it be intruding on your confidence to ask in what manner?"

"Sir, in you I see a mind of rare grasp and power," said Mr. Simkins, solemnly, "and naturally my soul meets yours in the realms of sympathy. I will confide in you, sir."

Mr. Fennel bowed to the compliment; and Mr. Simkins continued feelingly.

"The harpy-winged fate, sir, that blights the innocent tomato and cabbage plants in my flower-pots, pursues the roses of my existence. Do

---

[1]   The name of this Greek philosopher (4th century BCE) has become a byword for "cynic."

you observe a slight swelling and discoloration about my left eye?"

"Now that you speak of it, I do," answered Fennel, looking at the pale, blue orb in question, "but it isn't very remarkable."

"It was a dire spectacle one short week ago," said Mr. Archelaus Simkins. "It resulted, sir, from the treachery of a fair, but treacherous woman and goddess of classic lore, sir, with the heart of a 'Fierce Mermaiden,'[1] as Tennyson so beautifully puts it."

"She must have a fine biceps," remarked Fennel, smiling despite his efforts to look sympathetic. "A lover's quarrel, I suppose."

"A tragic ending to a glorious dream," said Mr. Simkins, looking into the coffee-pot to see if it were boiling; "but," he continued, darkly, "it is not all over yet. Ha! the lion is aroused and before his tail ceases to wag, there will be mischief! Take heed, take heed Seraphina Brown, take heed, Robinson Jones!" Mr. Simkins fell in his chair, and sneered at a time-table hanging opposite.

"Were it not for the interference of a stranger with a black beard and an arm of iron, I would have had his life on the spot," he said. "Yes, sir, Robinson Jones would have now been in a land of spectres and Seraphina a lovely relict, a blighted blossom!" said Archelaus sentimentally.

"One short fortnight ago, I was engaged to Seraphina," he continued in low intense tones, "and I was happy! What was it to me that her parents favored Robinson Jones? Like Romeo and Juliet, we laughed at such trifles, or at least I did, for alas! Seraphina nourished the serpent of deceit in her faithless bosom. What were my feelings when amid the passengers on the very train your inquiries were about, I recognized Seraphina, her lovely countenance framed in orange-blossoms, while beside her sat Robinson Jones in a new suit and hat as black as his own base soul! I said not a word, and Seraphina laughed in my face. 'Let's be friends all around,' says Jones; but I withered him with a look. Presently he got out of the car to buy candy for Seraphina, and the spectacle of the double-dyed villain ministering to her wants at the candy-stall possessed my breast with a sublime fury. I forgot the duties of my office. I forgot all earthly things but my rival, and I pitched into him, sir, with a sensation of intense joy. I would have slain him on the spot, but at this moment I felt a grasp of iron on my arm, and I was torn from my prey by the stranger with the immense black beard, and before I had time to understand things, Jones had fled to the arms of Seraphina,

---

[1]   See Tennyson, "The Sailor Boy" (1864) 6.

and the train had carried him from the reach of my vengeance. Sir, fancy if you can, my sensations. I turned to assault the stranger, but he was calmly perusing a poster just put up, describing the young lady you mention."

"Well," said Mr. Fennel, much interested in the tale of woe poured forth by Archelaus, "what did you do then?"

"I looked at him," said Mr. Simkins solemnly, "and being convinced that in some cases matter is superior to mind, I felt my eye, which had come in contact with Jones' fist, and came into the office here, in order to calm my tempestuous feelings. Presently the door opened and in walked the stranger. 'When does the next down train pass?' he said in a slow low kind of voice. 'I've missed this one.' I told him, and he walked out again and went to reading the poster."

"This was on the night-express from Toronto?" said Fennel, whose interest in the recital of his sorrows flattered Mr. Simkins vastly. "Does no train pass up at the same time, and might you not have missed seeing the girl in the confusion?"

"No, trains don't pass here, and the next one wasn't due for hours," replied Mr. Simkins. "She wasn't on it, and you may be sure, on reading the poster I kept a good look-out for her. Your grandmother must be very fond of her, sir?"

"Very," said Mr. Fennel, looking in through the open door of the stove at the blazing fire. "But what happened to your black-bearded friend?"

"He, and a lame Indian boy, took tickets for Scranton, and went on by the next train. The poor red-skin must have walked a good bit to the station for he seemed hardly able to crawl. He was blind of an eye, and as sickly a looking case as you'd see. They went," continued Mr. Simkins, relapsing into sentiment, "and left me to nurse my wrath in the cradle of indignation. You seem to find the room too warm, sir!"

Mr. Fennel had grown very red in the face, and answered that he did find it rather close, whereupon Mr. Simkins flung wide the door, and soon reduced the temperature. At the same moment the telegraph apparatus began clicking and he had to leave his guest to attend its signals. "A well-spent morning," said Mr. Fennel, with a little smile. "So Mr. Macer, you did not see her here, and you went to Scranton instead of Montreal. I think I've a clue now, worth having. Gracie, my dear, I won't be with you to-day, my pet, or perhaps to-morrow."

All which was, as a mental soliloquy, quite inaudible to Mr. Archelaus Simkins.

CHAPTER XXII

A Strange Betrothal

"What is going on to-night?" said Denville, as the footman flung wide open the door of one of the stateliest houses in or about Montreal, and welcomed his master with a start of surprise.

"Good evening, sir," said the man, respectfully. "Mrs. Denville has a dinner party and a reception afterwards. Shall I let her know that you have arrived, sir?"

"Not at present. Tell some of them to see to my luggage. I shall go to my room. How have you all been during my absence?"

"Very well, thank you, sir, excepting the bay 'oss. He's been pinin' like, but he looks first-rate now, and feeds as it would do you good to see him, sir. You're not looking very well yourself, sir."

"I'm quite well, thank you, Simon. A little tired, that's all. Is there a large party at dinner?"

"Not very, sir; there's Colonel Champlean and the Miss Champleans, and the Honorable Mr. Davenant and Major Skyer and Sir Bertram Ousely, belonging to the new regiment, and Mr. Armor and some more ladies. That's all."

"Very well," said Theodore. "Pay the cab-man and have my trunks sent to my room. I do not know whether I shall come down to-night."

At this moment a servant opened one valve of a lofty, arched folding-door, and came out, giving a brilliant glimpse of a magnificent room beyond, all dazzling light, glowing exotics, and glittering plate and crystal. An oval table occupied the centre of the apartment, and beyond the plateau Theodore could see the stately form of his mother, speaking graciously to a pale, distinguished-looking young man, whom, with a savage grinding of his teeth, he recognized as Armor. Servants were moving silently about, and a faint hum, broken frequently by silvery ripples of laughter, proclaimed that dullness certainly was not a guest at the board.

Like figures in a dream, he noted the flower-crowned heads of the girls and the faces of the men; but Armor's was painfully vivid and real, and seemed to shine out from amongst the others.

The great vestibule was very softly lighted, so that Theodore escaped the observation of the party, and as the door closed again he turned away and walked slowly towards the wide staircase, lighted by alabaster lamps held by laughing nymphs in bronze, their dusky beauties flung out well from the rosy-tinted walls behind them.

He passed the drawing-rooms, silent enchanted vistas of deserted magnificence, softly lighted by chandeliers like crystal fountains, holding mellow wax-lights that gleamed like stars in a summer sky. The ruby tide of firelight flowed out over every object that could gratify the most refined or the most sumptuous taste. Statues rising from banks of rainbow bloom, great vases of porphyry, dropping cascades of starry blossoms and emerald foliage to the white carpets, that glowed here and there with a flower or leaf that looked as though dropped from the hand of summer herself. Great mirrors, with gilded Cupids hiding in the tangled vines with blossoms of enamel that framed them, and in the distance the glitter of a conservatory seen between great draperies of rose-silk, caught back by two Arab women in bronze and oxydized silver, copied from a pair made for Eugenie.[1] The glitter of a fountain amongst the oleanders, and the flutter of brilliant-winged tropical birds, in a great cage, almost a portable aviary of fine, gilt wire.

In a shadowy corner of the farther drawing-room there gleamed the frame of a harp, and by it, as still as the statue of Diana,[2] with bow and crescent, behind her, sat a young woman in white, with jet black hair and a face as clearly cut and pale as ivory; and Theodore's step paused and his face changed seriously as he looked at her.

"Why not?" he said, with a smile of utter bitterness, and then he went in and walked noiselessly up beside her.

"Valerie!" he said, touching the ivory arm that rested on the rosy velvet of the low *fauteuil* on which she reclined.

"*Ciel!*" she said with a slight start, and speaking in French. "Theodore, you alarmed me! I was even now thinking of you."

The greatest coxcomb could hardly have mistaken the simple friendliness of Valerie's voice and manner, as she put out her slender hand, and Theodore took it in his as frankly as it was given. Whatever and how great his failings might be, he certainly did not err on the side of personal vanity.

"How is it you are here alone?" he said, drawing a chair close to her;

---

[1] Wife of the French emperor Napoleon III, Eugénie (1826–1920) was regarded as a great beauty and model of elegance, and became an object of sympathy in her exile in England following the revolution of 1870.

[2] Goddess of the moon and hunting in Roman mythology, often associated with chastity and the protection of women.

"but I am glad to secure you for a moment to myself," he added, "no matter from what cause."

"Thanks!" with a gay laugh that vibrated like fairy music from the harp at her side; "a bad headache detained me here, but it is gone now. Mamma did not expect you, Theodore, and it is undeniable that you look miserable. Eh! you have an appearance of illness, most extremely."

He glanced at an opposite mirror, and was forced to acknowledge that he did look rather ghastly, and a striking contrast to the woman at his side, in her fresh, white dress, and the glowing Bejaria[1] spray, clinging to the massive braids of her satin-glossy hair.

"I am not well," he confessed, "but it is only a trifling indisposition, a thing of no moment."

Valerie's brilliant black eyes travelled over his face, over his somewhat neglected dress, and her crimson lips, fine and firm, parted in a very faint smile. She put out her hand and touched his arm.

"Look at me, *monsieur mon cousin*," she said, "and listen to me. Your words are not of the well of truth, *mon ami. Ciel!* I possess eyes and a soul."

Theodore was silent. He ground his teeth together and involuntarily clenched the hand that rested on the arm of her *fauteuil*.

Valerie's eyes glittered.

"I am right," she said triumphantly; "stay! without another word from you I can read the secret of your indisposition. In the first place, it is a mental ailment."

"Valerie, do not seek to know its origin," said Theodore bitterly. "You have ever had my confidence. You may surmise what the cause of my present annoyance is, but keep the secret to yourself, my cousin, as you value my friendship."

"My dear Theodore!"

"Valerie, do not look at me with such reproach. I am utterly miserable, and it only racks my soul to speak of its cause. How did that cursed Armor become a guest under this roof?"

Astonished beyond expression at the sudden ferocity with which Denville asked this question, Valerie looked at him in silence. She began to fear that her cousin was slightly insane.

"There," he said, with a short laugh, "I have alarmed you!"

"Do not apologise," said Valerie, quietly, "but explain. As the confidante

---

[1]   The "Rose of the Andes," a genus of trees and shrubs known for its brilliant flowers.

and adviser of my cousin, he should not leave me to grope my way, perhaps to a false conclusion. What has this *Monsieur* Armor done to render himself so obnoxious to you?"

Denville's dark eyes absolutely glared like wells of fire.

"He is going to marry Olla Frazer," he said, as though these words were explanation sufficient. Valerie raised her hand, on which gleamed a plain gold ring guarded by a hoop of blazing diamonds and emeralds, with a gesture of astonishment. A crimson spot stained the ivory of her cheeks, and for a moment she was speechless.

"The traitor!" she said at length, looking at Theodore with infinite compassion. "I had no idea that the evil I guessed at was so great."

There was a sensitive conscientiousness about Denville, a keen sense of honor, that would not, despite his rage, allow of his permitting Valerie to apply this epithet to his rival.

"I hate the man," he said, gloomily; "but, Valerie, he is blameless in so far as that he knew nothing of my hopes concerning Olla; but while I hate him with all the strength of my soul, I cannot hate her, traitress as she is."

Valerie leant back in her couch, and clasping her jewelled hands, looked earnestly at her cousin, as he gazed up the long vista of the room, with set teeth and lowering brows.

She was a thoroughly practical, warm-hearted, picturesque kind of woman, doing sweet home duties in a cordial, effective kind of way, that when she poured you out a cup of tea left you under the impression that she was a kindly Grace presiding at some celestial banquet, to which her radiant smiles lent its chiefest charm. She looked dainty and lovely as a poet's dream, leaning back, with the soft glow on her upturned face, and her liquid black eyes full of pensive light; but, in fact, she was trying to take a common-sense view of her cousin's case, either to give him comfort if it were past cure, or to seek the remedy if such existed.

There be no such potent panaceas for the woes of man, short of their removal, as a great deal of sympathy from one we love, and a few whispers of common sense from the goddess Reason. Valerie was prepared to give both. She was several years older than her cousin, and had a keener insight into his wayward, jealous, slightly unreasonable disposition than she permitted him to suppose. She knew of his affection for Olla, and had often urged him to make his love for her known to the young girl, but half-secure, half-diffident, Theodore had deferred seizing his happiness until now it had flitted beyond his reach.

She knew Olla slightly, and had guessed from her speaking eyes and ingenuous face, that she loved Theodore, as Valerie, proud and fond of him as an elder sister, would have had him loved; hence these sudden tidings found her utterly unprepared for them.

"Tell me, Theodore," she said after a few moments' reflection. "How did you hear of Miss Frazer's engagement? From herself?"

"No," returned Denville, pulling his glossy moustache fiercely, as he recalled the scene, "Miss Bertrand, her whom we met at Murray Bay, you remember, told me of it. I had it from no one else."

Valerie sat up and looked at Theodore curiously. She had been in the fair Cecil's society sufficiently long to read with her keen eyes the poor little volume of that young lady's soul and character. Long enough to discover and laugh at the pretty little nets she was weaving for that well gilded young "catch" of society, and she felt as suspicious of the truth of the information so received, as one would feel of the good-will accompanying a gift of red gold from the arch-enemy of mankind.

"*Bien!*" she said, laughing one of her rare, sudden little laughs, and clapping her little hands together. "Then I wager you my diamond locket that it is false."

Theodore started violently, and his face flushed deeply. He looked at his cousin, but he did not speak.

"My good Theodore!" she said, "but you are stupid. Miss Bertrand, was a skilful archer when she launched that shaft!"

"She is a simple-hearted little thing," said Theodore, "and besides, what object—?"

"True, she looks like one of Correggio's Angels, so innocent, so *spirituelle*. Her object? to secure a thoroughly eligible *parti*. It is done every day. These little lies that sting to death are told and never discovered until too late by those lied about or lied to. They are the recognized weapons of what the English term, match-makers."

"Valerie!"

"Theodore! Your Miss Cecil is a pretty little *intrigante*. Leave it to me to prove it."

"Valerie, this is not worthy of you! If you could only see her sweet gratitude to me for the risk I ran in saving her life when the boat upset at Murray Bay, her lovely nature so childish and pure, you would not wound your own nobility by speaking thus."

"Theodore," cried Valerie in sudden alarm, "have you been betrayed into thinking you could love that wicked little butterfly?"

"Love her!" said Denville, "oh, no, Valerie."

"Pardon me, *mon ami*," said Valerie softly. The exceeding desolate bitterness of Theodore's voice convinced her of the great hold, firmer than she had fancied, that Olla had on her cousin's fiery heart.

She felt confirmed in her opinion of Cecil's duplicity, but she saw how useless it would be to urge it then. She watched Theodore silently as he rose and paced the room, looking down frowningly at the carpet.

A look of set bitterness had aged and darkened his handsome face, and his lips curved as though in deadly scorn of himself and all the world. Its sternness softened a little as he paused before her chair and looked at her.

"Valerie," he said suddenly, "are you not yet persuaded that your infamous husband is dead? Do you still doubt the newspaper notice of his death in New Orleans?"

Certainly she had not been prepared for this question. Her face became white as marble, and she bent her head, coroneted with shining braids, against the carved back of the *fauteuil*.

"I still believe that he is alive," she said quietly. "Why do you ask me this to-night?"

"Because," said Theodore, "I am going to ask you to believe yourself the widow you are, and being free, become my wife."

She rose and faced him, leaning her hand on the back of the couch, reading him with her astonished eyes. "Listen to me," he continued as he saw she was about to speak. "I love you dearly, my noble cousin, and from your hand I beg the boon of redemption of my life. I am standing on the brink of destruction and you alone can save me. I foresee for myself a few brief years of wildest dissipation in which I shall try to forget, for I know the weakness of my character, as no one else does. By becoming my wife, my loved and honored wife, Valerie! you can save me from this."

She knew how true his words were, and her very soul trembled in exceeding anguish.

"Ah," she exclaimed, raising her beautiful eyes full of tears to his, "what have I done that this new trial is thrust upon me? Theodore, I cannot, dare not marry you. I am no widow."

"It is a strange idea that clings to you, dear Valerie," said Theodore, almost pityingly.

"I feel it as a solemn truth," she said, laying her left hand, with the marriage ring, over her heart, "and, Theodore, unworthy as he proved, I loved him."

"Forget him," said Denville, "morally or legally he has no claim to you. A felon and fugitive, he dare not breathe the very air with you. Valerie, once for all, will you save me or not?"

"Ungenerous!" exclaimed the young woman, sobbing faintly. "Why do you not say, 'Valerie Lennox, you owe my mother a debt of gratitude that nothing can repay. I command you to marry me.' Oh, for once you fail to be yourself. You are ignoble!"

"Valerie," said Theodore, "if you do not marry me what shall I do, think you?"

His tone filled her with a great fear.

"I do not know," she said.

"I will go straight from this room to the street, and the first woman I meet, who is willing to take it, shall own the name of Denville."

"You are mad!" she cried, shrinking from him.

"I am mad," he answered slowly. "I know that I am. It has been creeping on me for days. But I am serious in my purpose, Valerie!"

"Your mother?" she said, looking at his blazing eyes with a shudder of terror.

His countenance changed.

"Will you promise?" he asked, and put out his hand to lift his cap, which he had inadvertently carried into the room.

She sprang to him and caught his arm.

"Rash boy," she cried, "I promise to become your wife in one short week if you should still wish it."

"Thank you, Valerie," he said simply, "you alone have power to save me."

"Go and lie down, Theodore," she said, looking anxiously at his sunken eyes and hectic flushed cheeks, "and sleep if you can. Your mother and her guests will be here in a few moments, and she would be inexpressibly shocked to see how ill you are looking." He lifted her hand to his lips and left the room. She went out into the corridor and watched him ascend the wide stairs towards his own apartments.

Then she came back and stood for a moment in deep thought.

"The boy is frightfully in earnest," she said with a deeply drawn sigh. "Should the worst come, I must sacrifice myself on the shrine of gratitude. Stay! I have an idea."

She rang the bell, and Simon answered the summons.

WINONA; OR, THE FOSTER-SISTERS   229

"I wish to send Pierre to the Telegraph Office, send him to the library in five minutes."

"Very well, Madame."

The message Pierre bore to the office was this:—

"Mrs. Frazer, I shall be with you to-morrow night on business of importance.

VALERIE LENNOX."

[PART 9—8 MARCH 1873]

CHAPTER XXIII

Mr. Macer's Accident

Valerie Lennox, a radiant figure in rich furs and cashmere and velvet of a royal purple, walked into the drawing-room of Captain Frazer's residence, and found Dolly sitting in solitary state, with her dainty feet on the fender, and a long strip of tatting slipping very slowly through her rosy-tipped fingers.

"Miss Dolly, asthore," said Mr. Murphy, who, in his character of general factotum to the establishment, had gone with the sleigh to the station to meet Mrs. Lennox, and now ushered her into the apartment, "would ye be after tellin' the misthress that the lady is here? I've got to put up them rattlin' bastes of ponies that turned me out into two snow-drifts like a murphy out ov a skib,[1] the rapscallions. They had the manners to behave like dacent Christians comin' home, out ov respect to the lady, but it's me heart's broke wid 'em entirely."

"Miss Dolly Frazer?" said Valerie with one of her sweetly radiant smiles. She had heard of the lovely creature, and though she had never seen her, she guessed her identity immediately.

Dolly was always self-possessed, and the air, quite natural, by the way, with which she rose and welcomed Mrs. Lennox was perfect. The latter was an able critic of men and manners, and inly she pronounced the girl's bearing perfection. To do Dolly justice, had she been born a dairy-maid, her style would have varied very little. She would have milked the kine and scoured the churns with the combined air of an empress and a saint. As our lively Gallic friends say, her manner was *tout naturel*.

She rang the bell, and directed the trim parlor-maid who answered its call to let her mother know of the arrival of the self-invited guest whose telegram had excited no little wonder and speculation in the family circle. She placed a lounging chair beside the fire, into which Valerie sank with a smile. She looked at Dolly, and her brilliant eyes sparkled.

---

[1] Like a potato out of a basket.

"My dear Miss Frazer," she said, as Dolly seated herself again, and raised her magnificent violet eyes with a little curiosity to the superb form and face opposite, the ivory skin tinged with rose from the bracing air, the gracious kindliness and soul-lit expression of every feature, the high-bred, easy grace of the tall form, all making a striking and pleasing picture. "My dear Miss Frazer, my presence must be utterly unaccountable to you all, and now that I am here, I really am almost at a loss how to introduce my errand."

If she expected Dolly to aid her in the least she found herself mistaken, for Dolly only smiled sweetly, clasped her white fingers on her lap, and said:

"Are you Mrs. Lennox?"

Fortunately the door opened and Mrs. Frazer came in, with a look of expectant curiosity, and followed by Olla, on whom the speaking eyes of Mrs. Lennox rested eagerly and anxiously.

Olla was much changed since she had seen her at the close of the previous winter in Montreal. She looked fragile in the extreme, and there was a pensive and mournful expression in the lovely brown eyes that struck her at once.

She rose and drew the girl to her side with a quiet grace, and kissed her on the cheek.

"Present me to your mamma," she said, and Olla, trembling she knew not why, did so.

The telegram, coming as it did from one who, though Theodore Denville's cousin, was nearly a stranger to her, and altogether so to the rest of the family, had filled her with forebodings that at one time almost assumed the rosy complexion of something nearly akin to hope, while again she was involved in presentiments of misery to result from the visit of Valerie Lennox.

She did not for a second doubt that Denville or herself was in some way connected with the business that brought Valerie the long journey from Montreal in such severe weather, and as Mrs. Lennox turned to her mother, with outstretched hand and attentive eyes that read Mrs. Frazer's face with serious scrutiny, Olla leant her hand on the back of Dolly's chair to support herself, for she trembled exceedingly.

The atmosphere of the room suddenly felt stifling to her, and, going to the door, she set it open, and then came back, and resuming her former attitude, watched Mrs. Lennox anxiously, while her heart beat loud and fast, and a mist swam before her eyes.

"I have ascertained," said Mrs. Lennox, looking at her watch, "that I can catch a return train in two hours from this time, so, Mrs. Frazer, I have exactly that period in which to learn whether three persons are to be made intensely miserable or extremely happy. Am I at liberty to speak?"

"Not until you have rested and refreshed yourself," said Mrs. Frazer, decidedly, "and as for leaving us to-night——"

"My dear madame," said Mrs. Lennox, "I am in the position, almost, of a fugitive. No one is aware of my absence from home but my aunt and one of the servants. It is urgently necessary that I return to Montreal to-night. A member of our little family is threatened with severe illness," she added, turning suddenly towards Olla, and fixing her grave eyes on the girl's face. They lightened triumphantly as the pretty face blanched suddenly, and as Mrs. Frazer looked on in astonishment, Valerie swept across to Olla and took her hand. She led her to a little couch opposite Dolly's throne, and seated herself, drawing Olla down beside her.

She had a view of the pretty hall as she sat thus, but her gaze was fixed on the downcast face at her side. She had thrown aside her velvet cloak, and her furs lay on the arm of the couch. She was evidently in haste.

It was perfectly true that before her departure from Montreal Denville had developed slight symptoms of fever, but Valerie was not to be much blamed if she slightly exaggerated matters, in hopes of reading Olla's sentiments more clearly in the light of the announcement.

"May I ask your meaning, Mrs. Lennox?" said Mrs. Frazer gently; "as you may perceive, I am quite mystified."

Mrs. Lennox hesitated. She felt the delicacy of her position——a perfect stranger, coming to thrust herself on the confidence of this family; but too much was at stake to risk anything through an overstrained sentiment, and with a sweetly deprecating glance at Mrs. Frazer she said:

"I have come all this way in order to ask a simple question, which I am perfectly aware I have no right to ask. Before I transgress, may I feel certain of your indulgent consideration?"

Mrs. Frazer bowed a little distantly. She was one of the proudest, as well as one of the humblest of women, and Mrs. Lennox's tone somewhat alarmed that pride which most women feel in keeping the real home history of the family, whether it be pleasant or sad, sacred from the touch and gaze of strangers.

Mrs. Lennox paused, secretly a little fearful and uncertain how to put the question she had come so far to ask.

The trouble in her handsome face appealed to Mrs. Frazer strongly, and she said kindly:

"I am altogether at your service, Mrs. Lennox, if I can in any way assist you in your present difficulty. I knew and esteemed your aunt as a girl, and, for the sake of my girlhood's friend, I would do her niece any good office that lay in my power."

"Then give me permission to speak freely in your presence to your daughter, and conjure her to answer me frankly," said Mrs. Lennox eagerly.

Olla attempted to rise. She dumbly felt that something was coming which, whether of good or evil to her, a blind impulse urged her to fly for the present, but Mrs. Lennox pressed her firm arm round her and detained her.

"Excuse me, Olla," said Dolly, looking up from her work, "but will you tell me how many stitches make the large circle?"

She was quite unaware of the disturbance in the moral atmosphere surrounding her, for she was quite incapable of following out two trains of ideas, and absorbed in her work, had lost the thread of the conversation.

"Twenty-four, dear," said Olla mechanically.

"Thank you," said Dolly graciously; "but really, Olla, you don't look well. Is there anything the matter with you, dear?"

"I am quite well," replied Olla hastily; "but I think the day is changing to even greater cold," and she shivered as she spoke.

"You look quite blue," said Dolly sympathizingly. "I've noticed Mr. Armor get quite blue when it's very cold," and she relapsed into silence.

Mrs. Lennox glanced at the exquisite face bent over the work with such infinite grace, curiously.

"Miss Frazer," she said, coloring deeply with agitation, "your sister has just spoken a name connected with the question I am about to ask you. Have you been, or are you at present engaged to this Mr. Armor?"

"No," said Olla, looking at Valerie in simple surprise, "how could you have heard that? Dolly and he are to be married in the spring."

She looked at Valerie questioningly. Was this the question that there had been so much trouble in asking?

Suddenly its bearing on herself struck her, and trembling with agitation, she sprang to her feet.

"Who told you such a false, wicked thing?" she cried, with an impetuosity that for a moment seemed to transform her to a thing of fire.

"Miss Cecil Bertrand told my cousin Theodore when he was in Toronto," said Valerie, speaking very slowly and distinctly, and without a trace of color even in her lips; "she said that it was your engagement to him prevented your visiting Toronto, as you had led my cousin to expect you would. You can imagine the result so far as Theodore is concerned."

Olla was never born to be a heroine. Here was the moment for denouncing vengeance on the wicked head that had wrought her such mischief, but she at once sacrificed all claims to heroic immortality by burying her face in her hands and sobbing over and over again:

"Oh, Cecil, how could you, could you do it?"

Valerie's face darkened as she gave a thought to Cecil, and brightened again as she rose and took Mrs. Frazer's hands in hers, while Dolly, in an anomalous kind of calm flutter, floated to Olla, and mistily conscious that her sister was in trouble, looked the sympathy she could not find words to express.

"Mrs. Frazer," said Valerie, radiant again as a southern constellation, "this is all a mystery to you, but a few words will make the affair clearer. In the first place, Olla, I am the most miserable woman in the world, and it lies in your power, my child, to render me happy again; at least," she added, as a shadow fell on her face, "as happy as I can ever hope to be. Will you do this for me?"

"If I can," said Olla, who had recovered her usual sweet composure. "Mamma," she added, turning to Mrs. Frazer, "you must think me so silly, but I did not think Cecil could have been so wicked."

"Well, Olla," said Valerie, "I must carry back your promise to Montreal, strengthened by the consent of your parents, that you will think more kindly of Theodore, than, I admit, he has any right to expect. In fact," said Valerie, with infinite candor, "he——"

"Behaved like a horrid donkey," said Sidney, who, in full walking dress, her cheeks crimson from the outer air, had been standing unobserved on the threshold for some moments, listening with profound attention. "Mamma, I can't help it! and, Olla, I told you Miss Cecil was telling fibs."

At this moment the door of the library opened, and a gentleman came out into the hall, carrying a fur cap in his hand.

Mrs. Lennox, looking at Sidney in the doorway, saw behind the bright head a dark face and flowing beard of ebon darkness, and the eyes of Mr. Macer, shaded by their blue glasses, rested for a moment on the radiant form of Valerie, as she stood, the central figure in the group of women who had clustered round her.

Excitement had kindled a warm rose in the pure ivory of her cheeks. Her liquid black eyes flashed with expression, and her lips, fine and coral-scarlet, were parted in a singularly sweet smile.

She made an exquisite picture as she stood thus, in the rich firelight and sunlight of the room, a glowing creature such as Titian or Rubens[1] would have loved to have painted, and such as smile from quaint old frames in the mellow light of Italian galleries.

Mr. Macer stood and studied her for a moment, and then turned back into the library.

Captain Frazer was writing at the escritoire, the front of which lay back, displaying rows of pigeon-holes containing bundles of papers, neatly arranged and labelled, for the Captain was, like most military men, the perfection of neatness in the ordering of his personal effects.

Androsia Howard sat basking in the full tide of sunlight pouring on her through the window, reading, her straight brows knitted over her brilliant eyes, which she raised from the page as Macer re-entered the room. Captain Frazer, absorbed in his task, did not notice his return.

Macer walked up to Androsia, who eyed his approach with extreme disfavor. Since his rescue of Sidney, he had been a very frequent visitor at the house, but while he was a lion and favorite with the other girls, Androsia's haughty reserve and evident dislike had not abated towards him by so much as a shade.

"Excuse me," he said, in his slow peculiar voice, "but I am all anxiety to know the name of Mrs. Frazer's beautiful guest. Will Miss Howard pardon my audacity in addressing her, and gratify my inquisitiveness?"

There was an undercurrent of mockery in his words and voice that Androsia felt like a sting. Her brows lowered, her head went up.

"Go away!" she said with that pitiless directness springing from her want of cultivation. "You can ask some of the servants. I am busy," and, with a face of utter scorn, she dropped her eyes on her book. It was plain that it would require an immense amount of "cultivation" to make Androsia, poor child of nature, gracious to those her instincts warned

---

[1]   The Italian painter Tiziano Vecellio Titian (1577–1640) and the Flemish painter Peter Paul Rubens (c. 1477–1576) are regarded as two of Europe's greatest Renaissance artists.

her against as base and ignoble. Mr. Macer's eyes sparkled behind his glasses, and a dull red glow showed on his swarthy face.

His long brown fingers clenched themselves stealthily, and, with a glance at Androsia's averted face, he left the room.

"I suppose I was what they call 'rude' to him," thought Androsia, with a slight pang of remorse; "but my tongue speaks of itself. I hate him!"

Mr. Macer walked out into the morning sunlight, and stood for a moment on the veranda, listening to the sound of Mike's saw as he busied himself with the wood-pile in the wood-yard behind the house. The sharp cutting sound of the saw was accompanied occasionally by a bar or two of "Molly Bawn"[1] or some hilarious remark to some person who was evidently engaged with a second saw in Mr. Murphy's neighborhood.

Mr. Macer's face expressed a great many things as he stood on the veranda reflecting on the rebuff he had just received from Androsia. There was amusement of a slightly diabolical character, malice, and, above and beyond all, a deadly resolve in the compression of the lips. The eyes were hidden by the tinted glasses, but the air of the man was deadly.

There was a look about his face, too, as of one who, in walking through the mists of evening, finds himself suddenly standing on the brink of some yawning and horrid chasm, and strains his gaze through the shadows to see if perchance, by a daring leap, he can gain in safety the opposing crest.

He had walked over this morning to borrow a book from Captain Frazer, and with a lingering step, that yet sounded firm and unfaltering as the snow crunched beneath his foot, he walked away, and was lost to sight amongst the pine-trees, watched curiously over the cedar-hedge, which divided the front lawn from the kitchen-garden and wood-yard, by Mr. Murphy and his companion.

"Now who may that be?" said the latter, pausing to oil his saw, while Mike shook his head after the retreating form of Macer; "one of the family, I'll be bound." The questioner was a slightly-built young fellow in a checked flannel shirt and an old fur cap set well back from his freckled and sunburnt face, one side of which seemed considerably

---

[1] A traditional Irish ballad.

swollen, while his jaws were bound up with a red cotton handkerchief, emblazoned with "Let dogs delight to bark and bite"[1] in yellow letters.

His eyes were sharp and bright, and his accent decidedly Milesian, a fact which had instantly commended him to the good graces of Mike, whose heart warmed instantly to anything or any one on which or whom the skies of Erin had smiled.

"You're out, Pat," responded Mr. Murphy, in a tone of some slight offence; "shure it's blind ye must be to be afther takin' that black-aired rapscallion—the divil fly off wid him this same day!—for kith, kin or relation to the swate young craythurs inside. It's Macer, as he calls himself, it is."

"An' who's he, now?" asked Pat, looking musingly at the cord-wood stick he had just placed across the saw-horse. "It's a mortial black-faytured craythur he is, any-ways."

Mr. Murphy shook his head, and proceeded to light his favorite "dhudeen"[2] as he answered:

"Sorra wan ov me knows, or any wan else in the house for that matther. He comes an' goes like wan ov themselves, an' exceptin' my Miss Drosia, he gets the heart's welcome from all. He says he's an hartist, an's takin' picthures ov the winter scanes about the river. He boords down at Mrs. Appleyard's that sent ye up here to get the job ov helpin' me cut the winter's wood. How cum it ye didn't persave him yerself?"

"It's meself was only there wan night, an' a man on the tramp for work isn't over an' above noticeful ov sthrangers," said Pat. "Och, Mike, but this toothache's a sore bother, an' the wind so keen," and Pat groaned.

"Come now!" said Mike, grinning jocularly, "it's in to purty Rosie there ye wants to be, gettin' her to doctor up that face ov yours, an' bedad! I'm not blamin' ye, considherin' the wind that's in it."

"What's that noise?" said the young man suddenly.

He raised his hand and leant forward in an attitude of eager attention. Mike, too, listened, and through the sharp clear air there came a loud shout, evidently for assistance, two or three times repeated,

---

[1] See Isaac Watts, *Divine and Moral Songs for the Use of Children* (1715), Song 16, "Against Quarrelling and Fighting":

> Let dogs delight to bark and bite,
> For God has made them so:
> Let bears and lions growl and fight,
> For 'tis their nature, too. (1–4)

[2] Pipe (Irish).

238   ISABELLA VALANCY CRAWFORD

"I wouldn't like to be over an' above certain," said Mike, coolly, "but it's mortial like Mr. Macer's voice; mebbe he slipt on that bit ov ice below the carriage-gate an' bruk his leg." There was an air of pleasurable speculation on Mr. Murphy's face that said more for his animosity towards Macer than a whole volume would have done. He applied a light to his pipe, and listened composedly for a repetition of the shout, and as soon as it came he smiled placidly as he observed:

"It's him, shure enough. Well! it's no day to lave a dog, let alone a gintleman, in disthress. His voice comes from the gate-ways, an' if he's bruk his leg we'll be afther wantin' that hand-sleigh. Fetch it along, Pat, ma bouchal!"[1]

Mike walked very leisurely round the cedar-hedge, followed by Pat with the sleigh, and led the way through the pine-grove to the gate. About a hundred feet to the right of the carriage gate there was a steep but short hill, now, owing to successive thaw and frost, completely shod with ice as glare as glass, and at the foot of this declivity, as Mike had foreseen, sat Macer, his hands grasping his foot, while he shouted loudly for assistance. "Is it hurt ye are, sur?" said Mike, with an air of great sympathy, as he approached the side of the road to which Macer had dragged himself. "Och hone! it's meself thought what had happened; but it's thankful ye ought to be that it chanced just here close by the house this shavin' day, sur. Is yer leg bruk, sur?"

"Only sprained," said Macer, turning a shade paler as he spoke, "but severely at that. I cannot move a step, I am afraid." He looked as though it gave him a sharp twinge as he spoke, and he compressed his lips firmly.

There was nothing for it but, as Mike suggested, an immediate return to the house he had just left, and, with the assistance of Pat, Mike managed to place him on the hand-sleigh and succeeded in dragging him up the hill.

He was quite unable to stand without assistance, and the family, who beheld his return from the drawing-room windows, ran out in dismay to learn the nature of the accident which had brought him back in this plight.

"I am afraid," he said, with a faint smile, to Mrs. Frazer, "that I must throw myself on your hospitality for the night, unless, indeed," he added anxiously, "you would allow Mike to drive me down to Scranton. Mrs. Appleyard, I have no doubt, would soon set me right again."

---

[1] My boy (Irish).

"Neither Captain Frazer nor myself could dream of allowing such a thing, Mr. Macer," said Mrs. Frazer, her face brightening, as she felt that now she would be enabled to return his service to Sidney in some degree; "you must be our guest until your ankle is well again." Perhaps in her maternal heart there was a faint wish dimly formed that they could have known something of the antecedents of this stranger, whom she, as well as her daughters, admitted to be one of the most fascinating men she had ever met.

And so it came about that Mr. Macer found himself thus unexpectedly domiciled in the bosom of the Frazer family.

Valerie Lennox watched him compassionately and curiously as Pat and Mike assisted him across the hall to the stairs, and became so absorbed in regarding him that Mrs. Frazer addressed her several times before, with a start, she heard and turned towards her.

"Pardon me," she said, crimsoning, "but, variable creature that I am! I have changed my mind, and will remain under your kind care for to-night, and telegraph to my aunt to expect me to-morrow. I will send no hint of the joyful news I have for Theodore," she said turning, with a rather broken and fluttering laugh, to Olla. "He deserves to be kept miserable a few hours longer. Don't you think so, Sidney?"

"I have no patience with such people," said Sidney severely, "and if I were Olla, I—"

"What would you do?" queried Valerie laughingly.

Sidney's loveliness and piquante sauciness delighted her. A really beautiful woman frequently takes genuine delight in the graces and attractions of another, despite all that may be said to the contrary.

"I don't know in the least," said Sidney gravely. "Dolly, you have owed Roddy a letter for this fortnight; come away and write it, or we shall have another embryo tragedy on our hands. *Au revoir* until tea-time, good people."

"If I had only something to say to him!" sighed Dolly, as she swept like a spirit from the room. "Oh, I wish he didn't ask me to write to him. It's worse than worsted work."

240   ISABELLA VALANCY CRAWFORD

CHAPTER XXIV

Mr. Murphy's Assistant

"Now, Pat," said Mike, as he lighted the stable lantern, "if ye can lave Rosie there, ye might lend me the loan ov yer company to the stables, and help me a bit wid them bastes ov ponies. Shure it'll do ye as much good to get a breath ov fresh air as sit cosherin in the corner there, wid Rosie."

"I guess you'd best mind your own business," said Rosie disdainfully, tossing her black head and looking daggers at Mr. Murphy, "it's not your ugly old teeth that's aching, and if it was I guess you might reckon on doing all your crying yourself."

"Now, whisht, Rosie, me posie," said Mr. Murphy poetically, winking at Pat, who sat toasting his bandaged jaw at the kitchen stove, "shure it's meself 'ud give a welcome to a toothache in every grinder, if it wor yer purty self 'ud condescind to wrap the hot bran round me face, wid yer own dawshy hands, as ye did for Pat, there. But, och! it's could enough charity is for an ould chap like me!" and Mr. Murphy heaved a labored sigh, and made a ridiculous effort to leer sentimentally at the saucy serving-maid, who, *pour passer le temps*, had instituted a very lively flirtation, based upon the toothache, with Pat, who responded rather bashfully to her coquettish attentions.

"You'd get all you deserve!" said Rosie, more graciously, however, somewhat appeased by Mike's compliment; "but I guess I'd best go where I'm wanted; and, Pat, while you're out just look to the door of the summer kitchen. I thought I shut it, but I heard it bang a little ago. Laws! but the wind's rosed powerful."

Rosie tripped out of the kitchen, and Mr. Murphy and Pat went out to attend to the ponies for the night, leaving the room to solitude with the exception of an old Tabby of majestic proportions, which lay blinking luxuriously in the warm glow of the great cooking-stove. Rosie had taken away the lamp, and the dry maple burning redly, threw an inexpressibly cheery light over the white walls, decorated with shining tins, and the painted floor. Three doors gave egress from the apartment, firstly to the summer kitchen, secondly to the wood-shed, through which Mike and Pat had to pass on their way to the stables, and the third opened into the house.

A door from the summer kitchen opened into the wood-shed, and as Pat and Mike passed it, the latter remembering Rosie's request, looked to see if it required fastening.

"Bedad, she must have been dhraming," said Mike, holding up the lantern to inspect the latch, "the dure's closed right enough, but I'll just put up this bit ov a chain to make it so, this windy night," and while Pat held the lantern, Mike secured the door on the outside by a stout chain, fixed to the post for the purpose, and then the two men took their way to the stable.

Hardly had the sound of their retreating steps died away, when the door leading from the summer to the winter kitchen, was noiselessly opened, and a face, dark and ghastly as some newly risen corpse, peered into the deserted apartment, and for a second took anxious survey of it. The appearance of the room seemed satisfactory, for the door was opened sufficiently to give entrance to the slender form of a tall Indian youth who stole like a shadow into the quiet room, and with a step as swift and soundless as the passage of light advanced towards a corner, where the outline of a trap-door made itself visible in the painted floor. Without a second's pause, he lifted it by an iron ring attached to it for the purpose, and disclosed a flight of steps leading into a spacious and airy cellar. Holding the trap in such a manner that it would descend noiselessly to its place he disappeared down the steps, and cautiously lowered the door over him. Hardly had it settled into its place when Rosie came back with the lamp, having been absent hardly five minutes. There was nothing in the appearance of the room to excite her suspicions of anything unusual having occurred in her absence, and taking up her knitting she seated herself in her wooden rocker and began to knit, and rock, and hum, a real picture of comfort, and a very pretty one too, with her apple-red cheeks, bright, shrewish, black eyes, and trim, rather gaily attired little figure. Despite the snapping of those eyes, and the sharp nimbleness of her tongue, she had a very pleasant smile and was a good-hearted little girl, much attached to the family of her employer, and inly much delighted with the evident impression her charms had made on the susceptible bosom of Mr. Murphy, who in this, "his sere and yellow leaf,"[1] had relinquished the memory of the faithless daughter of Erin, to worship at the shrine of the pretty

---

[1] See Shakespeare, *Macbeth* V.iii.22–23: "I have lived long enough: my way of life / Is fall'n into the sear, the yellow leaf...."

Canadian parlor-maid. He had visions of a "cleared farm" over which Rosie and he should preside at some future date, if that young woman could be prevailed on to become the partner of his life, and his savings, the latter being quite a handsome sum, on account of his long service with Colonel Howard.

Presently he and Pat came back from the stable, shivering and blue from the outer air, and Rosie looked up sharply as they entered the kitchen.

"Now, Pat," she cried, "just walk out and brush that snow off your boots! and you too! Mike. One'd think a body had nothing to do but sweep and clean after you men folks! I'm sure me and Sally hev trouble enough running after that there Macer and his lame foot without a sight more from you two!"

"Is the gintleman's foot rale bad, Miss Rosie?" said Pat, as he resumed his seat by the stove, after carefully obeying her injunctions. "Och bud it's meself wishes he had this toothache along wid it, the murtherin' torment that it is! Shure I wish it wor as aisy to cure as a sprain, any how!"

"I guess he don't feel very bright," said Rosie, "and if he isn't easier in the morning, Missus says, Mike there must go for the Doctor the first thing. Not that it looks much, but it do seem to hurt him quite a bit."

"The unfortunate craythur!" said Mike. "Well, well! it's a comfort to think that if it wor the will of a certain ould gintleman, the saints be betune us an' harrum! to invite him to his sate beside the nob down there, there's them about as could spare him, aisy!"

"You're a brute!" said Rosie, "people anyhow, don't die of sprains, do they, Mr. Pat?"

"I never heerd tell of any," responded Pat. "Begorra! me ould grannie larned me the thrick ov curing them in a jiffey, when a goose-berry skin 'ud have made me a night-cap, a'most. She wor a wise woman, the Heavens be her bed!"

"Is that so?" said Rosie, letting her knitting drop on her apron and gazing at Pat with rounded eyes.

"That she wor," replied Pat, retrospectively gazing into the fire, "an' no mistake. She could rade a tay-cup or scent a guager,[1] bad luck to 'em! wid any wise woman in the four parishes. An' as for love-charms, there warn't a colleen or gossoon in the county that wouldn't tramp her score ov miles, bare-fut, to get wan ov them."

---

[1] Tax collector (Irish).

"She didn't tell you anything about them last?" asked Rosie, much interested, "not that I reckon there's anything in such trash."

"In coorse not," said Mike, gallantly, "the red cheek an' the black eyes is the best love-charms. Eh, Rosie?"

"Shut up, do!" said Rosie, "and let Pat speak, can't you!"

"Oh," said Pat, looking a little sulky, "if ye don't belave me, Miss Rosie, where's the use ov tellin'? You'd be after laughin' your life out at me, I'll be bound."

"Seeing is believing," said Rosie, who was secretly dying to hear about the despised love-charms, "if you was to cure Macer's ankle, I guess I'd be readier to believe your grannie was so awful cute, above other folks."

"Now would ye?" said Pat, getting a little nettled as he saw Rosie's cherry lips, pouting scornfully. "Well, here's a bargain, Miss Rosie, if ye get me lave to thry the wise woman's charm on the gintleman up-stairs, I'll make ye a gift ov wan ov them others, that 'ud dhraw the fishes out ov the salt say, most nigh, an' giv ye the pick of the counthry. Red Injuns an' all! I'd like to let you persave that it's the thruth I'm discoorsin' to ye."

"Laws," said Rosie, tossing her head, "I don't want none of your trash, I'm sure; but it wouldn't be Christian to let Macer want the chance of gettin' around again, so if you like I'll ask him to let you try it."

"Do, yer sowl," said Pat, "it'll be doin' the poor gintleman a good turn anyhow."

"I've got to bring that there hot vinegar up to his room, right away," remarked Rosie, "and you can come up and stay outside the door until I ask him. He's a catchy kind of fellow, though he don't shew it out much, so don't you dare come in unless you get leave. Missus is in the drawing-room with Mrs. Lennox and the young ladies or I durstn't venture to fetch you up."

"I'll mind," said Pat.

"What a thing it is to have a feelin' heart," said Mike, grinning behind the cloud of tobacco smoke that issued from his favorite dhudeen. "Is it Macer's fut or them love-charms ye're thinkin' most ov, Rosie alannah?"[1]

"I wouldn't be such a fool as you, Mike, no, not for ten thousand dollars!" retorted Rosie, scarlet with wrath; "come, Pat, walk awful soft, for I wouldn't like Missus to hear."

---

[1] My child (Irish).

"What a quare fish a faymale woman is to be sure!" murmured Mike, as Rosie and Pat vanished, "an' the ways they hev of deludherin' themselves, let alone the boys! There's Rosie now, she's makin' belave to herself, that it's Macer's sprain she's thinkin' ov when we all know how much the same sprain has to do wid it. Och, but that Pat's a rale lad, he is. It's meself won't be sorry whin his job ov wood-cuttin' is over. A toothache's the Devil intirely for coortin' over."

Macer was seated in a great arm-chair drawn close to a blazing fire, and his injured foot rested on a pile of downy pillows, while a small stand stood at his elbow, bearing a reading-lamp, a small tea-equipage and a couple of magazines. He was alone, and his eyes were fixed on the fire as though he were plunged into a profound reverie, and his knitted brows proclaimed that either his injury or his meditations gave him some uneasiness. His eyes flashed and his lips were compressed, but while his thoughts were evidently concentrated on some subject of absorbing interest, there was mingled with his reverie a curious watchfulness, from which no movement in the quiet house seemed to escape.

Rosie's step and knock roused him with a start, and he called out "come in," with an impatient half-sigh.

Rosie entered with the embrocation, after warning Pat to remain perdu in the passage until she had sounded Macer on the subject of his willingness to permit the trial of the charm, the merits of which Pat was eager to prove in honor of the memory of the "wise woman" from whom he proudly claimed descent.

Pat, however, being the possessor of a most inquisitive and Paul-Pryish[1] disposition, no sooner found himself alone in the dimly-lighted lobby than he was seized with a strong desire to see the interior of the apartment into which Rosie had disappeared, and of which he had obtained a momentary glimpse as she had opened the door. The wind rattled and raved boisterously and the windows shook noisily, so that the turning of the handle of the door, escaped notice, and thrusting his face close to the aperture, he looked cautiously into the room.

Macer sat half-turned from the door, while Rosie knelt before him, bathing the sprained member with hot vinegar, her face screwed into an expression of profound sympathy as she plied her task.

---

[1] Nosy or wantonly intrusive, like the protagonist of *Paul Pry* (1825), a comedy by the English playwright John Poole.

"Do you feel it easier?" she asked, presently, "it do seem to hurt you awful though t'aint much swollen."

"Not much easier," said Macer, impatiently, "it's a wretched trifle though to keep a man chained in one spot when he ought to be about his business. My drawings will suffer for this enforced idleness."

"It's a real shame!" said Rosie, sympathetically, "now, if I was you, I'd send for the doctor right away."

"Those pretty little hands of yours ought to be equal to a charm, Rosie," said Macer, smiling, so far as his lips were concerned, but his eyes were gloomy enough as they rested for a brief second on the coquettish face of the little parlor-maid.

Rosie eagerly caught at the word.

"There now!" she exclaimed, as though for the first time struck by the recollection, "it was real mean of me to disremember it! There's a young man down stairs as says he has a charm that would cure that there sprain right off. When I was a little girl and lived with my father in the back townships, I remember them old squaws usin' sich things for sprains and ague, and some of them were right smart in making good cures."

Macer gave the girl such a savage look, that brave as she was, her heart leaped beneath her trim bodice.

"Do you take me for an idiot, woman?" he said, fiercely, and then as though annoyed at his own violence, he added more calmly, "excuse me, child, but you cannot imagine how utterly distasteful such superstitions practised by those old beldames are to me. Ugh! how I abhor the whole race of red-skins!"

"Well, you needn't get mad, Mr. Macer," retorted Rosie, as she rose indignantly from her knees. "I meant friendly by you; and Pat is as white as yourself if you don't take no account of freckles; and as for superstitions, it was chiefly berries, and bark and herbs that the squaws used, poor old things. Superstitions, indeed!"

"An' shure anyways, yer honer wouldn't be after comparin' an ould wise woman like my grannie, her soul to glory! to them ould copper-colored craythures?" said the voice of Pat, who in his interest in the conversation, forgetting Rosie's warnings, had thrust, first his head and then his body into the apartment, and with a deprecatory air was edging closer to Macer, who surveyed his approach with a look of haughty displeasure. Rosie, dumb with indignation and dismay, shook her head spitefully at Pat, who smiled serenely with his head on one side, not at her, but at Macer, who turned to Rosie.

"What is the meaning of this intrusion?" said the former in his slowest, lowest voice, a tone which always accompanied a certain compression of the lips and dilation of the finely cut nostrils. Signs to any who might hold the key of interpretation, of an anger deadlier than any that might be expressed in others by the most florid tokens of rage of which the countenance of man is capable.

"Shure it's no inthrusion at all, at all," said Pat, affably; "it's meself wouldn't dhrame of sich a thing! I just made bould to step up to see if yer honor'd let me thry a bit ov a charrum for that sprain ov yours. Och now, shure, a sprain is a bad thing, it is," and Pat bent down and peered at the foot which lay on the cushions.

"Leave the room, directly," said Macer, and he pointed to the door, his face quite livid.

"No offinse, sur," said Pat, "shure, afther all it don't seem much ov a sprain. Bedad, I've walked me five Irish miles wid a worse, but perhaps it's worse than it looks. So you won't thry the charrum, sur?"

"Get out, Pat, you great fool!" said Rosie, "how dare you come in where I told you not! You're not wanted here. Laws, Mr. Macer, don't you mind him. He don't mean anything."

"In coorse not," said Pat, shuffling slowly towards the door. "What should I mane? I daresay the sprain's worse than it looks. Bud it's meself didn't like to hear yees talkin' ov them ould hags, them squaws, in the same coorse ov connection wid a dacent Connaught woman like me grannie, who wint to her duty and ate taties and buttermilk like a dacent Christian woman," and with a somewhat offended air, Pat went out muttering his discontent, while Macer turned to Rosie.

"Who is that fellow?" he asked, anger in voice and eye.

"A hired man," said Rosie, stiffly. "I guess if you don't want anything, I'll go."

"Nothing, thanks," said Macer, "except that you will take care that I am not intruded on again in such an unwarrantable manner. I'll sleep in this chair all night, so you need not send Mike to me."

Rosie departed angry with herself, with Macer, and above all with Pat, who had roused Macer's wrath, and fully determined to give her admirer a stirring piece of her mind, a task into which she generally plunged *con amore*.

As the door closed behind her, Macer flung himself back in his chair and stared angrily into the leaping flames.

"The devil take the meddling dolt!" he muttered, "it would almost seem as though he suspected me! However, that is simply impossible, and with the prize to-night will place in my hands I cannot draw back. Great Powers!" he exclaimed, "if after all I should be mistaken, and that it should not be there! But I need not fear that evil. I have gathered enough from the old man to confirm my idea, and I feel the fore-glow of triumph upon me. To-night places the golden key in my hands. Let me but manipulate it properly and it gives me all the rest. The devil seems, according to the old adage, to have taken care of his own. I am guiltless of the blood that might have risen to bar the road to success, and in the future I can settle down into a thoroughly respectable life, with as clean hands as half the patriarchs of society who are held up as examples of cleanly living to those who are, perhaps, a thousand times better than themselves. Who knows in time but I too may ride in my juggernaut car of morality over writhing worshippers, who see nothing but the gilding of my chariot, under the golden wheels of which they are ready to grovel in the dust, grovel and worship. After all, perhaps, morality may not be altogether a name, there is something in the air of this house,

'A fragrance like that of the beautiful garden,
Of Paradise in the days that were;
An odor of innocence,'[1]

as Longfellow hath it that would almost convince one with its sweet logic. Well, to the rich all things are possible. If fate ordain me wealth I will ordain myself virtue, with old Jack Falstaff, I will, figuratively of course, for vulgar dissipation is not in my life,

'Forswear sack, and live cleanly!'"[2]

---

[1] These lines occur in a speech by Lucifer in Longfellow's *The Golden Legend* (1851) VI. [i] "The School of Salerno" 164–66.

[2] Sir John Falstaff is an old reprobate and the boon companion of Prince Hal in Shakespeare's two plays on Henry IV; see his speech in *1 Henry IV* V.iv.166–69: "I'll follow, as they say, for reward. He that rewards me, God reward him! If I do grow great, I'll grow less; for I'll purge, and leave sack, and live cleanly as a nobleman should do."

[PART 10—15 MARCH 1873]

CHAPTER XXV

Olla's Song

The Frazers were much interested in the beautiful Valerie, and as Mrs. Frazer reflected that the serene happiness in Olla's sweet face was altogether owing to the course pursued by Mrs. Lennox, her heart warmed towards the latter with a glow that was almost maternal in its nature. Captain Frazer also, who had been informed of all concerning Theodore and Olla, seemed to emerge from the restless melancholy which had of late so strangely clouded his placid and kindly disposition, and listened to her lively sallies with interest and evident pleasure, so that the drawing-room circle was on this evening an exceedingly vivacious one.

Androsia was pleased to be serenely gracious, indeed she seldom gloomed except when in the society of Macer, or when her thoughts were more than usually hopeless concerning the return of Winona, and to-night her low laughter mingled frequently with the lively tones of her companions.

Dolly, idle as she loved to be, sat on a low stool at her father's feet, nursing the tiniest toy terrier that had ever lived out of that time-honored fairy tale, in which the unreasonable old King commands his son to bring him a dog that will fit in a walnut shell.[1] Her golden hair drifting about her and the fire-light sparkling in her sweet, violet eyes, and on the betrothal ring glittering on her dainty hand.

Sidney, restless as Puck or Ariel,[2] hovered about Mrs. Lennox, her arch face full of inexpressible things, as she occasionally glanced at Olla, who sat demurely in a shady corner, busy at some dainty finery for Dolly's trousseau, her cheeks crimson, her brown eyes so full of humid light, that she dared not raise them, lest all should read the shy happiness that was welling to them from her very soul. Androsia, who despised

---

[1] This German story was translated into English as "Cherry, or the Frog Bride" in *Grimm's Fairy Tales*, trans. Edgar Taylor, vol. 2 (1826; London: Scolar Press, 1977) 97–107.

[2] Puck is a mischievous fairy in Shakespeare's *A Midsummer-Night's Dream* and Ariel "an airy Spirit" in Shakespeare's *The Tempest*.

needle-work heartily, and loved to be idle nearly as well as Dolly, sat on the hearth rug, her chin on her rosy palm, her great dreamy eyes studying Valerie, and admiring her heartily, as heartily as Mrs. Lennox admired the regal-looking creature, whose romantic story Sidney had taken the earliest opportunity of giving her, in a somewhat rambling fashion, it is true, but in a style sufficiently clear to interest Valerie not a little.

Captain Frazer had lived for some time, when a young man, in Paris, and Valerie's animated descriptions of the modern queen of cities amused him not a little. She spoke freely about herself except on the one subject of her marriage, and save that while living in Paris, she had married a Scotch gentleman, she was completely silent on that portion of her history, and, of course, delicacy forbade any questioning, where it was apparently her wish to be silent. Although the shadow that clouded her brilliant face as she casually mentioned her marriage, woke a feeling of sympathetic curiosity in the bosoms of Captain and Mrs. Frazer, while at the same time they carefully avoided the subject, as it evidently awoke unpleasant and sorrowful memories.

"As a girl, I remember well the gaiety of Montreal," said Mrs. Frazer, with a soft, meditative smile, "and the zest with which I mingled in it. It must be much changed, however, since I have had an opportunity of visiting it."

"I like it," said Valerie, with sparkling eyes, "the air of the place in winter is so clear and exhilarating, and it is very lively, I assure you. Ah! I have been almost happy during the three years I have lived with my dear aunt."

She kept back a heavy sigh as she spoke, and raised her slender hand as though to shade her fine eyes from the glow of the fire.

"She and I were educated in the same convent," said Mrs. Frazer. "As Mademoiselle DesLorges, she was exceedingly beautiful."

"Theodore is very like her," said Valerie, glancing at Olla, "and she is still extremely handsome."

"Theodore's lovely," said Sidney, looking in the same direction with mischievous eyes, "don't you remember Olla, when he spent a day here in spring, before Archie went away; Rosie said that he was the beautifullest young man she'd ever glimpsed! She actually did, Mrs. Lennox. Though apparently her capricious fancy has veered round in favor of Mike since."

Valerie laughed, and Dolly, looking up from her task of tying a pink ribbon round "Cupidon's" neck, opened her rosy lips, and with a glance of large-eyed reproof at Sidney, said, "I don't think Mr. Denville is in the least like Mike, Sidney. Mike is almost quite plain and has no air, and is so much older, and his clothes are not at all nicely made. I'm sure Mr. Denville would not wear a coon-skin cap like Mike. Cupidon carried it in here to me the other day, and it had a lame chicken in it, which Mike had put there to get well in the summer kitchen. I don't think Mr. Denville would put poultry in his caps, Sidney," and having raised her voice in defence of Olla's lover, Dolly resumed her decking of Cupidon, in his pink favors, with the exalted air of a priestess adorning a sacrifice.

Sidney was so overcome at the idea of Dolly's views of her speech, that she laughed until the infection caught the others, and the room rang with the merry peal, which so excited Cupidon that he barked from Dolly's lap as furiously as though possessed of the soul of a mastiff, his eyes flaming from under his tangled hair like spots of fire. Olla blushed and laughed, and blushed again, and Valerie, pitying her crimson cheeks, turned to her with one of her bright smiles.

"Come," she said, "I remember what a charm your voice had for me in Montreal. Sing for me, pray; see, the piano is open."

Olla's voice was indeed rarely beautiful, and had been carefully cultivated, and with ready grace she complied with Valerie's request, glad to turn her speaking face from the group about the fire.

As intense cold and intense heat scorch the flesh, so the extremes of happiness and sorrow are parted by so frail a barrier, that either most certainly partakes of the nature of the other, and as Olla placed herself at the instrument, the tremulous joy that filled her whole being was mingled with that quivering of the soul, which leaves it uncertain whether tears or laughter will triumph. Her fingers strayed over the keys, and involuntarily into the prelude of a Scotch ballad, a great favorite with Captain Frazer, and she began to sing, while Valerie listened, leaning back in her deep chair, her eyes fixed on the fire. The wind wailed a melancholy accompaniment of Aeolian chords round the eaves, and through the pine tops, and the plaintive melody gathered new sorrow from the sound.

> "A weary lot is thine, fair maid,
> A weary lot is thine;
> To pull the thorn thy brow to braid,
> And press the rue for wine;
> A lightsome eye, a soldier's mien,

A feather of the blue;
A doublet of the Lincoln green,
No more of me you knew,
My love,
No more of me you knew."

"This morn is merry June, I trow,
The rose is budding fain;
But she shall bloom in winter snow,
Ere we two meet again."
He turned his charger as he spake,
Upon the river shore;
He gave his bridle reins a shake,
Said "adieu for evermore,
My love,
Adieu for evermore!" [1]

Mrs. Lennox listened with hands clasped on her lap, and her ivory face intent upon the fire, and when the last cadence died away, she neither spoke nor moved; but Mrs. Frazer who sat facing her, saw a heavy tear sparkling on her jetty lashes, a tear that did not fall, but dried there, and was followed by no more. Anxious that no one should observe, the witness of an emotion that she felt was based on some sad and sorrowful page in the history of her guest, Mrs. Frazer rose and glancing significantly at her husband who, she perceived, had also remarked it, said as she touched the bell:

"I must be rude enough to disturb our circle. We will have supper and then you must all really go to bed. Poor Dolly is half asleep, and as for Mrs. Lennox and Olla, they must both be sufficiently fatigued. Is supper ready, Rosie?" to the smart parlor-maid who answered the bell.

"Yes'm," said Rosie, who looked very acid indeed, "leastways nearly, for I had to see to that there Mr. Macer. Not that some people's ankles is as badly hurted as they pretends to be, by a good bit," and Rosie sniffed the air disdainfully.

"What nonsense are you talking, Rosie?" said Captain Frazer, a little sternly. "Are you alluding to Mr. Macer?"

---

[1]   This song appears in Sir Walter Scott's narrative poem *Rokeby* (1813) III.xxviii.

"I'm not alluding to nobody, Captain Frazer, if you please," said Rosie, loftily; "but I'd be ashamed to make such a fuss about nothing. Supper'll be ready right away'm," and Rosie disappeared with a flounce, in the direction of the morning-room.

"My dear, that girl is allowed too much liberty of expression," said Captain Frazer, vexedly. "What does she mean, do you think?"

"She doesn't mean anything, papa," said Sidney. "She has been quarrelling with Mike, I daresay, and feels a little spiteful. That's all."

Valerie excused herself from supper, and in a few minutes was in the solitude of her own chamber. She locked the door with hands that trembled, and then flung herself on her knees, her face pallid as ashes, her black eyes dilated.

"Oh, heavens," she groaned. "How nearly I came betraying myself, when she sang that song. But to-night will end all. I dare not venture to hope, and I dare not turn and flee, when I see the hawk hovering over these tender doves. Is it my hand that will bring fiery vengeance? I could almost die, if by dying I could shake the sword that I feel fate has thrust into my grasp, from me. Oh, the woe for a soul to be brought to this strait!"

She flung her white arms up, in a paroxysm of mental anguish, and threw herself along the floor, with her face down, and long after the household was wrapped in profound repose, she lay thus, her form motionless except when convulsed by a dry sob, the pallid moonlight drifting over her through the window, in a ghostly pall. The firelight flickering, fading, dying on the walls and the wind playing weird funereal harmonies without.

Was she the only watcher in that quiet house?

CHAPTER XXVI

Husband and Wife

Macer looked from the fire to the clock, a small, bronze one over the mantle-piece.

"A quarter of one," he said, silently, "and the house is perfectly quiet. The night, however, is fortunately shrewish and loud voiced. Hark! how the wind surges across the river, and roars amongst the pines yonder

where that monument shines ghostly in all weathers. Queer old fellow to have such a melancholy sight constantly before him. It reminds one something of the medieval taste for skulls and cross-bones. 'To this favor ye must all come,'[1] and so on. What an old Bayard he is too! There is something in his silver hair and falcon eyes, old as he is, which has often made me quake either for fear that some mistimed feeling of reverence on my part, or those piercing glances on his should mar my little schemes. Even now I cannot quite cease regretting that success in them will bring his contempt on me. Pshaw! what nonsense to moralize and prate such sentiments when but half an hour separates me from the commission of as dastardly a crime, as I could almost well be guilty of! And I knowing myself so thoroughly, too! No, not if Heaven opened and proffered me an immortality of bliss, as the price of my desertion of my present hopes, I know that I would not turn aside from the path I have marked out for myself, by so much as a hair's breadth. Yet am I human! I would gain wealth hand in hand with Virtue if so I could, but if that is forbidden, welcome Vice, but welcome as an accomplice, not as a friend. I wonder what will this new complication of events lead to? No present danger, that is certain, for I went through the ordeal unrecognized, and I am not likely to see her again. Well, the fate that cast me a nameless waif on the world will either mar or make my fortunes soon. They will not miss the document soon, or should they, why suspect me? a cripple confined to my chair, and without an object in purloining it. The only danger I have to apprehend is that it is not in the escritoire, but I am convinced that it is. Once in my possession I will soon destroy all trace of it. As for recognition, I have had ample proof to-day how safe I am. Valerie! you are a cunning piece of nature's handiwork; but in truth I love you not! Go your ways in peace, pure and noble as I know your white soul to be and your spotless life, but cross not my path, or—"
A look of terrible darkness swept like the clouds of a hurricane across his face, and he clenched his hand as it lay on the arm of his chair until the muscles rose on the white skin, like whip-cord. He gazed into the fire, his face illumined by the lurid glow, working with stormy passion. It seemed as though across his foretaste of triumph, some spectre had

---

[1]   See Shakespeare, *Hamlet* V.i.211–13, in which Hamlet contemplates a skull: "Now get you to my lady's chamber, and tell her, let her paint an inch thick, to this favour she must come...."

stalked ominous of disaster. He was at once and without new cause disturbed and agitated. "As the wind bloweth where it listeth, and we cannot tell whence it cometh or whither it goeth,"[1] so across the securest moments of guilty triumph sweeps a hurricane that destroys the content of the hour, and is nameless, a bastard child of remorse and fear; remorse which does not lead to repentance; fear that yet stays not the hand from its work of evil. Such was the deadly wind that shook the soul of Macbeth, while the murder of his liege was yet but a fearful pageant pictured on the mists of the future.

As the smoke of a great fire is tossed to and fro by the rushing tempest the vast flames themselves attract, so the soul of the guilty man is shaken violently by the storms his crime has brought howling round him, but still, as the eager, naked flame leaps on to destroy, so his soul knows no relenting, and rushes in fiery billows on its path of desolation and destruction.

Macer was a bad man, but a bad man more from education and circumstances than from the moulding of nature. He would fain, as he said, gain his will, like Macbeth

"Holily, wouldst not play false,
Yet wouldst wrongly win,"[2]

but yet would bate no jot of that will, because virtue must needs fly in his gaining of it.

Gradually his wide brow resumed its usual placidity, and once more his eyes sought the clock. Its hands pointed to two, and a sombre smile crept over his heavily bearded lips.

"The innocent and young as a rule are not wakeful," he thought, "my time is nearly come. The house is quiet as the grave."

A low, but profound sigh, that almost stirred his hair, sounded behind him and with a start he lifted his head. His lamp he had extinguished an hour before, but the firelight threw a vast shadow across the floor and wall of the form standing motionless at his side, so close to him that

---

[1] See John 3.8: "The wind bloweth where it listeth, and thou hearest the sound thereof, but canst not tell whence it cometh, and whither it goeth: so is every one that is born of the Spirit."

[2] See Shakespeare, *Macbeth* I.v.21–23: "... what thou wouldst highly, / That wouldst thou holily; wouldst not play false, / And yet wouldst wrongly win ..."

the folds of her drapery almost touched his hand, as it lay on the arm of his easy chair.

His heart gave a great bound, like the swing of a mighty hammer, but at once his indomitable will was again master of the expression of his emotions, and his face expressed simple astonishment, but only such as would be natural in a man who finds his solitude invaded at midnight by a lovely and unknown woman.

"Madame," he exclaimed, "Mrs. Lennox! may I ask to what I am indebted—?" He paused and looked at her as though unwilling to credit the evidence of his senses. There was nothing theatric in his manner; no one for a moment could have suspected what a subtle piece of acting it all was; no one but the woman at his side.

She stood for a moment looking at him with piercing eyes; eyes of dumb accusation, of mental pain subdued by a strong will,—eyes, the changes in which were swift and inexplicable as the shiftings of the northern lights. The lines in her fine face were deepened, the mouth expressed invincible determination, illimitable sadness. A lofty and mournful compassion was shining on her calm brow. She moved forward, so as nearly to face him. "Malcolm," she said, in a low and guarded voice, stretching her hand towards him, as though to command his attention, "you see we have met at last!"

He looked at her curiously, with a smile of amusement and surprise, tempered with a courtly kind of deference that was always noticeable in his bearing towards women.

"There is some strange misapprehension at work in your mind, Madame," he said, gently. "My name is Harold Macer, Artist and Bohemian, and really I cannot recall ever having seen, before, a face which once known must remain for ever an integral part of one's memory." He looked at her with an air of respectful admiration, such as frequently falls to the lot of very pretty women from the tribe, a member of which he called himself; critically too, as though he were pleasing himself with thinking what a fine study she made in the red half lights falling on her ivory face and purple raiment from the fire.

"This subterfuge is useless, Malcolm Lennox," said Valerie, in the same hushed voice, and never for a second removing her large, dark eyes from his; "nay, more, it is fraught with danger to yourself. Your disguise would deceive any gaze but that of your wife. To me it was as none. The moment I saw you I knew you for the husband who deserted me, and—"

She dropped her head for one second and her cheek became ashy, but she reared it again and looked at him, "and plundered your employer," she breathed, rather than spoke.

Macer's very brow became livid. He made as though he would have risen, but sank back again with a half groan apparently extracted from him by the pain of his strained foot.

"Madame," he said, with a gesture of proud denial, and meeting her eye with his eagle glance, unflinchingly, "were you a man, I should know but of one reply to your extraordinary accusations; as it is I must beg of you not to give way to so unhappy an hallucination. I am the person I have stated myself to be and none other!"

"Oh," she said, with a sad and proud smile, "do not misunderstand me, Malcolm. I have no desire, in seeking you thus, to lure you to my side again. I can confess to you that you are still the dearly beloved of my heart, and in the same moment I can swear to you that no consideration of whatever kind could move me to let our lives flow in the same channel again. No, my purpose in coming to you thus is to warn you."

Macer's pallid face had recovered its healthy hue, but his eyes were full of fire and gloom as he looked at her.

"Not being in a position to claim the position you would assign me," he said deliberately, "I must beg, Madame, to decline pursuing the conversation. Were I not confined, as you see, to my chair, I should do myself the honor of opening the door for you. The hour is scarcely seasonable for such an interview."

For the first time a shade of disdain of him flitted across her perfect face, but it faded instantly, and a kind of tender anguish and compassion of him filled her radiant eyes instead.

"Listen to me, Malcolm," she said, in a voice that was not alone plaintive, but tremulous with the agony of a high soul who feels that pleading is useless to turn, even for a moment, the feet of one who errs from the precipice on the brink of which he totters. She stretched out her hands to him as she spoke. "Listen to me, for the sake of the love no longer existing, I know, in your breast, but strong and immortal in mine—strong and vital enough to risk all to save you, but one thing—Honor."

For the first time a hunted look stole into Macer's eyes, and, with unwilling steadfastness, he gazed at her as though spell-bound by her voice and manner. Even then he had sufficient command of his emotions to mask his agitation by a show of haughty surprise. He would have spoken, but she hurriedly waved her hand and continued:

"When you deserted me in France and fled, covered with the odium of a felony, the forgery of your employer's name, I felt neither anger nor scorn of you. I thought of the hard fate which had thrown you as a nameless waif from infancy on the world, and oh! Malcolm, it was with a great compassion for you that I weighed against your crime the fiery temptations which had surrounded you through life, the evil influences which, like a pestilence, had blighted the germs of good in your soul. When your utter desertion of me grew to be a fact that I could no longer doubt, I still loved you. That I still love you I have said, but, at the same time, I cannot, will not refrain from showing you the fearful position you have placed me in."

She clasped her hands together, and looked for a second upwards, when Macer broke in impatiently, as he glanced furtively at the clock.

"Really, Mrs. Lennox," he said, "I am utterly astounded that, in the face of my assertions to the contrary, you persist in mistaking my identity."

She looked at him with melancholy calmness and raised her hand commandingly.

"Hush!" she said; "your assertions but confirm the fears with which I sought this interview. You know that I have no desire to claim you as my husband. I married you because I loved, and thought that love returned. To me it would be insufferable degradation to force my affection on one who was capable of treating its bestower as you have done." Here a slight flush of lofty pride swept across her ivory face and faded. "And all this you know as well as I myself know it. Therefore, in your persistent denial of your identity to me, I see but a confirmation of my suspicions."

"May I ask what they are which you honor me by entertaining?" he said, looking at her with deadly eyes.

"That you are engaged in some plot disastrous to the happiness of the innocent family under whose roof I find you, disguised and bearing a false name," said Valerie quietly, steadfast under the baleful glitter of his gaze; "such are my suspicions. This is my warning: If so much as a hair of these innocent heads suffers through your machinations, I shall at once denounce you, even if in so doing I should break my heart. Otherwise," she added, lifting her superb head with an air of inexpressible pride, "I should be the first of my race who tarnished our pure annals by becoming the supine witness, and hence aider of wrong and treachery."

He bounded in his chair in a sudden frenzy of uncontrollable rage. For the first time in his life, in the light of her love and scorn, he saw what an abject wretch he really was, and he was stung to quick if passing madness by the real anguish of soul which for a moment possessed him. Then, too, the terror that his plans would be frustrated added its viper lash, and, pallid as the grave, he looked in her face, torn by such a whirlwind of contending emotions that his reason for a second seemed plunging headlong from her throne. To be a comfortable villain, it is not necessary to take "Lucifer, the fallen son of the morning,"[1] for one's model, for writers agree in placing his hell, not in material flames, but in the torments of a debased grand soul, torn by the refined anguish of an immortal remorse, which is not repentance,[2]—it is simply necessary to get rid of all impulses of good, murder the soul as far as possible, and cultivate one's mind and digestion. Your villain with a sickness of remorse upon him is but a pitiable knave, who, in making ruin for others, makes a hell for himself before he enters the shadowy bark of old Charon.[3]

Valerie was a brave woman, but only a brave woman, not an Amazon, and she moved back a step as her husband gazed at her dumbly.

"I will go now," she said, glancing towards the door. "I sought you at this hour in order that nothing would be suspected concerning you. Look to it, Malcolm, that you save yourself and me from the alternative I have pointed out. If I am mistaken in your designs, we meet no more; if not, I shall face you as your accuser."

She walked towards the door, and, gaining it, turned and looked at him, and her hand sought a fine chain of gold round her grand throat, and which she always wore. Indecision was written on her face, and after a moment's sharp conflict with herself, she drew a locket miniature from her bosom, and walked swiftly back towards Macer.

---

[1] See Isaiah 14.12: "How art thou fallen from heaven, O Lucifer, son of the morning!"

[2] The best-known such writer is Milton, in *Paradise Lost*; see Satan's long monologue at the opening of Book IV, especially lines 75–82:

> Which way I fly is Hell; myself am Hell;
> And in the lowest deep a lower deep
> Still threat'ning to devour me opens wide,
> To which the Hell I suffer seems a Heav'n.
> O then at last relent: is there no place
> Left for Repentance, none for Pardon left?
> None left but by submission; and that word
> *Disdain* forbids me ...

[3] The boatman who ferries souls of the dead across the river Styx, in Greek mythology.

"Keep it," she said, laying it on the stand at his side; "it is the miniature of our dead child. You loved her. Let her angel face plead with you as no human voice or words may," and before he could open his rigid lips to speak, Valerie was gone like a shadow from the room.

The hands of the little bronze clock were pointing to three, and Macer rose from his chair, in which he had sat motionless since Valerie left him. Without looking at it, he lifted the locket from the stand, and after kissing it again and again, thrust it into his bosom.

"I dare not look upon your face, my loved darling," he muttered, "not until its mute appeal shall be powerless to weaken my resolve. To-night must decide much."

From a pocket he produced a very small dark lantern and a skeleton-key, and noiselessly opening the door, he stood, for some five minutes, listening intently. The house was quiet as the grave. Long bars of pallid moonlight fell into the dim lobbies from the windows, and carefully closing the door behind him, he stole like a shadow towards the stairs. As he crept on, a spectre in the ghostly light, another shadow slipped from behind a projection of the wall close to the apartment he had just left, and, pausing when he paused, glided after him, silent as a snake writhing through dank grass.

[PART II—22 MARCH 1873]

CHAPTER XXVII

Face to Face

With the velvet tread of a panther Macer glided down the softly carpeted stairs, pausing every moment to peer through the darkness, or rather shadows, for altogether dark it was not, and to listen, with every nerve vibrating with the dread of discovery. So careful was he, that the stairs hardly creaked under his tread, and gaining the pretty entrance hall, he stole across the rich-hued checkers of rainbow light, falling through the stained glass windows, a black shape in the peculiar illumination, and laid his hand on the handle of the library door, which, as he knew, was never locked. It opened readily and silently, and looking behind him to ascertain that he was indeed alone, he glided into the room closing the door softly behind him.

The night was indeed favorable to those who would be secret, for the wind held a weird carnival abroad in the earth; sobbing and sighing through the pines, roaring along the frozen water-courses, howling over clearings, and rattling the doors and windows of the house noisily, so that even had Macer made any sound it would have been quite inaudible amid the din made by "the fierce Kabibonokka,"[1] in his flight over the land.

Faithful as his own shadow, the form we have mentioned glided down the stairs, but paused in the shade cast on them by the archway at the foot, and in this safe ambush watched Macer as he stole across the hall and into the library, and then, when the door had closed upon the latter, was about descending in his track, when from the passage leading from the dining-room and servant's offices a tall, slender form stepped suddenly, appeared phantom-like from the shadows, a figure of bronze in the fuller light of the hall. It was the figure of an Indian youth, with burning eyes which shone in the gloom like stars.

---

[1] The North-Wind; see Longfellow, *The Song of Hiawatha* (1855) II.82, and "Vocabulary" 664.

WINONA; OR, THE FOSTER-SISTERS   261

Arrested by this apparition the hidden spy peered through the bannisters on the unconscious stranger, and keeping cautiously concealed in the shadow of the arch followed every movement of the intruder with lynx-like watchfulness. It was well that the shadows were deep in his lair, for the Indian youth darted a piercing glance above and around him while he stood opposite the library door motionless as though hewn from granite. Apparently his scrutiny satisfied him, for approaching the partially closed door, he pushed it back about an eighth of an inch, and leaning against the framework as though to support himself, he looked earnestly into the apartment. So noiseless had been all his movements that the concealed witness might well have been excused had he taken the whole scene for some phantasy of his brain. No light issued from the library and for some twenty minutes, during which the patient spy made no sign, the Indian remained fixed in his attitude of profound attention, holding the door in his hand.

Macer entered the library, as we have seen, and closing but not fastening the door, so that he could more speedily obtain egress if interrupted, he groped his way cautiously towards the escritoire. So thoroughly had he made himself acquainted with every feature of the apartment that he found no difficulty in avoiding the different articles of furniture, for though a faint gleam through the heavy curtains shewed that the windows were unshuttered, it only served to "make the darkness visible,"[1] and had he not been endowed with an almost additional sense, he would have, to a certainty, dashed himself against some chair, table or flower-stand in his progress. He did not wish to use his dark lantern until the last moment.

Having gained the escritoire, he paused a moment to listen. Nothing but the voice of the wind was audible, and with a firm hand he disclosed the light of his lantern. He then placed it on a little stand close at his elbow, in such a position that while its light fell on the escritoire, a touch would be sufficient to dash it to the ground and so extinguish its tell-tale glimmer. He required the use of both his hands for the work he was about.

It had been a matter of little difficulty for him, as a guest of the family, to obtain an impression of the key of this receptacle of his host's private papers, and in another moment he gently let down the richly

---

[1]   See Milton, *Paradise Lost* I.62–64: "... yet from those flames / No light, but rather darkness visible / Serv'd only to discover sights of woe...."

carved front, and the yellow gleam of the lantern fell on the pigeon-holes and their orderly contents.

"It is well for my resolution," he thought, as his eagle-glance travelled rapidly over the array of papers, "that I have no time to think, and but little to act in. Ten minutes ought to suffice. If the will is here I shall speedily find it. Once in my possession, I can make my own terms."

With the swiftness and skill of an adept he examined hole after hole, proceeding regularly from the top compartments downwards, until the bottom row contained all that were yet to be explored. As yet what he sought had not rewarded his search, and he paused a moment before proceeding with it. His face, faintly touched by the red light of the lantern, was white as ashes, in startling contrast to his jetty beard and eyebrows, and on his forehead a clammy dew had broken, damping the heavy locks of ebon hair lying on its wide expanse.

"If, after all this fearful risk," he thought, as his eyes fixed themselves on the unexamined compartments, "it should not be here! or, if here, if the old man should have taken the precaution of having had it registered! How near one may be to success, and yet miss it by the width of a hair. Truly though, in any case, I am playing a very desperate game, but it is for two high stakes: wealth and love. Courage, *mon ami!*"

As he spoke he extended his hand and lifted a package of considerable size from the first of the remaining pigeon-holes. It was tied with black tape, and a fiery heat swept across his marble face as he glanced at the neat label, written in Captain Frazer's precise hand:

"The last will and testament of Colonel Howard, late of the— Cavalry."

"Mine," he said, silently, and for a second his brain reeled and his heart seemed to stand still.

In this, the foretaste of coming triumph, a horrid failing of the soul descended on him. He thrilled to the innermost recesses of his being, as one trembles when, on the perfumed air of a silent summer's day, affluent with the vivid beauty of fullest life, there peals the single melancholy toll of the passing bell. It was gone, this awful palsy of the soul, swift as the glancing wing of a bird, and, with a strong shudder, he thrust the stolen will in his bosom.

"So far, so good!" he said, "thanks to your loquacity, Mike, or I should not have so easily ascertained the fact of a second will having been made. This destroyed, by the terms of the first I am heir to the old man's wealth, and, above all, the guardian of Androsia. Let them identify me with Macer if they can, and then let them prove that it was Macer, crippled as he was, who stole and destroyed it."

He was in the act of closing the escritoire when his eye lighted on a small package lying in the hole from which he had taken the will, and his face changed suddenly, flushing with varied emotions.

"My mother's portrait!" he said; "how comes it here?"

He put out his hand eagerly to snatch it, and then drew it back with a half-groan.

"I dare not take it," he said bitterly; "'twould be too conclusive a proof against me were it missing with the will. I will take one look and no more."

He lifted the faded morocco case reverently and touched the spring. It flew open, and the lovely face of the miniature smiled up into his. A piece of paper lay on the glass, and his eyes fell on the writing on it. A few words in Captain Frazer's hand, slightly tremulous and uncertain, met his glance, and despite his wonderful self-control, a low cry of amazement and horror broke from his lips as his mind grasped their meaning.

"My first wife, Lady Flora Lennox Frazer, who died 18—, aged seventeen years, in giving birth to a son, who is now, in consequence of the death of his grandfather without heirs male, Earl of Tynemouth and Baron of Auton in Scotland. Disastrous to himself and others was the day which saw his birth!"

Nemesis had at length flung her thunderbolt!

In one glance the ambitious man read the lordly future which might have been his, and from which his crimes would now forever exclude him. He saw the numerous and tender ties which would have surrounded him had he but once listened to the promptings of the better nature which had so often pleaded in vain with the demon of his pride, which urged him to tear as a prey from the world what he could not otherwise obtain—wealth and love,—and in that moment of time he suffered the pangs of the deepest hell, of a thousand deaths, though on his stony face there was no sign or token of the awful despair within him.

A hand was laid on his arm. At another moment this sign that he was discovered would have driven him to a sudden frenzy, but now it was with a simple mechanical recognition of the presence of a spy on his actions that he looked up, and faced the tall form of the Indian, shadowy and gigantic in the dim, spectral light from the little lantern.

"Winona!" he said, in a low, level voice, which was like the mere mechanical utterance of an automaton.

"It is I, Andrew Farmer," said Winona, folding her arms across her chest and turning her blazing eyes upon him; "I yet live."

"I knew it," he said calmly. "I can guess your motive in seeking me thus. You seek revenge?"

Winona looked at him with a lofty smile. "The pale-face traitor speaks the truth," she said; "I seek revenge."

A slow frown darkened his face. With an effort he flung off the numbness into which his late discovery seemed to have stunned his physical being, and darted on her a terrible and menacing glance.

"Begone, girl," he said, "and do not tempt me too far. I cannot tell what force keeps me from slaying you on the spot, when for the second time you cross my path. Beware and depart!"

She smiled again, showing her white, sharp teeth, her eyes blazing on him with a terrible lustre.

"Winona's heart has become as iron, from which fierce words strike nothing but fire," she answered; "yes, from that night on which the paleface traitor shot her down as a dog, because she would have rescued her sister from his claws, as a dove from the beak of a kite; then Winona's heart changed within her, as the bright flower changes to the hard, unlovely seed."

"Oh?" said Farmer slowly, his worst passions gathering to a mighty and overwhelming tide as she stood, dauntless and defiant, facing him. "I remember your interference with my abduction of Androsia, my promised bride, whom the caprice of her mad old father was, I knew, even then plotting to deprive me of, and bestow upon another. What curse was on me that you escaped the death you rushed upon then!"

"It was the will of the Great Spirit," said Winona, her eyes flashing triumph through the sinister darkness. "And more, 'twas Winona who stole the white dove from thy snare, and hid her in the recesses of the forest, until, weary of seeking her trail, thou turned thy feet towards the abodes of men. Then was Winona partly avenged!"

"In truth, yes," said Farmer sombrely; "and now—"

Winona lifted her dark head with infinite majesty.

"Winona is the daughter of a great chief. For many days she has followed her white enemy with the thought in her heart to slay him, as she slew Hawk-eye, the half-breed, when he found out the place where she had hidden her sister in the forest by the great lake, and would have torn the white dove from her lurking place. Winona hung his scalp to her belt."

She laughed with a sombre, deadened glow in her dark eyes, and her slender brown hand clenched itself in her bosom.

Looking at Farmer steadily, she pointed to the still open escritoire.

"What brings the traitor pale-face under the same roof with the white doves? Is it to work some evil to the sister of Winona?"

Farmer looked at the open cabinet, and the remembrance of what brought him there returned like the flow of a tide of lava over his soul.

All that was Satan's own rose up armed within him.

With eyes literally flaming in their murderous glare, he tore a revolver from his breast and fired full at her.

She dropped with a heavy sound, as a pillar of a ruin falls, silent, as became a daughter of her haughty race.

Even as his finger touched the trigger, he stood transfixed, gazing beyond her, a slow horror gathering on his face, spell-bound under the falling sword of the swift vengeance which had crept to his side, silent, unperceived, but terrible.

He was no coward, but what man can stand unmoved and hear the dread cry in his soul, "Behold, sinner, thine hour hath come."[1]

Behind Winona, his foot touching her as she lay, the centre of a ghastly pool, stood Fennel the detective, no longer in his Milesian disguise, but cool, alert, watchful, his dark eyes holding Farmer's.

"Mr. Farmer," he said, "or Macer or Lennox, I arrest you on two charges. One of a forgery committed three years since, the other of burglary. You are my prisoner."

Winona, breathless, with dilated eyes and panting bosom, lay motionless, though not senseless, while Fennel walked past her and faced Farmer, whose splendid figure seemed actually to dilate as the officer approached. He stood for a second, measuring him with his eyes, and then, as a resistless breaker rushes upon and overwhelms a storm-tossed vessel, he rushed upon the detective.

They fell to the ground in a silent and deadly struggle. There was the sudden sharp crack of a pistol, and Farmer sprang erect, stood for

---

[1] See Mark 14.41: "the hour is come; behold, the Son of Man is betrayed into the hands of sinners"; and John 5:25: "The hour is coming, and now is, when the dead shall hear the voice of the Son of God: and they that hear shall live."

half a second motionless, and then fell headlong to the ground, shot through the heart.

Fennel sprang to his feet.

"Great heavens!" he cried, "I have shot him!"

In the struggle the detective's revolver, which he had held concealed in his hand, had accidentally discharged itself, and the husband of Valerie Lennox lay dead beneath the roof of his father.

CHAPTER XXVIII

Winona's Story

"There is little doubt of her ultimate recovery, though there has been a great shock to the nervous system," said the family physician, putting his gold spectacles into their case, and himself into his luxurious cutter, piled up with valuable furs and "tooted" by an old young man in a respectable, funeral kind of livery, "tell your mother so, Captain Archie, and don't let her worry more than she can help. Good morning. I'll be round again to-morrow, or perhaps to-night."

The doctor dashed away, and Archie, summoned home by a telegram the day before, turned, and went into the house.

He passed the closed door of the library softly, and with a fixed awe upon his face, and in the ruby light, Sidney ran noiselessly to him, with loosened, golden hair, and eager face.

"What does he say, Archie dear?" she asked, in a hushed whisper, "will she get better?"

"I trust so," answered Archie, and there was almost an agony of concentrated anxiety in his eyes. "The disgrace if she were to die, to our good name!"

His face flushed hotly, but Sidney's little soft fingers closed on his sympathizingly.

"He was our brother," she said, softly; "don't think of anything else just now."

Archie sighed profoundly. The worst thing of all lay in that fact, but it softened him a little towards the dead man lying in the silent room, and the sudden fire died from his face and eyes.

"How is—Valerie?" he asked, drawing Sidney away with him.

Sidney's face became awed and puzzled. "I don't know," she answered, "it's dreadful to watch her. She will not leave Winona, and goes quietly about, but her face is awful. Fixed and white like marble, and her great black eyes, dilated and shining. Isn't it strange she should care so much for him?"

Strange indeed to the pure, bright child whose soul, like a folded lily bud, had yet to expand in the new and fervid light and warmth of the love a woman, a noble and true woman, bears her husband.

Archie understood Valerie, for he held the key to this knowledge, because he also loved.

"Poor thing!" he said, with a man's trite expression of a sympathy more felt than expressed. "Do you think mother could come down to me for a little? There is so much to be arranged and father is too prostrated to be disturbed on any account."

"I'll go and see," whispered Sidney, slipping like a sunbeam up the darkened stair, and stealing across the lobby to Androsia's room.

She opened the door gently and peeped in.

The pretty room was partially darkened, but rosy fire-light flowed over its draperies of maiden white, and across the snowy couch by the window.

Sharply outlined against the pillows, the majestic profile of Winona showed, motionless as some rare thing moulded in bronze; her long, fine hands crossed on her bosom, her unfathomable eyes shining, with a startling and dusky splendor, into space. By the hearth sat Mrs. Frazer, pallid and anxious, and intently watchful, not only of Winona, but of Androsia, who, worn out with grief and watching slept heavily, her lovely head pillowed beside Winona's, her cheeks blazing into fervid scarlet, as her knitted brows shewed how haunted by horror her dreams were.

Valerie, like some rare statue of ivory, sat facing Mrs. Frazer, fearfully self-contained in her anguish of grief, and that utter anguish of the soul which is the growth of but one emotion, a love which will not die and finds its object unworthy.

There is a strain of solemn joy in our farewell to those of whom we can think as our "glorified dead"[1] which brings into our desolation the glorious cry "O, death where is thy sting? O grave where is thy victory?"[2] Through our tears their starry crowns strike upon our dazzled senses. Our

---

[1] See John 17.4–5: "I have glorified thee on the earth: I have finished the work thou gavest me to do. And now, O Father, glorify thou me with thine own self with the glory which I had with thee before the world was."

[2] 1 Corinthians 15.55.

cries of mortal agony at separation, are mingled with the triumphant sound-ings of their song of victory which returns to us across the chasm between. The desolation of Valerie's lofty soul was complete, she could not hope, she dare not even think. She tried to concentrate her mind on nursing Winona, hoping to snatch her back from the death her husband had nearly hurled her upon, and thus have one crime less heaped upon his memory.

Sidney's entrance did not disturb the Indian girl, who was under the influence of an opiate, administered by the doctor, who had managed to extract the tiny bullet which had lodged in her chest, dangerously near the heart. Neither did Androsia waken from her sleep of exhaustion.

And so the day wore down from its radiant winter beauty, into the calm of evening, with a sky of opal, emerald and rose, and so into a night, gemmed and glorified with moon and stars, shining as they only do in winter, a cold, celestial splendor, a fitting dome for the earth in her pure vestments, white and stainless as those of a priestess of the great Diana.

Quiet feet stole through the house. Voices were hushed to whispers, for the Angel crowned with amaranth[1] was brooding on outspread wings above, and his shadow fell on all.

Once a sound reached the sick room above, the heavy, muffled tramp of strange feet bearing in something which was laid softly down in the library beneath.

Valerie heard it, and her stricken heart sickened and died within her. Androsia heard it and her vivid face paled. She looked with startled eyes at Winona, whose eyes suddenly opened on hers.

"What is that sound?" she asked in the Indian dialect, a look of such command on her features that Androsia's unwilling lips were forced to frame an answer.

"His coffin," she said in the same tongue, "Winona, you must sleep!"

Winona moved her head on the pillow and fixed her dark eyes on Valerie, who was standing in the light of the fire, listening to the sounds below, her hands locked convulsively, her glance glazed and vacant. Her whole mental being was in the room below.

"Who is that woman?" asked Winona, in the same tone of quiet and measureless force, which compelled an answer. "Why is her soul full of tears for the dead, and why does her spirit linger beside him? Answer!"

No one had anticipated this question, and Androsia was alarmed at

---

[1]   The Angel of Death; see Longfellow, "The Two Angels" (1858) 7.

the effect its answer might have on the passionate nature of the Indian girl. At the same time not to reply was as dangerous.

"My sister," she said, reading Winona's face intently, "no longer loves him. Is it not so?"

"I go to the hunting grounds of my father," said Winona evasively, "the spirits of the white men do not come thither. Answer me, my sister."

"The white woman is his wife," replied Androsia tremulously.

A sudden and exquisite crimson swept like a tidal wave over the delicate bronze of her foster-sister's face, and a wild light sprang luridly to her eyes. They died, both flush and flame as suddenly, and she lay looking at Valerie, studying her with solemn eyes, mournful and splendid in their mingled lustre and shade. Androsia sat patiently beside the bed hour after hour, hoping and fearing, as Winona slept and wakened and slumbered again; but at length Mrs. Frazer insisted on her retiring, and as there was no immediate danger, she crept away to Olla's room and was soon asleep.

Valerie insisted on watching alone with Winona, and in her soul guessing what influence was at work upon her, the fear and anxiety consuming her, Mrs. Frazer yielded, and in the solemn midnight Valerie and Winona were left together, and the house sank to perfect quiet.

Valerie's tender hands touched her, her true soul, pitying, compassionate, looked at her clearly from those soft and mournful eyes, and from hour to hour Winona lay awake watching her steadfastly, and framing a purpose in her untutored soul.

Why should this tender and lovely woman weep for the dead who had been so utterly false to her? If she knew all, would she not scorn him and take comfort? This was not so clearly argued in Winona's mind. It was more an instinct guiding her than reason understood and accepted.

Valerie knelt by the fire, softly drawing the ruddy logs together, when Winona called to her softly, and she approached the bed, across which the flickering light fell warmly.

Winona stretched out her round, dusky arm, and caught Valerie's rosy, jewelled, hand in hers.

"The pale-faced woman is good," she said regarding her fixedly. "Winona loves her."

"Rest," said Valerie in her sweet low voice, "rest, my child. You must not speak."

Winona's great eyes read her face, she still held her soft hand firmly and determinedly.

"Winona must speak," she said, "and her white sister must listen. The Great Spirit wills it."

Valerie considered an instant. She saw invincible determination in the girl's face, and afraid of exciting her by opposition to her wishes yielded.

"I will listen," she answered gently, "but do not excite yourself."

Valerie seated herself on the edge of the bed. An engraving of Carlo Dolci's most exquisite Madonna and Child[1] hung at the head on the wall. Its tender and saintly beauty soothed and quieted her inexpressibly as she raised her eyes to it; but the calm fled as her glance fell on Winona. The girl's face was alive with fire and some degree of passionate rage. She held Valerie's hand, but her eyes were fixed on space. Her crimson lips were drawn back, laying bare the white pointed teeth, and her dusky cheeks were crimsoned to richest rose.

Valerie was alarmed and would have risen, but the bronze hand tightened round hers like iron bands.

"Stay," uttered Winona imperiously. "Winona will speak."

Valerie trembled a little, she knew not why. Winona smiled with a haughty kind of pitying tenderness.

"White sister is mourning for him below!" she said, "the white-hearted fox who assassinated squaws and tore the white dove from her nest."

Valerie bowed her graceful head in mute assent. She knew but little of Winona's previous history; but there came a sudden dread of unknown evil upon her. The impulse was strong on her to rise and fly, but Winona's dazzling eyes held her chained.

"Mourn no longer," she said; "who shall weep for a dead dog?"

A blush that was hot and sickening as a furnace blast came to Valerie's marble face. She sighed shudderingly.

Winona spoke again, after, with a violent effort, raising herself against the pillows. There was no light but that from the fire, rich, fantastic and ruby-hued in the room, but it illumined every corner and the two women, each so exquisitely yet differently beautiful, with a broad and mellow glow.

"Listen and believe," said Winona, a passionate scorn in her melo-

---

[1] Dolci (1606–86), a Florentine artist, produced several paintings of the Madonna and Child. The one referred to here may be his "Madonna of the Veil" (oil on canvas, Palazzo Corsini, Rome), which had appeared in a full-page reproduction in the *Canadian Illustrated News* on 23 December 1871, not many months before Crawford entered *Winona* in *The Hearthstone*'s story competition; see Appendix E.

dious voice; "Winona will tell the tale of the White Fox, who twice struck at her heart."

Valerie had heard a few meagre outlines of her husband's previous life in Canada, and the baneful influence he had had on the two girls lying within a few yards of each other, and a feeling she could not resist forced her to listen to the burning words which flowed in passionate melody of speech from Winona.

"Winona is the daughter of a great chief," said the beautiful creature, lifting her proud head majestically; "and his squaw took to her bosom a little white dove. When Winona had grown tall as a young osier by the water-courses, her mother died and her father left her in the nest of the White Dove, whose feet were like snow upon the young grass, and whose locks were snares for the sun. Through many moons the White Dove and Winona ran through the forest and guided the canoe together, and their hearts were as two springs meeting in one stream. Like the stream, they laughed in the sun and their hearts were clear to each other as its waters. Then the White Fox crept to the Dove's nest and she was betrothed to him by her father, whose heart was frozen like a great icicle hanging over a river. The White Dove hid nothing from her sister, but Winona hid from her the love and the hate which the White Fox won from her. She loved him, for it was the will of the Great Spirit; she hated him, for his soul was naked before her. He whispered in her ear, 'I mean no evil. Your white sister is a stranger to my heart. I breathe with your breath.' With her heart Winona believed him; with her head she thought, 'He is false as the southern wind, promising eternal summer to the foolish reeds by the little lakes and marshes;' and she waved her head from side to side, to watch him as the rattlesnake watches the prey it would strike.

"When the White Fox saw that the heart of the Dove's father saw his snares, he said to himself, 'What is this red maiden to me? I will tear the Dove from her nest, and the red leaves of the maple and sumach will soon fall upon the grave of Winona.'

"Winona felt the thing in the air. The nee-ba-naw-baigs[1] sang it in the streams, and her heart became iron to save her sister. Her shadow fell in the footprints of the White Dove. The hate and the love for the

---

[1] Water spirits; see Longfellow, *The Song of Hiawatha* (1855) XVIII.20, and "Vocabulary" 665.

Fox tore her as an eagle rends a fawn. Every day she died and lived again, because the voice of her sister called her back.

"When the wily Fox sent the red-skins to carry off the Dove, Winona shielded her in her arms, and would have saved her but for the mighty arm of the Fox. He threw his arm across the eyes of her sister, and—" Here Winona paused, a young Pythoness,[1] an embodied flame. Her eyes blazing into space, past Valerie, whose every sense was absorbed in one feeling of black and rayless horror. She suddenly tore the cambric and lace from her magnificent throat. A little below its stately column, a deep scar showed itself. She struck her hand against it fiercely and laughed triumphantly.

"The bullet ploughed the flesh," she said, looking at Valerie. "Does my white sister love him still?"

Valerie dropped her head upon her breast. The long-suffering and mighty love was dying, but oh! the pity of it!

Winona's voice fell to its exquisite minor cadences again, and she resumed.

"When the pale-faced brave and Mike came and found Winona clinging to the canoe, the heart of the Fox had leaped into her bosom. She said to herself, 'I alone will track him and tear the Dove from him.'

"Winona dived like an otter under the canoe and swam to the opposite shore, and while the young brave and Mike thought the White Fox was lying in the heart of the stream, she fled like a shadow along his trail, her hand upon the hunting knife in her belt, the leaves of the Odahmin[2] shivering as her blood fell upon them, her heart a fire-stone in her breast. When he lay at rest outside the wigwam of bark where the White Dove lay caged and bound, she said to the Snow Spirit, 'Lend me thy foot-fall, oh, white Jeebi!'[3] and while he slept, her knife cut the White Dove's fetters of doeskin, and like shadows upon the white pathway of the ghosts across the sky, they fled into the forest. Winona knew a cave hidden by tall ferns, and in it she lay for a moon, while the White Dove fed her with berries and squirrels snared by herself at night. When the moon was down and the rain fell, the half-breed, Hawk-eye, stole upon them, and Winona, whose heart was strong, slew him when he

---

[1]   A prophetess or woman with the power of divination.
[2]   Strawberry; see Longfellow, *The Song of Hiawatha* (1855) V.35, and "Vocabulary" 665.
[3]   Ghost; see Longfellow, *The Song of Hiawatha* (1855) XVII.164, and "Vocabulary" 664.

would have torn her sister from her, and hung his scalp to her belt; and, her wound being healed, led her sister forth to the dwellings of the white men. Does my white sister tremble?"

Valerie was shuddering from head to foot. Winona looked at her with grave wonder.

"He was a dog," she said, emphatically; "it was right he should fall by the hand of a squaw!"

She lay silent for a few moments; and had Valerie not been overwhelmed with a flood of miserable emotions, she would have seen a mysterious shadow darken the proud face and shining eyes. It passed, and Winona raised her hand slowly and pointed downwards.

"When Winona saw the face of the White Fox at the window in the great wigwam in Toronto her heart beat like a war-drum, for she saw evil to the White Dove. She whispered to her heart, 'Oh, fawn heart! Why did thy knife not seek his heart before?' When she had seen the new nest of her sister she went out to slay him, and came upon his trail after many days; but her heart turned to water and she said, 'Wait, if he seeks not the haunt of the White Dove, well, he shall live.' Wrapping a mist round his head so that none should know him, he entered the nest; and the heart of Winona spoke to her hunting-knife and said, 'I am ready, oh friend.' She stole after him and found him stealing the writing of the Dove's father, and—"

She pointed with a terrible gesture to her heart. A smile wonderful and tender burst into her eyes. She took Valerie's hand and raised it to her lips.

"Let the withered flower blossom in another sun," she whispered, and closed her eyes as if to sleep.

Across the sky another day was stealing. Androsia, roused by a cry uttering her name, sprang from Olla's enfolding arms and across the corridor into the room where Winona lay.

Winona sat up in the bed, her face transfigured in the rosy glory of the dawn, her deep eyes smiling with an awful radiance on Androsia, her long arms stretched towards the door.

Androsia sprang to their embrace. They closed round her, faithful, firm and tender to the end; and the first arrow of morning gold shooting athwart the sky fell on the foster-sisters, the dark face radiant, beautiful beyond expression in the majesty of death, the fair one lying against it as still and lovely in the blessed unconsciousness of grief.

The schooner had been engaged by Farmer to remove Androsia from the pursuit of her friends. A useless precaution, as we have seen.

[PART 12—29 MARCH 1873]

CHAPTER XXIX

The Fate of Miss Cecil Bertrand

"You wicked, unprincipled boy!" cried Cecil, flushed like a wild rose, and angry sparkles in her violet eyes; "wanting to marry your cousin! You ought to be ashamed of yourself."

"Ashamed of myself!" exclaimed Percy Grace. "Cecil, you glittering Vivien,[1] is this the coyness of a girl or the heartless thrust of a— jilt?"

"Upon—my—word!" said Cecil, breathless, her eyes wide with astonishment, her little hands uplifted, "you dreadful story! I treated you like a brother, and you turn on me like this. Why, you know as well as I do that I am to marry Mr. Horneyblow next week."

It was most pitiable to see the boy writhe and cower under this sudden lash; his sensitive face paling to ashes as he looked at her, lovely, audacious, triumphant in her young beauty and its cruel power over him. He put out his hands towards her as though she stood in a mist whole leagues away.

"Cecil!" he gasped, "have mercy. Remember how you have led me on to this."

"I led you on," said Cecil; "you silly creature, because I taught you to dance and told you where to buy your neckties, did you expect me to be so dreadful as to dream of marrying my cousin? Why, all my wedding things are ready, and every one says I am just one of the luckiest girls out. Old Horney owns two millions, and he's seventy if he's a day. I wonder how those odious widow's caps will suit me."

She looked at him, sparkling and dimpling with laughing delight and triumph.

"My guerilla dash to aunty's, in New York, was a success, you see," she said. "All the girls are just dying with envy, and it's the jolliest thing

---

[1] That is, a malevolent temptress like the damsel Vivien in Tennyson's *Idylls of the King*; see "Merlin and Vivien" (1859) 958: "Her eyes and neck glittering went and came …"

276 ISABELLA VALANCY CRAWFORD

out to watch them while mama is showing them my trousseau and jewels. They're fit for a princess—"

He looked round the bowery little drawing-room, bright in the morning sun, and he saw that her words were true. It was one graceful litter of rare things, bright and white as for the bridal of a fairy queen. Over the arm of the chintz couch hung a great veil of priceless Mechlin,[1] and resting on it a coronal of orange-flowers[2] mocked in pearls and softly gleaming emeralds. Something cut his eyes, like a biting blast of January sunlight. On a little stand by the window the flash of diamonds, lying like a constellation on a bed of white velvet, Cecil's monogram in gold and coral glittering above them in the lid of the case, an exquisite gem in itself, of ivory, inlaid with gold.

The cruel glory of the baubles struck him like the gleam of a destroying sword. He covered his eyes for a single moment with his hands and stood motionless, and during that brief space Cecil drank as deeply of the intoxication of gratified vanity as she had ever done in her life—perhaps more so—for there was the air of being wounded to the death about him as she watched him greedily, with shining eyes.

She would not have spared him a single pang, not for all the fine gold of California, in that moment of extremest delight.

A coquette has many of the points of the tigress, the iron claws shod in softest velvet, the fierce hunger and thirst for blood, in the guise of broken hearts. Rather a singular anomaly,—a perfectly heartless person having sufficient imagination to draw pleasure from pangs in another of which she is as incapable of forming a just idea as the snake is of the anguish of the animal it charms first and crushes afterwards.

He dropped his hands from his face—a boyish face, with curls of bright gold about the white temples and the sharpest beauty of a young

---

[1] A type of lace originally made at Mechlin, in northern Belgium.

[2] A wreath of natural or artificial orange blossoms became a standard part of bridal costume in the Victorian era; see Tennyson, *In Memoriam* (1850) xl:

As on a maiden in the day
When first she wears her orange-flower!

When crowned with blessing she doth rise
To take her latest leave of home,
And hopes and light regrets that come
Make April of her tender eyes;
(3–8)

Greek of the most ideal type ever struck into vivid reality by the chisel of Praxiteles[1]—and looked at her.

At its very best it was a very weak face, passionate, perhaps, with scarlet lips and delicate tints, like a girl's, and large, azure eyes, uncertain in their glance, if brilliant with genius, fickle and capricious as that genius was; but in that moment of silence the beginning of a change showed itself.

He pointed past her to the diamonds, his eyes and voice strangely steadfast.

"Your purchase money!" he said, looking at her, not at the jewels. "Cecil, answer me, on your soul, if that is sacred to you, did you never love me?"

"No," said Cecil promptly, "and if you can't stop being unpleasant you'd better go home. I didn't ask you to fall in love with me, you great goose."

This was not Miss Bertrand's usual formula of rejection; but he was her cousin, and only eighteen.

"Don't stare at me," she went on irascibly. "If you weren't my cousin ever so much, I wouldn't marry you or any mortal man who couldn't give me all I wanted."

"What is your God, Cecil?" he said, in the same even tone, the curious change deepening in his face.

"Myself," said Cecil, with an aspect of the most entire honesty. She was exhilarated in the view of the diamonds and laces, and a little off her guard.

"Can you feel remorse?" he asked her, "when you inflict such tortures as I feel now, knowingly, remember, Cecil, oh, remember that!"

"You're perfectly ridiculous!" said Cecil, rippling into sudden laughter; "I don't feel anything but that I adore diamonds and *bonbons* and lovers, and that old Horneyblow can give them to me. Don't stare, sir! When I'm a married woman, you may sigh at my feet if you like and only be fashionable. Now, don't try to talk goody to me! I have no heart, and I'm very glad of it, and no principle, and I'm very glad of that, and I don't care about anything in the world but being pretty and having people say so!"

With which synopsis of her views, Cecil twisted the violet bows in

---

[1] Praxiteles was a Greek sculptor of the 4th century BCE, famous for his studies of figures like Aphrodite (at Knidos, Greece).

her fluffy golden hair, and gave a more coquettish sit to the silk cord and tassel round her dainty waist.

"Noxious and beautiful," he said, but in a tone too low for her hearing; "deadly, and with the poison but coming to its full power."

"Sit down and be sensible," said Cecil, rolling a shell-like chair towards him. "Take care of my veil, you careless thing. Recollect you have promised to take me out on the bay to-night. The moonlight's glorious now."

"I will come for you," he said, going towards the door. On the threshold he looked back at her with a singular smile; and as she watched him from the window he was smiling still.

"The ridiculous young monkey!" said Cecil, spitefully, "I don't believe he cares much after all."

"I don't believe he does," remarked Lina, crawling in a dishevelled condition from under a table, where she had lain hidden to enjoy the interview; "I've ten minds to tell Mr. Horneyblow all you said, just to spite you for getting ma not to let me on the ice-boat party to-night, Miss Cecil."

"Perhaps you want the old wretch yourself, minx!" cried Cecil, in a rage. "Well, it's one comfort, he has eyes in his head."

"Has he?" asked Lina, with great interest. "How funny! Has he got any teeth, Cecil?"

"I don't know, and I don't care," replied Miss Bertrand, disdainfully. "It's nothing to me."

"Cis, if anything happens to you, I'll try and get the reversion of old Horneyblow."

"Much good may he do you, Miss Black-a-moor!"[1] said Cecil, sweeping away with her laces and diamonds, in a whirlwind of wrath, to torment the two sempstresses upstairs at work on her trousseau.

★ ★ ★ ★ ★ ★

There had been a genial thaw, followed by a biting frost, and between the shore and the ebon line of the Island, the Bay showed a plain of silver,[2]

---

[1]   Black African, or any dark-skinned person.

[2]   The Island and the Bay are Toronto Island and the bay or harbour of the Port of Toronto. The extensive harbour is protected by several islands, of which Toronto Island, linked by ferry service to the mainland, is the largest.

glittering to a full moon, rolling through a sky of deepest blue. A faint shade of turquoise ran gleaming through the glare ice, and out beyond the island a sea of jet, spangled with great patches of silver, lapped the glittering rim of the ice.

A steady, strong breeze set from the shore, and like phantoms crowned with light, five or six ice-boats swept over the shining plain, their sails pearl in the moonlight, a stained glass lantern cresting each lofty mast.

Faint laughter and merry voices mingled with the wind, and occasionally the refrain of some gay song caught up by several voices and tossed to and fro from boat to boat, as they glided past each other; long shafts of rainbow light falling from their differently hued lanterns across the pellucid floor, in dazzling tracks of ruby, gold, green and rose.

No one who has not felt it can imagine the exhilaration of dashing on before the wind on one of these winter-birds over a shining plain of glare ice, either by day or night.

"To whom have you lent the *Ruby*?" asked Prancer of Spooner, who was his companion on his own boat, the *Regina*.

"To young Grace to take the little Bertrand out on," responded Spooner, a voice in a huge capote. "He don't seem a bit cut up about her going off, after all."

Spooner sighed dismally. The lovely Flora had "gone off," *i.e.*, married young Damask, the week before, and the Ensign was "wearing the willow."[1] The allusion touched a sore place.

"Hum!" said Prancer thoughtfully. "I don't know. Did you notice how his eyes were sparkling to-night? Mischief there, Spoon."

"Oh! Come now," said Spooner. "I should say,—mint juleps. Listen to him."

The *Ruby* swept by like a comet, Cecil's lovely face glorified in the moonlight, Percy Grace's voice ringing out wildly in a weird burst of melody, which Cecil caught up in her jubilant young voice. She waved her little hand to the young men as they flew past, the ruby lantern leaving a track, red as blood, behind them.

It was all weird, lovely and dream-like as a scene of enchantment.

The air was full of a kind of falling glory of frost, like diamond-dust in the broad moonlight. The aurora flung phantom banners tinged with hues of ghostly rose and green across the purple arch, and, swept from the land

---

[1] Grieving for the loss of a loved one.

behind, delicate snow-wreaths, faint and fine, whirled across the gleaming ice, and were lost, disappearing like ghosts on the ebon tide beyond.

Behind lay Toronto, its silvery spires lancing the sky, its thousands of lights gleaming, like some constellation dropped earthward from the dome above. A band was playing some distance away, and now and then the riotous wind tore across the bay, hurrying out lakeward with fragments of the far-away harmony in its clutch.

Prancer suddenly altered the course of the *Regina*, bringing her round with a mighty sweep, until she stood out in the track of the *Ruby*.

"What is that for?" queried Spooner, as the ice-boat obeying Prancer's skillful hand, whizzed like an arrow out towards the Island.

"What a—excuse me, Spooner,—muff you were to lend your boat to that hare-brained boy," was Prancer's irrelevant remark. "The mad young fool is steering past the Island, beyond which there are not more than ten or twelve feet of ice, and with this wind behind him, too."

Prancer had usually one of those dark, unreadable faces which might pertain to a human sphinx did such a monster exist, but when he was fairly roused his countenance was—either diabolically or heroically— in earnest. At this moment there was a touch of both in his eyes and about his coarse and firm lips.

"Let's shout and warn them," said Spooner, his face chalky in the moonlight, with sudden terror.

The same impulse was at work with the occupants of the other boats, and a strong shout, "Take care! Come back!" went thundering out along with the wind.

"Percy!" cried Cecil, "there is no ice beyond the Island. What are you doing?"

The moonlight and ruby lantern lighted the boy's face sufficiently for her to read her answer in it. Yet he was smiling as he had smiled back at her from the door earlier in the day. What was it that cleared the scales from her eyes so that she might read that look aright, at last and too late?

She gave a sudden shrill, awful scream, and with her feeble hands tried to tear his grasp from the rudder. Useless. His muscles were iron. His face marble. His eyes relentless, tender, scornful, mad, all things at once.

He shook off her fragile fingers, and moved the rudder. They were rounding the Island.

"Pray!" he said, looking down at her, as she flung her arms out towards those behind.

"Save me!" she shrieked in answer, as the *Regina* flew towards them, and Prancer's voice came back.

"Courage, Miss Bertrand! Drop the rudder, you madman."

Prancer had one hope. To head the *Ruby* and cut off her course. He had about a minute to do it in. If the ice-boat were only lighter! "Spooner!" he said appealingly. "My good fellow, lighten her."

They were rushing over the glare ice with a sickening rush, their ears filled with the savage roaring of the wind. To jump from the flying thing meant—Death perhaps.

"All right," said Spooner, simply, and the next moment was lying bruised, half-stunned, an arm broken on the glittering floor, and the *Regina* shooting far ahead.

Had Spooner lived in good old times, he would have leaped into the chasm without half the parade of Marcus Curtius,[1] with the Roman equivalent for "all right," whatever that may be, on his lips.

Prancer knew the lad best, but as his appeal was answered, and the lightened thing bounded upon the ice, his dark face went like ashes, but he dared not remove his eyes from the *Ruby*, indeed he could not.

He was gaining on them.

Cecil's face was turned towards him, and he had liked her a little once.

He set his teeth desperately and then shouted.

"Stop I say! or I shall run into you."

Percy Grace turned his head, and the madness in him burst out in one horrible, lance-like laugh, a shrieking sound utterly and entirely awful.

"Too late!" he shrieked back, and Prancer had just a second to alter his course and save himself.

As the *Regina* swept away, as he tried with furious strength to stop her, he looked back and saw it all.

He saw the *Ruby* bound from the ice, like a thing of life, and Percy Grace clinging to her, flash downward into the ebon tide, and disappear, the ruby lantern, like a drop of luminous blood, shining redly for a second in the black waste.

He saw Cecil, at the last sublime flash of time, rise with a mighty cry,

---

[1] According to Roman legend, the oracles declared that a chasm that had appeared in the forum would not close until it had received Rome's most valuable possession. Realizing that Rome's most valuable possession was her citizens, Marcus Curtius rode his horse into the abyss, which immediately closed over him. See Crawford's poem "Curtius" (1881) in *The Collected Poems of Isabella Valancy Crawford* (1905; rpt. U of Toronto P, 1972) 256–60.

and as the ice-boat bounded shuddering to the dark embraces of the lake, fling herself back upon the glittering deadly ice, and lie there a little dead form, in richest velvets and furs, a hideous bruise on the dainty temple, and a little stream of blood trickling over the gleaming ice.

She lay in the bowery drawing-room three or four days in all the pomp money could buy. In a white casket wreathed with silver, a cross of starry tube-roses at her feet, and her bridal wreath lying in the golden tendrils of her hair.

They placed virginal lilies on her cold breast, and Mr. Horneyblow wept over her and thought how pretty Lina looked in her sisterly grief, and friends came in and out and said how beautiful she made Death, and Prancer and Spooner came, and held their hats in their hands, and looked at her in silence and went away silently, Spooner with tears in his honest eyes, and his arm in a sling. And on the day she was to have been wed, the white casket was drawn under nodding plumes of white to a little grave under a leafless willow, and while a wintry sun gilded the lake where Percy Grace lay, and played with the snowy plumes which honored her maiden estate, Cecil Bertrand was laid away in the embraces of the tomb, crowned and garlanded with the jewels she had loved.

CHAPTER XXX

Marrying and Giving in Marriage

Who forgets the charm of the fairy lore of one's childhood, when every tale wound up with, "and so they were married and lived happy ever afterwards," despite the malevolence of the spiteful old fairy, who had insisted years before on coming, an uninvited guest, to the christening of the royal heroine? Who forgets with what a sigh of satisfaction the old romance was laid down which concluded amidst the ringing of joybells and the clatter of the post-chaises which whirled off all the principal characters to the four quarters of the globe on what, in those good old times, were called "marriage jaunts."

Of course it's very frivolous and all that, my dear Miss Cross-patch, and you, Mr. Singlestick; but I can't help it, if in the good old style "there comes the sound of wedding-bells"[1] across the concluding words of this modest

---

[1] See Tennyson, "The Letters" (1855) 48: "There comes a sound of marriage bells."

tale. Shut your ears and so it please ye and hearken not, close your eyes and see not;[1] but to the dimpled Hebes,[2] the gay young bachelors and the blooming matrons of the land, I turn sure of consolation and encouragement when I relate what befell some eighteen months after the events related in the foregoing chapter.

It was July, and in the pretty drawing-room of Captain Frazer's residence a large and brilliant party was assembled. A clergyman in white vestments stood beside a richly carved reading stand on which lay open the wedding service, and though there was a restless flutter of expectation amongst the guests, every voice was mute as the door opened and a band of white robed beauty drifted in surrounding three forms whose coronals of orange blossoms proclaimed them brides.

First came Olla, almost beautiful in the rosy dawning of her coming life, then Dolly to describe whom at this crisis words totally fail, and lastly Androsia Howard, magnificent, regal, bearing herself like a Queen pacing to her coronation.

The pretty room was like a temple of Flora. "Roses, roses everywhere,"[3] and billows of golden light flowing over all.

Mrs. Denville was there, a magnificent looking woman in mauve satin, talking earnestly to Captain Frazer, who in his invalid chair was seated near the clergyman. His face was placid and cheerful, but his hair had become as white as snow and thinner about the temples. Mrs. Frazer, with sparkling eyes and flushed cheeks stood beside him, her hand resting fondly on his arm, but her eyes watching the door, and it would have been strange indeed had any one blamed the gleam of fond pride which swept across her beautiful eyes as the group we have mentioned floated up the room.

Roderick Armor, Theodore Denville, and Archie were talking to Valerie Lennox and three or four magnificent dames, strangers to these pages, but friends of the two families. Valerie, if she had suffered had made no sign, but as she looked from Theodore to Olla, her black eyes sparkled through tears.

---

[1] See Jeremiah 5.21: "Hear now this, O foolish people, and without understanding; which have eyes, and see not; which have ears, and hear not...."

[2] Hebe is the goddess of youth in Greek and Roman mythology.

[3] Unidentified; but see George MacDonald, *Phantastes; a Faerie Romance for Men and Women* (1858): "Roses, wild roses, everywhere!" (intro. C.S. Lewis [Grand Rapids, MI: Wm. B. Eerdmans, 1981] 65); and Harriet Beecher Stowe, *Oldtown Folks* (1869): "O, what a world of white roses over that portico,—roses everywhere, and white lilacs" (ed. Dorothy Berkson [New Brunswick, NJ: Rutgers UP, 1987] 477).

"Now, Dolly," said Sidney, who had shot up into a tall, young beauty, and was radiant as first bride's-maid, "do try and remember that you're to put up your veil for Roddy to kiss you when it's over, and don't forget whereabouts you're to say 'I will.' I feel quite safe about Olla, but you and Androsia are just dreadful! As for those other ridiculous creatures no one will be foolish enough to expect anything graceful or distinguished of them." With which distinguished compliments to her brother and brothers-in-law elect, Sidney leant forward to arrange Androsia's veil which had become disarranged.

Then through the perfumed, sunny stillness of the room came the rich voice of the old clergyman, commencing the service, and in a few moments, the silence fell again to be broken by the buzz and flutter of congratulations, the rustling of rich robes and the subdued sound of silvery laughter, as the three brides received the embraces and good wishes of their friends.

"God bless you, Theodore," said Valerie, fondly, as Denville turned to her, with his wife on his arm, and she smiled to keep back the tears which rose to her eyes. She put back Olla's rich veil, and perused her sweet, blushing face, and then drew her to her heart, with silent grace. "May your lot be happier than mine, dear child!" she whispered softly, and Olla's heart dumbly echoed the prayer.

Dolly leant on Armor's arm, watched critically by Sidney, but Mrs. Armor's deportment was a study in its way, and left nothing to be desired. Her faint blushes were like reflections from the roses of Paradise, her eyes beamed with a holy lustre just tinged with a faint expression of exquisite pensiveness, due altogether to a doubt as to whether she ought not to have chosen blue in place of ashes-of-roses for her travelling dress, but the effect was charming.

Androsia drew Archie out through the rose-draped window, to the shadowy veranda. Her great eyes were full of tears, joy and sorrow struggled together in her lovely face.

"Is it done?" she said looking wistfully at him.

"Come and see, my darling," said Archie gently.

He led her round the veranda and out across the sunny lawn to the pine-grove.

Standing in its shadow, was the life size statue of Winona, hewn in the purest marble and evidently but just placed there. It stood at the head of a narrow, grassy mound on which lay a wreath of purest camelias. A small foot-stone bore a name and a date.

"Winona, aged twenty years," and beneath:

"I am the Resurrection and the Life, saith the Lord."[1]

Androsia stood for a moment looking fixedly at the life-like face of the statue gleaming whitely on her in the shadows, and then turning she hid her face on Archie's arm, and he drew her tenderly away.

"Come, my wife," he said. "See! our way lies through the sunshine. Let us leave the shadows behind."

And with the full glory of the summer day upon them, he led her back to the house.

———

A few words will explain the mystery of Captain Frazer's first marriage.

He had married privately, a cousin of his own, Lady Flora Lennox, the only child of a man as stern as he was proud.

They did not dare make their union public, and with a heart full of dire forebodings Captain Frazer accompanied his regiment to Canada to receive there the news of her death and that of the son, whose birth had caused her death.

This last, as we have seen was false, but the deathly rage of her father had been so aroused, that he had sworn that his grandchild should never succeed to his title and estates.

He had given him into the charge of an old valet of his own, who had taken him to France and reared him there until he came to man's estate, giving out, and telling the lad himself, that he was the illegiti- mate son of a gentleman in Scotland.

There he had grown up; there he had lived like Ishmael, "his hand against every man and every man's hand against his,"[2] and the manner of his death was as his life.

FINIS.

---

[1]   From "The Order for the Burial of the Dead," *The Book of Common Prayer According to the Use of The Church of England ... in the Dominion of Canada* (London: Cambridge UP, n.d.) 368.

[2]   In the Old Testament, Ishmael is less favoured by God than his younger half-brother, Isaac; before his birth it is prophesied that "his hand will be against every man, and every man's hand against him" (Genesis 16.12).

Appendix A: The Discourse of Womanhood

[Two of the following articles are opinion-pieces from the British press on the freewheeling behaviour of young women in the later Victorian era, while two are essays from the Canadian press on stereotyped female characters in nineteenth-century fiction. As a group, they illustrate the circulation of character types in various forms of writing, across national boundaries, during the later nineteenth century. All four deal with conceptions of women that bear upon characters in *Winona*.

Eliza Lynn Linton's "The Girl of the Period" (1868) was controversial in its day for its strong condemnation of the "modern" young Englishwoman's faddism, materialism, and abrogation of the "natural" female role. The anonymous—but evidently male-authored—"Fast Young Ladies" (1872) presents a more ambivalent view, in letting slip a measure of admiration for the self-confidence, conversational skills, and flamboyance of its subject. The relevance of both pieces to Crawford's characterization of Cecil Bertrand is obvious.

More than a decade later, Sara Jeannette Duncan offers a comic perspective on the evolution of the heroine in popular fiction. She defines the "heroine of old-time" as a painted, wooden figure around whom the fictional plot pivoted, a figure broadly parodied in Crawford's depiction of Dolly Frazer. By the mid-1880s, Duncan suggests, this kind of protagonist has been replaced by a young woman who "bears a translatable relation to the world" and who is thereby raised in human stature. Despite imperfect evidence, it is tempting to see in Dolly's younger sister Sidney a potential avatar of this later figure.

Finally, E. Pauline Johnson's searing essay of 1892 looks at the ways in which Native women have been depicted by white Canadian authors. Defining the phenomenon of "the inevitable Winona" but apparently unaware of Crawford's novel, she recounts various examples of the "book-made Indian," identifying a pattern of negative representation and descrying a cultural ideology that reduces such figures to stereotypical, groveling, and "convenient personage[s]." Johnson's powerful indictment provides an indispensable perspective on the antecedents and defining features of Crawford's Native protagonist.]

WINONA; OR, THE FOSTER-SISTERS 287

1. Eliza Lynn Linton, "The Girl of the Period," *Saturday Review* 25 [London], 14 March 1868: 339–40[1]

Time was when the stereotyped phrase, "a fair young English girl," meant the ideal of womanhood; to us, at least, of home birth and breeding. It meant a creature generous, capable, and modest; something franker than a Frenchwoman, more to be trusted than an Italian, as brave as an American but more refined, as domestic as a German and more graceful. It meant a girl who could be trusted alone if need be, because of the innate purity and dignity of her nature, but who was neither bold in bearing nor masculine in mind; a girl who, when she married, would be her husband's friend and companion, but never his rival; one who would consider their interests identical, and not hold him as just so much fair game for spoil; who would make his house his true home and place of rest, not a mere passage-place for vanity and ostentation to go through; a tender mother, an industrious house-keeper, a judicious mistress. We prided ourselves as a nation on our women. We thought we had the pick of creation in this fair young English girl of ours, and envied no other men their own. We admired the languid grace and subtle fire of the South; the docility and childlike affectionateness of the East seemed to us sweet and simple and restful; the vivacious sparkle of the trim and sprightly Parisienne was a pleasant little excitement when we met with it in its own domain; but our allegiance never wandered from our brown-haired girls at home, and our hearts were less vagrant than our fancies. This was in the old time, and when English girls were content to be what God and nature had made them. Of late years we have changed the pattern, and have given to the world a race of women as utterly unlike the old insular ideal as if we had created another nation altogether. The girl of the period, and the fair young English girl of the past, have nothing in common save ancestry and their mother-tongue; and even of this last the modern version makes almost a new language, through the copious additions it has received from the current slang of the day.

The girl of the period is a creature who dyes her hair and paints her face, as the first articles of her personal religion; whose sole idea of life is plenty of fun and luxury; and whose dress is the object of such thought and intellect as she possesses. Her main endeavour in this is to outvie her

---

[1] Eliza Lynn Linton (1822–98) was a popular novelist and journalist in London, England, whose fiercely anti-feminist views about how women should conduct themselves aroused much controversy in her time. Often reproduced in contemporary anthologies, this essay was unsigned when it first appeared in the *Saturday Review*.

neighbours in the extravagance of fashion. No matter whether, as in the time of crinolines, she sacrificed decency, or, as now, in the time of trains, she sacrifices cleanliness; no matter either, whether she makes herself a nuisance and an inconvenience to every one she meets. The girl of the period has done away with such moral muffishness as consideration of others, or regard for counsel and rebuke. It was all very well in old-fashioned times, when fathers and mothers had some authority and were treated with respect, to be tutored and made to obey, but she is far too fast and flourishing to be stopped in mid-career by these slow old morals; and as she dresses to please herself, she does not care if she displeases every one else. Nothing is too extraordinary and nothing too exaggerated for her vitiated tastes; and things which in themselves would be useful reforms if let alone become monstrosities worse than those which they have displaced so soon as she begins to manipulate and improve. If a sensible fashion lifts the gown out of the mud, she raises hers midway to her knee. If the absurd structure of wire and buckram, once called a bonnet, is modified to something that shall protect the wearer's face without putting out the eyes of her companion, she cuts hers down to four straws and a rosebud, or a tag of lace and a bunch of glass beads. If there is a reaction against an excess of Rowland's Macassar,[1] and hair shiny and sticky with grease is thought less nice than if left clean and healthily crisp, she dries and frizzes and sticks hers out on end like certain savages in Africa, or lets it wander down her back like Madge Wildfire's,[2] and thinks herself all the more beautiful the nearer she approaches in look to a maniac or a negress. With purity of taste she has lost also that far more precious purity and delicacy of perception which sometimes mean more than appears on the surface. What the *demi-monde*[3] does in its frantic efforts to excite attention, she also does in imitation. If some fashionable *dévergondée en evidence*[4] is reported to have come out with her dress below her shoulder-blades, and a gold strap for all the sleeve

---

[1] Advertised as the original and genuine hair oil, Rowland's Macassar was a popular means of grooming. It was alluded to in Lewis Carroll's *Alice Through the Looking Glass* and was so widely used that by the 1860s it had become a commercial synonym for "greasy" or "slick".

[2] A sympathetic and powerful character in Sir Walter Scott's *The Heart of Midlothian* (1818), Madge Wildfire is a fallen woman who meets a melancholy fate because of her devotion to her aristocratic lover. She is closely associated with nature, loyalty, and vulnerability. Later in the century, her name became a popular designation for ships and boats.

[3] (French) A class of persons, particularly women, of doubtful reputation who live on the outskirts of society. Alexandre Dumas *fils*'s novel *The Demi-monde* (1855) helped to locate that shadowy world of actors, artists, dancers, and libertines in the backstreets of Paris.

[4] (French) A woman who offers evidence of loose morals and improper behaviour.

thought necessary, the girl of the period follows suit next day; and then wonders that men sometimes mistake her for her prototype, or that mothers of girls not quite so far gone as herself refuse her as a companion for their daughters. She has blunted the fine edges of feeling so much that she cannot understand why she should be condemned for an imitation of form which does not include imitation of fact; she cannot be made to see that modesty of appearance and virtue ought to be inseparable, and that no good girl can afford to appear bad, under penalty of receiving the contempt awarded to the bad.

This imitation of the *demi-monde* in dress leads to something in manner and feeling, not quite so pronounced perhaps, but far too like to be honourable to herself or satisfactory to her friends. It leads to slang, bold talk, and fastness; to the love of pleasure and indifference to duty; to the desire of money before either love or happiness; to uselessness at home, dissatisfaction with the monotony of ordinary life, and horror of all useful work; in a word, to the worst forms of luxury and selfishness, to the most fatal effects arising from want of high principle and absence of tender feeling. The girl of the period envies the queens of the *demi-monde* far more than she abhors them. She sees them gorgeously attired and sumptuously appointed, and she knows them to be flattered, fêted, and courted with a certain disdainful admiration of which she catches only the admiration while she ignores the disdain. They have all for which her soul is hungering, and she never stops to reflect at what a price they bought their gains, and what fearful moral penalties they pay for their sensuous pleasures. She sees only the coarse gilding on the base token, and shuts her eyes to the hideous figure in the midst, and the foul legend written round the edge. It is this envy of the pleasures, and indifference to the sins, of these women of the *demi-monde* which is doing such infinite mischief to the modern girl. They brush too closely by each other, if not in actual deeds, yet in aims and feelings; for the luxury which is bought by vice with the one is the thing of all in life most passionately desired by the other, though she is not yet prepared to pay quite the same price. Unfortunately, she has already paid too much—all that once gave her distinctive national character. No one can say of the modern English girl that she is tender, loving, retiring, or domestic. The old fault so often found by keen-sighted Frenchwomen, that she was so fatally *romanesque,*[1]

---

[1] (French) This early nineteenth-century coinage by art historians referred to the study of medieval art and architecture, often in a Christian context; here it seems to suggest the sense of "excessively romantic."

so prone to sacrifice appearances and social advantages for love, will never be set down to the girl of the period. Love indeed is the last thing she thinks of, and the least of the dangers besetting her. Love in a cottage, that seductive dream which used to vex the heart and disturb the calculations of prudent mothers, is now a myth of past ages.[1] The legal barter of herself for so much money, representing so much dash, so much luxury and pleasure—that is her idea of marriage; the only idea worth entertaining. For all seriousness of thought respecting the duties or consequences of marriage, she has not a trace. If children come, they find but a stepmother's cold welcome from her; and if her husband thinks that he has married anything that is to belong to him—a *tacens et placens uxor*[2] pledged to make him happy—the sooner he wakes from his hallucination and understands that he has simply married some one who will condescend to spend his money on herself, and who will shelter her indiscretions behind the shield of his name, the less severe will be his disappointment. She has married his house, his carriage, his balance at the banker's, his title; and he himself is just the inevitable condition clogging the wheel of her fortune; at best an adjunct, to be tolerated with more or less patience as may chance. For it is only the old-fashioned sort, not girls of the period *pur sang*, that marry for love, or put the husband before the banker. But she does not marry easily. Men are afraid of her; and with reason. They may amuse themselves with her for an evening, but they do not take her readily for life. Besides, after all her efforts, she is only a poor copy of the real thing; and the real thing is far more amusing than the copy, because it is real. Men can get that whenever they like; and when they go into their mothers' drawing-rooms, to see their sisters and their sisters' friends, they want something of quite different flavour. *Toujours perdrix*[3] is bad providing all the world over; but a continual weak

---

[1] Compare John Keats, "Lamia" (1820): "Love in a hut, with water and a crust, / Is—Love, forgive us!—cinders, ashes, dust" (2.1–2).

[2] (Latin) Silent and pleasing wife.

[3] (French) Literally, this phrase means "always partridge"; proverbially, it means "having too much of the same thing." More particularly, Linton appears to play on its association with sexual misconduct in a story attributed to Horace Walpole (1717–97): "the confessor of one of the French kings reproved him for conjugal infidelity, and was asked by the king what he liked best. 'Partridge,' replied the priest, and the king ordered him to be served with partridge every day, till he quite loathed the sight of his favourite dish. When the king eventually visited him, and hoped he had been well served, the confessor replied, '*Mais oui, perdrix, toujours perdrix.*' 'Ah! ah!,' replied the amorous monarch, 'and one mistress is all very well, but not *"perdrix, toujours perdrix"*'" (Ivor H. Evans, ed., *Brewer's Dictionary of Phrase and Fable*, 14th ed. [New York: Harper & Row, 1989], 841).

imitation of *toujours perdrix* is worse. If we must have only one kind of thing, let us have it genuine; and the queens of St. John's Wood in their unblushing honesty, rather than their imitators and make-believes in Bayswater and Belgravia.[1] For, at whatever cost of shocked self-love or pained modesty it may be, it cannot be too plainly told to the modern English girl that the net result of her present manner of life is to assimilate her as nearly as possible to a class of women whom we must not call by their proper—or improper—name. And we are willing to believe that she has still some modesty of soul left hidden under all this effrontery of fashion, and that, if she could be made to see herself as she appears to the eyes of men, she would mend her ways before too late.

It is terribly significant of the present state of things when men are free to write as they do of the women of their own nation. Every word of censure flung against them is two-edged, and wounds those who condemn as much as those who are condemned; for surely it need hardly be said that men hold nothing so dear as the honour of their women, and that no one living would willingly lower the repute of his mother or his sisters. It is only when these have placed themselves beyond the pale of masculine respect that such things could be written as are written now; when they become again what they were once they will gather round them the love and homage and chivalrous devotion which were then an Englishwoman's natural inheritance. The marvel, in the present fashion of life among women, is how it holds its ground in spite of the disapprobation of men. It used to be an old-time notion that the sexes were made for each other, and that it was only natural for them to please each other, and to set themselves out for that end. But the girl of the period does not please men. She pleases them as little as she elevates them; and how little she does that, the class of women she has taken as her models of itself testifies. All men whose opinion is worth having prefer the simple and genuine girl of the past, with her tender little ways and pretty bashful modesties, to this loud and rampant modernization, with her false red hair and painted skin, talking slang as glibly as a man, and by preference leading the conversation to doubtful subjects. She thinks she is piquante and exciting when she thus makes herself the bad copy of a worse original; and she will not see that though men laugh with her they do not respect her, though they flirt

---

[1] St. John's Wood, Bayswater, and Belgravia are neighbourhoods in the West End of London, England. During the Victorian period, St. John's Wood became associated with elite brothels and the lodgings of kept mistresses, while Belgravia and Bayswater were respectable areas known for their impressive residential squares and stately homes.

with her they do not marry her; she will not believe that she is not the kind of thing they want, and that she is acting against nature and her own interests when she disregards their advice and offends their taste. We do not see how she makes out her account, viewing her life from any side; but all we can do is to wait patiently until the national madness has passed, and our women have come back again to the old English ideal, once the most beautiful, the most modest, the most essentially womanly in the world.

2. "Fast Young Ladies," *Canadian Illustrated News*, 28 September 1872: 195[1]

Some few years ago a great deal was heard about the "girl of the period." She was sketched in many newspapers and pamphlets, and badly-drawn and cleverly-drawn caricatures of her might have been seen hanging up in numerous shop-windows. She was invariably depicted as the naughtiest, most eccentric, and generally most useless representative of the sisterhood the world had seen for many ages. While it was pointed out that her vices and failings were numerous, it was shown that her virtues were only conspicuous by their absence. The thing was overdone, and thus though at first the general public was amused, after a time they grew weary of seeing the womanhood of England held up to ridicule and often something worse. Justice was at no time done to English girls. The idiosyncrasies of a small minority were accepted as pertaining to the whole class, and nearly all were embraced under the wholesale condemnation. This was a pity, apart from its injustice. Had the section which alone deserved censure been singled out, much good might have been the result; as it was, people who felt that the cap fitted them, disposed of the allegations by alleging that they were the utterances of reckless and thoughtless writers. But, for all that, the condemnation was not, and is not, altogether uncalled for. There existed then, as there exists now, a large and growing class of "fast" young ladies, who might advantageously be checked in their onward careers. They may be encountered without much trouble, for they ostentatiously thrust themselves upon public notice. They have, generally, plenty of self-confidence, lots of lung power, and a certain amount of personal attractiveness, enhanced by their style of dress which, though "loud" and generally, extremely inartistic, has

---

[1] Reprinted from *The Liberal Review of Politics, Society, Literature and Art*, an English magazine published from 1868 to 1882.

charms for men of a certain type. It can be compared to nothing so well as that adopted by the *demi-monde*; indeed, it seems the desire of the "fast" young ladies to imitate the latter in many particulars besides dress, so much so that people may well be excused for occasionally mistaking them for what they are not. They have many accomplishments. Provided they get with a congenial companion, their conversational powers do not fail them. They go galloping on from topic to topic in a merry, devil-may-care fashion. No doubt, were they wise, they would avoid vulgar slang and some of the topics upon which they touch, and refrain from expressing sentiments which do not sound well coming from lovely and presumably innocent maidens. They would be more charitable towards their neighbours, less sparing of hostile criticism upon those who do not affect the same kind of life as they do. Their sisters, who lack such personal attractions as themselves, should not be cuttingly alluded to; nor young men, of studious habits and steady mien, be dubbed "muffs," and other uncomplimentary epithets—notwithstanding the fact that, in the majority of instances, they may be incorrigible blockheads. No man living likes to hear a woman speak ill of anybody—unless it be a dangerous rival for her favour. All instinctively feel that, from feminine lips, especially when the owners and the lips are alike beautiful, nothing but sugar-plums should fall. Thus, it is far more jarring to hear a woman speaking ill of her neighbour than it is to listen to a man so doing. The "fast" young ladies, then, defeat their own purposes, in being sarcastic at the expense of other less-gifted beings than themselves, in expressing a preference for dubious pleasures, and in sneering at Mrs. Grundy's laws of propriety.[1] But the fact remains that they can talk, which, though talking is reputed to be a purely feminine attribute, is what many young ladies are unable to do, except under the most advantageous circumstances. Frequently, they can sing and play fairly, though their style may be, to use a dramatic term, stagey to the last degree. They are, generally, great adepts at croquet, and if they have pretty feet, can show them in the most charming manner, during the progress of this interesting game, to great advantage. They use violet powder, and the various cosmetiques known to ladies, with considerable skill, and manipulate false hair, sufficient, one would almost think, to stock a hairdresser's shop, with marvelous dexterity. A cigarette—may we whisper a cigar—is no stranger to their ruby lips, and strange to say,

---

[1] Mrs. Grundy is a personage too much concerned with being proper, modest or righteous; hence, a self-appointed and tiresome arbiter of social rules and standards of conduct. The name originated in Thomas Morton's *Speed the Plough* (1798), not as a character who appears in the play but as a figure referred to and described by some of the characters.

does not cause them to betray symptoms of internal uneasiness. They understand betting, and, unlike most gamblers, win a good deal more than they lose. Fortunately, however, their wagers are confined to such trifles as gloves and feminine articles generally. They can frequently ride, row, and indulge in other masculine pursuits. But, perhaps, the accomplishment in which, of all other, they mostly excel, is that of flirtation. You can get up a flirtation with them—if you are an Adonis[1]—a really desperate affair, with little difficulty. Without committing yourself to an engagement, you may squeeze their little hands, encircle their dainty waists and press kisses upon their rosy lips and it will not follow as a natural consequence that "mama" is made acquainted with all the circumstances. Nor need you fear that the injured ones will be mortally offended with you. Rest assured, if you can enjoy a bit of fun, so can they; and if you can keep good counsel, so can they. It will thus be evident that "fast" young ladies have many accomplishments.

The *summum bonum*[2] of existence of the "fast" young ladies is to get as much pleasure out of life as possible. That is paramount to duty by a long way. Their chief idea of what pleasure consists in is to secure as much male admiration as possible, and to triumph over many feminine rivals. Hence some of their eccentricities and follies. They have small regard for any one but themselves. They enjoy eating and drinking, and are not ashamed to do either, publicly or privately. Indeed, they rather delight in setting the ordinary usages of society at defiance. Yet they are snobbish and insufferably proud. They would laugh heartily at the idea of love in a cottage, and have no hesitation in roughly squelching the aspirations of humble devotees. They do not profess to believe in sentiment to any very great extent; indeed, they are professedly worldlings. Such girls shine for a few years. The "fast" men of the set in which they move are loud in their praises, and court their society. But they do not marry. They are passed over for less extravagant and quieter creatures. Their admirers argue justly that it would need a millionaire to support them. By-and-by their beauty fades, their vivacity becomes forced, and their admirers few and far between. If they do not elope with the coachman or the footman, they often do what is, perhaps, quite as bad—become disappointed women. Defend us, then, from "fast" young ladies, and may their numbers become less.

---

[1] The beautiful youth in Greek mythology who was loved by Aphrodite, the Goddess of Love and Beauty.
[2] (Latin) The highest or greatest good.

3. Sara Jeannette Duncan, "Saunterings," *The Week*, 28 October 1886: 771–72[1]

Has it occurred to nobody, in his struggles to keep abreast of the tide of new activity that sets in fiction, as in every other department of modern thought, to cast one deploring glance over his shoulder at the lovely form of the heroine of old-time, drifting fast and far into oblivion? It would be strange indeed if we did not regret her, this daughter of the lively imagination of a bygone day. By long familiarity, how dear her features grew! Having heard of her blue eyes, with what zestful anticipation we foreknew the golden hair, the rosebud mouth, the faintly-flushed, ethereal cheek, and the pink sea-shell that was privileged to do auricular duty in catching the never-ceasing murmur of adoration that beat about the feet of the blonde maiden! Wotting[2] of her ebon locks, with what subtle prescience we guessed the dark and flashing optics, the alabaster forehead, the lips curved in fine scorn, the regal height, and the very unapproachable demeanour of the brunette! The fact that these startling differences were purely physical, that the lines of their psychical construction ran sweetly parallel, never interfered with our joyous interest in them as we breathlessly followed their varying fortunes from an auspicious beginning through harrowing vicissitudes, to a blissful close. So that her ringlets were long enough, and her woes deep enough, and her conduct under them marked by a beautiful resignation and the more becoming forms of grief, it never occurred to us to cavil at the object of Algernon's passion, because her capabilities were strictly limited to making love and Oriental landscapes in Berlin wool.[3] Her very feminine attributes were invariably forthcoming; and if the author by any chance forgot to particularise the sweetness of her disposition, the neatness of her *boudoir*—they all had *boudoirs*—or the twining nature of her affections, we unconsciously

---

[1] Sara Jeannette Duncan (1861–1922) was an Ontario-born writer who initially acquired a reputation as a journalist. In the late 1880s she wrote a column under the title "Saunterings," as well as poetry, book reviews, and political journalism, for a Toronto paper, *The Week*, before embarking on a distinguished career as a novelist. The leading Canadian literary periodical of its era, *The Week* was founded by the essayist Goldwin Smith and published from 1883 to 1896.

[2] Knowing.

[3] This light wool used in the making of clothing, gloves and tapestries was perfected in Berlin, Germany early in the nineteenth century. Its uses, much celebrated in ladies' magazines, led to a vogue in the United States for its application in fine work such as embroidering and needlepoint.

supplied the deficiency, and thought no less respectfully of Araminta.[1] She was very wooden, this person for whom gallant youths attained remarkable heights of self-sacrifice, and villains intrigued in vain; her virtues and her faults alike might form part of the intricate and expensive interior of a Paris doll;[2] and we loved her perhaps with the unmeaning love of infancy for its toys. She was the painted pivot of the merry-go-round—it could not possibly revolve, with its exciting episodes, without her; yet her humble presence bore no striking relation to the mimic pageant that went on about her. She vanished with the last page, ceased utterly with the sound of her wedding-bells; and we remembered her for a little space, not the maiden, but the duels in her honour, the designs upon her fortune, and the poetic justice that overtook her calumniators.

But extinction in time overtook this amiable damsel. Mere complexion began to be considered an insufficient basis upon which to erect a character worthy of public attention in the capacity of a heroine. So we were introduced to the young creature of "parts"—the parts consisting of an immoderate desire to investigate the wisdom of the ancients, as Plato has expressed it, an insatiable appetite for metaphysical conversation, and a lofty contempt for the frivolities of her sex. To keep the balance between these somewhat laudable peculiarities and proper womanly accomplishments, she was usually invested with a powerful and melodious vocal organ, whose minor notes frequently depressed her frivolous associates of the drawing room to tears, and reduced the hitherto invincible heart of the interesting woman-hater of the volume to instant and abject submission. To preserve the unities, charms of feature and philosophical tendencies being somewhat incompatible, she was given a rather wide mouth, and a forehead too high and thoughtful for beauty's strict requirements; while her dark expressive eyes and straight nose sufficed to secure our regard from an aesthetic standpoint. Then came that daring innovator who gave us a countenance all out of line, with freckles on it, a look of restless intellectuality, and a vague charm that was beyond his power to analyze or ours to conceive. The conduct of this young person was usually characterised by the wildest vagaries. She held communings with herself, which she reluctantly

---

[1] Algernon and Araminta (whose name in Hebrew means "lofty"), together with Adolphus, Genevieve, Rosabel, etc., later in the essay, are Duncan's ironically typical names for the generic hero and heroine of the "old-time" romantic novel.

[2] Mannequin.

imparted to the interesting youth in whom she recognised her mental superior, and therefore her fate; and the sole end of her existence appeared to be to make his as wretched as possible. The plot, of which this ingenuous maid was the centre, usually turned upon a mood of hers—the various chapters, indeed, were chiefly given over to the elucidation of her moods, and their effect upon her unfortunate admirers.

Just about here, in the development of the heroine, do we begin to see that she is not a fixed quantity in the problems of the novelist, but varies with his day and generation. Araminta was the product of an age that demanded no more of femininity than unlimited affection and embroidery. The advent of the blue-stocking suggested the introduction of brains into her composition, though her personality was not seriously affected by them, as the blue-stocking was but a creature of report in the mind of the story-teller, the feminine intelligence not being popularly cultivated beyond the seminary limit.[1] As dissatisfaction with her opportunities infected the modern young lady, her appearance in fiction with a turned-up nose and freckles, solely relying upon her yearnings after the infinite for popular appreciation, followed as a matter of course.

We are not talking, O captious soul—with a dozen notable heroines of the past at your fingers' ends!—of the great people in the world of fiction, but of the democracy of that populous literary sphere. We are discussing the short-lived Ethels and Irenes who have long since gone over, with their devoted Arthurs and Adolphuses, to that great majority whose fortunes are to be traced only at the second-hand book-stalls now; but whose affections formed the solace of many an hour in the dusty seclusion of the garret, while the rain pattered on the roof, and the mice adventured over the floor, and the garments of other days swayed to and fro in dishevelled remembrance of their departed possessors. Ah, Genevieve and Rosabel, Vivien and Belinda, how fare ye now whose yellow-bound vicissitudes were treasured so carefully from the fiery fate that awaited them at the hands of stern authorities diametrically opposed to "light reading!" By what black ingratitude are ye reduced, alas! to the pulp of the base material economy of the age on which, perhaps, the fortunes of damsels less worthy and less fair are typographically set forth for the fickle amusement of a later generation!

Hardly less complete is the evanishment of Rosabel and Belinda than

---

[1] The term "blue-stocking" was used during the nineteenth century to refer to a woman having intellectual and literary interests, and was frequently applied in a derogatory way.

that of their successors in fiction, and the time-honoured functions they performed. A novel without a heroine used to be as absurd an idea as the play of Hamlet with Hamlet left out.[1] But the heroine of to-day's fiction is the exception, not the rule. The levelling process the age is undergoing has reduced women with their own knowledge and consent to very much the same plane of thought and action as men. It has also raised them to it, paradoxical though the statement be. The woman of to-day is no longer an exceptional being surrounded by exceptional circumstances. She bears a translatable relation to the world; and the novelists who translate it correctly have ceased to mark it by unduly exalting one woman by virtue of her sex to a position of interest in their books which dwarfs all the other characters. It has been found that successful novels can be written without her. The woman of to-day understands herself, and is understood in her present and possible worth. The novel of to-day is a reflection of our present social state. The women who enter into its composition are but intelligent agents in this reflection, and show themselves as they are, not as a false ideal would have them.

4. E. Pauline Johnson, "A Strong Race Opinion: On the Indian Girl in Modern Fiction," *Toronto Sunday Globe*, 22 May 1892: 1[2]

E. Pauline Johnson of the Iroquois Makes Some Remarks—The One Distressful Type—Winona—Her Suicidal Tendency—Mair's 'Tecumseh'—'The Algonquin Maiden'—A Chance for Writers.

Every race in the world enjoys its own peculiar characteristics, but it scarcely follows that every individual of a nation must possess these prescribed singularities, or otherwise forfeit in the eyes of the world their nationality. Individual personality is one of the most charming things to be met with, either in a flesh and blood existence, or upon

---

[1] William Shakespeare's *Hamlet* is likely the best-known play in the English language; its protagonist, Prince Hamlet, is massively central to the play's dialogue and action.

[2] E. Pauline Johnson or Tekahionwake (1861–1913) was a poet, journalist, and performer. Born near Brantford, Ontario of a Mohawk father and a white mother, she became not only a popular international entertainer but also a well-recognized spokesperson for Native issues and concerns. Johnson's modern editors have suggested that the title for this article "may have been created by the *Globe* staff, rather than by Johnson," an observation equally pertinent to its subheadings (see E. Pauline Johnson, Tekahionwake, *Collected Poems and Selected Prose*, ed. Carole Gerson and Veronica Strong-Boag [Toronto: U of Toronto P, 2002] 323).

the pages of fiction, and it matters little to what race an author's heroine belongs, if he makes her character distinct, unique and natural.

The American book heroine of today is vari-coloured as to personality and action. The author does not consider it necessary to the development of her character, and the plot of the story to insist upon her having American-coloured eyes, and American carriage, and American voice, American motives, and an American mode of dying; he allows her to evolve an individuality ungoverned by nationalisms—but the outcome of impulse and nature and a general womanishness.

Not so the Indian girl in modern fiction, the author permits her character no such spontaneity, she must not be one of womankind at large, neither must she have an originality, a singularity that is not definitely 'Indian.' I quote 'Indian' as there seems to be an impression amongst authors that such a thing as tribal distinction does not exist among the North American aborigines.

Tribal Distinctions

The term 'Indian' signifies about as much as the term 'European,' but I cannot recall ever having read a story where the heroine was described as 'a European.' The Indian girl we meet in cold type, however, is rarely distressed by having to belong to any tribe, or to reflect any tribal characteristics. She is merely a wholesome sort of mixture of any band existing between the Mic Macs of Gaspé and the Kwaw-Kewlths of British Columbia, yet strange to say, that notwithstanding the numerous tribes, with their aggregate numbers reaching more than 122,000 souls in Canada alone, our Canadian authors can cull from this huge revenue of character, but one Indian girl, and stranger still that this lonely little heroine never had a prototype in breathing flesh-and-blood existence!

It is a deplorable fact, but there is only one of her. The story-writer who can create a new kind of Indian girl, or better still portray a 'real live' Indian girl will do something in Canadian literature that has never been done, but once. The general author gives the reader the impression that he has concocted the plot, created his characters, arranged his action, and at the last moment has been seized with the idea that the regulation Indian maiden will make a very harmonious background whereon to paint his pen picture, that, he, never having met this interesting individual, stretches forth his hand to his library shelves, grasps the first Canadian novelist he sees, reads up his subject, and duplicates it in his own work.

300   APPENDIX A

After a half dozen writers have done this, the reader might as well leave the tale unread as far as the interest touches upon the Indian character, for an unvarying experience tells him that this convenient personage will repeat herself with monotonous accuracy. He knows what she did and how she died in other romances by other romancers, and she will do and die likewise in his, (she always does die, and one feels relieved that it is so, for she is too unhealthy and too unnatural to live).

The Inevitable 'Winona'

The rendition of herself and her doings gains no variety in the pens of manifold authors, and the last thing that they will ever think of will be to study 'The Indian Girl' from life, for the being we read of is the offspring of the writer's imagination and never existed outside the book covers that her name decorates. Yes, there is only one of her, and her name is 'Winona.' Once or twice she has borne another appellation, but it always has a 'Winona' sound about it. Even Charles Mair, in that masterpiece of Canadian-Indian romances, 'Tecumseh,' could not resist 'Winona.'[1] We meet her as a Shawnee, as a Sioux, as a Huron, and then, her tribe unnamed, in the vicinity of Brockville.

She is never dignified by being permitted to own a surname, although, extraordinary to note, her father is always a chief, and had he ever existed, would doubtless have been as conservative as his contemporaries about the usual significance that his people attach to family name and lineage.

In addition to this most glaring error this surnameless creation is possessed with a suicidal mania. Her unhappy, self-sacrificing life becomes such a burden to both herself and the author that this is the only means by which they can extricate themselves from a lamentable tangle, though, as a matter of fact suicide is an evil positively unknown among Indians. To-day there may be rare instances where a man crazed by liquor might destroy his own life, but in the periods from whence

---

[1] Charles Mair (1838–1927) was a prominent journalist, poet and playwright, a key figure in the nationalist movement known as "Canada First" in the years immediately following Confederation, and a friend and correspondent of Johnson. His Shakespearean verse tragedy, *Tecumseh* (1886), about the renowned Shawnee chief who died in battle supporting British forces against an invading American army in the War of 1812, was well received, and remains a landmark of early Canadian drama. While Mair's Native heroine in *Tecumseh* is named Iena, the play does include a secondary character named Winona among its "Indian Maidens."

'Winona's' character is sketched self-destruction was unheard of. This seems to be a fallacy which the best American writers have fallen a prey to. Even Helen Hunt Jackson, in her powerful and beautiful romance of 'Ramona,' has weakened her work deplorably by having no less than three Indians suicide while maddened by their national wrongs and personal grief.[1]

To Be Crossed in Love Her Lot

The hardest fortune that the Indian girl of fiction meets with is the inevitable doom that shadows her love affairs. She is always desperately in love with the young white hero, who in turn is grateful to her for services rendered the garrison in general and himself in particular during red days of war. In short, she is so much wrapped up in him that she is treacherous to her own people, tells falsehoods to her father and the other chiefs of her tribe, and otherwise makes herself detestable and dishonourable. Of course, this white hero never marries her! Will some critic who understands human nature, and particularly the nature of authors, please tell the reading public why marriage with the Indian girl is so despised in books and so general in real life? Will this good far-seeing critic also tell us why the book-made Indian makes all the love advances to the white gentleman, though the real wild Indian girl (by the way, we are never given any stories of educated girls, though there are many such throughout Canada) is the most retiring, reticent, non-committal being in existence!

Captain Richardson, in that inimitable novel, 'Wacousta,' scarcely goes as far in this particular as his followers.[2] To be sure he has his Indian heroine madly in love with young de Haldimar, a passion which it goes

---

[1] Helen Hunt Jackson, (1831–85), born Helen Maria Fiske, was a Massachusetts writer who moved west to Colorado after the death of her first husband, Captain Edward Hunt, and became fascinated by the plight of the American Native tribes. She became a tireless advocate for them in her later years, publishing (among many other works) a scathing indictment of the U.S. government's Indian policy in her book A Century of Dishonor (1881), and a number of novels, of which the best known is a study of Native mission life, Ramona (1884).

[2] Canadian-born John Richardson (1796–1852) wrote a number of novels combining historical and gothic elements. His most highly regarded work is Wacousta; or, the Prophecy, A Tale of the Canadas (1832), which used events during the Pontiac war of 1763 as the backdrop for a tale of love, betrayal, murder, and old-world duplicity. One of its principal characters, Captain Frederick de Haldimar, the elder son of the (fictional) English commander of Fort Detroit, is the object of unreciprocated love by the young native woman Oucanasta (the novel's "regulation Indian maiden"), who betrays her people in a vain attempt to win his affection. Wacousta remains today a classic of nineteenth-century Canadian literature.

without saying he does not reciprocate, but which he plays upon to the extent of making her a traitor to Pontiac[1] inasmuch as she betrays the secret of one of the cleverest intrigues of war known in the history of America, namely, the scheme to capture Fort Detroit through the means of an exhibition game of lacrosse. In addition to this de Haldimar makes a cat's paw of the girl, using her as a means of communication between his fiancée and himself, and so the excellent author permits his Indian girl to get herself despised by her own nation and disliked by the reader. Unnecessary to state, that as usual the gallant white marries his fair lady, who the poor little red girl has assisted him to recover.

Mercer Adam's Algonquin Maiden

Then comes another era in Canadian-Indian fiction, wherein G. Mercer Adam and A. Ethelwyn Wetherald have given us the semi-historic novel 'An Algonquin Maiden.'[2] The former's masterly touch can be recognized on every page he has written; but the outcome of the combined pens is the same old story. We find 'Wanda' violently in love with Edward MacLeod, she makes all the overtures, conducts herself disgracefully, assists him to a reunion with his fair-skinned love, Helene; then betakes herself to a boat, rows out into the lake in a thunderstorm, chants her own death-song, and is drowned.

But, notwithstanding all this, the authors have given us something exceedingly unique and novel as regards their red heroine. They have sketched us a wild Indian girl who kisses. They, however, forgot to tell us where she learned this pleasant fashion of emotional expression; though two such prominent authors who have given so much time to

---

[1]   Pontiac (c1720–69), a powerful chief of the Ottawa tribe, became convinced in the early 1760s that it was necessary to resist the English who occupied a chain of strategically located forts along the Ohio frontier and the upper Great Lakes, including Fort Detroit (site of the city that bears the same name today) and Fort Michilimackinac (now Mackinaw City, Michigan). His alliance of tribes, including Ojibwa, Huron, and Potowatomi, proved successful on several fronts but failed to take Fort Detroit. Through the ruse of a lacrosse game, a force of Native warriors did gain entrance to Fort Michilimackinac, massacred part of the garrison, and occupied the fort for a year before the English recovered it.

[2]   *An Algonquin Maiden: A Romance of the Early Days of Upper Canada* (1887) was co-authored by Graeme Mercer Adam (1839–1912) and Ethelwyn Wetherald (1857–1940). Adam was a prolific writer on Canadian and American topics while Wetherald was an Ontario-born poet, novelist, journalist, and literary critic. Wetherald's "Introduction" to John Garvin's edition of Isabella Valancy Crawford's poetry (Toronto: Briggs, 1905) helped to confirm Crawford's reputation as an important Canadian poet two decades after her death.

the study of Indian customs and character, must certainly have noticed the entire ignorance of kissing that is universal among the Aborigines.

A wild Indian never kisses; mothers never kiss their children even, nor lovers their sweethearts, husbands their wives. It is something absolutely unknown, unpractised.

But 'Wanda' was one of the few book Indian girls who had an individuality and was not hampered with being obliged to continually be national first and natural afterwards. No, she was not national; she did things and said things about as un-Indian like as Bret Harte's 'M'liss:' in fact, her action generally resembles 'M'liss' more than anything else; for 'Wanda's' character has the peculiarity of being created more by the dramatis personae in the play than by the authors themselves.[1] For example: Helene speaks of her as a 'low, untutored savage,' and Rose is guilty of remarking that she is 'a coarse, ignorant woman, whom you cannot admire, whom it would be impossible for you to respect;' and these comments are both sadly truthful, one cannot love or admire a heroine that grubs in the mud like a turtle, climbs trees like a raccoon, and tears and soils her gowns like a madwoman.

The 'Beautiful Little Brute'

Then the young hero describes her upon two occasions as a 'beautiful little brute.' Poor little Wanda! not only is she non-descript and ill-starred, but as usual the authors take away her love, her life, and last and most terrible of all, her reputation; for they permit a crowd of men-friends of the hero to call her a 'squaw,' and neither hero nor authors deny that she is a 'squaw.' It is almost too sad when so much prejudice exists against the Indians, that any one should write an Indian heroine with such glaring accusations against her virtue, and no contradictory statements either from writer, hero, or circumstance. 'Wanda' had without doubt the saddest, unsunniest, unequal life ever given to Canadian readers.

Jessie M. Freeland has written a pretty tale published in The Week; it is called 'Winona's Tryst,' but Oh! grim fatality here again our Indian girl duplicates her former self.[2] 'Winona' is the unhappy victim of

---

[1] An American author of the mid to late nineteenth century, Bret Harte (1836–1902) was well known for his stories of life in the early days of the American west. His 1863 tale about "M'liss," an uncouth but spirited orphan girl living in the mining region of the Sierra Nevada, was collected in *The Luck of Roaring Camp and Other Sketches* (1870).

[2] Jessie M. Freeland, "Winona's Tryst," *The Week* 6 Feb 1891: 155–57; a subheading reads: "Fourth Prize Story, by Jessie M. Freeland, Brockville, Ont."

violent love for Hugh Gordon, which he does not appreciate or return. She assists him, serves him, saves him in the usual 'dumb animal' style of book Indians. She manages by self-abnegation, danger, and many heart-aches to restore him to the arms of Rose McTavish, who of course he has loved and longed for all through the story. Then 'Winona' secures the time honoured canoe, paddles out into the lake and drowns herself.

But Miss Freeland closes this pathetic little story with one of the simplest, truest, strongest paragraphs that a Canadian pen has ever written, it is the salvation of the otherwise threadbare development of plot. Hugh Gordon speaks, 'I solemnly pledge myself in memory of Winona to do something to help her unfortunate nation. The rightful owners of the soil, dispossessed and driven back inch by inch over their native prairies by their French and English conquerors; and he kept his word.'

Mair's Drama 'Tecumseh'

Charles Mair has enriched Canadian Indian literature perhaps more than any of our authors, in his magnificent drama 'Tecumseh.' The character of the grand old chief himself is most powerfully and accurately drawn. Mair has not fallen into that unattractive fashion of making his Indians 'assent with a grunt'—or look with 'eyes of dog-like fidelity' or to appear 'very grave, very dignified, and not very immaculately clean.' Mair avoids the usual commonplaces used in describing Indians by those who have never met or mixed with them. His drama bears upon every page evidence of long study and life with the people whom he has written of so carefully, so truthfully.

As for his heroine, what portrayal of Indian character has ever been more faithful than that of 'Iena.' Oh! happy inspiration vouchsafed to the author of 'Tecumseh' he has invented a novelty in fiction—a white man who deserves, wins and reciprocates the Indian maiden's love— who says, as she dies on his bosom, while the bullet meant for him stills and tears her heart.

> 'Silent for ever! Oh, my girl! my girl!
> Those rich eyes melt; those lips are sunwarm still—
> They look like life, yet have no semblant voice.
> Millions of creatures throngs and multitudes
> Of heartless beings, flaunt upon the earth,
> There's room enough for them, but thou, dull fate—

Thou cold and partial tender of life's field,
That pluck'st the flower, and leav'st the weed to thrive—
Thou had'st not room for her! Oh, I must seek
A way out of the rack—I need not live,
★ ★ ★ ★ but she is dead—
And love is left upon the earth to starve,
My object's gone, and I am but a shell,
A husk, and empty case, or anything
What may be kicked about the world.'[1]

After perusing this refreshing white Indian drama the reader has but one regret, that Mair did not let 'Iena' live. She is the one 'book' Indian girl that has Indian life, Indian character, Indian beauty, but the inevitable doom of death could not be stayed even by Mair's sensitive Indian-loving pen. No, the Indian girl must die, and with the exception of 'Iena' her heart's blood must stain every page of fiction whereon she appears. One learns to love Lefroy, the poet painter; he never abuses by coarse language and derisive epithets his little Indian love, 'Iena' accepts delicately and sweetly his overtures, Lefroy prizes nobly and honorably her devotion. Oh! Lefroy, where is your fellowman in fiction? 'Iena,' where is your prototype? Alas, for all the other pale-faced lovers, they are indifferent, almost brutal creations, and as for the red skin girls that love them, they are all fawn eyed, unnatural, unmaidenly idiots and both are merely imaginary make-shifts to help out romances, that would be immeasurably improved by their absence.

A Chance for Canadian Writers

Perhaps, sometime an Indian romance may be written by someone who will be clever enough to portray national character without ever having come in contact with it. Such things have been done, for are we not told that Tom Moore had never set foot in Persia before he wrote Lalla Rookh? and those who best know what they affirm declare that remarkable poem as a faithful and accurate delineation of Oriental scenery, life and character.[2] But such things are rare, half of our authors

---

[1] This speech by Iena's lover Lefroy occurs in *Tecumseh*, Act 5, Scene 6.

[2] The most popular Irish poet of the first half of the nineteenth century, Thomas Moore (1779–1852) was highly regarded in North America where his *Irish Melodies* (1807–34) and *National Airs* (1818–27) were sung and celebrated in concert halls and homes. His Oriental poem *Lalla Rookh: An Eastern Romance* (1817) created a sensation upon its publication.

who write up Indian stuff have never been on an Indian reserve in their lives, have never met a 'real live' Redman, have never even read Parkman, Schoolcraft or Catlin;[1] what wonder that their conception of a people that they are ignorant of, save by hearsay, is dwarfed, erroneous and delusive.

And here follows the thought—do authors who write Indian romances love the nation they endeavour successfully or unsuccessfully to describe? Do they, like Tecumseh, say, 'And I, who love your nation, which is just, when deeds deserve it,' or is the Indian introduced into literature but to lend a dash of vivid coloring to an otherwise tame and somber picture of colonial life: it looks suspiciously like the latter reason, or why should the Indian always get beaten in the battles of romances, or the Indian girl get inevitably the cold shoulder in the wars of love?

Surely the Redman has lost enough, has suffered enough without additional losses and sorrows being heaped upon him in romance. There are many combats he has won in history from the extinction of the Jesuit Fathers at Lake Simcoe to Cut Knife Creek.[2] There are many girls who have placed dainty red feet figuratively upon the white man's neck from the days of Pocahontas to those of little 'Bright Eyes,' who captured all Washington a few seasons ago.[3] Let us not only hear, but

---

Through much of the nineteenth century, Moore had a stature among the Irish similar to that granted to Sir Walter Scott in Scotland and Shakespeare in England.

[1] These three writers were crucial figures in early scholarship on North American Native peoples. Francis Parkman (1823–93) wrote influential histories of the English-French-Indian wars of the eighteenth century, including *The Conspiracy of Pontiac* (1851). Henry Schoolcraft (1793–1864) was an explorer and surveyor in the American Midwest who in 1822 became Indian agent at Sault Ste. Marie. His interest in and curiosity about the tribes he worked with led to his 6-volume *History and Statistical Information Respecting ... the Indian Tribes of the United States* (1851–57). In the mid-nineteenth century Schoolcraft was regarded as the foremost pioneer of Native American Studies and as such influenced Henry Wadsworth Longfellow's popular narrative poem *The Song of Hiawatha* (1855). George Catlin (1796–1872) was born in Pennsylvania but devoted his career to painting Native Americans in their own settings and championing their cause as a mistreated people. Both in his realistic paintings and in his book, *Letters and Notes on the Manners, Customs and Conditions of North American Indians* (London, 1844), he left powerful representations of the Native population.

[2] A number of Jesuit missionaries were captured and killed by the Iroquois during the destruction of the Huron nation in 1648–49 in the Lake Simcoe area south of Georgian Bay. At the Battle of Cut Knife Hill on 2 May 1885, during the North West uprising in what is now the province of Saskatchewan, Cree warriors led by Fine Day repelled an attack on their village by units of the North West Field Force under Lieutenant-Colonel William Otter.

[3] Pocahontas is the name of a legendary "Indian princess" (c. 1595–1617) who aided British settlers in Virginia during one of their earliest colonial forays into North America. Bright

read something of the North American Indian 'besting' some one at least once in a decade, and above all things let the Indian girl of fiction develop from the 'doglike,' 'fawnlike,' 'deer-footed,' 'fire-eyed,' 'crouching,' 'submissive' book heroine into something of the quiet, sweet womanly woman she is, if wild, or the everyday, natural, laughing girl she is, if cultivated and educated; let her be natural, even if the author is not competent to give her tribal characteristics.

Eyes was the popular name given to Susette LaFlesche Tibbles (1854–1903) or Inshata-Theumba, a woman of mixed blood belonging to the Omaha tribe in eastern Nebraska who became a celebrated advocate of Native rights after serving as interpreter at the landmark 1879 trial of the Ponca chief Standing Bear that resulted in the judicial recognition of Native Americans as persons. During the 1880s she and her husband Thomas Tibbles conducted lecture tours in the eastern United States, Scotland, and England.

Appendix B: Editorials on Literature and Publishing from Desbarats's Papers

[These anonymous editorials from three periodicals published by George-Édouard Desbarats in the post-Confederation era address both topical issues and perennial problems in Canadian literary culture. The untitled piece from the *Canadian Illustrated News* on "the state of Canadian literature" is typical of nineteenth-century discussions of the subject, resembling many of those collected by Carl Ballstadt in *The Search for English-Canadian Literature: An Anthology of Critical Articles from the Nineteenth and Early Twentieth Centuries* (U of Toronto P, 1975). In noting a tendency among Canadians to dismiss work by their own writers while embracing work from abroad, the editorial identifies a syndrome that persisted for decades, and that has not completely disappeared even in twenty-first-century Canada. Its censure of American publications and reference to "the sensational and often immoral trash which comes flooding the country from over the line" are amplified in the leader "Artistic Filth," published the following year in *The Favorite*. This later piece represents a minor, decidedly Victorian, but nonetheless resonant episode in the long and continuing struggle to nurture domestic Canadian publishing in the face of massive competition from the United States. The essay on "Sensation Literature" from *The Hearthstone* intersects with these two editorials in criticizing the vogue for sensational journalism, while in commenting on sensation novels it offers a shrewd assessment—allowing for some hyperbole—of the background, characteristics, and popular appeal of the genre that most significantly informs *Winona*.]

1. ["The state of Canadian literature"], *Canadian Illustrated News*, 13 July 1872: 22

There has lately been one of those periodical outcries respecting the state of Canadian literature which, from time to time, arise and occupy a considerable amount of space in newspaper columns, and a wonderfully disproportionate amount of the attention of newspaper readers. On every side we hear cries that our literature is not what it ought to be. Now and then, in reading the papers, we stumble upon an indignant communication demanding why in the name of Heaven we have not a national literature of our own, and protesting against our inability to compete in the literary field with our neighbours across the line. Even in the course of conversation one too often hears—even from Canadians at times—a sweeping denunciation of Canadian writers as being utterly destitute of the first qualities necessary in the making of a successful author, and an impatient sneer at the hinted possibility of our country ever becoming rich in literary representatives.

Such a state of affairs could hardly be more discouraging. It is but an evil omen for the literary future of the country that aspiring authors, possessed of good parts and sound education, should be deterred from using their pens by the sneers and gloomy prognostications of soured prophets of evil, with whom the fact of a work being Canadian is equivalent to a certainty of failure, while a foreign brand is an equally sure guarantee of success. And that these croakers, while doing their best to damage the literary status of the country, should actually venture to complain of the evil themselves are working is certainly surpassing belief. To them is due in great measure the primary cause of the comparative poverty of our national literature— want of support. No one can close his eyes to the fact that home literature is most insufficiently supported; that the literary career is too frequently looked down upon. Were there a sufficient demand, a supply would immediately be forthcoming. We have no lack of writers, both in prose and poetry, whose works would compare favourably with many of those issuing from British and American presses. More than that, we have some whose works are known and appreciated better abroad than in their own country, thus fully carrying out the moral of the old adage that a prophet is not without honour, save in his own country and among his own kindred. Further still, we have actually writers amongst us—Canadians whose name and fame are known wherever the British language is spoken—whose parentage and birthright are utterly unknown to the great majority of general readers. Take an instance. How many of the many thousand Canadian readers of "The Dodge Club" and "Cord and Creese," are aware that the author of those popular works is a Canadian, living in a Canadian city, who has been unable to find a market in his own country, and has been compelled to send his works abroad because his country-

310   APPENDIX B

men will not support native talent?[1] There seems to be among the class of readers coming under the denomination of "general," or "average," a rooted dislike to anything in the shape of native productions, and a proportionate attraction to the sensational and often immoral trash which comes flooding the country from over the line. What the ultimate cause of this antipathy to moral and instructive reading may be we have not now time to consider. It may be education. It may be vicious tastes. But whatever it is we are convinced of one thing, viz., that a certain portion of the press of the country is greatly to blame for fostering and tending this aversion to wholesome literature. Now and then we see in the columns of some patriotic journal an urgent, vigorous appeal to the people to support Canadian literature, but for every such appeal, for every single call upon the patriotism of the people in the matter, we find twenty invitations to support foreign talent, foreign enterprise, and too often foreign rubbish. Until this kind of thing has ceased, until on the one hand the croakers are all killed off, and on the other patriotism becomes more generally preferred to profit; until Canadians from Gaspé to Vancouver Island unite in advancing, each in his own way, the literary interests of the country, we may look in vain for the Golden Age of Canadian Literature.

2. "Sensation Literature," *The Hearthstone*, 3 August 1872: 4

In nothing is the high pressure under which the present generation is living more noticeable than in the style of literature needed for the mass of the reading public. The style of writing has changed so completely that if some of the "bright particular lights" of the last generation could be brought to life again and given a modern novel to read, or a modern "sensational" newspaper to look over, they would start in amazement at the wonderful flights of fancy which are now indulged in, even in recording ordinary, every-day events, or horrible and atrocious crimes. The sensation reporter of the day is a genius after his own peculiar manner; he is an epitometical[2] novel writer, and crowds into a report of a column,

---

1 *The Dodge Club* (1859) and *Cord and Creese* (1869) are adventure novels by the Canadian author James DeMille (1833–80), a Professor of History at Dalhousie University whose novels, numbering more than thirty in all, were much read in his time. All DeMille's serialized stories and books were published in the United States. Today he is remembered particularly for his posthumous utopian/dystopian novel, *A Strange Manuscript Found in a Copper Cylinder* (1888).

2 A mistake for, or perhaps a jocular version of, "epitomical," i.e., of the nature of an epitome, meaning in this instance "a novel writer in miniature."

WINONA; OR, THE FOSTER-SISTERS   311

or a column and a half as much agony, as many adjectives, as much harrowing pathos, as many telling situations, and more exclamation points than would have sufficed to furnish material for an old fashioned three volume novel.[1] How he glories in a murder; with what gusto he enters into all the horrible details, and gloats over the most barbarous and atrocious portions. He fairly howls with delight over an execution, and "does up" the unfortunate victim with "double heads" and "cross heads," and embellishes the effusion, if possible, with a miserable caricature which is misnamed a picture.[2] The sensation reporter must write in the most florid style; he must be an adept at verbal ornamentation, must be prepared to go into ecstacies at a moment's notice, if given a ball or other pleasurable entertainment to "write up;" or must be gloomy, pathetic or witty if given a murder, or suicide, or elopement, or anything else out of which he can make, that which most editors are ever so anxious for, a good sensational article. He is no respecter of persons, and he will "do up" his bosom friend if he can only make a good article out of him. The sensation reporter is not a bad fellow, he generally enters into his work *con amore*, but he very seldom has any personal feeling with reference to the victims he holds up as "villains of the deepest dye," he simply fills a want in newspaper literature, a want which has grown out of the feverish, unhealthy appetite which has been engendered in the public mind by a constant perusal of sensation novels. Our grandfathers were content to have facts recorded in the newspapers without any garnishing; but the present generation must have their facts highly spiced and served up with sauce *piquante*; therefore, the sensational reporter is a necessity growing out of the public taste. There are dozens of papers in the States which exist almost entirely on their "sensations;" and if any crime of more than ordinary interest is committed, the circulation of these papers is largely increased, because the public think they will get the horror served up rather more horribly in these papers than in tamer sheets.[3]

Sensation novels antidate the sensation reporter, and indeed it is the former which has occasioned the necessity for the latter. Novel writers

---

[1] Victorian novels were often published in three volumes and were of enormous length by today's standards.

[2] "Cross head" is printing terminology for a heading set within the body of a text to divide it into easily comprehensible portions; "double head" perhaps refers to a heading spanning two lines or columns of text.

[3] Notable among cheap magazines that specialized in reports of crime and scandal were the *National Police Gazette* and *The Day's Doings*, both emanating from New York City; see the following editorial, "Artistic Filth."

312   APPENDIX B

began early to drift from the path of mere story-tellers, and commenced embellishing their narratives with striking situations, wonderful escapes, &c.; but it was not until serial stories came into fashion, and the cheap weeklies began to make their appearance, that the sensation writers commenced to come out in full force. With the penny magazines, and their weekly instalments of stories, came the necessity for more spice in the intellectual food; it was found that more thrilling incidents, more diabolical plots, more mysterious circumstances and other ingenious devices must be introduced to keep up the interest from week to week. A climax must be reached, not at the end of the novel, but every week, and when the imagination of the author could conceive no more "telling situations," then the story could be finished in any quiet humdrum style. But gradually the straining for sensation became greater and greater, until now the story serves simply as a thread on which to hang any quantity of impossibilities; murders, seductions, forgeries, burglaries, suicides, arsons, and every variety of crime chase each other with kaleidoscopic rapidity through the pages of the sensation novel, and the story either ends at last in a sort of general firework display, or meekly and quietly fizzles out like a burnt out pin wheel; it makes a few revolutions in darkness and then is taken from its peg, and the reader is ready for another string of impossible circumstances. The main objections to purely sensational novels are that they unfit the mind for good wholesome literature—just as constant dieting on highly seasoned French dishes and fancy sweetmeats causes the stomach, metaphorically speaking, to turn up its nose at plain roast beef and plum-pudding, —and also that they compel good writers to abandon, to a certain extent, the plan of their story to accommodate the public taste by introducing some startling incidents. In the sensation novel little or no attempt is made at character sketching, there is no effort at teaching a moral lesson; it is simply an endeavour to introduce a few personages, make them go through a series of wonderful adventures and hair-breath [sic] escapes, and then march them off the scene again, just as a troupe of acrobats, bound on the stage, go through a series of unnatural contortions, make their bows and disappear. These books can have no good effect, indeed their effect is highly injurious to the mind, for they leave nothing to think over with pleasure; we never get on intimate terms with the characters in a sensation novel; we never feel as if we knew them well, and looked on them as friends; we simply gaze at them and their marvelous performances in wonder and astonishment, and when they are gone we scarcely regret them, for we were never really interested in them, but only in their wonderful gyrations. We can feel as if we had known Mr. Pickwick personally; Little Nell is to us a sweet little angel whose loss we mourn; but who ever felt, after he had finished a sensation novel, that he had known the people he had been reading about, or had any desire to know them.[1] We by no means wish to entirely expunge the sensational element from our novels; all our best writers of fiction are to some extent sensational writers, it is necessary to a limited degree to sustain the interest in three or four hundred pages of printed matter; but with them sensation is a secondary consideration, and introduced merely to assist the pleasant progress of the story. With the genuine sensation writer the story, morality, character sketching, and even good English, are all minor considerations scarcely worth a thought, and the only aim is to crowd as many horrible incidents and marvelous circumstances as possible into the smallest space. Sensation literature is undoubtedly the taste of the day, and is hourly gaining popularity; and it is well worth our while to reflect for a moment on the effect which it will have on the coming generation. Already it is an old and well worn saying that "there are no children now," and there are not; not in the sense that we knew children when were young; they are simply little men and women. There is no doubt that a great deal of this quick aging of children is due to the class of literature on which their minds are fed; watch any group of boys or girls of ten or twelve years of age who happen to be studious and see what they are reading; Indian tales, which must make Fennimore Cooper[2] shiver in his grave; love stories, which ought to bring a blush to the cheek of mature womanhood; romances, where under a thin film of so-called morality, subjects of the most delicate—or indelicate—nature are handled without gloves. Look at this and cease to wonder that our boys and girls are getting to be only little men and women. It is often asked, "What will the 'coming man' be like?" we are not prepared to say what he will be like, but whatever he is, depend on it that the formation of his character will to a great extent have been influenced by the present deluge of sensation literature.

---

[1] Samuel Pickwick is the plump and cheerful major character in Charles Dickens's *The Pickwick Papers* (serialized in 1836 and published as a book in 1837). The doings of Pickwick, his servant Sam Weller, and other members of the Pickwick Club established Dickens's reputation as a writer and humorist. Little Nell Trent is the sympathetic, childlike heroine of Dickens's *The Old Curiosity Shop* (1841); her pathetic fate galvanized readers of the novel, especially when the story first appeared in serialized form.

[2] James Fenimore Cooper (1789–1851) was an American writer who became famous for his tales of forest life, pioneering, and adventures at sea in early nineteenth-century America. In his Leatherstocking series of novels, his protagonist Natty Bumppo lives and works closely with Native figures.

3. "Artistic Filth," *The Favorite*, 1 February 1873: 56

One of the most prominent artists engaged on one of the vilest illustrated papers published in New York has given the above title to his own
work, and it is an apt one. There are numbers of illustrated papers
published in the States, the contents of which are nothing but filth, and
one of their most dangerous characteristics is the fact that they are artis-
tically got up and present an attractive appearance calculated to please
the eye. These publications have been introduced very freely into
Canada, and have, undoubtedly seriously injured the morals of the rising
generation. It is, therefore, with great pleasure that we notice the action
of Mr. E.J. Russell, agent for the Lower Provinces for the Favorite and
Canadian Illustrated News, who has induced the Collector of Customs at
St. John, N.B., to seize a large number of *Police Gazettes, Days Doings*,
and other kindred publications, on the ground that they were indecent
and immoral.[1] We hope that the action of the Collector at St. John, will
be followed by a similar action of other Collectors, and that the dissem-
ination of artistic filth throughout Canada may be effectually stopped.
A few spasmodic efforts will be of comparatively little avail, but we hope
to see the action of Mr. Russell followed up by a persistent effort by our
agents and the Collectors of Customs to drive indecent literature out of
Canada. There cannot happen to any country a worse curse than to be
flooded with indecent and immoral books and papers, and there is little
doubt that the moral laxity of Paris and New York is to a great extent
due to the too great liberty with which artistic filth has been published
in both places. It is a painful and pitiable sight to see boys and girls
scarcely in their teens eagerly devouring the contents of publications
especially intended to appeal to the lowest and most degrading passions,
and it is high time that some vigorous measures were taken to sweep the
vile stuff away. The record of crime is always sad to read, and where it is
necessary to record it, it should be done seriously and for the purpose
of warning others by the example, not made attractive by fancy pictures
and fine description so that the imagination is excited and all abhor-
rence of the crime is lost in the interest in the subject.

---

[1] The *National Police Gazette*, founded in 1845 by Enoch Camp and George Wilkes, and
The Days Doings, published under this title by Frank Leslie from 1868 to 1876, were weekly
pictorial papers specializing in reports and lurid illustrations of violent crime, sensational
trials, and scandal, with particular emphasis on female vice and threatened female virtue.

Appendix C: Prospectus for The Favorite

[These two items appeared in the special Christmas issue that constituted the debut of *The Favorite*, which featured Crawford's short story "The Silvers' Christmas Eve" on its front page. Two weeks later, the initial installment of *Winona* appeared in the paper's first regular number, dated January 11, 1873. The intentions declared in this prospectus for the contents and conduct of *The Favorite* are, aside from its pointedly Canadian perspective, typical of the nineteenth-century North American story papers, as is the international roster of prospective contributors, many of whom were never actually published in the paper. The number of "Peterboro" and area writers on this list is striking, almost equaling the number of those identified with the much more populous and prosperous city of Montreal. In addition to Isabella Valancy Crawford there are her sister Emma Naomi, Catharine Parr Traill's married daughter Mary Muchall (whom Traill was encouraging in her writing career), and the widowed Susanna Moodie, who visited the Traills in Lakefield every summer. Ultimately, while Muchall and Emma Crawford, as well as Isabella, placed stories in *The Favorite*, neither Moodie nor Traill appeared in its pages.]

1. "Our First Bow," *The Favorite*, 28 December 1872: 8

A merry Christmas and a happy New Year to all; and, in the general joy and enjoyment of the festive season, may you find room in some warm little corner of your hearts to welcome the new candidate for your favor. We make no excuse, nor offer any elaborate arguments as to the necessity for launching THE FAVORITE on the sea of literature; we only have two reasons; first, a desire to furnish a thoroughly good paper, perfectly moral in its tone and tendencies, to take the place of the trashy publications with which the country is deluged; and, secondly, we have what we conceive to be a very reasonable desire to make a little money by the transaction. In order to accomplish our purpose we shall spare neither pains nor expense to make the FAVORITE the *best*, as it is the *largest* and *cheapest*, weekly story paper printed on this continent. We shall constantly have three or four serials by the best authors, a number of short stories, interesting sketches, spicy editorials, and entertaining

316   APPENDIX C

selections from the contemporaneous press. We shall run the FAVORITE emphatically as a *live* paper; there will be nothing in it to induce drowsiness; every article will be well written and entertaining, and our stories will be of the most absorbing interest. THE FAVORITE will be conducted essentially as a *family* paper; it will be pure and elevated in tone, and not a word or line will appear in it which could call a blush to the cheek of virtue, or sully the purity of thought of the most innocent. It will be designed especially for entrance to the family circle, and may safely be placed in the hands of childhood. The stories we publish, while interesting and full of adventure and incident, will be free from any of the vulgar sensationalism of the day, and will tend to elevate, improve, and instruct as well as humor. As a fair sample of the class of paper we intend having, we refer to the present number; future numbers will be constructed on the same model, only they will contain parts of several serial stories. Politics and religion—that is religious discussions—will be excluded from our columns, as we do not think them suited for a purely literary paper; current topics will be discussed in an independent and liberal spirit, and no partisanship or sectarianism allowed to creep into our reviews of the most interesting questions of the day. We intend to publish a thoroughly good paper, as good as money and talent can make it, and we trust to the public to give us that earnest and cordial support which alone can insure our enterprise being a success. We desire to supplant the indecent and immoral publications which now circulate so freely, and to supply in their place pure, healthy, invigorating literature; and we call on every one who wishes to see the literature of his country elevated and improved to assist us.

2. "Who Will Write for *The Favorite*," *The Favorite*, 28 December 1872: 8

Our number of 4th January, to be issued in a few days, will commence the first volume of *The Favorite*. It will be rich in story and verse, and will contain an immense amount of interesting reading matter. Three new serials, two of them written expressly for *The Favorite*, will commence in this number which will contain the following, and other articles:

HARD TO BEAT; a tale of Canadian life, By J.A. Phillips, of Montreal, author of the popular stories "From Bad to Worse," "My Reporter," &c. &c.

WINONA; OR, THE FOSTER-SISTERS 317

WINONA; or the Foster Sisters. By Miss Isabella Valancy Crawford, of Peterboro', Ont., author of "The Silvers' Christmas Eve," "Wrecked; or, The Rosclerras of Mistree," &c.

TALES OF MY BOARDERS, By A.I.S., of Huntingdon, Q.

DEATH ON THE OCEAN. By E.A. Sutton, of Quebec.

The continuation of "The Clevedon Chimes" and "Christmas in Sunshine and Shadow," and other interesting articles.

In this number will also be commenced a novel of great power and absorbing interest now appearing in England, entitled:

LESTELLE. By the author of "The Rose and the Shamrock," which we publish from advance sheets.

We have a large number of interesting tales on hand which will be produced in rapid succession; and we are always ready to encourage native talent by purchasing at the highest rates anything in the way of stories, sketches, poems, provided they are good.

The Favorite is the largest and cheapest literary weekly published on this continent, containing as it does sixteen pages of four columns each, or sixty-four columns of reading matter, being one fourth larger than the New York *Ledger* or *Weekly* or any of that class of papers.

Amongst the many authors whose works will appear in *The Favorite*, we may mention the following:

CANADIAN

Miss Isabella V. Crawford, of Peterboro', Ont.
Mrs. Alex. Ross,   Montreal, Q.
Mrs. M.E. Muchall,   Peterboro', Ont.
Mrs. Susanna Moody,   Lakefield, Ont.
"Effie,"   Clarenceville, Q.
Kate Seymour   Montreal, Q.
Miss Emma N. Crawford,   Peterboro', Ont.
A.I.S.,   Huntingdon, Q.

Mrs. J.V. Noel,   Kingston, Ont.
J.A. Phillips,[1]   Montreal, Q.
Robert Brydon,   Hespeler, Ont.
John Lesperance   Montreal, Q.
Rev. W. Lumsden,   Oakville, Ont.
E.H. Griffith,   Montreal, Q
E.A. Sutton,   Quebec
Geo. S. Burnham,   Ottawa.

&c., &c., &c.

ENGLISH

Wilkie Collins, Edmund Yates, Ernest Brent, Miss M.E. Braddon, James Greenwood, John Ingelow, &c., &c., &c.

AMERICAN

Rev. Henry Ward Beecher, William Ross Wallace, Dr. Oliver Wendell Holmes, Dr. J.G. Holland, Mark Twain, Bret Harte, Louisa M. Alcott, &c., &c., &c.

---

[1] John Arthur Phillips (1842–1907), the editor of both *The Favorite* and its predecessor *The Hearthstone*, was a prolific Montreal writer whose serialized novels appeared in both papers.

Appendix D: Reports of the 1873 Autumn Assizes, Peterborough, Ontario

[This section reproduces, in their entirety, the two Peterborough newspaper reports of the action brought by Isabella Valancy Crawford against her Montreal publisher, George-Édouard Desbarats. The longer report illustrates a stock phenomenon of the newspaper business then and now, a capable court reporter recounting the events in an objective, authoritative manner. Lacking sensational matter and clear local interest, the Crawford suit received only perfunctory attention, while a local murder trial in the same Assizes was reported in much greater detail in both newspapers. Apparently, neither reporter saw any special significance in a young woman writer's battle to receive a promised prize, and other earnings, from a prominent metropolitan publisher.]

1. From "The Assizes," *Peterborough Examiner*, 30 October 1873: [2]

The next case was Crawford *vs* Desbarats. This was a case in which Miss Crawford of Peterboro' was plaintiff, Mr. Desbarats of Montreal, defendant. The plaintiff brought an action to recover $605.48 for stories or novels written for defendants papers, the *Hearthstone* and *Favorite*. It appeared that in 1872, Mr. Desbarats published that he would pay certain premiums for a certain class of stories to be published in his papers. Miss Crawford competed, and after examination was informed by the Editor of the *Hearthstone* that she had been awarded the first prize of $500 for her story entitled "Winona," she wrote several other short stories for the same papers, for which she charged $3 a column. The whole account came to $605.48. There was simply no defence, except that the plaintiff had not shown that premiums were offered or agreed to be paid, as letters were not proof, as they might not be from the person at all. The jury returned a verdict for plf. of full amount.

320   APPENDIX D

2. From "The Autumn Assizes," *Peterborough Review*, 31 October 1873: [2]

CRAWFORD *vs.* DESBARATS

This was an action brought by Miss Crawford to recover the amount of a premium of $500 offered by the defendant for a novel, and which was awarded to the plaintiff; also, an account amounting to $99.50, and interest $5.98, in all $605.48. Verdict for plaintiff. Boultbee, Fairbairn & Poussette for plaintiff; F.E. Burnham for defendant.

Appendix E: Illustrations

[These six pictures are a sample of the visual culture that surrounded Crawford and informed her writing. The first, "Winona's Return," is the most melodramatic of eight woodcut illustrations that accompanied the original serial installments of *Winona*. The next three, "The Clytie Bust," John Everett Millais's "The Black Brunswicker," and the lithograph reproduction from the *Canadian Illustrated News* of Carlo Dolci's "Madonna of the Veil," are mentioned or alluded to in the text of the novel. The final two drawings, "A Moonlight Excursion on the St. Lawrence" (apparently done by the same hand that produced the illustrations for *Winona*) and "Ice Boats on the Bay, Toronto" (by the well-known local artist William Armstrong), were both published in the *Canadian Illustrated News* in 1871 and correspond closely to specific scenes in *Winona*. Together with the reproduction of Dolci's painting and similar evidence in Crawford's other fiction, they suggest the importance of this illustrated paper as a stimulant to her imagination and a source of material at this early stage of her career.]

1. "Winona's Return," woodcut illustration from *Winona*, Part 4, Chapter IX, *The Favorite*, 1 February 1873: 57; see p. 140 in the present edition

2. The Clytie Bust, marble, Roman, c. CE 40–50, Townley Collection, British Museum; see *Winona*, p. 127

3. John Everett Millais, "The Black Brunswicker," 1860, oil on canvas, Lady Lever Art Gallery, Liverpool, England; see *Winona*, p. 212[1]

[1] Millais depicts an officer from the German duchy of Brunswick parting from his beloved before the Battle of Quatre Bras (1815). In the course of this engagement preceding the Battle of Waterloo, a French army under Marshal Ney decimated a contingent of black-uniformed troops led by the Duke of Brunswick. On the wall behind the couple hangs an engraving of Jacques-Louis David's famous painting "Napoleon Crossing the Alps" (1800).

4. Full-page reproduction of Carlo Dolci, "Madonna of the Veil" (c. 1630–86, oil on canvas, Palazzo Corsini, Rome) from the *Canadian Illustrated News*, 23 December 1871: 408; see *Winona*, p. 271[1]

"PARCE SOMNUM RUMPERE."

---

[1] The Latin caption "Parce Somnum Rumpere" means "forbear to interrupt sleep" or, in Alexander Pope's rendering, "spare my Slumbers" ("Inscription" [1735] 3). While the ultimate source of this phrase is likely the "antique" Latin inscription translated by Pope, there is also an engraving titled "Parce Somnum Rumpere" by the eighteenth-century Scottish artist Sir Robert Strange that resembles the "Madonna of the Veil"; perhaps the caption, together with the comment "After Carlo Dolci," was intended to suggest a link between the latter's painting and Strange's work.

5. "A Moonlight Excursion on the St. Lawrence," cover of the *Canadian Illustrated News* for 24 June 1871; compare *Winona*, pp. 115–16

326 APPENDIX E

6. William Armstrong, "Ice Boats on the Bay, Toronto," *Canadian Illustrated News*, 18 February 1871; see *Winona*, Chapter XXIX

Select Bibliography

Principal Works by Isabella Valancy Crawford

Collected Poems. Ed. J.W. Garvin. Intro. Ethelwyn Wetherald. Toronto: William Briggs, 1905. Rpt. Intro. James Reaney. Literature of Canada: Poetry and Prose in Reprint. Toronto: U of Toronto P, 1972.

Fairy Tales. Ed. Penny Petrone. Ottawa: Borealis, 1977.

The Halton Boys. Ed. Frank M. Tierney. Ottawa: Borealis, 1979.

Hate. [Serialized] *Frank Leslie's Chimney Corner*, 1 May—11 September 1875.

Hugh and Ion. Ed. Glenn Clever. Ottawa: Borealis, 1977.

Malcolm's Katie: A Love Story. Ed. D.M.R. Bentley. London, ON: Canadian Poetry Press, 1987.

Old Spookses' Pass, Malcolm's Katie and Other Poems. Toronto: James Bain, 1884.

Selected Stories. Ed. Penny Petrone. Canadian Short Story Library. Ottawa: U of Ottawa P, 1975.

Winona; or, The Foster-Sisters. [Serialized] *The Favorite*, 11 January—29 March 1873.

Wrecked! or, The Rosclerras of Mistree. [Serialized] *Frank Leslie's Illustrated Newspaper*, 26 October 1872—29 March 1873.

Works about Isabella Valancy Crawford

"Antrim" [Mrs. Annie Sutherland]. "Old Paisley Landmark Once Writer's Home." *London Free Press* [London, ON], 2 July 1927: 6.

Bentley, D.M.R. "Introduction." *Malcolm's Katie: A Love Story.* By Isabella Valancy Crawford. London, ON: Canadian Poetry Press, 1987. xi–lxi.

——. "Isabella Valancy Crawford, *Malcolm's Katie*." In D.M.R. Bentley *Mimic Fires: Accounts of Early Long Poems in Canada.* Montreal and Kingston: McGill-Queen's UP, 1994. 272–91.

——. "Sizing Up the Women in *Malcolm's Katie* and *The Story of an Affinity*." *Studies in Canadian Literature* 14.2 (1989): 48–62.

Bessai, Frank. "The Ambivalence of Love in the Poetry of Isabella Valancy Crawford." *Queen's Quarterly* 77 (1970): 404–18.

Brooks, Marshall. "*Malcolm's Katie*: The Interior View." *Canadian Literature* 76 (1978): 134–35.

Brown, E.K. *On Canadian Poetry.* Toronto: Ryerson, 1943. 41–45.

Burns, Robert Alan. "Crawford and Gounod: Ambiguity and Irony in *Malcolm's Katie*." *Canadian Poetry: Studies, Documents, Reviews* 15 (1984): 1–30.

——. "Crawford and the Indians: Allegory in 'The Helot'." *Studies in Canadian Literature* 4.1 (1979): 154–61.

——. "Crawford, Davin, and Riel: Text and Intertext in *Hugh and Ion*." *Canadian Poetry: Studies, Documents, Reviews* 37 (1995): 62–78.

——. "The Intellectual and Artistic Development of Isabella Valancy Crawford." Diss. U of New Brunswick, 1982.

——. "Isabella Valancy Crawford (1850–1887)." *Canadian Writers and Their Works*. Ed. Robert Lecker, Jack David, Ellen Quigley. Poetry Series. Vol. 1. Toronto: ECW Press, 1988. 19–71.

——. "Isabella Valancy Crawford's Poetic Technique." *Studies in Canadian Literature* 10.1–2 (1985): 53–80.

——. "The Poet in Her Time: Isabella Valancy Crawford's Social, Economic, and Political Views." *Studies in Canadian Literature* 14.1 (1989): 30–43.

Burpee, Lawrence J. "Isabella Valancy Crawford: A Canadian Poet." *Poetlore* 13 (1901): 575–86. Rpt. abr. in Lawrence J. Burpee *A Little Book of Canadian Essays*. Toronto: Musson, 1909. 1–16.

Campbell, Wanda. "Isabella Valancy Crawford and Elizabeth Barrett Browning." *Canadian Poetry: Studies, Documents, Reviews* 29 (1991): 25–37.

"A Canadian Contribution." Rev. of *Old Spookses' Pass, Malcolm's Katie and Other Poems*, by Isabella Valancy Crawford. *Spectator* [London], 18 October 1884: 1381. Rpt. in *Evening Telegram* [Toronto], 8 Nov 1884: 3.

Cogswell, Fred. "Feminism in Isabella Valancy Crawford's 'Said the Canoe'." Tierney 79–85.

Daniells, Roy. "Crawford, Carman, and D.C. Scott." *Literary History of Canada: Canadian Literature in English*. Ed. Carl F. Klinck et al. 2nd ed. Vol. 1. Toronto: U of Toronto P, 1976. 422–37.

Dellamora, Richard. "Isabella Valancy Crawford and an English-Canadian Sodom." *Canadian Literature* 173 (2002): 16–32.

Devereux, Cecily. "'And let them wash me from this clanging world': Hugh and Ion, 'The Last Best West' and Purity Discourse in 1885." *Journal of Canadian Studies* 32.2 (1997): 100–15.

——. "Canada and the Epilogue to the *Idylls*: 'The Imperial Connection' in 1873." *Victorian Poetry* 36 (1998): 223–45.

——. "Documenting His/story: Towards a Feminist Reading of *Malcolm's Katie*." *Canadian Poetry: Studies, Documents, Reviews* 41 (1997): 85–101.

——. "Repetition with a Vengeance: 'Imitations' of Tennyson in the Poetry of Isabella Valancy Crawford." Diss. York U, 1996.

——. "The Search for a Livable Past: Frye, Crawford, and the Healing Link." *ReCalling Early Canada: Reading the Political in Literary and Cultural*

Production. Ed. Jennifer Lynn Blair et al. Edmonton: U of Alberta P, 2005. 346–67.

Dudek, Louis. "Crawford's Achievement." Tierney 123–25.

Dunn, Margo. "Crawford's Early Works." Tierney 19–32.

——. "Crawford's gisli, the chieftain." *CV/II* 2.2 (1976): 48–50.

——. "A Preliminary Checklist of the Writings of Isabella Valancy Crawford." Tierney 141–55.

——. "Valancy Crawford: The Lifestyle of a Canadian Poet." *Room of One's Own* 2.1 (1976): 11–19.

"Editorial Notes." *Arcturus: A Canadian Journal of Literature and Life* 19 (February 1887): 83–84.

Farmiloe, Dorothy. "Isabella Valancy Crawford, Canada's Emily Dickinson." *Kawartha Heritage: Proceedings of the Kawartha Conference, 1981.* Ed. A.O.C. Cole and Jean Murray Cole. Peterborough, ON: Peterborough Historical Atlas Foundation, 1981. 127–35.

——. *Isabella Valancy Crawford: The Life and the Legends.* Ottawa: Tecumseh, 1983.

——. "I.V. Crawford: the Growing Legend." *Canadian Literature* 81 (1979): 143–47.

——. "New Light on Crawford's Early Years." *Canadian Literature* 90 (1981): 168–74.

Frye, Northrop. "The Narrative Tradition in English Canadian Poetry." 1946. Rpt. in Northrop Frye *The Bush Garden: Essays on the Canadian Imagination.* Toronto: Anansi, 1971. 145–55.

Fulford, Robert. "Isabella Crawford: Grandmother Figure of Canadian Literature." *Toronto Star,* 10 February 1973: 77.

Galvin, Elizabeth McNeill. *Isabella Valancy Crawford: We Scarcely Knew Her.* Toronto: Natural Heritage/Natural History, 1994.

Garvin, John W. "Isabella Valancy Crawford." *Canadian Bookman* 9 (1927): 131–33.

Godard, Barbara. "Crawford's Fairy Tales." *Studies in Canadian Literature* 4.1 (1979): 109–35.

——. "The Forces of Light." Rev. of *Fairy Tales* and *Hugh and Ion* by Isabella Valancy Crawford. *Essays on Canadian Writing* 9 (1977–78): 52–54.

——. "The Quest for the Elusive Crawford." Rev. of *The Crawford Symposium,* ed. Frank M. Tierney. *Essays on Canadian Writing* 20 (1980–81): 61–67.

Hale, Katherine. *Isabella Valancy Crawford.* Makers of Canadian Literature. Toronto: Ryerson, 1923.

Hathaway, E.J. "Isabella Valancy Crawford." *Canadian Magazine* 5 (1895): 569–72.

Hughes, Kenneth J. "Democratic Vision of 'Malcolm's Katie'." *CV/II* 1.2 (1975): 38–46.

———. "'The Helot' and the Objective Correlative: Ontario and Greece." Tierney 87–96.

———. "Isabella Valancy Crawford: The Names in 'Malcolm's Katie'." *Canadian Notes & Queries* 14 (1974): 6.

Hughes, Kenneth James, and Birk Sproxton. "Crawford's 'Malcolm's Katie' and MacLachlan's 'The Emigrant'." *Canadian Notes & Queries* 19 (1977): 10–11.

———. "Malcolm's Katie: Images and Songs." *Canadian Literature* 65 (1975): 55–64.

Johnson, James F. "'Malcolm's Katie' and *Hugh and Ion*: Crawford's Changing Narrative Vision." *Canadian Poetry: Studies, Documents, Reviews* 3 (1978): 56–61.

Johnston, Nancy. "Garvin's Crawford: The Editing of Isabella Valancy Crawford." Thesis (M.A.). York U, 1988.

Jones, Rev. Harry. "Railway Notes in the Northwest; or, Dominion of Canada." Rev. of *Old Spookses' Pass, Malcolm's Katie and Other Poems*, by Isabella Valancy Crawford. *Leisure Hour* [London], March 1885: 165.

"The Library." Rev. of *Old Spookses' Pass, Malcolm's Katie and Other Poems*, by Isabella Valancy Crawford. *Evening Telegram* [Toronto], 11 June 1884: 4.

Lighthall, William Douw, ed. *Songs of the Great Dominion: Voices from the Forests and Waters, the Settlements and Cities of Canada*. London: Walter Scott, 1889. xxvi–xxvii, 450.

"Literary Notes." Rev. of *Old Spookses' Pass, Malcolm's Katie and Other Poems*, by Isabella Valancy Crawford. *Globe* [Toronto], 14 June 1884: 10.

Livesay, Dorothy. "Crawford's Stories." Rev. of *Selected Stories*, by Isabella Valancy Crawford. *Canadian Literature* 73 (1977): 103–05.

———. "The Documentary Poem: A Canadian Genre." *Contexts of Canadian Criticism*. Ed. Eli Mandel. Patterns of Literary Criticism 9. Chicago: U of Chicago P, 1971. 267–81.

———. "The Hunters Twain." *Canadian Literature* 55 (1973): 75–98.

———. "The Life of Isabella Valancy Crawford." Tierney 5–10.

———. "The Native People in our Canadian Literature." *English Quarterly* 4.1 (1971): 21–32.

———. "Tennyson's Daughter or Wilderness Child? The Factual and Literary Background of Isabella Valancy Crawford." *Journal of Canadian Fiction* 2.3 (1973): 161–67.

Macdonald, Mary Joy. "Inglorious Battles: People and Power in Crawford's *Malcolm's Katie*." *Canadian Poetry: Studies, Documents, Reviews* 23 (1988): 31–46.

MacGillivray, S.R. "Garvin, Crawford and the Editorial Problem." Tierney 97–106.

MacMurchy, Archibald. "Isabella Valancy Crawford." In Archibald MacMurchy *Handbook of Canadian Literature (English)*. Toronto: William Briggs, 1906. 144–47.

Martin, Mary F. "Another View of 'The Hunters Twain'." *Canadian Literature* 71 (1976): 111–12.

———. "The Short Life of Isabella Valancy Crawford." *Dalhousie Review* 52 (1972): 390–401.

Mathews, Robin. "'Malcolm's Katie': Love, Wealth, and Nation Building." *Studies in Canadian Literature* 2.1 (1977): 49–60.

Mazoff, C.D. *Anxious Allegiances: Legitimizing Identity in the Early Canadian Long Poem*. Montreal and Kingston: McGill-Queen's UP, 1998. 103–22.

Morgan, Henry James, ed. "Miss Isabella Valancy Crawford." *Types of Canadian Women and of Women Who Are or Have Been Connected with Canada*. Vol. 1. Toronto: Briggs, 1903. 64.

O'Brien, Sister Patricia. "Isabella Valancy Crawford." *Peterborough, Land of Shining Waters*. Ed. Ronald Borg. Peterborough, ON: City and County of Peterborough, 1967. 379–83

"Old Spookes' Pass." Rev. of *Old Spookes' Pass, Malcolm's Katie and Other Poems*, by Isabella Valancy Crawford. *Toronto Evening News*, 13 June 1884: 2.

"Old Spookses's Pass, and other Poems." Rev. of *Old Spookses' Pass, Malcolm's Katie and Other Poems*, by Isabella Valancy Crawford. *Week* [Toronto], 11 September 1884: 653.

Ower, John. "Bentley's Katie, Bachofen, & Psychology." *Canadian Literature* 122–23 (1989): 288–94.

———. "Crawford and the Penetrating Weapon." Tierney 33–47.

———. "Crawford's Move to Toronto." *Canadian Literature* 90 (1981): 168.

———. "Isabella Valancy Crawford and 'The Fleshly School of Poetry'." *Studies in Scottish Literature* 13 (1978): 275–81.

———. "Isabella Valancy Crawford. 'The Canoe'." *Canadian Literature* 34 (1967): 54–62.

Paolucci, Anne. "Crawford's Achievement." Tierney 127–29.

Petrone, Penny. "The Imaginative Achievement of Isabella Valancy Crawford." Diss. U of Alberta, 1977.

———. "In Search of Isabella Valancy Crawford." Tierney 11–18.

"Poetry." Rev. of *Old Spookses' Pass, Malcolm's Katie and Other Poems*, by Isabella Valancy Crawford. *Illustrated London News* [London], 3 April 1886: 360.

Pomeroy, Elsie M. "Isabella Valancy Crawford (December 24th, 1850—February 12th, 1887)." *Canadian Poetry Magazine* 7 (June 1944): 36–38.

Radu, Kenneth. "Patterns of Meaning: Isabella Crawford's 'Malcolm's Katie'." *Dalhousie Review* 57 (1977–78): 322–31.

Reaney, James. Introduction. *Collected Poems of Isabella Valancy Crawford.* Ed. J.W. Garvin. 1905. Rpt. Literature of Canada: Poetry and Prose in Reprint. Toronto: U of Toronto P, 1972. vii–xxxiv.

——. "Isabella Valancy Crawford." *Our Living Tradition.* Ed. Robert L. McDougall. 2nd and 3rd ser. Toronto: U of Toronto P, 1959. 268–88.

"Recent Poetry and Verse." Rev. of *Old Spookses' Pass, Malcolm's Katie and Other Poems*, by Isabella Valancy Crawford. *National Graphic* [London], 4 April 1885.

"Recent Verse and Translations." Rev. of *Old Spookses' Pass, Malcolm's Katie and Other Poems*, by Isabella Valancy Crawford. *Saturday Review* [London], 23 May 1885: 693.

Relke, Diana. "The Ecological Vision of Isabella Valancy Crawford: A Reading of 'Malcolm's Katie'." *Ariel: A Review of International English Literature* 22.3 (1991): 51–71.

Ross, Catherine Sheldrick. "Dark Matrix: A Study of Isabella Valancy Crawford." Diss. U of Western Ontario, 1976.

——. "Isabella Valancy Crawford and 'this clanging world'." *Kawartha Heritage: Proceedings of the Kawartha Conference, 1981.* Ed. A.O.C. Cole and Jean Murray Cole. Peterborough, ON: Peterborough Historical Atlas Foundation, 1981. 119–26.

——. "Isabella Valancy Crawford: Solar Mythologist." *English Studies in Canada* 4 (1978): 305–16.

——. "Isabella Valancy Crawford's 'Gisli the Chieftan'." *Canadian Poetry: Studies, Documents Reviews* 2 (1978): 28–37.

——. "I.V. Crawford's Prose Fiction." *Canadian Literature* 81 (1979): 47–58.

——. "'Narrative II'—the Unpublished Long Narrative Poem." Tierney 107–22.

Rudzik, Orest. "Myth in 'Malcolm's Katie'." Tierney 49–60.

Seranus [Susie Frances Harrison]. "Isabella Valancey [sic] Crawford." *Week* [Toronto], 24 Feb 1887: 202–03.

Skretkowicz, Victor. "Where Isabella Valency [sic] Crawford Died." *Studies in Canadian Literature* 10:1–2 (1985): 177–82.

"Some Recent Poetry." Rev. of *Old Spookses' Pass, Malcolm's Katie and Other Poems*, by Isabella Valancy Crawford. *Literary World* [London] 19 March 1886: 272–74.

Stich, K.P. "*The Rising Village, The Emigrant*, and *Malcolm's Katie*: The Vanity of Progress." *Canadian Poetry: Studies, Documents, Reviews* 7 (1980): 48–55.

Suo, Lynne. "Annotated Bibliography on Isabella Valancy Crawford." *Essays on Canadian Writing* 11 (1978): 289–314.

"A Talented Lady Dead." *Globe* [Toronto], 14 February 1887: 8.

Thomas, Clara. "Crawford's Achievement." Tierney 131–36.

Tierney, Frank M., ed. *The Isabella Valancy Crawford Symposium.* Reappraisals: Canadian Writers. Ottawa: U of Ottawa P, 1979.

Tracy, Collett. "Gender and Irony in Isabella Valancy Crawford's *Malcolm's Katie*." *Literature of Region and Nation: Proceedings of the 6th International Literature of Region and Nation Conference ... 2–7 August 1996*. Vol. 2. Ed. Winnifred M. Bogaards. University of New Brunswick in Saint John, 1998. 114–28.

The Varsity [Toronto] 23 January 1886: 116. Item regarding the serialization of a novel by Isabella Valancy Crawford in the Toronto *Globe*.

Warkentin, Germaine. "The Problem of Crawford's Style." *Canadian Literature* 107 (1985): 20–32.

Waterston, Elizabeth. "Crawford, Tennyson and the Domestic Idyll." Tierney 61–77.

——. "Crawford's Achievement." Tierney 137–38.

West, David S. "*Malcolm's Katie*: Alfred as Nihilist not Rapist." *Studies in Canadian Literature* 3:1 (1978): 137–41.

Wetherald, Ethelwyn. Introduction. *Collected Poems of Isabella Valancy Crawford*. Ed. J.W. Garvin. Toronto: William Briggs 1905. Rpt. Literature of Canada: Poetry and Prose in Reprint. Toronto: U of Toronto P, 1972. 15–29.

Wilson, Maud Miller. "Isabella Valancy Crawford." *Globe* [Toronto], 15 April 1905: 8; 22 April 1905: 8. Wilson's middle name is mistakenly given as "Wheeler" in the byline to the first installment of this two-part article.

Yeoman, Ann. "Towards a Native Mythology: The Poetry of Isabella Valency [sic] Crawford." *Canadian Literature* 52 (1972): 39–47.